LINDA KAGE

A PERFECT TEN

A FORBIDDEN MEN NOVEL
BOOK 5

A Perfect Ten

Contact Information : linda@lindakage.com

Publishing History
Linda Kage, March 2015
Print ISBN: 1508511934
Print ISBN-13: 978-1508511939

Credits
Cover Artist: Kage Covers
Editor: Stephanie Parent
Proofreader: Shelley at 2 Book Lovers Reviews

Published in the United States of America

DEDICATION

FOR

SHI ANN CRUMPACKER

&

ALAINA MARTINIE

PROLOGUE

TEN

I STARTED OUT with good intentions. I'm serious.

That's fucking whack to hear, I know. Me and those two words strung together like that just don't mix. But in this case, I actually did want to do what was best.

It was probably some stray brotherly vibe left over from days long past. I do still get weird when I learn a chick I'm with is someone's sister. If I don't know about it, I'm cool; I can proceed with my typical asshole ways. But if she has to go and mention it, I start itching with respect and shit, which ruins the wicked intentions I usually have.

So knowing *she* was a little sister before I ever laid eyes on her doomed everything from the get-go. What's worse, she wasn't just anyone's little sister. She had to go and be *his* little sister. But meeting her as he was carrying her from a bathroom where she'd been deathly ill all night was what really cinched it for me. She looked like death warmed over with her skin so pale and translucent, strands of damp blonde hair falling out of a loose ponytail, and thin arms limp with exhaustion as she wrapped them around her brother's neck.

After seeing her like that and listening in on what she'd told him had happened to her, I got all these freaking, pansyass reactions. The strongest was...what's that one word? That thing that's never applied to me. Oh, yeah. Protective. I turned protective. I wanted to yank her out of his arms, into my own, and kick anyone who came close to us right in the nuts.

I was ready to murder for this girl.

And that was before she even lifted her face from his shoulder and looked at me. Talk about a slap on the ass. I wasn't expecting to experience a damn thing from merely making eye contact with some chick. But I did, and so much more. Her unforgettable blue eyes were bruised with sleeplessness, her perfectly shaped cheekbones were tinged with a sick kind of gray, and her lips were chapped until dried blood flaked off her delectable mouth. Yet even so, she was so damn beautiful in one of those hauntingly ethereal ways it stole my breath.

Yeah, yeah, I'm being all flowery and dramatic and bullshit, but it's fucking true, so shut it.

I know what else you're thinking. I'm Oren Tenning; I think a lot of women are gorgeous. What else is new? I can't step outside my apartment without listing off attributes I appreciate.

Check out her ass.

Love the titties on that one.

Hey, let me run my tongue over that lip for you, honey.

Oh yeah, I'd do her in a New York minute.

That one's so hot I'd even do her again.

But for me it's rare when the appearance of any particular girl punches me so hard it leaves a hole in my gut and sticks in my mind.

Caroline Gamble left a gigantic hole burning right through the center of my stomach. The place still singes when I see her, or when someone talks about, or when I think, or even dream about her. Shit, I've invested stock in antacids because my entire digestive tract is one constant, sweltering mess.

I should've never been nice to her. That's what really fucked me. I realize that now...now that it's too *freaking* late.

See, I always—*always*—behaved when she was around. I watched what I said. I treated her politely, all things that are out of the norm for me, yeah, but I didn't want her to know what a creepy perv I really was. I wanted her to think I was a nice guy. Plus her brother would've kicked my ass if

I *hadn't* been perfectly behaved around her.

But, fuck, did being nice backfire in a major way.

The damn girl tried to kiss me. Twice.

I know. The nerve.

There I was, *attempting* to be good for once in my life. I was already uncomfortable and irritated with all the respect and protectiveness I had going for her. Add that to how wildly attracted I was and the fact that her older brother—my best goddamn friend on earth—warned me away from her on a daily basis, and what do you get? You get one tempted motherfucker, that's what you get. How dare she put the moves on me when I was trying to play good despite the fact I wanted to fuck her two hundred ways to Tuesday.

Worst moment of my life was turning her down on both of those occasions she tried to lay a wet one on me. Okay, fine. The *second* worst moment of my life. Whatever. But we're not talking about *número uno* on my shit list. So, just drop those curious little thoughts already. We're talking about that lost expression that invaded Caroline's face the moment I said, "Don't," and "stop," and "this is not going to happen."

Yeah, *don't*. First and last time I ever said *that* to a woman.

A light dimmed from her eyes, the smile dropped from her lips, and her shoulders curled protectively in around herself. I had never been so bothered about hurting someone as I was in those two moments. I think they crushed me more than they did her.

Thank God she spun away and ran off both times (though there were—*dammit*—tears in her eyes) before I could react. I probably would've fallen to my knees and apologized, or hugged her, or some crap. And I definitely would've finished that kiss I hadn't let her start. Who knew what would've followed, but I'm sure it's something her brother would slaughter me for even thinking.

I had to bring out the big guns after that. She was Noel Gamble's one and only sister; I could not fuck her. No matter what. I needed to take drastic measures to keep her at arm's length. I needed to...okay, fine. Fuck. I just needed to be me. Not really so drastic once you think about it, even though it probably seemed that way to her.

So I let her have the full intensity of Ten. I stopped watching what I said when she was around, and I let all my base, disgusting thoughts bleed out of my mouth like I usually did. I stopped smiling at her, stopped paying her special attention with little courteous things like holding doors open for her or asking her how her day went. I completely stopped being a nice guy. I backed off and pretty much ignored her, unless I could think up something crude to say in her direction. I made sure to chase other women when she was around. And I felt like shit every night I lay in bed, unable to get to sleep, because I'd relive every awful thing I'd done to her that day.

No matter how deeply my actions bothered me, though, it didn't stop me from making her hate me and killing any soft feelings she'd ever had for me.

It should've been easy to accomplish. Everyone who knew me understood how fast I could piss off a woman.

But nothing about Caroline has ever been easy.

That's the curious thing about temptation. It festers and grows. You feed that bitch enough and she morphs into craving, and then craving turns into obsession. Pretty soon, nothing in your life is as important as that one thing you want but can't have.

I wanted her and I couldn't have her, so I fed the temptation, I flooded the craving, I would've fucking nursed the obsession from my own tits if I could've. I made sure I got little doses of her here and there. Except something incredibly enlightening happens when you spend enough time in one woman's company. You start noticing shit about her, little useless crap that actually begins to mean everything, like how she brushes the hair out her face—even if there isn't any in her eyes—whenever she's unsettled, or how she chews on the end of a pen during class whenever she's listening to something that captures her attention. You learn all her different laughs and know what each one means. You learn what pisses her off the most, or what makes her the happiest. You discover how smart and witty and sarcastic she is, and that her mind is almost as dirty as yours. You see how passionate she becomes when she defends those she loves, and you start to fall. Hard.

So, this is my Pathetic Loser's confession: I am Oren Tenning, and I have fallen. Hard.

Damn, I can't believe I just admitted that about a girl I've never even kissed, much less fucked. But I'm almost out of tricks here. I know I need to keep on keeping her away, except I'm getting desperate. I want her so goddamn bad.

It's my own damn fault, really. I could've and *should've* turned her off of me for good by now. It's just that every time I think I've finally done something that will make her hate me forever—something she'll never forgive me for—the panic sets in. I can't bear the thought of her hating me and never forgiving me. So then I have to go and do something to ensure her forgiveness.

She always forgives me, too, even though she shouldn't. But I love that about her, that sweet, beautiful, overforgiving, dirty-minded heart of hers. And so I keep plowing down this destructive path, knowing good and well I'm running myself insane, and probably her too.

Something's gotta give soon or I'll explode...most likely inside her.

I just hope it doesn't end up with me dead at the hands of my best friend.

CHAPTER 1

Caroline

"Ooh, he's cute. Caroline, don't you think he's cute?"

I sighed as Blaze—and yes, she'd given herself that name—shoved me in the arm for like the tenth time in the past five minutes, almost making me upset the glass of cola I was nursing.

"Yeah," I said, not even bothering to check out the newest hottie she'd spotted. "He's...adorable."

Usually, I was all for checking out anyone within my age range who possessed a Y chromosome. But tonight, I was anti-Y, so freaking anti-Y that I'd rather throw a vat of flesh-eating acid on the lot of them than check out one of their annoying, irritating, cute smiles, or asses, or packages, or pecs.

Across the table from us, Zoey covered her mouth with her hand and tried not to laugh out loud over my lackluster response. I scowled at her and mouthed, "*Shut up.*"

She had nothing to be moody about. Her boyfriend was frigging perfect. Gorgeous, considerate, sweet, faithful, Quinn Hamilton was exactly the kind of guy I should crave. But no...oh no. The idiot I coveted was a loudmouthed, politically incorrect jerk who shoved his penis into any willing woman who batted her eyelashes at him.

Except me. Me, he had turned down flat.

Twice.

Yeah, I said twice...because I was idiot enough not to get the hint the first time around.

Wrapping myself with my own arms, because just remembering his rejections made me feel all ugly, worthless, and gross, I glared at my drink, wishing I had even a hint of a bourbon in my cola. But my brother was working the bar, so that was a no-go.

Typically, his coworkers would slip me a little alcohol, but not if Noel was on the clock. No one crossed Noel Gamble where his eighteen-year-old sister was concerned, not even the biggest loudmouthed, politically incorrect jerk of the century.

"No, wait. Check *him* out instead. Now there's a stallion I'd like to mount and ride." Blaze literally licked her lips as she gazed hungrily across the crowded club. "Just look at how thick that chest is. And those arms. Mmm, God. You gotta know the rest of him is just as big. Dayum. I want to see him naked."

"Hey," Zoey spoke up, her tone annoyed. "That one's my boyfriend."

I glanced over to find Quinn's hulking figure up by the stage as he talked to Asher.

Ready for the evening's performance, Asher had a guitar strapped to his back. He swept a long piece of hair out of his face before gesturing with his hands as he spoke to Quinn. And like Quinn, he was another amazing guy, a hot rocker dude with a voice that made your hormones hum along with him every time he sang.

But he didn't want me either, which brought up another reason I was so anti-male these days. The good guys who might actually treat me right stayed away, weren't interested or already had a woman. The only asshole who'd actually taken a chance on me had used me, turned me into his dirty little secret, and then thrown me out like yesterday's trash. Was it any wonder I hadn't had sex in almost a year?

Oh, hell. Had it already almost been a year? Not cool.

I sank deeper into my chair as Blaze gasped. "What?! That hunk of walking orgasm is your boyfriend? Since when can *you* attract a guy?"

"Whoa!" I sat up straighter, scowling at Blaze. "What the

hell? Zoey could attract any man she wanted."

Zoey was my best friend on earth. She and I had come here tonight with Quinn to watch Asher's band play. Blaze was merely a passing acquaintance I shared a couple classes with, who'd approached us tonight, probably just looking for a table to sit at.

"But she's just so..." Blaze motioned to Zoey as she made a sour face. "So..."

"Sweet?" I guessed snidely, arching an eyebrow while my gaze dared her to say one more negative thing about my friend. "Beautiful? Smart? Loyal?"

"*Shy,*" Blaze burst out as if that was something horrid. "Seriously, I don't know why you hang out with such losers. You're not like them, but I swear you try to be. You just need to live a little, Caroline. Find yourself a man. A hot one-night stand. I haven't heard about you hooking up with anyone since we met last semester, and I know you're not into chicks. I'm worried your poor vagina's going to wrinkle up and dry out if you don't give it a little pampering."

Zoey's eyes grew big as she darted glances between me and Blaze. Unlike Blaze, though, she knew I had a temper and wasn't afraid to use it, so she also knew I wasn't going to let Blaze get away with saying all that shit unscathed.

One freshly clawed face coming up.

Sniffing up some oxygen into my nostrils, I nodded and sent Blaze a pleasant smile. "You know what? You're absolutely right."

"I know." She lifted a hand and motioned toward Quinn. "I say you take her man and show him what a real woman's like."

"No." I shook my head. "Not about that. You were right about me hanging out with too many losers. I totally need to stop that shit. They're such a drain. So...bye-bye now...you fucking loser."

Blaze's mouth fell open. "What the hell? What'd *I* say?"

Was she for real? "What did you *not* say? You just belittled my best friend and then told me to go cheat on her with her boyfriend. I don't care who you are, that's wrong, honey. And since when does a girl need a man in her life to be considered *living*? I don't need some useless dick around to prove I'm somebody."

"Well, damn, you didn't have to be such a bitch about it. I was just looking out for you, Care." With a huff, Blaze shoved her chair back and hopped to her feet. "I don't have to take this from you." Arching her chin up, she pulled her shoulders back and pushed her chest forward. "Only a girl who can't get a guy would say that, anyway. You're *both* losers."

As she flounced off, I snorted. Good riddance. I turned to Zoey to apologize for letting Blaze sit with us in the first place, but she was already sending me a regretful wince as she bit her lip. "I'm sorry, Caroline."

I blinked. "*You're* sorry? About what? She was the one who insulted *you*."

"But she insulted you too, and I said nothing. If I was just a little more outgoing or—"

Reaching across the table, I clasped her hand. "Zo, you are perfect just the way you are. And I don't want you to change a thing. Besides, how can you listen to a word she said, about you or me? She's headed over to hit on your man as we speak."

"She's what?" Zoey twisted in her seat to watch as Blaze boldly approached both Asher and Quinn, but Quinn was the one she turned to. She moved in close enough to brush up against his arm as she sent him a flirty smile.

Bouncing in her seat, Zoey clapped happily. "Oh, this should be fun to watch. I hope he's really cold and rude when he rejects her."

I shook my head, amused. Ninety percent of the women I knew would turn jealous and insecure when another woman hit on her boyfriend and end up blaming *him*, but not Zoey. She was completely confident about her relationship with her man, and she knew Quinn would never cheat...which only made me feel worse about my own pathetic relationship status.

Without my consent, my gaze strayed to another part of the bar where one dark-headed guy flirted with four—not one, or two, or even three, but *four*—women at once. He'd looped his arms around two of their waists while he said something to the other pair in front of him. When the two girls in front of him moved together and began kissing, he hooted in approval as if he'd asked them to do it and was pleased about getting his wish granted.

The sleaze ball.

I rolled my eyes and tore my attention away before I puked. Oren Tenning was the epitome of the male chauvinist pig. Every word to spew from his mouth was laced with all his crude, promiscuous thoughts. I wanted to hate everything about him with every fiber of my being, except he stirred each molecule in me into wanting to pounce and take him instead.

Humiliated that I'd actually tried to kiss him a few months ago, and even more humiliated that he'd stopped me—*twice*—I clenched my teeth. He and his harem were the very reason I was so pissy this evening.

But seriously, *four* women? Was that not a bit excessive?

I would almost swear he went out of his way to make himself look like the biggest man-whore asshole on the planet whenever I was around just to keep me away from him. But then, that was probably wishful, presumptuous thinking on my part. I'd worked out some big romantic plot in my head where he was desperately in love with me but he had to stay away because his best friend—my overprotective big brother—would kill him for even looking at me wrong, thus he went to ridiculous lengths to make me disapprove of him. If I hated him and stayed away, he wouldn't feel so tempted into falling for my wonderful self.

Yeah, I only *wished* that were the case. In reality, he probably didn't even know I was in the building and his only passing thought of me was that he had to be nice to me or my brother would lob off his dick with a butter knife.

My shoulders slumped. God, my life sucked. Maybe Blaze had been onto something when she said I needed to live a little. Because really, it *had* almost been a year since I'd stepped out of my comfort zone. I didn't agree that I *needed* a man to make myself something, but Zoey seemed more fulfilled to have a special someone to share everything with her. And since Noel had met Aspen, there something different about him, as if her presence settled a restless part of him. Having one certain someone around to talk to might not be so bad, someone to hang out with, to tell secrets to and lean on when I needed support, someone to support when he needed a boost. That didn't sound bad at all.

So why wasn't I getting back on that horse and trying out the dating scene to find that kind of companionship? Maybe because the last time I'd searched for that in a guy, it ruined me. Maybe I was letting myself obsess over Oren because unconsciously I knew I could never have him. I could safely pine for him without putting my heart at risk...again.

I did miss kissing, though. And certain parts of touching. Being physically close to someone and drowning myself in a little bit of pleasure.

"Maybe I *should* have a one-night stand," I said aloud.

Zoey swerved around in her seat to blink at me from large, startled green eyes. "Say what?"

"It's been almost a year since Sander," I told her, feeling funny just saying his name.

Sander Scotini had broken me so badly I hadn't been able to speak his name aloud but a handful of times in the past twelve months. I hated how much power I'd given him just by my inability to vocalize his existence... and by how wary of the opposite sex in general I'd been since him, or how overprotective of me my scandal had made Noel. I wanted my freaking power back. I wanted to be able to live again.

"And I don't want a dried-out, wrinkled-up old vagina," I said with maybe a bit too much vehemence.

Zoey sniffed and waved her hand. "That's just absurd. Mine wasn't used for eighteen years, and Quinn has no complaints about it now."

I snorted out a laugh, loving it whenever my quiet, reserved best friend said something shocking.

"What's so funny?" Quinn asked, popping up behind Zoey and slipping his arms around her waist from behind.

As he kissed the side of her neck and nuzzled his nose into her ponytail, I couldn't help but gag a little, in a very jealous, I-hate-you-for-being-so-disgustingly-content-while-I'm-miserable way. A part of me still adored watching them together, though, because I did love a good happily ever after.

Separated, Quinn and Zoey were usually too shy to do much but bleed back into the sidelines. Together, however, they lit up like Christmas tree lights, and I loved Christmas tree lights. Best lights in the world.

Watching Zoey's face brighten with pleasure as she ran her hand up his arm and pulled him in tighter behind her, I shook my head. "I totally love your girlfriend, that's what."

Quinn cuddled his cheek against Zoey's. "Sorry, but she's already taken."

I sniffed. "Hey, don't be so selfish, Hamilton. Can't you share her at least every other weekend? I bet she's a hot piece of ass."

"Oh, she is." He grinned, looking proud of himself. "So I'm definitely not sharing."

While we all laughed, I slid my attention past them to the stage where Blaze had approached him. I was a little disappointed I'd missed the big rejection he'd given her; I'd been too concerned about glaring at the man-whore with his four skanks.

Damn, I was pathetic.

Spotting Blaze coming on to Asher now, I shook my head, disgusted. When Asher caught me watching him, I rolled my eyes and gave him a thumbs down, letting him know the woman talking to him wasn't worth his time. He sent me a wink, telling me in return that he got it and would be keeping his hands off my exacquaintance. I could even hear his voice in my head saying, "*You got it, babe*," like he usually did.

I preened rather smugly. I'd just showed that bitch.

It was nice to know I had some kind of influence, which made me adore Asher for giving in to me. If only *he* could've been the guy I wanted more than anything. He might've actually risked the wrath of my brother to be with me. Or maybe not. I wasn't exactly sure about him, because neither of us had attempted anything with each other. I think he suspected where my heart already lay. My stupid, idiotic heart that had no sense of decency or self-preservation whatsoever. Seriously, what kind of heart fell for an annoying, obnoxious, loud-mouthed male slut?

Probably a weak, too-forgiving, clueless heart, because no matter how much it hurt to watch him drool over four other women, I always came up with a reason to fall for Oren Tenning again and again. Every freaking day. Just when I decided I hated him, and meant it this time, he'd come up with one huge redeeming quality that made me look past all the bad and just see...him.

Like now. He caught sight of Quinn and Zoey and let go of one of his whores to point to them. "Blondie!" he called with a big, happy grin.

Zoey and I were both blonde, but I knew he was greeting her. For some reason unknown to me, he refused to call her by her first name. He'd even go as far as to describe her in terms of "that girl" or "the one Hamilton's dating" to keep from saying Zoey. But mostly, she was Blondie to him.

The boy had issues if you asked me.

But then, I had even more for wanting him as badly as I did.

Once again unwillingly warmed to him because he was so nice and accepting of my shy best friend, I sighed. He and Zoey had a close friendship. He'd never once made her feel freakish for how introverted she was, and I couldn't outright hate him because of it.

I *could* hate him for making me jealous of a bunch of nasty sluts who absolutely wouldn't stop pawing at him, though. I wanted to slap the smirk right off the little witch who was leaning in to nuzzle her nose against his neck. I itched to stalk over there, yank her away by the hair and nuzzle her nose against the first wall I found...as hard as I could.

Okay, fine. I had a whole boatload of issues instead of just a couple. Sue me.

But, ooh, was that bastard sliding his hand over the other one's ass while the first one sucked on his neck? He *was*! Grr. I hated him so much.

Wishing Oren Tenning a long, slow, painful venereal disease-ridden death, I glanced away. "He is such a freaking man-whore."

Both Quinn and Zoey glanced at me, their gazes full of sympathy, which made me want to pull my hair and scream, because I also hated how so many people knew how much of a crush I had on Oren. It wasn't fair.

"That's it," I announced. "I'm doing it."

Zoey and Quinn looked at each other, frowning in confusion, before turning back to me. "Doing what?" they asked together.

I blew out a breath. "I'm living again. I... I..." Glancing frantically around the place, I paused on the first guy I spotted. "I'm going to go talk to him."

Zoey glanced over and winced. "Him? Are you sure...?"

I gave a very decisive nod. "I'm positive."

"Who is he?" Quinn wondered, eyeing the guy censoriously. He was another friend of my brother's and was probably guessing how many times Noel would kill the guy for even talking to me.

I was thinking Noel had way too many freaking friends.

"No clue," I said, not caring who he was at all. "How about I go ask him."

To be on the safe side, I snatched up the piña colada Blaze had abandoned at our table for a little liquid courage and gulped it.

Slamming the empty glass down, I let out a refreshed breath. "Please excuse me while I get my groove on." Standing up, I threw a flirty little wave at Zoey and Quinn—or Zwinn, as I was going to call them henceforth—and I turned to make my way toward Mr. Lucky, whoever he was.

Except I couldn't spot him anywhere. Crap. Where had he gone? Didn't he know he was a possible candidate for clearing the cobwebs from my vagina? My own personal cobweb duster.

"Um..." Zoey cleared her throat before she helpfully offered, "He went that way."

I jerked around to scowl at her. Then I pointed at Quinn. "Stop laughing. My groove's been on an extended vacation."

He immediately pursed his lips tight, holding in a grin. I narrowed my eyes and waited a tick to make sure another laugh didn't slip out. Then I glanced at Zoey. She pointed me in the right direction. I nodded my thanks and turned that way, grateful when I spotted my possibly first one-night-stand man straight ahead.

CHAPTER 2

Caroline

I CLOSED IN ON my target, a determined woman on a mission. I was going to get my life *and* my girl power back tonight if it was the last thing I did. Fuck Sander Scotini and what he'd turned me into. And fuck Oren Tenning for rejecting me. I wasn't going to let those assholes get me down.

The stranger's back was to me as he talked to two other guys. I'm not sure why I'd singled him out. Maybe because he was the antithesis of Oren. Shorter, pale-headed, not at all sporty-looking in a polo shirt and dark gray pleated slacks. I doubted Oren even owned a pair of slacks.

With one last glance back at Zwinn, I sent them a *"watch this shit"* grin and plowed ahead until I rammed into my target's back, making him lurch forward and dump the lager he was holding all over the front of his pretty yellow polo shirt.

"Oh my God. I'm so sorry." Forcing myself not to snicker in triumph, I grabbed up a handful of napkins from the table next to us. "Are you okay? I can't believe I did that." Or that I'd nailed him so perfectly.

He turned to me slowly, his face molted with rage, only for his expression to clear when he saw me. I batted my lashes and cooed out my sympathy as I took in his soaked shirt. "Oh, you poor thing. Let me get that for you." I dabbed at his chest a few times—not a bad chest, but not the best either—before I bent in front of him to sop up the spilled beer on the floor by his feet. Once I had the floor reasonably dry, I stayed kneeling but lifted my face to meet his gaze.

"Did I get everything?" I'm not sure if it was how close my face was to his junk, the breathiness in my voice, or the complete innocence I tried to blink into my eyes, but the guy fell for it, hook, line, and sinker.

"Uh..." His attention darted from my face, to the front of his pants, and then back to my face as I rose back to my full height.

"Let me buy you another drink." He didn't seem to notice I wasn't wearing a legal-to-drink wristband like he was, meaning I wasn't able to buy him shit, unless it was plain soda. If he had, he might've known how severely I was tricking my way into a meet-cute.

Instead, he stepped right into my trap. He lifted his hand to stop me from turning toward the bar. "No, that's okay. How about I get *you* a drink instead?"

"Really?" Wow, this was almost too easy. "That'd be great. Thanks." I glanced surreptitiously toward the bar as I tucked a long piece of bangs out of my face.

My stomach swarmed with nerves. Most of the crowd had gathered around the stage as Asher and his band began to set up their instruments, which left the bar area less congested. I could see Noel from where I stood as he served someone a bottled beer. Mason Lowe was behind the bar with him, but neither of them noticed me, so I took a small step to the side to hide myself a little better and kept smiling at Mr. Mission Accomplished.

"I'm Caroline," I called over the noise as I held out my hand.

"Trey," he answered, shaking with me and tugging me just a little closer to him before he let go.

Asher chose that moment to interrupt us. He turned on his mike and introduced the band, Non-Castrato. The crowd grew rowdy until the drummer counted off the first song and all the guitars started in. When people realized they were playing an original, something Asher had written called "Slingshot," the female fans began to scream.

Then Asher leaned in to sing, and the female fans promptly shut up so they could hear him. I grinned at how captivated he could hold an audience.

Trey nudged me in the arm to get my attention. "Have you heard them before?"

I could've told him any number of things—how well I knew Asher, that I owned their album and had all their songs memorized, that I came to watch Non-Castrato play just about every Friday. But I kind of wanted to be a little more mysterious and illusive.

"Oh...a couple times," I answered, smiling evasively.

He smiled back, though his eyes had a hard time staying on mine. They liked to wander and dip, checking out my chest. He definitely wasn't uninterested. If I wanted him, I could probably snag him. Now, I just had to figure out if I really wanted him.

"What about you?" I asked.

He paused before answering, flagging down a waitress and taking two bottles off her tray before paying for them.

As he turned back to me, offering me one of them, I bit my lip. He hadn't bothered to ask if I wanted this brand of beer, or even if the drink I preferred *was* beer. That had to be a mark on the con side of my list. But he did have an awfully pretty smile and very expressive eyes that let me know just how much he liked what he saw when he looked at me. That tallied two checkmarks on the pro side. I decided to give him another chance before I made my final decision.

"Thanks," I said and reached for the bottle. But before I could gain possession, another hand swooped in and took it from him.

My stomach sank into my knees.

Busted.

I looked up, expecting to find a furious Noel, but was shocked to see Oren instead. Ignoring me, he glared down my prospective one-night stand as if he wanted to kick Trey's ass.

A bubble of excitement bounced around in my chest. Was he jealous? He kind of looked jealous. A mad jealous. I hoped he was jealous and swept me away, forgetting about his four skanks, and took *me* home with him instead.

"Are you fucking blind, asshole?" Grabbing my elbow, he lifted my arm and waved my bare wrist in Trey's face. "Do you want to go to jail tonight for giving alcohol to a minor?"

My mouth fell open as hypocrite Tenning continued to glower at Trey, because Oren just happened to be one of Noel's coworkers who gave me free alcohol whenever he was working the bar and Noel was not.

"I...I..." Face flooding a bright, embarrassed red, Trey glanced at me, his eyes wide with alarm. I could tell by the look on his face he'd just realized I'd played him. "I didn't know she was a minor. I'm sorry."

"Well, maybe you would've gotten the clue if you'd been able to stop staring at her tits long enough to see that she wasn't wearing a wristband, fuckwad."

I tried to jerk my arm out of Oren's grip, but he refused to let go. Taking a step closer to Trey, he asked, "Do you even know who her brother is?"

Oh God. He just *had* to go there, didn't he?

Even more worry lit Trey's face as he gulped, his Adam's apple bobbing quickly. "N-no." He darted a glance toward me. "Who's her brother?"

Oren grinned. "The name Noel Gamble ring a bell?"

"Shit," Trey croaked. "You mean the football quarterback?"

"Mmm hmm." Oren hitched his face to the side, motioning toward the bar. "And he's right over there, behind the bar."

We all looked—Trey, his two friends, me, even Oren—and yep, there was Noel watching us, his expression pissed and his arms crossed stonily over his chest in his signature disappointed big brother stance.

The three guys Oren was intimidating whimpered, "Oh shit," together.

"I'm sorry. I'm so sorry." Trey turned to me to offer his apologies, but I guess he was too worried about talking directly to me because he hesitated and promptly turned back to Oren. "I'll never talk to her again. I swear."

"You better not, scumbag. Now get lost." When he made a dismissive motion with his chin, Trey and his friends cleared out, tripping over each other in their haste.

My face flooded with heat. I wasn't sure if I'd ever felt so humiliated in my life, like a little girl who'd just been reprimanded for misbehaving.

Oren puffed out his chest in self-congratulations. "Damn that was easy." He grinned at me. "But what a bunch of pussies, huh?" Then he took a big, long swig of the beer that had been meant for me.

As I watched him laugh and wipe his mouth with the back of his hand, my humiliation morphed into red, hot rage.

"What...the...*hell*?" I shoved him right in the chest, using both hands and trying not to notice how defined *his* pecs felt under my palms. So much better than Trey's had been—even though that was so not the point.

My beer he had confiscated sloshed onto him, in his face and down his shirt.

He leapt back, jerking the bottle upright. "Easy, woman! This is my favorite shirt."

Of course it was. It said, "*I support single moms*," and showcased the silhouette of a curvy, naked woman swinging from a stripper pole.

"Do I look like I care?"

He glanced up at my dry tone and lifted an eyebrow. "Let me guess. You're not going to offer to wipe me dry like you did that dipshit, are you?"

I shoved him again for being a total jerk *and* for buying such an offensive shirt. "Why did you do that?"

He snorted and glanced after Trey. "Because the dude looked like a douche."

I rolled my eyes. "Well, I obviously don't have a problem with douches. I'm talking to *you*, aren't I?"

He frowned. "Harsh, Caroline. I was just looking out for you."

"No." I set my hands on my hips and sent him the laser-beam depth of my glare. "You were cock-blocking me."

Lifting his hands in completely unrepentant negligence, he said, "Fine, whatever you want to call it. He's not going to bother you again. *You're welcome*."

"I wasn't *thanking* you." I made a face after him as he turned away and sauntered off. "You ass."

"Love you, too," he called back, blowing me a kiss over his shoulder. Then he took another swig of *my* damn beer.

I ground my teeth, frustrated with myself for letting him get to me so much that I had such a childish response and had to add to it by sticking my tongue out at him. But he could just make me so...mad.

As he strolled to the bar where Noel was watching us and sat on a stool, I glared after him. He and my brother spoke, and Noel glanced my way. Pointing at his own eyes, he then turned his fingers to tell me he was always watching me.

I sent him my own sign language and flipped him off. And the entire time, Oren sat facing the bar with his back to me as he finished off my drink.

Jerks. The both of them.

I guess that showed me for trying to get some action while they were around. But I'd come here to see Asher play; the action had been a spur of the moment thing.

I had a bad habit of running with spur of the moment ideas. And a year ago, I'd paid big time for it. It should've taught me my lesson. But like every other Gamble I knew, I had a hard head about learning lessons.

Needing to cool off and gather my self-control, I spun away and stalked toward the bathrooms. I waited until I was safely inside the ladies' room before I breathed again. Pressing my back to the door, I closed my eyes, glad for a moment free from Oren.

Sucking in a nice, refreshing...*eww*! Who the hell was spraying such rank perfume?

I opened my eyes and immediately frowned at the three ladies gathered in front of the mirrors. They just happened to be three of the very four whores—I mean, fine, upstanding young women—who'd been huddled around Oren mere minutes ago.

Awesome.

Maybe we could all get together sometime and just have us a slumber party.

"I still can't believe he picked *you*, you lucky bitch," the girl teasing her hair complained as she puckered her mouth and studied her lipstick job.

"I know," the one leaning in to examine the blackheads on her nose added before she tried to pop one. "I was totally feeling this vibe between us too. I was so sure he'd pick *me* tonight."

"You just...suck," muttered the third one who was, yes, still applying that awful perfume. "I've never had him before. It should've been *my* turn."

Behind one stall door, a toilet flushed, and the fourth whore appeared as she opened the door. "Face it, ladies. I simply rule. Ten's *always* preferred me."

At the mention of Oren—or rather his stupid nickname

everyone called him—I froze and focused on her a little harder. So, *she* was the chosen one for this evening, huh?

I hated her.

I really, really hated her.

"I heard he only does it in the dark," perfume girl said, her eyes wide with wonder.

My mouth fell open. *Say what*? I should not be listening to this crap. So, I edged in a little closer, hungry for more.

"Mmm hmm," the winner, I guess we were calling her, said. "He's almost weird about it. But it's so kinky you can't really care, because, oh my God, he makes up for the lack of sight by using all his other senses."

I almost whimpered as I imagine it. Oren learning me by touch, by taste, by scent. I shivered, growing a little warm under my clothes until the winner ruined the moment by speaking again.

"If you know what I mean." She smirked and wiggled her eyebrows.

Yes, honey, we all knew what you meant. But...hell. Listening to them talk about Oren's sexual preferences was...probably really forbidden, but even as it chipped off pieces of my heart to think of him doing those things with *them*, it still made my stomach tighten and my entire body tingle embarrassingly.

Stupid body.

"And it's always from behind. I've never talked to anyone who *hasn't* gotten it from him doggie style."

I clamped my legs together, because hello, they were talking about my Oren...in different positions. Yes, it was disheartening to hear he had such a following that they all knew his...proclivities. I couldn't believe I was half a second from being in love with such a freaking man-whore. But damn, I still wanted him to take *me* from behind like that.

"I'm supposed to meet him at his place at midnight tonight," the chosen one announced as she began to check herself in the mirror right along with the other three, fluffing her boobs up into her cleavage. "It's always so mysterious and thrilling when I go there."

"He leaves his apartment unlocked," pimple pincher explained to perfume girl, "and you're supposed to just walk right in and down a dark hall to his dark bedroom. You never know if someone's going to jump out and grab you."

The chosen one fanned herself. "And then he *does* jump

out and grab you."

All four of them giggled and then sighed. I rolled my eyes, deciding I'd had enough.

"I'm sorry." I waved my hand to get their attention. "But are you guys talking about...Oren Tenning?"

Four faces turned my way. I'm sure they found me lacking in my comfy blue jeans and V-neck T-shirt. I never dolled myself up. In fact, I purposely dressed down to avoid attention from the opposite sex. I hadn't really fixed myself up since the school dance last year where Sander had invited me to be his date, way back when he'd still been kind and sweet. But it turned out he hadn't ever planned on taking me to that stupid dance. I'd spent all the money I'd scrimped together and saved over the years to buy the dress, and after two hours of beautifying myself for him, he'd taken me straight to the infamous make-out spot to get lucky in the backseat of his Dodge Challenger. Not since then had I used clothes, makeup, or perfume to impress anyone.

"We sure are, honey. Do you know him?" Perfume girl sniffed and tipped up her face in a haughty kind of way, as if she couldn't believe I was good enough to even associate with him.

"Oh..." I gave her a brief, tight smile. "Barely." I bet I knew him a hell of a lot better than *she* did.

I doubt she had any idea that his favorite food was chocolate mints, or that he preferred a bottle of Sunny Delight over coffee every morning to drink with his breakfast. Or that he hated spiders and loved cats. I bet she had no clue that every extra dollar he made at the nightclub where he worked went into a savings account from which he someday wanted to build his own dream home...that he'd already designed himself. I bet she would never know what an extremely talented artist he was or what lengths he went to just to help his friends.

The bitch probably knew nothing about him at all...except how he felt inside her, which, okay, was more than I knew. Damn it.

"But one of my friends...," I went on, lifting my eyebrows so they'd think my friend had all the carnal knowledge of him that I did not, "...is still taking treatments to get over...whatever he gave her."

All four women gasped. "No," one said, her eyes wide.

"Oh my God. I was with him only two *weeks* ago."

"Oh, sweetie," I said with all the fake sympathy I could muster as I reached out as if to pat her arm. "You really need to go get yourself checked." And she probably needed to anyway, so I didn't feel bad about suggesting that at all.

"Is it herpes?"

"Syphilis?"

"AIDs?"

I almost rolled my eyes. How the hell did I know which disease to choose? "I don't know, but it was nasty, whatever it was. She was all red, bumpy, and itchy and..." I leaned in closer, lowering my voice dramatically. "Yellow stuff was dripping...if you know what I mean."

My four little puppets pulled back in horror. "Eww," they chorused, making me want to throw my head back and cackle.

I nodded, getting into character a little bit too enthusiastically. But hey, if Oren was going to cock-block me, I was going to vagina-block him. "I know," I cooed to his band of skanks. "The doctor told her she couldn't safely have sex again for a whole year."

More horrified gasps followed. "*A year*?"

Damn, was I good or what?

"Well, I can't meet him *now*," the chosen one squawked, looking panicked. "What do I tell him if he's still out there whenever we leave the bathroom? I can't even look him in the eye without seeing..." She shuddered. "No. Just, no."

Pimple popper slid her arm around her friend in comfort. "It's okay, Kelly. We'll sneak you out of here. He'll never see you."

"Ohmigod, *thank you*." Kelly stepped toward me for a hug. "I don't know how I could ever repay you for this." She looked really grateful too. I probably should've felt my first twinge of remorse right about then. But nope. I didn't.

I hugged her back, glad Oren wouldn't be feeling those really big boobs pressing against *his* chest later on. "I'm just glad I warned you before it was too late."

After getting a round of hugs from the other three girls—all with overly huge boobs that put my C-cups to shame when they embraced me—they hunched their shoulders together, formed a tight circle around Kelly, and hurried from the bathroom.

I had to watch this, so I followed them out and propped myself against the back wall of the bar.

Folding my arms over my chest, I snickered at how obvious they were about making Kelly duck down within their group and hide from him.

But Oren was absolutely clueless to their pathetic attempts as he stood way on the other side of the room, talking to Quinn. He didn't even notice their hasty exit. But he would eventually, and that made me smirk.

Things were about to get interesting.

CHAPTER 3

Caroline

I STUCK AROUND Forbidden a while longer and watched Oren from a safe distance. He glanced toward the hall opening to the bathrooms with a slight frown a few times, probably looking for Kelly and her sidekicks, but he didn't seem all that perturbed that he never spotted her again. He just kept mingling through the crowd and talking with everyone who stopped him.

"You're being really obvious tonight," Zoey said from beside me.

I didn't even glance at her. "Hmm?"

"With your Ten-watching," she cautioned. "You're not even bothering to hide it. Did he tick you off that much when he chased that guy away from you?"

"Oh, I'm over that," I said, though I wasn't. I still wanted to hurt him, not only for turning me down and then going to other women like Kelly, but for keeping me from the exact thing he would've done with her.

I finally glanced at Zoey. "I just heard a couple girls talking about him in the bathroom earlier. My ears are still ringing from the things I learned."

Zoey shuddered. "I can only imagine. Actually..." She wrinkled her nose. "I don't even want to imagine. His idea of fun no doubt goes beyond what I could even fathom."

The idea of that seemed to disgust her, but it turned me

on. That probably meant I was a freak. Well, yeah, I had to be a freak. I wanted Oren Tenning. That could not be normal. But still, why did I crave such dirty things? With him?

I checked the time on my phone. Eleven thirty. If he truly meant to meet Kelly at midnight, he'd have to leave soon. But he was still here. Maybe this meant he wasn't—

"Yo, Ham. I'm heading out." He appeared out of nowhere beside me to tap the top of our table and get his roommate's attention.

I yelped because I hadn't even noticed him moving our way. With a low growl, I scowled at him for startling me...or maybe for leaving now, because that meant he was still planning on meeting Kelly. The ass.

He met my gaze and paused. Reading something— though I'm not sure what—from my expression, he leaned close to talk into my ear.

"What? You're not still mad at me for chasing off that little boy, are you?"

I sniffed and lifted my chin. "You're just as bad as Noel. I mean, you're never going let me date anyone without any kind of interference, are you?"

He watched me a moment longer, his intent expression harboring all his thoughts. Then leaned in again. "How about this? If you ever find anyone good enough for you, I will step back and let you at him without even a single fuck-off glare in his direction." Then he leaned even closer. "Problem is, I don't think anyone will ever be good enough for the likes of you."

When he reached out slowly and caught a tendril of my hair, the achiest look entered his eyes. He studied the lock he was methodically winding around his finger, and the way he watched it was just...I knew that look and recognized it intimately. Every time I saw him, I felt it rising from my own core, wanting, yet helpless to take.

A shudder wracked me. Once upon a time, I'd told Zoey that if I knew for certain Oren really, truly liked me—liked me the way I liked him—I wouldn't let Noel keep us apart. And I'd meant it.

I still meant it.

"Even you?" I asked him.

His eyes flashed at the question. "Especially me." Dropping my hair, he stepped back and straightened before he cast a quick glance toward the bar, as if testing whether my brother could see us or not. When he seemed to realize Noel hadn't spotted him touching me, he turned away and strolled off.

I stared after him, my lips parting. And that's when I knew, or at least I convinced myself I knew. My theory wasn't a theory at all; Oren honestly *did* want me, and he really was an ass to me sometimes because he was trying to keep me away so he wouldn't fall into temptation and go against Noel's wishes.

Well, screw that. My brother wouldn't have befriended Oren if he thought he was such a bad guy. And Oren had done so many good things for him—which was another reason I'd grown obsessed with him. I swear, the only reason Noel didn't want me to date his friend was because he didn't trust me not to mess my life up royally, as I had the last time I'd gotten involved with someone.

But Oren was nothing like Sander. And I wanted him. I wanted him so bad. Even suspecting that he wanted me back made my heart ache.

It made Blaze's words echo through my head.

"Live a little, Caroline. Find yourself a man. A hot one-night stand."

A one-night stand, huh? On the heels of her echoing comment, I heard Kelly's, *"He only does it in the dark... I'm supposed to meet him at his place at midnight."*

"He always leaves his apartment door unlocked, and you're supposed to just walk right in and down a dark hall to his dark bedroom."

As everything I'd heard tonight crowded into my head, an idea formed. It was crazy. Insane. The worst idea I'd ever had. But I couldn't push it from my mind.

I shouldn't even consider it.

Then I did, anyway.

Seriously, though...if I arrived at Oren's place tonight at twelve o'clock and entered his dark bedroom, and he really honestly always did it with the lights off, he'd never know it was me. He'd think I was Kelly. Right?

My heart pounded. Yeah, that was a crazy idea. Too crazy. I was going to stop thinking it now.

Then again, what would the harm really be? He'd get his sex. I'd get what I'd been craving from him for months. Blaze would be happy my vagina wasn't going to dry out and shrivel up, not that I was sure why she was even worried about my vagina. But honestly, everyone would go away happy. Wouldn't they? Not even Noel could freak out over what happened because he would never be the wiser. Oren could still have me, and he wouldn't have to worry about keeping it from my brother.

The sweetest part of the whole idea was that I could have exactly what I wanted, and the immature chauvinist pig who pissed me off as much as he turned me on would go away absolutely clueless. I didn't want him to know how fixated on him I was. This could be the perfect solution, which really tempted me into wondering—

Oh, hell. The entire notion was crazy. I would never in a million years actually go through with such a thing.

Half an hour later, thousands of voices in my head shrieked. "*For the love of God, Caroline. What're you doing?*"

"Shh," I hissed at the annoying shits. "I'm doing this."

I slipped inside the front door to Quinn, Oren, and Zoey's apartment and then closed it behind me with trembling fingers. To be discreet, I'd parked my sister-in-law's car that I'd borrowed tonight a block down the street. And if anyone caught me inside, I already had an excuse handy. I was here to see Zoey. To talk important girl stuff. Yeah. That sounded good. And I really would talk to her if I was caught...about the fact that I'd lost my everloving mind!

Pausing at the beginning of the hall, I took a moment to bolster my nerve. Oren's bedroom was the first door on the right. Only ten feet away. Drawing in a deep breath, I started to step forward when an idea hit me. Scrambling, I reached under my skirt I'd raced home to change into for my panties, and I peeled them down my legs.

I know, I know. They were the nicest underwear I owned. Why was I taking them off before he could even see the goods? Well, probably because, if we stayed in the dark like we were *supposed to*, he'd never see them anyway. And tonight, I just wanted to be bold and promiscuous. If I was really going to do this, I was going to do it right.

Pantyless, I stopped in front of his door and lifted my palm, but instead of knocking, I set my fingers against the wood. He was on the other side of this door, waiting for me.

Okay, fine, waiting for some *other* girl. But if I knocked and went inside, it'd be *me* he took.

A thrill raced up my spine, and butterflies danced in my stomach.

I knocked.

Oh my God. I'd just knocked on Oren's bedroom door. What the hell was I doing?

Without waiting for an answer, I reached for the doorknob and turned it. It was also unlocked. The hallway was dark, so he wouldn't be able to see me as I entered. And just as the girls in the bathroom had gossiped, his bedroom was unlit too.

They'd been spot-on about the spooky yet thrilling aspect of it all. I was half scared out of my mind and yet completely turned on all in the same breath. Tense with anticipation and fear, I waited for him to accost me.

Gah, this was going to kill me.

No, no, it was going to be like walking a tightrope, I told myself, with a nice safety net under it. Yeah, because if I changed my mind, I could just tell him who I was, and he'd stop. Instantly. There was no doubt in my mind he'd stop. His best friend was my big brother. If he didn't want to be murdered, he'd definitely stop.

But I was sure I didn't want him to stop, so I'd have to be very careful not to let him figure out who I was. Still, that security of knowing I could halt this at any time was a nice benefit in case I did chicken out at the last moment.

"Hello?" I kept my tone low and husky, hoping he wouldn't recognize my voice.

"You're early."

I jumped like a startled mare before silently cursing myself. Damn, I hadn't expected him to be so close already.

Thank God it was pitch black. He couldn't see how flighty I was.

Accusation laced through his words and made me start to say, "sorry," but I stopped myself at the last second, not wanting to sound like a complete pushover. Only the *s* sound leaked out, making an adept impersonation of a deflating tire.

"What was that?" he asked, his voice even closer now. It moved through me and made my nipples bead.

I cleared my throat as silently as possible, and pulled forth all the courage I could muster. Then I lifted my chin. "I think you're the only one here we have to worry about coming too early."

He chuckled in my ear, making my nerves wrench once again because I hadn't sensed him getting quite that close. I could actually feel his breath in my hair.

"So you're going to be a smart-ass tonight, huh?" His voice held approval. "You know what I do to smart-asses, little girl?"

I didn't move but to turn my face his way. His breath shifted to my cheek, and his unique minty yet musky scent wafted up my nostrils. My belly fluttered with excitement as the cloth of his shirt brushed my bare arm. Oh...God. Maybe we did have to worry about me coming too early. Was it possible for girls to prematurely ejaculate?

Shivering, I nodded to myself, bolstering my nerve. Trying to lower the pitch of my voice to disguise it and maybe make it more sensual, I said, "Why don't you just *show* me what you do to them?"

It took him a second to respond. Damn, my fake voice had sounded terrible and way too much like my own. Positive he'd figured me out, I froze and waited, bracing for him to flip on the light and expose me, ruining the entire charade. My heartbeat pounded through my ears.

But then he murmured, "You got it, honey." Warm fingers, strong and confident, grasped my elbow. "This way." He nudged me to walk in front of him, not deeper into the room toward the bed, but off to the side toward... who-knew-what.

When I bumped into something, I huffed out a startled breath and stuck out my hands, blindly checking things out until I realized what we'd encountered.

"Table," I cautioned, thinking he'd direct me around it.

But, no. He bent me over it. "Good. Brace your hands and spread your legs."

A lightning bolt of heat spread through me, and something deep in my womb clenched tight, aching to feel him there.

"So, it's true then?" I gasped, gripping the table for dear life as I widened my stance. I didn't have to do anything to alter my voice that time. It went high all on its own, because oh my God, I was opening my legs for Oren. "You really do like it in the dark and from behind."

As soon as the words left my mouth, I realized I'd messed up. The girl meeting him tonight had already been with him, meaning I should already know about such inclinations.

He didn't call me on it, though, which made me frown in confusion after a second of petrified horror, waiting for him to figure it out. He merely leaned in to smell my hair. "Since you still showed up, I'm guessing that idea doesn't totally disgust you."

Unable to help myself, I jumped when he set his palm on my hip. The heat from his fingers scorched viciously through my dress until it had my already hard nipples tightening into oversensitive nubs.

He paused. And I knew—just knew—he was going to figure me out, turn on the light and force Noel's misbehaving little sister from his room. But an unimaginably long breath later, he shifted his hand, sliding it around to the front of my abdomen.

"What're you so jumpy about, honey?" His chest pressed lightly into my back, urging me to bend over the table some more. Moving naturally with him, I shifted my legs farther apart and rested my elbows on the smooth wooden top. My palms were damp and slipped a little across the surface until I found a nice sturdy grip around the beveled edge.

"Not scared," I answered. "Worried...just worried you're not going to be able to get me off. I'm kind of a hard nut to crack." Sander had only managed to make me come once, and that had been with tongue and fingers, never his cock.

That was so not what I was worried about with Oren, though. But it made me sound a lot less unsure about this entire thing than I felt. Made me sound confident, sexy, in charge.

I was Caroline. Hear me roar.

"Oh, I'll get you off, sweetness. You don't need to worry about that."

He gathered my skirt up to my waist. And ohmigod, ohmigod, ohmigod, this was really happening. A light breeze wafted between my bare thighs. My head went light from freaking myself into a dizzy mess!

Should I stop him?

I should totally stop him.

Oh God. I didn't stop him.

Warm, slightly roughened hands gripped my legs and slid up, and yeah...we definitely wouldn't have to worry about him not being able to get me off.

"Oren," I moaned, bowing my head down and biting my

lip. My eager thighs quivered in delight under his caress.

Until he stopped moving. Damn it! I really need to remember to check my voice.

But he didn't mention that. Instead, he muttered, "It's just Ten."

"What?" I blinked my eyes open and lifted my face, even though I still couldn't see a damn thing, and I wouldn't have seen him even if a light had been on since he was behind me.

"Just call me Ten."

Crinkling my brow, I said, "I like Oren better."

His hands left me completely. "Well, tough shit. I hate that fucking name. Only family is allowed to call me that."

Huh. *Really?* He didn't seem to mind when *Caroline* called him Oren. Did that mean he considered me family? Because I'd never called him anything but that, and he'd never once corrected me.

I wasn't sure if that was a good thing or a bad thing. Maybe he only saw me as a sister figure. That was creepy. If he ever found out about tonight, he'd be disgusted, thinking he'd done his surrogate sister.

"Fine." I straightened, refusing to voice my disappointment. "I guess I'll go, then." It'd been stupid to think we could be anything more anyway.

What the hell had I been trying to accomplish? Even if I'd been able to sleep with him, I'd still never *have* him, have him. Going through with this would've led to nothing but heartbreak.

I pushed away from him, and he fell back a step, letting me go. Angry at myself for being a complete idiot and angry at him for letting me leave so easily, I stumbled through the dark until I rammed my fingers into the door. With a pained curse, I fumbled for the knob, but when I couldn't find it within two seconds I growled out more of my frustration and flopped onto the floor in defeat, sitting with my back to the door as I cradled my head in my hands.

"What's such a big deal about saying Oren, anyway?" I felt sulky and yet heartbroken, realizing I still wasn't going to get the one thing I wanted most. Him.

"Because," he mumbled, sounding reluctant. "It's the last word to leave my sister's bloody lips before she *died* in my arms."

"Oh." I shuddered, my voice barely a whisper. "Oh, hell."

"Yeah," he murmured.

Gulping with unease and sorrow, and shame, I wondered what I was supposed to do now. I blew out a breath and tried to control the sudden shaking in my entire frame. But what the hell? Why did he have to go and confess something like *that* to me? I hadn't even known he'd *had* a sister. Shit, I didn't know he had family at all. As far as I was concerned, he could've sprouted fully horny out the side of some Zeus dude's head.

I covered my mouth with a shaky hand. How could I not already know about this? I'd made it a point to know everything there was to know about him. I doubt Noel even knew, because my brother would've mentioned it at some point. Right?

Discovering it now, though, told me how much it had left him traumatized. He hadn't told anyone in our group, or I'd know. That meant he still couldn't talk about it, was repressing the pain. I wondered how long ago—

"So..." he said in a conversational tone that I swear was laced with worry. Did he regret telling me what he'd just told me? "I can't help but notice you're still here."

I sniffed and wiped my face, even though I wasn't crying. I just *wanted* to cry. A lot. "Sorry," I mumbled. "I'll go."

But as soon as I put my hands down on the floor to push myself up, he said, "I didn't say you had to go."

Shuffling in the dark told me he was coming closer. And then I swear he knelt in front of me. "Shit. You're not crying, are you?"

"No." My face heated with shame, horrified he even knew I wanted to. I felt so stupid...and small. "But I am sorry. About your sister. I didn't know."

"Well, *no one* knew, so..." He trailed off as if he was shrugging.

"Why didn't you ever tell anyone about it?"

"Because I didn't want to talk about it. Why are you still here, not-crying on my bedroom floor?"

"I don't know," I mumbled. "Because I feel like a big, stupid failure, I guess. This was my one and only chance to be with you, and I...I royally fucked it up."

I caught my breath, realizing I'd slipped again. This wasn't the one and only chance *Kelly*—who I was still supposed to be—had gotten to be with him. Why did I keep butchering this?

And why wasn't he catching any of my mistakes?

"I wouldn't say royally." His voice seemed to move closer, seemingly clueless about my failed impersonation. "I mean, I'm still here. You're still here. And I'm not exactly hard to get."

I snorted. Yeah, he was *so* easy. This was only my third failed attempt to get into his pants.

"Damn. You really wanted me tonight, didn't you?" The idea seemed to amaze him.

With a roll of my eyes, I sighed. He seriously couldn't be so oblivious about how much women wanted him, could he? "If you could feel how wet I am, you wouldn't even have to ask that."

"Well...okay." He sounded as if he'd just accepted an invitation. When his hand landed on my ankle, I jumped out of my skin with a started yelp.

"What the hell? What're you doing?"

His fingers stole up my calf. "You just told me to feel how wet you are. Invitation accepted."

"No, I didn't. You know what I meant. *Oren!*"

"Shh," he warned, reminding me I wasn't supposed to call him that. "You know you want this."

"Oh, good Lord." I groaned and slapped a hand to my forehead. "Of all the corny things to—"

I broke off with a gasp when Oren discovered just how wet I was.

"Holy fucking shit. You're not wearing any panties." His fingers were sure but gentle as they moved between my legs, swiping through the moisture before finding my clit.

"Wait. You can't..." I grabbed his wrist but didn't stop him. I didn't *want* him to stop.

"I can't what?" he asked.

"I don't know." I panted, my legs loosening as his thumb rolled over the most sensitive little muscle in my entire body with a merciless precision. "Was I talking?"

He chuckled. "You really are this wet just for me, aren't you?"

"Who else?" I moaned and arched up my hips. That's why I was here, why I was risking everything to be here. Learning about his sister only made me feel closer to him. I wanted to soothe his soul, tame the poor, wild, hurting boy, and experience every physical intimacy with him while I was at it.

Even if he was only here to get off in some random chick— Wait. Thinking of it that way didn't help anything.

I squeezed my eyes closed. Could I be any more of an idiot than I was now?

"Damn," he breathed. He pressed at least two fingers inside me and we both sucked in a breath. My eyes flew open as I panted through the pleasure and ground against his hand, needing more.

He groaned. "I want to smell it." Abandoning my pussy to grip my hips, he tugged me away from the door and toward him. "Slide this way, will you, sweetness?"

Once he had me where he wanted me, he gathered my skirt up to my waist, split my legs open wider, and then gripped my ass cheeks to lift me a couple inches off the floor. A second later, his breath heated me there.

I damn near came. "Oh God. Oh God."

"Fuck," he gasped. "You smell good. Makes me want to...taste."

The mere word had my eyes rolling into the back of my head. But then a wet heat touched me. Knowing it was his tongue—*him*—I couldn't take it. I came hard, gasping and grabbing his hair, quivering out of control.

What? It'd been a freaking year since a male had been anywhere near there. I couldn't help it. And knowing it was Oren made it...yeah. No way was I holding that baby back.

So, I didn't.

And Oren lapped it up until I was an exhausted, panting mess under him. "Christ, woman. You're fucking sensitive. Too sensitive. I was kind of hoping to feel you go off around me, let these sweet, tight walls here milk my cock while I thrust inside you."

When he lightly circled the opening of my pussy, I gritted my teeth and bowed up, taut and ready again.

The movement of his finger slowed. "Holy shit. Are you...?" As if experimenting, he slid two fingers in me. I gasped and squeezed my thighs around his wrist. "Goddamn." He sounded amazed. "You *are* ready again?"

"I... I..." I wasn't sure. I was still riding the last orgasm he'd given me, but I also felt like a live wire. If his cock wasn't in me within thirty seconds—

His fingers jerked free, and I cried out from the loss. "*No.*"

"Just...hold on. I'm...damn. Fuck. Where did I put the

condom?"

"*What*?" I sobbed, nearly in tears. If he lost his condom, I was going to hurt him. No one had riled me up like this before. I was so turned on I felt like a hair trigger. Just one more touch and I could blow...again.

"Oh yeah. I had it on the table." A split second later, arms were lifting me. I was carried a few feet to the table he'd bent me over before. He didn't have to say anything this time; I just slumped over it and hiked my ass into the air, beyond ready.

The sound of his zipper lowering made me jerk. I had no idea even a sound could set things off. But when you were as turned on as I was, he could probably exhale right about now, and I'd likely come. The rasp of tearing foil and the hiss of his breath as he rolled latex over his length made my thighs tremble. I bet he had his hand around himself right now. He had to be hard and pulsing, ready to enter me.

I swallowed, unable to believe this was happening. Oren was going to put his cock inside me.

"Ready?"

I shuddered, a full-body shiver from head to toe...toes that were already curling because they tingled so badly. "Okay," I chanted, boosting and trying to calm myself from the anticipation, all in one word. "Okay."

"Okay," he echoed. He almost sounded as eager and nervous as I felt, which only synched me in with him more. So when he touched me there with the blunt head of his cock, I whimpered.

"Oh God. *Please*."

The head entered me and I sucked in a breath, bowing my face as I soaked in the sensation. He slowly applied pressure, filling me and stretching my womb to accommodate himself. I felt every freaking centimeter.

"Holy...*fuck*," he gritted out, gripping my waist hard enough that his fingers bit into my skin. "You're so...damn...tight." He blew out a breath as he seated himself completely, all of him in all of me.

I couldn't remember ever feeling this full with Sander. Not that I was thinking about *him*, but he was my only other point of reference, and I had definitely never experienced this much stretching before. Oren felt so...I don't know, huge, maybe. He was crammed in almost too tight, as if there was no room for anything else. All I could feel was him, and it was delicious and perfect and—

"Oh God!" I yelped as he shifted ever so slightly, hitting something that shot off a spasm that consumed me entirely. "Right there. Right there. You found it. Don't move." I wanted to freeze this moment in all eternity and memorize the feel of him lodged deep, filling me, and consuming me. I just needed a second to appreciate the wonder—

"Don't *move*?" he yelped, repeating my instructions. "Are you *insane*? You can't let a guy into pussy heaven and then tell him not to move."

So, of course, he moved, sliding most of the way out, until I was gasping and clutching the table harder, pressing my forehead to the flat wooden surface. And then he shoved right back in.

"Oren," I whimpered. Seated deep, he'd felt amazing. But moving and rubbing his cock against every nerve ending in my channel was pure torture, amazing, marvelous torture. Inner muscles were quivering and contracting out of control around him. None of my previous orgasms—not even the self-inflicted ones—had ever had such an extreme buildup.

Grabbing my hair—and not too gently—he thrust again and growled into my ear. "Stop...calling...me—"

But I was too busy coming to care what name I was shouting, so I just kept chanting, "Ohmigod, ohmigod, *Orrrrrennnn.*"

He cursed and pounded harder, pulling my hair snugger and growling out his own release as I pulsed around him, my nipples throbbing and core convulsing with every tug on my scalp.

It was the single greatest orgasm to ever claim me... and definitely the strangest. Who knew hair pulling would get me off like that?

After I finally stopped coming, Oren slumped onto me, making the small table wobble perilously under us. His damp chest stuck to my back and pushed my breasts forward, smashing them against the cool wood.

Panting in my ear, he sounded sapped of all energy. "Holy...fuck."

"S-sorry, I...I called you Oren again," I tried to say, though it was nearly impossible from the way he was squishing out any air that might've circulated through my lungs.

He hissed out an amused sound. "I didn't mind it so much that time."

I smiled. "I guess it was time to give that name a new kind of memory."

"Hmm." His voice went distant as if he didn't want to share such an intimacy with me.

Making new memories was only meant to happen with friends and lovers, not strangers humping in the dark.

That's when the first wave of queasy reality sliced through me. This hadn't meant to him what it had meant to me. In my head, I'd known that all along. But now that it was all said and done, I was actually *living* it. He was still buried inside me, and to me, it was intimate and bonding. To him, it was empty, emotionless fucking.

I bit my lip, forcing myself not to cry. What the hell had I just done?

I pressed my forehead to the table a bit too hard and made it thump.

Oren's fingers eased back into my hair. "Did pulling your hair really make you come?"

I'm pretty sure it had been an accumulation of everything that had made me come, but the hair thing...oh yeah, my muscles quivered around his length, remembering how it had felt when he'd done that. So I said, "Yeah. Weird, huh?"

"What? Hair pulling's never turned you on before?"

"I...no one's actually pulled it before, you know, during..."

He gave another experimental tug. My body clamped around his and we both sucked in a breath as he started growing inside me.

"Damn." Once again hard enough to pull out and nudge his way back in, he groaned. "I'm going to need another condom." But instead of leaving me, he thrust forward the next time he backed his hips away. "Fuck, you feel good."

"Oren," I sobbed, my body growing tingly and tense all over again.

"Yeah," he growled. "Say it again."

"Oren."

He reached around and pinched my clit lightly. I convulsed and started coming, calling out his name. I was barely finished when he yanked out of me abruptly.

"*Wha*—?" What was he *doing*?

"New condom," he choked. As he abandoned me completely, leaving me chilled, I straightened and rubbed my arms briskly, still coming down from the tingles seizing me.

When I took a step from the table, I winced. "Ouch. I think your table just left a permanent indention in my hip."

"Poor baby," he murmured, returning to me. "Here. The bed will be more comfortable."

I sighed, thinking he'd pull back the covers and we'd climb in together and snuggle a bit, maybe finally kiss. But no. He bent me over the bed exactly as he'd bent me over the table. I wasn't prepared when he entered me. The startling penetration caused me to jump. "Oh God! Oren..."

Moving deep and slow with each pass, he leaned into me heavily and even braced his arms on either side of me so he could press his front to my back. "You know," he murmured into my ear as he began to stroke his fingers through my hair. "Kelly's only ever called me Ten."

I frowned, wondering who the hell Kelly was and why he was talking about her while he was inside me. I really didn't want to kill him before he could give me a fourth orgasm.

"She has short, coarse, curly locks, too," he added as he continued to comb my hair with his fingers. "Nothing this long, or straight, or silky soft."

"Oh, shit." Now I remembered who Kelly was.

I was supposed to be Kelly.

CHAPTER 4

TEN

My MYSTERY visitor tried to squirm out from under me, but I covered her completely, pinning her to the bed. No way was I letting her up until I drew Big O Number Four from her. So I pushed into her deeper, literally imprisoning us together. God, that felt good. The tight, wet, warm clasp of her pussy was pure nirvana.

You wouldn't think one woman would feel all that different on the inside from another. But she did. Holy fuck, did she ever. She felt better than any other woman to let me into her body.

I tightened my grip in her silken hair, because I needed to latch on to something and also because I loved the way it seemed to set her off. Then I began to thrust with more intensity. She gave a startled sound and panted harder, getting closer to that next orgasm I was so hungry to claim. I could tell by the clenching of every muscle in her body she only had seconds to go. When she threw her head back, I sank my teeth into the tightly corded muscles of her shoulders, reveling in her approaching explosion. She sounded good when she came. Real good.

"I knew the second you walked into this room you weren't Kelly," I murmured into her ear, and then pressed my lips against her temple because the familiar scent from her hair had my balls tightening. "But that's okay. I like fucking a stranger."

That was a lie, though, since fucking a stranger wasn't what I felt like I was doing at all. What I really liked was imagining she could be whoever I wanted her to be, not who she really was.

"Not knowing who you are just makes this hotter." Imagining she was *Caroline* was what made it hotter.

And just like that, she came. The hot little muscle squeezing my cock quivered and constricted, and I couldn't hold back. I poured into her, grinding my hips into her ass as I submerged myself as far as I could and just let it all go. She buried her face into my sheets and screamed. I felt my own moan rising, so I bit the back of her shoulder again and slid my palms up her arms until I reached her fingers where she was gripping the sheets. Then I covered her hands and clutched the sheets right along with her.

The storm rolled through us, and I kept holding her that way long after it was over.

I wanted to kiss her. I wanted to roll her onto her back so I could press my chest up against her tits and stamp my mouth to hers, part her lips, and wet my tongue against hers. I wanted to taste her and share our next thousand breaths together. Which scared the fucking shit out of me. Because I never wanted to kiss them. I was never this sweet and tender with them.

And that meant I knew she was different. She was—

She wiggled under me. "Get...*off.*"

"What? *Ouch.* Shit, woman." She rammed her ass back, dislodging me from inside her, and caught me in the stomach. It didn't hurt, but it did surprise me enough to rear up. "What the hell?"

I reached for her, but she was a little escape artist when she wanted to be. She shot out of the bed and scrambled for the door while my seeking fingers grasped nothing but cool air.

"Hey!" I finally caught an elbow but didn't get a good enough hold because she immediately wiggled free. Her shoes clattered across the floor before my bedroom door burst open and then slammed shut. I listened to her race down the hall and slam the front door as well.

Blowing out a long breath, I rolled onto my back and stared up at my dark ceiling, seeing basically nothing.

What had just happened had been...yeah. That had been something else.

I'd known she wasn't Kelly immediately. The lack of giggling and constant talking had kind of tipped me off. Then she'd gone and let it escape that she'd never been with me before. Her mentioning rumors of me only doing it in the dark from behind let me know she had to be someone from Kelly's clique, though.

I'd been a little bored lately, you see, so I'd started up this game with myself where I fucked each girl from the same group in a specific position. For example, I did all the Alpha Delta Pi sorority sisters in reverse cowgirl. Teaching majors were strictly oral. And the athlete groupies got it doggie style. That way, when they talked amongst themselves, they all realized I did them the same way, and they began to think I had some weird tick, or something.

Not really sure why I'd started up such a bizarre game with myself, but it amused the hell out of me to fuck with their heads.

So, that's why I assumed my new midnight visitor was another football groupie... Until the first moment she'd forgotten to disguise her voice or when she'd said my name in that tone I'd recognize anywhere.

I'd frozen solid, with my hand on her warm, bare thigh, not sure what to do and completely unable to believe *Caroline* was in my bedroom, bent over my table. Suddenly harder than I'd ever been in my life, I shook my head, trying to deny it. I mean, no possible way could that have been Caroline's flesh that had heated my palm. Uh-uh.

First of all, she wouldn't have the audacity. Okay, scratch that; she definitely had the nerve. That was one of the reasons I was so hot for her. She could be a gutsy little spitfire whenever she put her mind to it.

But she wouldn't...damn, she wouldn't stroll in here posing as Kelly, would she? She'd been pissed at me earlier this evening; I would've thought she'd be more likely to smash my nuts into a hand vise than give my cock the ride of its life.

So, yeah, I had to be wrong. It hadn't been her, no matter how much her voice had sounded like Caroline's, no matter how much she'd smelled like Caroline, and no matter how much she'd felt as I would imagine Caroline would feel. Silky hair, soft skin, perfectly firm but malleable breasts, and the tightest, hottest pussy to ever squeeze my cock.

Oh, shit. Had I just had my cock *inside* Caroline's pussy? I'd definitely treated her as I'd never treated a woman in the sack before, admitting that personal shit about my sister, kissing her temple, holding hands while we came together.

But no. No fucking way. It couldn't be.

Still...the idea of it turned me on like nothing else.

I lay there in my bed that felt extra empty without her and I started to grow hard again, just thinking about the possibility that I might've just had my dick in *the* woman I'd been craving for nearly a year.

I shuddered. No, no, no. It hadn't been her. I'd only been giving her Caroline's qualities because she was the one woman I wanted more than anything and I didn't know who she *really* was.

Sitting up on my mattress, I flipped on my bedside light. But no matter how fast my midnight visitor had lit out of here, she hadn't left anything behind; nothing to prove she'd been Caroline, but nothing to disprove it either. I was fleetingly tempted to race after her and find out who she'd really been—I could probably still catch her in the parking lot—but then...did I honestly want to know?

I ran my hands through my hair and then I squeezed my head hard, telling myself Kelly had just switched off with one of her friends this evening because...hell, who knew why. Who cared? I still couldn't get over how good it'd been.

But getting off from hair pulling? Hmm. Interesting.

I finally got around to tossing my condom, then I flopped onto my bed, naked. I stared up in the direction of my dark ceiling, reliving every minute of my midnight visit.

My brain was still tangled with thoughts of her the next morning...until some asshole interrupted my fond memories.

"Hey, how do you spell informative?"

"Hmm?" I grunted when Gamble kicked me under the table. "What?"

"Informative," he said. "How's it spelled?"

We were accustomed to hanging out on Saturday

mornings; it used to be football practice morning. But with us both being seniors and the season long over, we no longer had practice to attend; we wouldn't be back next year to play. So, we'd been meeting up at the local coffee shop every Saturday morning. And boring-ass old men that we were becoming, we usually did homework together.

Yeah, I said homework. My homeboy had turned into a homework-finishing machine in the past year. It was a little embarrassing, but I went along with it because, hell, I don't know. He was my friend, and friends sacrificed for each other and did shit like *homework* with their buddies who'd turned into pussies for the women they loved and wanted to impress with good grades. So, I sacrificed my precious Saturday mornings and did homework with my pal instead of what we used to do together, which was hit on chicks.

I kind of missed the hitting-on-chicks era, and yet, I kind of didn't. It'd gotten a little monotonous and stale lately. I don't know if it was Gam's settling down that had changed things, or something in me. Damn, maybe I was getting as old and boring as Gamble was. Shit, that couldn't be good. So, in an effort to preserve my Ten-ness, I still tried to put some effort into flirting with every girl who passed our table for the both of us, even though my heart was no longer in it.

"*E, n,* formative. Fuck, I don't know." I sent him a scowl. "Aren't you the one married to the goddamn English teacher?"

"I can't ask *her*." Gam stared at me as if I was whack. "If she helped me out, the dick administration would know it's not my work by the quality of the writing."

"Then purposely spell it wrong. Or better yet, use a dumber word you *can* spell and would actually use in a sentence." I shook my head. *What a freak.*

Gam ground his teeth and scowled. "But I want to amaze Aspen and make a good grade. English is her thing; I can't suck at an English essay."

I sighed and held up my index finger. "Reason number one why I will never fall for a fucking English teacher: because I refuse to pretend to like English essays."

As my buddy grumbled obscenities at me, I went back to ignoring him and chewing on my pen, wearing the end down to a mangled nub. It was still weird that he was married now. He'd tied the knot with his woman on New

Year's Day, three months ago.

The moment they'd repeated their vows echoed through my brain. As his best man, I'd had to stand right up there with a front-row view so I could hear their words, plain as day. Up until that moment when he was pledging his life to his woman, I'd done a damn fine job of not looking across them toward the maid of honor. But when Noel's clear voice started promising to love and cherish, and all that shit, I'd caved in and glanced at her.

Caroline.

Fuck me, but she'd been glancing back, and looking stunning in her maid of honor dress. So I'd stared at her through the rest of the entire freaking service. If she would've looked away first, I might've too, but she hadn't, so there I was, screwed into staring back and getting a stiffy in the middle of a wedding because I'd so desperately wanted to mount my best friend's little sister.

"Ha!" Gam crowed suddenly, making me jump out of my freaking skin, the douche. "It's *I, n,* formative, you fucker." He set the smartphone he was consulting on the table by his laptop and began to type, copying the spelling.

I scowled at him. "Good for you." I found myself frowning at him a lot lately. But I couldn't help it; sometimes I just wanted to wring his idiot neck for so constantly telling me to stay away from Caroline. Didn't he know that forbidding me only made me want to crowd in as close as I could until I was fucking *inside* her?

But thinking about being inside her made me think of last night, which made me even more irritable because I knew it couldn't have been her, no matter how much I'd wanted it to be.

I sniffed and stared at the opened page of my calculus book without seeing a fucking thing. "Wow, Gam can spell. *Yay.*" My voice was dry as I lifted my fisted hands like fake pom-poms and waved them for him.

He kicked me under the table again. "Douche."

I kicked back harder. "Finger banger."

"Rotten crotch." His shoe caught me in the shin, but I refused to flinch.

"Brown diver." I slammed my heel down on the tip of his sneaker, hoping to catch his toes. Success came when he winced.

Yes! I rule. Gamble drools.

Rolling his tongue over his teeth, he scowled. "You're not going to give up, are you?"

I shrugged. "I could do this all day, motherfucker."

"What a loser." He shook his head and returned to his assignment, taking the high road to maturity.

I snorted, betting myself he'd kick me again before our homework session was over.

I was about to call him a prick when a pair of ladies passing our table cooed, "Hey, Noel," and then, "Hi, Ten," as more of an afterthought.

"Hey," Noel said, not even daring to lift his face and make eye contact as he waved his pen at them in a halfhearted greeting. I waved too and watched them continue past as they got into the end of the line for a drink.

Instead of slipping out of my chair and following the lovely ladies who'd just waved at us, though, I went back to chewing on my pen and staring at my calculus assignment.

"Hey." Noel kicked me again—just as I knew he would—right in the soft spot on my shin that he'd gotten before. Fucker hurt.

"What the hell?" I snapped, glaring at him. "Stop kicking me."

He blinked as if my request was completely unfounded. Then he shook his head. "What is *wrong* with you?"

I hoped I didn't pale, but it felt like I did, like every ounce of blood in my face drained down to irritate the knots forming in my stomach. Then I panicked, my palms turning all cold and sweaty, and I didn't know why. But I felt instantly guilty, as if I had fucked his sister the night before. And I hadn't. I *knew* I hadn't, because the woman I'd been inside had *not* been Caroline. End of discussion.

So I scowled at the fucker for making me freak out.

"You're the one who can't keep his feet to himself," I countered. "What the fuck is wrong with *you*?"

He tipped his head toward the growing line at the barista's counter. "Why didn't you chase after them?"

I frowned, momentarily confused. "After who?"

"*Who*?" he repeated incredulously. "Those two girls who just eye-fucked the shit out of you, man. That's who. On a normal, average day in the life of Ten, you would've already been over there, panting and drooling by now."

I shrugged, refusing to take issue with the terms *panting* and *drooling*. "They said hi to *you* first."

He snorted. "As if that's ever held you back before."

Okay, so he might've had a point. I glanced at the two women still gossiping together, close enough that they were touching. They looked good from the back. Nice tight asses with enough junk in the trunk to interest me. I pictured both of them together, teaming up on me. But, yeah, not even that roused me enough to leave my chair.

I turned back to Gamble. "Meh."

His mouth dropped open. "What the hell? Oren Tenning does not say 'meh' to tits and ass. Ever. So...what the hell is up with you? Shit. Are you dying?"

"What? No." He wouldn't stop staring at me as if he really was afraid I had cancer or something, so I hissed out a sigh and glanced around before I leaned across the table toward him. "Have you ever..." I scanned the coffee shop again, on the lookout for spying ears. I debated whether I should say anything. But then, I told myself that it wasn't like I was really talking about his sister to him. This could be my proof to myself that it *couldn't* have been her last night. I'd never give details to a guy about his own sister. Plus I always gave him details; he'd think something was up if I didn't.

So, I lowered my voice and continued. "Have you ever gotten *more* turned on when you were arguing with a girl while doing her?"

Gamble stared at me with his mouth open before he shook his head and blinked. "Why would you argue with a girl while you were doing her?"

"Because..." I growled out my frustration and waved my hand, hoping to get him past that issue. He wouldn't understand why I couldn't stand hearing anyone but my parents or Caroline call me Oren. "It doesn't matter *why*. It just...happened. And it was hot. Really weird. But like, extremely hot."

He rolled his eyes toward the ceiling. "Jesus. You *would* like something strange like that."

"I'm serious, man." I scowled at him hard.

"So am I." He blurted out a laugh. "And only you would start up an argument with a woman while you were inside her. Damn, Ten." He shook his head again, but this time, he was at least grinning while he did it. "You're a piece of work."

Disappointment lanced through me. I was hoping he'd

have experienced something at least similar before. "What about hair pulling, then?" I pressed. "You ever get your woman to come by pulling her hair while doing her?"

Eyebrows shooting into his hairline, Gamble sniffed. "As if I'm going to let you know about anything that gets my woman off."

I opened my mouth to argue, but he held up a finger. "Let me get this straight. You argued with some girl *and* pulled her hair during sex? Wow. What are you? Five?"

"No," I muttered, growing more irritated than ever. I didn't like him bashing what might've possibly been the best sex of my life. "I'm Ten. And she liked it. A lot. Like, *four* times within twenty minutes a lot."

Gamble pulled back, clearly impressed. He whistled between his teeth, but then his face filled with disbelief. "She probably faked it."

I lifted my hands. "Why fake four times? Why not just once so I'd stop and leave her alone?"

He shrugged. "Good point, but I don't know. To make you feel better, maybe?"

"Whatever." I rolled my eyes. "She didn't fake them. Trust me. There was no way to fake this. It was..." I shook my head, still stunned by everything that had happened. "Fucking incredible."

A knowing grin lit Gamble's face. "Well, holy shit. One specific woman finally left an impression on my Ten. What'd you say her name was? Anyone I know?"

I winced and sucked my bottom lip in between my teeth. "I don't know."

He blinked. "You don't know what? Her *name*?"

With a shake of my head, I said, "Nope. I do not know her name."

"Well, what'd she look like? Was she one of the usual football groupies?"

I shrugged. "Not sure."

"You're not sure about...*what*?"

"I'm not sure what she looked like."

He scratched at the five o'clock shadow on his jaw and frowned at me. "How can you not know what she looked like? How drunk were you?"

"I wasn't drunk at all. I just didn't...*see* her."

"You didn't..." He shook his head, clearly confused. "*What*?"

"It was dark."

"Okay, but... Wait, wait, wait." He waved his hands. "Start from the beginning."

So I did, telling him about my meeting with Kelly at the bar. He knew who Kelly was and how tightly cork-screwed her hair was. Then I told him about our darkened meeting plans. "But the thing was, the girl who came into my room had long, straight hair that was really soft." *And silky. And she'd smelled amazing...like Caroline.*

Gamble studied me for a good ten seconds after my story before saying, "So, basically, you could've fucked...*anyone*?"

"Yeah," I said. "I guess. I mean, it was definitely a female, but other than that...yeah."

His eyes went wide. "It wasn't Hamilton's woman, was it?"

I started at him a moment to wait for him to grow up. Then I said, "Really?"

He shrugged. "Well...it's not an impossible suggestion. She lives in the same apartment as you and has long, straight hair. What if she got up in the middle of the night, and...I don't know, used the restroom and was so tired when she came out, she mistakenly walked into the wrong room and crawled into bed with the wrong roommate."

I stared at Gam, sure he'd lost his mind.

He snapped. "What? It's not that unreasonable of an idea."

"Yes, it is! Because it sure as hell was *not* Blondie." Even though, okay, the body type and hair did kind of match. Oh, shit. It hadn't been Blondie, had it? My stomach roiled. Quinn would never forgive me if I accidentally—

"Wait. No." My shoulders slumped in relief. "It *couldn't* have been her. She kept calling me Or—by my first name. So, the chick definitely knew who was doing her, which totally cancels out your theory that Ham's woman accidentally crawled into bed with me and screwed the wrong guy. Twice."

"Hmm. Yeah. I guess." He continued to think about it before saying, "But did the girl realize you didn't know who *she* was?"

"Yeah." I sat forward again, lowering my voice. "That's the strangest part. It totally spooked her when I told her I knew she wasn't Kelly. She actually *wanted* me to think she was someone else. She even tried to buck me off and stop when I told her. And we hadn't even finished round two yet."

"Wait. You told her *during* sex?" Gamble gasped out. "And holy shit. It wasn't even the first round? Can you possibly say anything else more bizarre right now?"

Yes. I think it might've been your sister.

But, yeah, I didn't say that shit. I freaked myself out for even thinking it. So I blew out a breath. "It was the best fucking sex of my life."

I *was* able to admit that.

Gamble snorted. "And you still don't know who she was?"

I shook my head, not sure if I wanted to know. Yeah, I'm pretty sure I didn't want to know. Because if it'd been who I wanted it to be, I'd be seriously fucked. And if it hadn't been who I wanted it to be, I'd be seriously... disappointed. "She lit out of there like her tail was on fire as soon as we finished. I'm telling you, she didn't want me to know her identity."

But that idea didn't faze my friend. "Well, I don't really blame the poor girl there," he said with an obnoxious grin. "If I were a woman who had a thing for you, I'd be too humiliated to let anyone—even you—know about it."

"Fucker." It was my turn to kick him under the table.

He rolled his eyes as if he was way past such childish antics. "So, it was the best sex of your life, and you'll never be able to get a repeat because you have no idea who to go to for night two. Nice, man. Way to fuck yourself over."

"Oh, shit." I fell back in my chair, staring at him with my mouth open. "You're right."

I'd never get to fuck that mystery woman again.

Not cool.

"Hey, guys." A breathless Hamilton interrupted us by pulling out the free chair between us and slumping down with an exhausted pant.

Since he was only a sophomore, he still attended the team's Saturday morning training sessions. Decked out in sweats and a T-shirt with his face shiny red with exertion and his hair wet from a recent shower, he'd obviously come straight from practice.

"What'd I miss?" he asked.

Gamble snickered, and I knew he was going to say

something I'd have to beat his ass for a split second before he asked, "Hey, your woman didn't get up in the middle of the night last night to, I don't know...get a drink or go to the bathroom or anything, did she?"

"Jesus," I muttered, tipping my head back and squeezing my eyes shut. He just had to go there, didn't he?

"Uh..." Confusion clouded Ham's voice as he glanced between the two of us. "I don't think so. Why?" His gaze settled on me before moving back to Gam.

"Because Ten here had a midnight visitor in his room. Some chick came to him in the dark, fucked his brains out, then ran out before he could get her name or even see her face, and he has no clue who it was."

I ground my teeth at the vulgar way he put it. Which was strange, because on any other occasion, I would've phrased it pretty much the same way. But since I was picturing her with Caroline's qualities, it suddenly didn't seem so funny to say it like that.

Hamilton's eyebrows crinkled in confusion before they shot straight up into his hairline. He whirled to me with an incredulous glance. "And you think it was *Zoey*?"

"*No*." I lifted my hands in immediate surrender. I mean, I wasn't puny by any stretch of the imagination. But Ham was huge, and I was pretty sure he could take me if I offended his woman in any way. "I *know* it wasn't her. And I never thought it was. That asswipe over there came up with that idea all on his own."

Ham zipped his stern glare to Gamble.

"Whoa," Gamble said, lifting his hands too, but laughing as he did so. "I was just fucking with you guys. Jesus. Who would've been *your* first guess?"

"Some football groupie," Hamilton said immediately.

Caroline, I didn't say at all.

I groaned into my hands before dropping them from my face. "The fact of the matter is, I have no idea who Miss Midnight Visitor was, and I'm sure I never will. So let's just drop it already. Okay? Good."

Knowing I was never going to dip my wick in that sweet honeypot was beginning to irritate me.

Jesus, why was everything irritating me today?

Ham and Gam glanced at me. Then they glanced at each other. When they gave one another a knowing grin, I rolled my eyes. But God...damn. I missed the days when all my friends had been as single and available as I was. Now that they were all pussy whipped, they seemed to think I should be too, like fucking one woman for the rest of my life was such a grand, amazing thing.

Dear God. The horror. Unless maybe that one woman felt like the woman last night had felt. Then maybe—nah. I shuddered at the thought, and leaned forward to pay attention to my calculus book. "Coach still lining you up as the first-string quarterback next year?" I asked Ham.

He cleared his throat, glanced at Gam, and then nodded. "Yeah."

Gamble had been the star QB of our team until he'd broken his collarbone on the second to last game this last year. So Hamilton had needed to step in and bring us the rest of the way to the national championships. We all knew it bothered Gamble because he hadn't been able to play that last game, and he'd lost his shot to try out for the pros. Even though he said he was happy settling down here with his woman and taking care of his three younger siblings— whom he'd taken away from his mother after she practically abandoned them—we knew it bugged him.

"Aspen find a job yet?" Ham asked him, hopefully.

When Gam looked up, we knew she hadn't from the tightening in his jaw. "No," he muttered.

She'd been unemployed for going on a year now, ever since she'd been fired for starting a relationship with him. Which brought up another sore issue with Gamble. He felt like a personal failure every time she applied for a new job and wasn't hired. But then he wouldn't even let her apply for jobs that he found "beneath" her. If their money was as tight as I knew it had to be, you'd think he'd just suck it up and let her be...well, whatever, for a while. But nope. He stayed stubborn. And she knew how much it would bother him if she "lowered" herself, as he called it, so she stayed unemployed and they just kept scrimping along. And I kept pretending it was my turn to pay for all our Saturday morning drinks at the coffee shop. And Gamble just kept letting me.

I knew Caroline offered him money on a regular basis. She'd gotten a little nest egg last year—though I never learned just how many eggs—after she'd gotten involved with that rich prick from her hometown and his parents had paid her off. But Gamble adamantly refused to touch a cent of that money.

I think each and every one of his rejections tore off a piece of her soul and left her bleeding a little more each time. She'd gone through a lot of bad shit to get that money; she should get to spend it however the fuck she wanted to. And if she wanted to help her family with it, her big brother should let her. That was one of the reasons she'd taken it in the first place...because of Gamble and their two younger brothers.

Gamble forcing her to spend it on no one but herself killed a part of her, and sometimes, I just wanted to wrap my hands around his throat and shake some sense into him, force him to accept some of her money already. It would've made her happier.

But I had no business in their family affairs, and I knew better than to butt in, no matter how many times I watched Caroline stiffen her spine, lift her chin and try to keep the pain from her eyes whenever *he* refused her help. The too-proud, stubborn ass.

"I think I'm going to change my major," Gamble spoke up suddenly.

"What?" Hamilton and I glanced at him in unison.

He nodded. "Aspen and I have been talking, and... business administration isn't my thing. I know I won't ever go pro, but I miss the football field. That's where I belong. So, I'm thinking...I'm going to enroll again next year and get a teaching certificate, maybe become a coach."

While Hamilton nodded, letting him know what a great idea that was, my jaw dropped. "What?" I couldn't be the only one of us three graduating and moving off to find a real job. I was the least mature of our group, the perpetual college party boy. I didn't want to be the first to grow up.

Gam shrugged and sent me a solemn glance. "Since Pick's raised my wages at the bar, we're doing...okay. We can make it for another two years until I graduate, and Caroline already has money for college taken care of, so I don't have to worry about her. I seriously think it's for the best if I did this."

"Well, fuck." Now I really felt crappy. Not only had I had the best sex of my life and had just realized I'd never have it again, but now I was hearing that I'd be moving off while all my friends would remain here together... without me.

That shit just wasn't right.

CHAPTER 5

Caroline

THE SECOND semester of my freshman year at ESU was drawing to a close in a month. A *month*. I would turn nineteen a week after the last day of class, I had a minimum wage job cleaning an insurance office downtown after hours, and I'd just tricked the asshole of my dreams into having sex with me.

Yeah, I was a complete mess.

The soreness between my legs was the first thing I felt when I opened my eyes the next morning. Which flooded my head with flashbacks of the night before. Oren's hand running up my thigh. Oren's teeth digging into the back of my shoulder. Oren's cock making me come all over his room. I shuddered and clamped my legs together as I hugged one arm over my tingling breasts.

Well, I'd been curious what he'd be like. And I'd gotten my curiosities appeased.

But now I ached for seconds.

"Way to go, Caroline," I muttered aloud. Way to *not* get him out of my system but to embed the craving for him even further into my soul.

Studying the ceiling of my room, I blew out a slow

breath. The sheetrock was painted white and had a delicate-looking ceiling fan hanging directly over my bed. There wasn't a hole or even a water stain of an approaching hole in sight. This was the best ceiling of the best bedroom I'd ever had. It was my room alone, too. I didn't have to share it with my two younger brothers, who rolled over constantly at night and always managed to jack me in the face with an arm or elbow.

It was all mine.

The trailer house we'd lived in before really couldn't even be classified as a home. The morning Noel had arrived on our front steps and seen how we were surviving, he'd bundled the three of us up and brought us all back to college with him. I hadn't seen my worthless mother once since then.

Though I knew how much Aspen and Noel squeezed and budgeted to keep us here and cared for, everything I had in Ellamore was a million times better than what I'd had back home. My big brother was my personal savior. He'd saved me in more ways than one by bringing me here.

And how had I repaid him? I'd slept with his best friend.

There went my sister of the year award.

With a little whimper of guilt, I squeezed my eyes closed and rubbed a hand over my aching forehead. I was so conflicted about last night. I think I was every contradiction in the book. Ashamed and yet thrilled. Scared I'd be discovered, but then totally comforted to know how good it felt to be held in Oren's arms. Satiated by everything he'd given me last night, while hungry for more. Anxious to see him again, but totally horrified by the same idea. Guilty and elated, depressed but ecstatic, wide-awake yet exhausted by my whirling thoughts.

Knowing I could lie here all day and worry myself into a freaking panic attack, I threw off my covers and climbed out of bed. The first three months I'd been here, I'd been a hollow shell. I hadn't left my room unless I was forced to, and that had been miserable. It hadn't been until I'd started college and met Zoey, and Reese, and Eva and just all of Noel's crew that I'd really started to live again. But I remembered what it felt like to want to burrow under my covers every day, all day, and just wilt away.

That was the main reason I wasn't going to stay in bed and think about what I'd done.

I'd already done it, anyway. There were no take backs now.

But as I took a shower and rubbed soap over me, my tender body just wouldn't allow me to let it go. I would never forget it. My breasts pebbled and my core swelled with lust.

I wasn't big on masturbation. I thought Sander's dumping me had killed everything sex-related in my life. It wasn't until Oren's presence slowly made me awaken to my desires that I'd ever touched myself in the first place...months and months ago. And the only time I ever did was when I thought of him. Like I was now. Except *now* I knew what it felt like to really *be* with him.

Oh God. How could he turn me so wanton? I'd never felt needs this strongly before he'd come along. I kind of liked it, but then it also scared me. What if I turned into my mother who ignored her own children in favor of finding the next dick to fill her? What if—

Damn it. Liking sex with one guy did not make me my mother. Touching myself in the shower did not make me my mother.

I pressed my back against the shower wall and rubbed myself with one hand as I pinched an inflamed nipple with the other. Water streamed over me and I pretended it was his hands, touching me everywhere. Just when my thighs trembled and my pussy clenched, preparing to come hard, a pounding fist on the bathroom door obliterated my ecstasy.

"Jesus Christ, Caroline! How long are you going to be? I gotta take a shit."

"Damn it, Brandt," I yelled back. "I'm almost done." Or more accurately, I wasn't going to finish at all now. Little butt licker had killed a perfectly good moment. "*Grr.*" I rinsed and snapped off the water.

There were three bedrooms and two baths in this house, but sometimes, I still felt as cramped as we'd been at the trailer park back home. Finding a better-paying job and moving out on my own was looking better and better each day. Noel would freak and fight me the entire way—he was still overprotective and worried about me—but he was no longer my legal guardian, so I guess I didn't need his approval.

I just *wanted* it.

After totally disappointing him last year, I still craved

his absolute love and acceptance of me.

More impatient knocking came as I wrapped a towel around my breasts.

"I really, really gotta go," my fourteen-year-old brother whined.

With a sigh, I slung my hair up in a towel turban and then yanked the door open to glare out at my brother who—*ack*, was taller than me now. When the hell had he grown so much?

He glared right back.

I arched an eyebrow and waited for him to step out of my way so I could exit and let him in. "Why couldn't you use Noel and Aspen's bathroom if you had to go that bad?" They had a private bath connected to their bedroom, and it was like ten times nicer than this one.

"Because Aspen's already in there." Brandt knocked me aside as he bulldozed inside.

I huffed out an indignant breath and stepped into the hall, shutting the door behind me because I had a feeling he wasn't going to wait for me to leave before he started his business. Disgusting, I know. Made me wish for the bajillionth time that I had three sisters instead of three brothers.

After I retreated to my room to change into clothes for the day and brush my hair dry, I made my way toward the kitchen, where Aspen was up and fixing breakfast. I stopped in the doorway and watched her, realizing I actually did have a sister now, didn't I?

She was nothing like Noel; I wasn't even sure how they found a reason to hook up in the first place, but you could tell from the intensity of their love when they were together, none of that mattered. So, to each their own, I guess.

I was just glad Noel had fallen for and managed to keep her, because she was an absolute godsend. She'd taken all four of us Gamble siblings into her home and let us crowd into everything until we'd completely rearranged her entire life. And she seemed freaking *thankful* about it, like she was actually pleased to have us ruin all her neat, orderly plans.

As if sensing my presence, she glanced over her shoulder and jumped. "Oh! Good morning, Caroline." She sent me the sweetest smile as she carried a pitcher of juice to the table. "Breakfast is almost ready."

When two halves of a bagel popped up from the toaster,

I moved toward it to spread on some of Colton's favorite strawberry cream cheese.

"Thanks," Aspen said. "You didn't have to do that."

I tucked a piece of damp hair behind my ear and shrugged. "It's fine. I don't mind." Honestly, I wanted to feel more useful than I usually did around here.

A year ago, I'd taken care of most of Colton's and Brandt's needs. Back home, I'd been the one to feed them, wash their clothes, make sure they took baths, and purchase all their necessities. But as soon as we'd moved here, Aspen had seamlessly taken over all those duties. I hadn't been in any shape at the time to do them myself, so I hadn't balked. And because of it, I'd backslid so much in the last year, I think I'd actually become less independent than I'd ever been.

I know that was crazy, but it just highlighted how much of a mess I was.

Still feeling awkward about doing kitchen stuff while Aspen was there too, I scraped on the cream cheese as fast as I could and carried the bagels to the table where Aspen already had everything set out for four people. I glanced at the empty spot where Noel usually sat. No plate or cup or silverware lay in his spot, which told me exactly where he was.

"Is Noel at the coffee shop again with—"

"The guys," Aspen finished for me with a smile and roll of her eyes. "I don't know why he feels as if he has to go there to work on his English assignments. It's not like I stand over his shoulder and correct his grammar or anything."

I snickered, because that's almost exactly what she'd done this year every time Brandt or Colton or I had worked on anything involving English homework. But we younger Gambles had actually appreciated it and gotten awesome scores because of it. And Aspen really did thrive on sharing her knowledge on the subject. So it was a win-win for all of us. Noel was the only stubborn ass who didn't want any involvement from her. I think that hurt her feelings as much as it tickled her. She knew how much he wanted to impress her with his own work.

Seating myself in my spot at the table, I chewed on my lip, still eyeing Noel's vacant place. It felt weird knowing he was with Oren right now. What if Oren— Oh God. Of *course*

Oren would tell him about last night. Oren was exactly the kiss-and-share-with-everyone type.

Fudge nuggets. My own brother was going to know every kinky, delicious thing I'd done. If Oren told him about the hair pulling, I was going to absolutely die. Why hadn't I thought about this possibility until just now?

Probably because I'd been too worried about getting my first taste of Oren Tenning. Nothing else had mattered. Not my pride, my common sense, my sanity, my brother. Nothing.

There was no way Oren could find out who I was now. This was so freaking embarrassing. And I had no one to blame but myself.

"Aspen! *Aspen*," Brandt hollered, dashing into the kitchen with the morning's newspaper rolled up and tucked under his arm. He skidded to a halt in front of her in his socks as he lifted and waved the newspaper roll. "You'll never guess what?"

"What? Are you okay? Where's Colton?"

"He's fine. We're all fine. This is...something totally different." Brandt shooed away her concerns before he flicked off the rubber band holding the newspaper together and opened it across the top of the table and right over my breakfast plate. "Sarah just texted me with the news."

"What news?" I asked, curious to know what he was babbling about.

Aspen, on the other hand, must not have a curious bone in her body. She gave a soft smile and sat one hand on his shoulder and the other on her heart. "You know, I think it's so amazing that you've befriended Mason's little sister."

"Yeah. Whatever." Totally distracted, the fourteen-year-old waved her quiet. "Check this out." He flipped pages until he came to a listing of obituaries. Then he paused and pointed. "There. That guy."

Aspen and I leaned in. "Roger Martin Rowan?" Aspen read slowly, her eyebrows pinching in confusion. When she glanced at me, I shook my head, letting her know I had no idea who he was either.

"Yes!" Brandt announced proudly, his grin spreading from ear to ear. "He's dead."

"Umm..." Aspen blinked and glanced at me again. I shrugged, still clueless why it was such good news to see someone dead.

I arched my brother a dry look. "Yeah, we kind of got that part...because of the whole *obituary* thing."

"He was an English teacher at Ellamore High School," Brandt said, rolling his eyes as if that was obvious to us, which it might've been if we'd actually read his obituary. But we hadn't. "Sarah said she was scheduled to take his class next year when she pre-enrolled for high school."

Aspen cooed sympathetically. "Oh, no. Did she know him well? Poor Sarah."

Brandt's shoulders slumped. He sighed and shook his head. "She'd never met the guy before in her life. That's not the point."

"Then what's the point?" I demanded, tired of him not getting to one already.

"The *point* is that they're going to need a new fucking English teacher there next year."

"Brandt." Aspen instantly frowned. "Language, please. I know your older brother curses all the time, but you can't just go around talking like that in..." Her scolding trailed off as his words seemed to finally take root in her brain. "Wait. Did you just say—" She snagged the paper and brought it closer to her face to read Roger Martin Rowan's obituary in more detail. "Oh my God," she murmured, lifting her gaze from the printed words. "There's going to be a new opening for an English teacher at the Ellamore High School next year. *There's going to be an opening for an English teacher!*"

The paper went flying as she literally jumped up and down. I'd never seen her hop before. It was kind of strange but really amusing. Then she snagged Brandt and hugged him into a happy circle. After that, she pulled me from my chair to envelop me into her excited arms.

"I'm going to get this job," she declared, looking so certain and jubilated that I felt my own excitement rising for her. "I *have* to get this job. It's like...I think it was *meant* to be. Oh my God. I feel so awful. But I've never been so happy to see someone die before." Tears began to stream down her face. I'm not sure if they were from guilt, excitement, jittery nerves or maybe a mixture of all three.

Clearly overwhelmed, she babbled and sobbed some more. "I need to...I need to update my resume. Oh my God. I don't even know what I did with my interview suit. Excuse me. I should..."

"Go." I laughingly waved her from the room, and she followed my instruction without hesitation.

Brandt and I grinned at each other, and all the irritation I'd felt at him for killing my shower orgasm melted away. I kind of wanted to give him a hug for making Aspen so happy.

"So, what're the chances that she'll actually get the job?" he asked.

I scowled because he suddenly sounded too serious. "Oh, she'll get it. She's like *over*qualified. She *has* to get it."

He moved in close, not only serious now, but worried-looking. "Yeah, but what if they've heard some of the rumors about her and Noel?"

I straightened, shocked senseless by the question. "You know about that?" I had no idea he knew about that.

With a snort, he rolled his eyes. "I'm fourteen, not stupid. Of course I know she was fired because of him. I was there when her old boss came to his hospital room after he broke his collarbone and threatened to expose them. Remember?"

"Yeah, but..." I sighed. He was right; he was fourteen, not a little kid anymore. Shit yeah, he understood what was going on, and he knew exactly how much trouble dating a student had gotten Aspen into.

"Well, even if they do somehow, miraculously catch wind of it, maybe it won't be such a big deal since she ended up *marrying* the student she had an affair with. Besides, they were both legal adults, and...and it had been at the college level. I mean, come on. Surely they'd know she wouldn't do anything like that with a piddly *high school* kid."

"Hey." He lifted his hands in offense. "I'm going to be one of those *piddly* high school kids, thank you very much."

"Exactly," I said. When he punched me lightly in the arm, I laughed. "Honestly, if they don't hire her...then we'll just have to kill off another English teacher somewhere else to get her another opening."

Aspen was a Gamble now, and we Gambles looked after our own...at least this generation of Gambles did. We weren't above stooping to devious measures to get what we wanted, either. We wouldn't honestly commit murder for Aspen, no, but we did appreciate the power of a good lie.

After all, one well-placed lie had gotten "Kelly" away

from Oren's bedroom last night so I could take her place.

I swallowed nervously, letting my mind wander back to him. I wondered what he thought of his Kelly impersonator. I wondered—

"Oh, yeah. I like the way you think." Brandt's voice snapped me back to the present. Holding a fist up for me to bump, he nodded his approval. "I'll come up with a way to take out the next teacher...if we have to."

I clashed my knuckles with his. "Just don't make it too bloody." He knew I had an aversion to blood.

He laughed and started talking about different poisons and ways to "accidentally" electrocute someone. I shook my head, wondering how boys got into such gory things so much. I'd grown up around it, so I was used to it by now, but still. I could never think up some of the strange shit that had at one time or another entered all three of my brothers' heads.

Brandt and I were halfway through our breakfast when Colton finally stumbled into the room, rubbing his bleary eyes and yawning.

"Morning, sleepyhead," I called to the nine-year-old.

I was continually stunned by how much he'd grown in the last year. He'd been a frail waif of a thing back home, and he'd gotten sick a lot. I'd been worried about him making it to ten. But ever since we'd moved here, he'd bloomed. Under Aspen's guiding influence, he'd become so healthy and happy, I started to think he might end up being the biggest Gamble brother of the three.

Which just went to show how awful I'd been about taking care of him. And Brandt too. Brandt hadn't gotten one black eye from being in a fight since we'd come here, whereas he'd gotten in them constantly back home. I must've had the worst motherly instincts ever to let the three of us fall to such depths.

Noel liked to reassure me and tell me that I'd done a fine job, that compared to our mother, I'd been amazing. But the truth remained, he was so much better at being a caretaker than I'd ever been.

That was another reason I wanted to impress my big brother. I'd felt as if I'd failed him. If only I'd taken better care of Brandt and Colton, he wouldn't have had to rearrange his entire life to scoop us up and move us to Ellamore with him.

As much as I blamed myself for that, Colton didn't seem to hold it against me, though. After glancing around, probably looking for Aspen—his first love—he padded over to me and crawled into my lap. He was getting way too big for me, but I didn't care. I curled my arms around him and cuddled him close as I slid his waiting bagel and favorite strawberry cream cheese over to sit before us.

"I had a nightmare last night," Colton told me, his voice accusing. "But you weren't in your room."

It was both a headache and flattering that he came to me in the middle of the night when he had a bad dream. While Brandt, who shared a room with him, might adamantly refuse to let his younger brother crawl into his bed with him, I'm sure Aspen wouldn't have kicked him out if he'd gone to her. But he always sought me. Probably because he was still a bit intimidated around Noel, and Aspen slept beside Noel. Still...I liked knowing he continued to need me in some capacity, even though letting him hog my bed, because he usually slept right against me with an arm or leg draped over me, was never comfortable.

Across the table, Brandt lifted his eyebrows. "Oooh, big sister wasn't home late last night? Where'd you go, huh, Caroline?"

I rolled my eyes and commanded myself not to blush. "I went out with Zoey to listen to the band at the club. Duh." And then I'd turned into a devious, dirty slut who'd hooked up with Noel's best friend.

Yeesh.

I cringed, and all-too-smart Brandt seemed to realize I wasn't telling the entire truth.

"Mmm hmm," he murmured as if he knew better. "Whatever."

I made a face at him and then smoothed Colton's hair across his forehead before kissing his temple. "What'd you dream about, honey bear?"

"Mama." His soft confession had both Brandt and me sitting up straighter. Brandt even stopped chewing. "She showed up and took us away from here." Colton shuddered and tucked his face against my chest. I tightened my arms around him and nearly dropped a tear or two. But it didn't pass my notice that my own brother was terrified of our mother. It'd been just as long since he'd seen her as it had been for me, but I guess the fear of being forced to move back there still clung to him.

"You don't ever have to worry about that happening," I said. "Aspen and Noel are your legal guardians now. And even if Daisy showed up and wanted you, she couldn't have you without going through them and an entire courtroom. And not without going through me either."

"And me too," Brandt spoke up. "We don't have to worry about her ever again. Okay, bud?"

Colton nodded, but I could tell the nightmare had left him rattled. A shiver passed up his spine. I began to rub his back and he kept his cheek on my shoulder. My earlier idea of maybe moving out soon moved to the back of my mind.

Maybe I wasn't such an expendable member of the family after all. Maybe there was something worthwhile about me, and Noel would regain some of the confidence he used to have in me. But one thing was certain; to accomplish that, I could never let him find out what I'd done with Oren...even if I did kind of want to do it again.

CHAPTER 6

Caroline

I STAYED AWAY from him for as long as I possibly could. Really, I did! But there was just something about Oren Tenning that kept me going back for more. I liked how he'd been all sweet and nice to me when we'd first met a year ago, but then, I also liked how he'd turned into a loud-mouthed smart-ass later on, even more. The only thing I never liked was his constant horny attention to other women. That, I could live without.

My obsession was the antithesis of healthy, but then, I'd never been known for following the healthy, *correct* path, had I?

By five that evening, I was craving him like a junkie tweaking for her next hit. I knew Noel had to work tonight— I'd heard him mention it to Aspen earlier today. And Asher would no doubt be on the clock. He liked to work on Saturdays since they'd become karaoke night, and anything to do with music at the club was his brainchild. But Saturdays had also become so crowded lately they now needed three bartenders instead of their regular two.

I copped a peek at Noel's work schedule and, yep, Oren worked this evening.

That meant I needed a reason to visit the Forbidden

Nightclub.

I chewed on my lip, panning through the options I gathered in my head. I couldn't go alone; Noel would definitely know something was up. Damn, why did *he* have to work tonight, too?

I shook my head, shrugging off that little obstacle. It was fine if Noel was working. What was one more challenge to overcome to get what I wanted? Wasn't like I was going to just jump Oren right there at the bar, anyway. I still didn't want him to know I was the woman he'd been with the night before.

I just needed to see him, and it made no difference if my brother was around for that or not. But it did mean I needed someone with me—a wing woman—or Noel might get suspicious. So I dialed up my trusty best friend.

Zoey answered on the third ring. "Hello?" She sounded a bit breathless, making me wonder what exactly I'd interrupted.

I winced. Great. Oren working meant Zwinn had the apartment they shared with him all to themselves for the evening.

Well, they'd just have to get their snuggle time on some other night. They already had *their* happily ever after; they had the rest of forever to be together.

"I need you," I said.

"Oh, no. What's wrong?" Worry instantly lit her voice.

Damn, I loved her.

"I've done the craziest thing in my entire life, and right now, I really need your support and acceptance, and...and help. I need your help."

"Okay," she said slowly. "Do I need to grab my hiking boots, shovel and some lime, or...bail money?"

I laughed and relaxed. "Neither. I didn't kill anyone... and I'm not in jail. I didn't even break the law."

"Well, that's a start. What'd you do, then?"

"Um...I think I have to tell you this one in person. Can we go to Forbidden in, say...half an hour?"

"Sure."

I bit my lip and took a deep breath before adding the hardest part of my request. "And...can you *not* bring Quinn?"

A pause followed. Then she finally asked, "Why can't I bring Quinn?"

"Because...this is a girl thing, and I...I just can't talk about it with you when there's this hulking, hot pile of walking testosterone sitting between us."

"But, he's not—"

"Zoey, please."

She sighed. "Okay...fine. Quinn can stay home."

I fisted my hand and pumped the air. Yes! I so rule. "Thank you, thank you, thank you! Pick me up at my place, bye."

After rushing the last few words, I hung up before she could come up with a way to back out. Zoey hated doing anything without Quinn. But I wasn't about to let that stop her.

Half an hour later, the headlights of her car blared through the front window and swung across the walls of the living room when she pulled into the drive. I popped up from the couch where Colton had been cuddling with me, watching *Goonies*.

"There's Zoey. I gotta go. See you guys tomorrow."

Aspen lifted her face from her laptop, where she was probably still nitpicking and perfecting her already flawless resume to death. Sitting cross-legged in a side chair, she wore one of Noel's old T-shirts and a frayed pair of shorts.

"Oh!" Surprise lit her voice as she took in my outfit. "You're going out?" After sending Colton a reassuring smile, as if to let him know she was still here for him, she returned her attention to me. "Have fun."

Thank God she was so much less inquisitive than Noel. She didn't ask where I was going, who would be there, what I'd be doing, or when I'd be home. It was nice to know someone in this household could treat me like a quasi-adult and gave me a little trust.

I hopped over Brandt who was sprawled in a beanbag on the floor, where he was watching the movie. I even managed to evade his foot when he purposely kicked out his leg to trip me.

Once outside, I paused to draw in a deep breath. Was I really going to do this? Just...hang out and stalk some guy I liked? That sounded really lame and desperate. But honestly, I didn't think much else could top my rating on the crazy scale after what I'd done last night. And the more I kept thinking about all the skanky, half-dressed sluts who'd be crawling all over the bar, trying to flirt with him, the more I just couldn't stay at home, watching eighties movies with my sister-in-law and younger brothers.

Nodding my head with reaffirmed purpose, I strode to the car waiting on me. I really loved Zoey's car. It was one of those nice, clean, pristine new luxury sedans. She came from money, but you couldn't tell unless you caught sight of what she drove. I wished I had a car. I actually had some money to get one, but Noel had convinced me to only buy *meaningful* things with that money...like college tuition. And since he'd finally been able to get himself a rattletrap truck, meaning we had two vehicles in the household—his and Aspen's—I usually didn't need my own automobile.

Zoey was clicking through channels on the radio when I opened the passenger side door. She looked up as I slid in and pulled on my seat belt.

"Hi." Her voice was too cheerful, her smile too bright. It all felt like one big, guilt-ridden inquisition. I just couldn't take the pressure.

So I blurted, "I had sex with Oren last night," in one, long, massive, run-on breath, only to moan in misery and slink lower in my seat as I clapped my hands to my head in defeat.

Forget Chinese water torture and thumbscrews; just have one innocent best friend smile at me, and I was spilling everything.

Damn, she was good.

But, oh, was it a relief to finally confide in someone.

"Umm..." Zoey wrapped both hands around the steering wheel as if she needed to hold on to something stable to brace herself. "If that's code for something else, I don't...I don't understand."

Glancing around to make sure no one was listening in, even though we were sitting alone in a closed car in the dark—hey, she might've stashed Quinn in the back-seat—I leaned over the center console and confessed, "That wasn't code. For *anything*. I truly, honestly had sex with him. Last night."

"But that doesn't..." She shook her head. "Wait. What?" Her eyes flew open wide and she slapped both hands over her mouth. "You mean, *you're* Midnight Visitor?"

"Who?"

"Quinn told me... Oh good Lord, Caroline. Please don't tell me you snuck into his room last night in the dark and...and...well, without him even knowing it was you. Did you?"

"I snuck into his dark room without him knowing it was me and had sex with him last night...twice. Well, twice for him. Four boom-booms for me."

Zoey sucked in a breath and clutched her hands to her chest. "Holy shit," she said, a girl who'd probably only spoken three curse words aloud in her entire life. "Oh God. Why did you tell me this?" she began in a chanting kind of voice as she spoke more to herself than to me. "You shouldn't have told me this. I should not know this."

"I had to tell *someone*," I argued. "Because, wow, my mind is completely blown right now. It was good. Oh my God, it was *sooo* good, Zoey. Like...I want to build a room inside my panties and force him to live there permanently kind of good. No way in hell can I keep this to myself. And you're my best friend. Who else *could* I tell?"

"But he's my *roommate*," she cried. "And Quinn's—oh, no. Quinn. I can't keep this from Quinn."

"Uh, *yes*, you can. No way can Quinn know about this. He'll tell Oren, or worse...Noel."

"*Noel*," Zoey gasped. "Holy shit. If Noel found out—"

"I know," I hissed. "So you're just going to have to keep this between the two of us."

Zoey gulped, but backed us from the driveway. "Why?" she finally asked. "Why did you put me in this position? Really? What did I ever do to you?"

I patted her arm, suddenly feeling less stressed and more cheerful now that I'd gotten the secret off my chest. "Just a perk of being my best friend."

When she sent me a dry glance across the car's darkened interior, I grinned. Finally, she sighed and loosened her shoulders. "So...why did you do it? I mean, I know how much you like him, but this just seems...a bit extreme."

A bit? Ha! I adored her understatements.

Not really sure how to explain it because it'd been one of those rash, didn't-take-the-time-to-think-it-through ideas, I shrugged. "Once upon a time, you said he liked me back."

"He does, Caroline, but I also told you *why* he stays away."

I snorted and glanced out the side window. "And I told you if he really liked me as much as I like him, then I wasn't going to let my brother come between us. And I didn't, did

I? By doing it this way, I can protect both Noel and Oren. Noel will never know, and Oren won't either, so he never has to feel guilty about it. It's basically the perfect solution."

"Riiiight."

I scowled at her for the sarcastic tone. *I* was supposed to be the witty, sarcastic one of the two of us. She was the sweet, supportive friend. Why was I not feeling the sweet support?

Oh, yeah. Because I'd finally gone off the deep end, and no way could anyone—even Zoey Blakeland—support this.

"You know, he already told both Quinn *and* Noel about you. They're calling you the Midnight Visitor."

I cringed as nausea churned in my stomach. "He did tell Noel, then? Damn. I was afraid of that."

"Well, what did you expect? This is *Ten* we're talking about. He's not exactly the private type when it comes to sharing sex details."

"I know." I groaned. "But...I just couldn't help it, Zoey. He's...he's so...he's *Oren.* Everything inside me comes alive whenever he's around. I've been crazy about him for so long, wanted him for months, it was starting to drive me batty. And he was never going to do anything about it. You *know* that."

Zoey gave a thoughtful nod. "You're right. He wouldn't have. Despite all his flaws—"

"And there are many," I agreed.

She grinned. "He's always been one of the most loyal people I know when it comes to his friends. He's gone above and beyond for them. And he'd never knowingly betray one of them."

I gulped. "Are you trying to make me feel guilty?" Because it was working.

"No," she was quick to say. "I just...I guess, in a way, I'm glad you did it this way, too. I want you two together so much. You both deserve love and happiness. I'm in awe of your...your..."

"Stupidity?" I guessed.

"Brash courage," she corrected as she pulled into the parking lot across the street from the club. As she killed the engine, she turned to me. "But seriously." She winced. "How exactly do you foresee this turning out?"

I cringed back at her and in a small voice answered, "Badly. Probably epically...disastrously...badly."

I was so sure she'd nod and agree, but she chewed on her lip a moment before murmuring, "I don't know. Maybe it'll come out okay. I mean, I never in a million years thought Quinn and I would end up together when I first met him. So, maybe..."

I took her hand and squeezed it gratefully. "I love you. You know this is going to end as awfully as I know it's going to end, and you think I'm crazy and probably stupid, yet here you are, supporting me anyway. Thank you."

Zoey squeezed back, and looked out the window at the flashing lights of the bar across the street. "So, I know Ten's working tonight. I assume we're here to make sure no other woman gets her dirty paws on him, right?"

"Wow. You know me so well."

She sighed and opened her door. "It's scary, isn't it?"

There was a line to get in tonight. After we bounded across the street and waited for a couple minutes in the warm evening, Harper, the doorman, shook his head when he saw us. "Ah, hell. I smell trouble brewing."

"Always," I answered happily and leaned up to kiss his cheek.

Harper grinned but swatted me away. "Hey, now. None of that. Your brother's just inside. You want me to die a slow and painful death? Now, quick. Give me something to look at so it seems like I'm checking your IDs."

We did and thanked him for letting us in without having to pay. Zoey grabbed my arm as soon as we started past him. She squeezed hard. "Wait. You didn't tell me *Noel* was working tonight, too."

I shrugged and immediately slid my attention to the bar, but damn it, there were too many people in my way. Didn't they realize I needed an Oren fix, like, *now*?

"A minor hiccup." I waved a hand at Zoey, letting her know I wasn't concerned about my brother.

But she shrieked, "*Minor*?"

Muttering what sounded like a prayer under her breath, she took my hand and started to lead me toward the bar.

I resisted, accidentally jerking her off balance, and just as she turned back to me with question in her gaze, there he was. It was as if the crowd parted and the blue neon lights overhead beamed down upon him. My stomach muscles instantly convulsed with pleasure, and I squeezed my legs together. I was almost tempted to cover my throbbing breasts with my arms.

"What's wrong?"

I couldn't even answer Zoey's question. I was too busy feeding the craving. But, wow.

I'd seen him nearly every day since we'd met a year ago. He was a frequent visitor at the Gamble house. My younger brothers treated him like their personal tackle mat—and speaking of tackle...I so wanted to tackle him right now.

It didn't matter how many times I'd seen him before, though, or how familiar I was with his appearance; tonight he looked better than ever.

His perpetually messy hair appeared extra dark in this lighting and really lit up the fact that he needed to shave. I have no idea how he managed to groom himself so that he always seemed to possess a five o'clock shadow, but it looked good on him. It highlighted the masculine angles in his jaw and framed his full plush lips to perfection.

Damn. I wanted him so bad. My fingers curled, eager to run their way up his toned arms. My mouth watered, wanting to suck on his Adam's apple.

You knew a girl had it bad when even a guy's straight, dark eyebrows turned her on. And his definitely did.

"I think I'm going to come," I told Zoey. My hand clamped down on hers as my breathing picked up.

She yelped, "Holy..."

"Shit," I finished. My core tightened painfully. I couldn't believe I was so turned on just from looking at him and remembering. "This is embarrassing."

When a group of girls approached the bar, Oren smiled at them with lips that had been on *my* flesh last night, flashing teeth that had sunk into the back of *my* shoulder. Arms spread wide, he rested his hands—those hands that had been all over me, pulling my hair, toying with my clit, pushing inside me—on the edge of the counter and leaned in toward them to hear their order. I snarled at them for getting so close to my man, even though he was the one moving in toward them.

"Who the fuck are *they*?"

"They're customers. They just want a drink. Down, girl." Zoey tugged on my hand and led me away, dislodging my perfect view of my perfect man.

I scowled at her, even though I was grateful for the reprieve. My body still throbbed for release, but without seeing him, the intensity of each pulse was beginning to lessen.

When we found a bare patch of wall to lean against in the darkest part of the club, I sucked in air and willed myself to calm down.

"Better?" Zoey studied my face with concern wrinkling her brow.

I nodded. "Yeah. Thank you."

She nodded too. "So...what now?"

My face crumpled when I looked at her. "I have to see him again. I mean, not as me. As *her*. I only wanted last night to be a one-time deal, but Zoey, you don't understand. It was so... It—"

She sent me a sad smile. "Actually, I do understand. Completely."

I guess she did. It was hard to believe now, but just a few months ago, Quinn had been completely forbidden to her since he'd been dating someone else. No matter how much everyone else could tell they belonged together, I'd had a bad feeling they would never hook up because they were both too honorable. But here they were now, together and happier than ever.

That should've given me some kind of hope.

Except it didn't. My situation was a tad different than theirs. And I was in no way as honorable as they were.

"I have to somehow sneak back into his room without him knowing it's me."

Zoey snickered. "The return of Midnight Visitor?"

"Yeah." I nodded before her words sank in. And just like that, one of my crazy, spur-of-the-moment, off-the-wall ideas hit me. "Yeah," I murmured again, eyeing her probably a bit maniacally. "Midnight Visitor. Zoey, that's *brilliant*."

"Oh God," she moaned, already cringing. "What did I just start?"

I grabbed her forearm, squeezing excitedly. "Can you get his phone?"

She began to say yes, when she realized what I really meant. "What? You mean *right now*?"

CHAPTER 7

Caroline

FIVE MINUTES later, Zoey was weaving back to me through the crowd with the biggest grin on her face. "I did it! I got his phone." She looked so excited and proud of herself, it was adorable. "I can't believe I really did it. I feel like such a rebel right now."

"Oh, baby, you are. You *so* are." I rubbed my hands together. "Now gimme."

She handed the cell phone over. The smooth plastic was cool in my hands. It looked like any other smartphone with a plain blue cover. But it felt almost electrified in my touch, as if its hallowed surface crackled against my fingers.

This was *Oren's* phone.

Yeah, I was a freaking spaz for getting my jollies off just by holding his phone. But I didn't care. *I was holding his phone!*

"You're not going to change anyone's number, are you?" Zoey asked.

"What? No. Of course not." Realizing she was watching me be a total creeper, I cleared my throat and quickly flipped the phone over before I pushed the *home* button. When I unlocked it, a passcode request came up. I whimpered.

But what the hell? He actually password protected his phone?

No!

I glanced at Zoey. She looked up and bit her lip sympathetically.

"Any idea what it is?" I asked.

"No. But I can't see Ten having a difficult password. It's probably something like one, two, three, four."

I nodded. Yeah, that sounded like him. I punched it in.

No go.

After a second of thinking, I tried another.

"Damn. That wasn't it, either."

"What'd you try?" Zoey asked.

"Six, seven, three, six. You know, the numbers for O-R-E-N."

"Oh, yeah. That's what Quinn does for his password too, but you know...he uses nine, six, three, nine for... Zoey." She blushed and smiled until her eyes widened. "Oh! Can I try one?"

I frowned suspiciously but handed the phone to her. "Okay. Sure."

She immediately punched in four numbers. Sadness entered her gaze, but then she nodded. "I'm in."

"What? *Really*?" I leaned in to see his home screen with a football-themed background. My stomach pitched with excitement and then disappointment because *she'd* known him better than I had. "What numbers did you use?"

"What?" She zipped her face up quickly, her eyes wide with guilt.

I pulled back, frowning hard. What the hell was she trying to hide from me?

Before I could grill her, though, his phone rang in her hands. She yelped and almost dropped it. She had to fumble to keep it from slipping through her fingers, but once she had it securely back in her hands, her face drained of color. "Oh my God, it's ringing. What do I do?"

"Silence it!" I hissed, glancing around in the hopes that no one important heard the distinctive ring tone of 2 Live Crew's "We Want Some Pussy". But the place was so loud and the karaoke was so bad, I didn't think we'd have a problem with anyone hearing much of anything we were doing over here in our private corner.

Zoey continued to freak, though. "How do I shut it off? I

don't know where—" Her words cut off as her attention focused on the screen. And just like that, her entire face lit up. "Oh, it's Quinn."

She pushed *Answer* and lifted the receiver to her ear.

"No!" I yelped, reaching to snag it away.

Too late.

It was natural instinct for her to talk to her man. She was already saying, "Hi!" A split second later, her eyes grew wide and she flashed her gaze to me. *"Oh crap,"* she mouthed as she realized she'd just answered Oren's phone.

I could hear Quinn's voice on the other end of the line, no doubt asking her what she was doing, answering *his* phone.

Panic filled her face. "Um...because I just helped Caroline steal it," she said, only to wince and press her fisted hand against her head. *"Sorry,"* she whispered to me. Then she kept on confessing everything. "Because she's Midnight Visitor...and I'm helping her set up one of those Google Voice phone numbers in his contacts list and—"

"Zoey!" I ripped the phone from her hand before she could tell him everything...even though she just had.

"I'm sorry," she wailed again, clearly distraught. "But I can't lie to him. I just...I *can't*. I swear his voice is like truth serum to me."

I growled at her and pressed the phone to my ear, my mind racing over how I could cover damage control. "Quinn?" I said hesitantly before I bit my lip.

"Caroline." He was usually nice and polite to me, but the hard tone in his voice as he said my name let me know he wasn't feeling very nice...or polite. Then he exploded. "What the hell did you just pull my girlfriend into?"

"I'm sorry," I instantly gushed. I really was sorry for putting her in such an awful position. "But she was the only person I knew I could count on. You know, you should be honored to have such a reliable, supportive woman."

"Yeah, well, I'm a bit too ticked at the moment because you just sucked her into some devious little nest of lies. Zoey *hates* to lie."

"I know. I know." I winced, feeling even more guilt from everything I was doing.

If I was smart, I'd call this off now and go home, pretend last night never happened. But when it came to Oren, I was never smart. I was way too emotional for that shit.

"I feel like crap for sucking her into this, but...it's too late now. Please just tell me you're not going to tell Oren...or Noel."

"Are you seriously asking me to lie to my two closest friends on earth?"

Oh, boy. I was screwed. But I said, "Yes, I guess I am. I'm sorry. But please." *Please, please, please.*

Of course he'd tell them, though. Why *wouldn't* he tell them? His loyalties would always lie with both Oren and Noel before they'd ever lie with me.

It felt as if my life had just ended. Things started sinking into the pit of my stomach. Evil, awful things that didn't belong anywhere near a stomach.

Panic, dread, hyperventilation.

Noel was going to find out what I'd done.

Oh shit. *Oren* was going to find out. What would he do when he learned last night had been me? Would he ever talk to me again? Would he be...disgusted?

"Dang it, Caroline," Quinn muttered in my ear. "As much as I think they both deserve to know what you did, you just had to go and pull *Zoey* in on it, didn't you? I can't let her catch any heat from this."

I blinked, shocked speechless. But, oh my God. I'd completely forgotten there was one more person with whom he'd always side, with whom his loyalties were even stronger than the ones he had for his two closest friends on earth.

A slow smile spread across my face. I had Zoey on my side, which meant I had *him* on my side, too. Yes! "So, you're not going to tell them?"

"*Only* because you've already gotten my girl involved."

"Oh my God!" Relief made my eyes throb with happy tears. "Thank you. Thank you so much. I love you."

He laughed. "Sorry, but I'm already taken." And thank God he was. His love for Zoey was the only thing ensuring his silence right now. "Let me talk to her again," he demanded.

"Sure." I happily handed the phone over.

I watched Zoey spew out apology after apology before she gushed on about her love for him. I was beginning to think it was unnatural how quickly those two forgave and made up by the time she finally finished the call. But whatever. I liked seeing them make up probably more than

I'd like to see them fight...if they ever *did* fight.

It was also unnatural how they never fought.

"Don't forget to erase his call from the phone's history," I cautioned.

She did and then handed it over. I had to take my own from my pocket to retrieve the new number I'd given myself, and then I plugged the details into Oren's. A thrill raced through me as I saved my new information.

I was about to click out of his address book when I noticed the name Marci Bennett. My fingers froze as I stared at the name of the bitch who'd ratted Aspen and Noel out to Aspen's boss and gotten her fired. I didn't like seeing her name in Oren's phone. And I liked even less knowing what it meant by being in there.

Sick nausea swamped me. Had he *been* with Marci Fucking Bennett? I suddenly wanted to cut his penis off. But then I loved his penis. I loved how it had felt in me, how it had moved and—damn it! Why did he have to go and share it with every fucking woman he met?

Before I could stop them, my fingers started to delete the number. But Zoey caught my wrist. "What're you doing?"

"He has Marci Bennett's name in here. *Marci... Bennett.*"

Zoey blinked blankly. "Who?"

"The bitch who wanted Noel for herself, so she took pictures of him and Aspen together to get my sister-in-law fired from her job."

"Oh." Zoey's mouth fell open. "*Her*. Well..." She bit her lip and looked down at Marci's name in Oren's address book, wincing.

"This is his little black book, isn't it? All the women he's ever slept with have their digits in here. I can't believe I was so stupid to think...I don't know. I don't know what I was even thinking to accomplish by coming here tonight and breaking into his phone."

"You can't blame him for women he had in the past, Caroline. I mean, Cora is the last person on the planet I want to have carnal knowledge of Quinn, but she's probably the one who taught him half of the stuff we do together. And yes, that *does* bother me. But if I let it consume me, it would. If you can't get over what Ten did before he ever *met* you, then—"

"But what if he does it tonight? Or tomorrow or...hell, Zoey. I was just another Friday-night hookup to him. Nothing—absolutely nothing is keeping him from moving on to his next score."

"I thought that was why you put your new number into his phone." Zoey motioned to it, looking suddenly uncertain. "You were going to keep his attention on you so he wouldn't..." But her words drifted off as if she too realized that probably wouldn't work.

Oren wouldn't just out-of-the-blue decide to become monogamous to some stranger in the dark who refused to show him her face or tell him her name.

"I can't text him, saying, 'Your dick is now mine. Get it near any other woman, and I'll physically remove it from you and keep it in a jar by my bedside.' That would sound a bit creepy."

"Actually, I was thinking it sounded *a lot* creepy."

I huffed out a breath and shoved at her shoulder. "Whatever. I can't...I just can't..."

But then I glanced toward the bar. No one had started up on karaoke since the last person had finished singing, so a regular song was playing through the speakers and Ten was bobbing his head to the beat as he filled a pitcher with beer at the tap.

After he handed it over to the waiting customer and accepted the payment, he danced his way toward the cash register where Noel was counting out change. Oren said something to my brother before he turned his back to Noel, pooched out his ass and pretended to booty grind against Noel's leg.

I couldn't help it; I laughed while Noel shoved him away before letting out a reluctant grin and shaking his head.

That right there was what always drew me back to Oren: his lighthearted, carefree, potty-mouth ways that made him uniquely him. It didn't seem to matter what anyone thought of him; he just went his own way, did his own thing, and managed to build up loyalties for those he called friends that were unbreakable.

"Okay, maybe I can handle his...filthy past," I told Zoey.

I glanced at her, feeling bolstered. I'd been waffling all day, knowing what I'd done was wrong and wanting to do it again anyway. But now...now I felt totally certain. I had to see him again.

"We need to get this phone back where you found it."

Zoey nodded and began to reach for it, but I shook my head. It had been beyond lucky she hadn't gotten caught the first time she'd gone to the bar. A second trip would be too risky.

Skimming my gaze over the bar to make sure Noel or Oren hadn't spotted us yet, I froze when I made eye contact with the third bartender. Asher smiled and started to wave, but I shook my head frantically and slashed my hand across my throat, asking him to stop.

He did, frowning slightly. Then he glanced toward my brother and turned back to me to cock his head in a curious manner. I set my finger over my mouth and motioned him to come to us. He once again checked out what his coworkers were doing. Then he turned back to me with a nod as he held up a finger, telling me to wait a minute.

"Incredible," Zoey murmured beside me. "I think I actually followed that entire conversation you guys had. You and Asher would make awesome spies."

I winked at her. "If only we could use our powers for good."

I barely caught Asher giving me the go-ahead to meet him over by the hallway as he lifted a tray full of used glassware.

"Come on." I grasped Zoey's hand and jerked her after me, weaving through people so we could stay out of sight from the bar. Our mission grew more perilous as we had to move close to it to reach the hall, but Oren and Noel seemed busy without Asher on hand to help. So, they didn't notice us.

Asher waited with his arms still laden with dirty glasses. I slowed to a stop, Zoey catching up to my side. Frowning at the dishes he was lugging toward the back kitchen, I shook my head. "Didn't Pick just buy you guys a new one of these sanitizing machines where it washes those right under the counter?"

Asher sighed and rolled his eyes. "It's on the fritz, and the new one is on back order. Pick is pissed." Then he glanced curiously between Zoey and me. "What's up, ladies? Finally decide to give up on your men and be my favorite band groupies?"

My shoulders sagged. It'd probably be better for my mental health if I did give up on Oren to follow Non-

Castrato around, but...I'd already come this far. "Unfortunately...no." I lifted Oren's phone to show it to him. "Can you sneak this back behind the bar?"

Asher glanced at the cell phone and lifted an eyebrow. "That's Ten's."

I nodded and sent him a cringe.

An ornery grin lit his face. "Do I even want to know what you did to it?"

This time, I shook my head no.

He laughed. "Cool. I'm in. Slide it in my front pocket here, sweetness."

Since his hands were full, holding the tray of cups, I reached for the front pocket of his black T-shirt and slid the phone in before patting it gratefully.

"And a little sugar?" he encouraged, tipping his face down and to the side to show me his cheek.

I rolled my eyes but leaned up to kiss his cheek. He nodded his approval and then turned to Zoey. "You too, princess. Don't be shy."

Zoey reluctantly stepped forward and kissed his cheek too.

Asher straightened, looking rather proud of himself. "Ladies," he murmured. "It was good doing business with you." Then he turned away and was off.

I wanted to stick around to make sure he got his job done. But I trusted Asher, so I gripped Zoey's arm. "Let's get out of here before we're caught."

I had some text messages to write.

CHAPTER 8

Ten

"HOLY SHIT." I gaped at the screen of my phone as I read the text that had been sent to me while I was working.

The bar had closed nearly twenty minutes earlier, and all of us left behind to clean up were just about done with our duties for the night. I'd just grabbed my phone where I'd left it sitting by the cash register when I'd noticed I had a waiting message.

Have you been a good boy since our first encounter? I'll only give you a repeat of last night if you've been a good boy.

The sender showed up as...Midnight Visitor.

"Holy fucking shit."

"What?" Noel asked curiously as he came up to me from behind.

I spun toward him, feeling the instinctive need to shield my screen from his eyes. But then I told myself that was stupid. There was no need to keep this from him. No reason at all. So I turned the phone around to let him read the message.

"She somehow got hold of my phone and added her name and number." I turned it slowly back to me and wondered aloud, "That's so totally whack. And how the fuck did she know you guys had been calling her Midnight Visitor?"

Unless it really was Caroline. Maybe Gamble had mentioned it to her, or Ham had told Blondie, who'd told her.

As I wiped a suddenly shaky hand over my mouth, Gam laughed and slugged me in the shoulder. "Well, aren't you a lucky son of a bitch? Who the hell cares how she got in? She's going to let you see her again. Isn't that what you wanted?"

"Yeah," I murmured absently. "I guess." But fuck, I couldn't believe she'd contacted me. The way she'd lit out of my room last night, I was sure that was the last I would hear from her. I began to sweat, nervous and elated at the same time.

Gamble nudged me again. "What're you waiting for? Write her back."

I scowled at him, not wanting to text her in public like this. But, oh...I would definitely be writing her back.

"Write who back?" Asher asked, strolling up with his attention on my phone I held in a still trembling hand.

I scowled at him and shoved it into my back pocket, out of sight. "Nothing," I said at the same moment Gamble blurted, "Ten's got a secret admirer."

Though I rolled my eyes over the term, it reminded me of what I'd done last semester, leaving little pictures of Caroline on her chair in art class for her. Damn, I was such a loser when it came to her. I'd honestly left her sweet little trinkets...just to make her smile.

It was impossible to think she might be doing the same thing back to me...with midnight rounds of hot, wild sex instead of stupid drawings.

"Oh, really?" Hart quirked a curious eyebrow and folded his arms over his chest. "Do tell."

I didn't want to tell him shit. I hated how close of a friendship he had with Caroline. It irritated the piss out of me until I just couldn't like the guy. But Gamble seemed to think he was just aces. He started blabbing about my entire encounter with Car—I mean, Midnight Visitor. And the more my good buddy spoke, the more intrigued Hart seemed to grow.

"So when do you think she broke into your phone and slipped you her number?" he asked.

"How the fuck should I know?" I sent him one last cranky glower and muttered, "I'm taking off."

I turned away, and Gamble and Hart laughed after me as if they thought my moodiness was cute. I flipped them the bird over my shoulder and pushed my way out into the warm April night. It was after two in the morning and the streets were quiet and dimly lit. I yanked my phone back out of my pocket and immediately checked my address book as I jogged across the street to the parking lot where my truck was.

First, I checked Midnight Visitor's number, then I scrolled up to the C's and checked out Caroline's contact link. I was actually expecting the two numbers to be the same. But they weren't. A strange disappointment funneled through me. I slowed to a stop on the curb and stared at Caroline's name on my screen with a totally different number than Midnight Visitor's.

I shook my head and breathed deeply through my nostrils. Almost tempted to delete the message and then Midnight Visitor's number completely, I ground my teeth and glanced up at the sky. A billion stars peered down at me, almost mocking me with their delightful *twinkling*.

I couldn't believe I'd been so sure she was Caroline.

A long, drawn-out sigh eased from my lungs. Well... did I want to see the woman again, or not? It wasn't like me to say no to free pussy. But knowing that last night really had been a complete stranger made me uneasy. I didn't like feeling the connection I'd felt with a woman who wasn't Caroline. I already had enough stupid-ass emotions swirling in me because I was pining after one woman. I didn't want to add another girl to the list.

Then I reminded myself I'd only felt close to Midnight Visitor because she'd reminded me so much of Caroline, so...what was wrong with giving her another go? No strings, great sex, so why was I standing here debating with myself? I could just keep pretending she was who I wanted her to be, and everything would be okay. This was probably as close to Caroline as I'd ever get anyway.

Making up my mind, I drew in a breath and reopened the message I'd been sent.

Define good, I typed, and then walked the rest of the way to my truck.

I'd just opened the driver's side door when my phone

buzzed. My dick jerked in response, knowing my correspondence directly involved him.

The definition of good: You have not had your penis in any other woman since it's been in me. So...have you been good?

With a laugh, I shook my head. *It's barely been twenty-four hours since I was in YOU. Just how much do you think I get around?*

"*I know exactly how much you get around. Answer the damn question.*"

I knew I was having more fun with this than I should, but I grinned. *You have a dirty mouth. I like that.*

For some reason, I thought she'd like that comment. Instead, she wrote, *I take your avoidance of my question to mean that you've been a very bad boy and dirtied your dick in some other whore. So bye-bye now.*

I sniffed, not liking her ultimatum-type threat. *Actually, no, I haven't been with anyone since you. But if you want a different answer, give me an hour. I'm sure I can find some chick to screw.* I growled as I jabbed the *send* button, wondering who the hell she thought she was to demand monogamy from me.

Instantly, she answered, *No! Please don't.*

I didn't immediately respond. I let her sweat. I didn't want to lose my shot with my Caroline wannabe, but I wasn't going to let her boss me around either.

I started the engine of my truck and muted my phone, muttering under my breath about how no one owned me.

She'd written another message by the time I'd driven home and parked in front of my apartment building. Since I wasn't the patient type, I opened it before heading up to my apartment.

I'm just asking you not to fuck anyone else while you're still fucking me. She sounded much more humble this time around, which made me smug. *If that's acceptable with you, then...Tuesday night. Midnight. Your room. Keep the lights off. I'm doing a sniff test, and if your cock smells like anything but Ivory soap, I'm leaving, and you're never touching me again.*

Okay, that second part wasn't quite as meek. My scowl returned, but then I realized something else and pulled back in surprise. "Holy fuck." How did she know I used that brand of body soap? I could've sworn I'd never had her before last night, but this chick had been in my apartment, in my very bathroom. Fuck, she'd figured out my passcode on my phone. She knew my buddies had dubbed her Midnight Visitor. And not only that, she knew my work schedule because Tuesday was the next night I had off.

Damn, I had a freaking stalker.

I grinned, because having a stalker was kind of hot. Crazy chicks were so much more interesting than the sane ones.

See you then, I said.

To which she immediately responded, *No, you won't. You better not see shit. I said no lights.*

I shook my head and chuckled under my breath. This woman really did have a mouth on her. That was so awesome. *Fine. Touch you then? Lick you then? Fuck you then? Which term do you prefer, princess?*

Any of those will do. Thank you.

Okay, fine. Lick you later then, baby.

Looking forward to it. Goodnight, Oren.

A bit of sadness and regret gnawed at my stomach. I stared at her smart-ass, kinky comments and realized I'd actually had fun sparring with her. I didn't particularly want to have fun doing anything but fucking this woman. My heart already belonged somewhere else. I didn't want the stupid organ straying on me.

But it felt wrong not to respond, so I typed, *Night, Midnight Visitor.*

I WAS STRESS drawing on Monday in the campus's main courtyard between classes when Gamble and Ham found me. I'd been doing that more and more lately, absently drawing when my mind wouldn't stop thinking shit it shouldn't be thinking. And I knew exactly what it was about, but I was in serious denial.

Four years ago, a part of me had died. The biggest part. The fucking *best* part. To combat the pain that was left, I'd closed off other parts because I could never picture myself loving any girl, in any capacity, ever again. Hell, I'd never really even planned on making friends with dudes, either. But Noel Gamble had obliterated that plan the day I met him.

We'd been two complete strangers forced together as freshman dormitory roommates, and he'd just kind of swept me in. After he'd realized I'd played some ball in high school, he'd coaxed me outside for a game of catch, then he'd told me how impressed he was by my skill, and before I knew it, I was a walk-on for the team and we were starting in games by the end of our freshman year.

It never felt as if I'd had a choice in becoming his friend. It just happened without me even noticing. He'd dragged me along with him to my first party, and after I realized how easily I could immerse myself in this place, in this life, that I could forget about all the pain in a much funnier, way more pleasurable way, I was a goner. From that point on, we'd become a team. When he needed work and found a job at Forbidden, he'd told me they were looking for another bartender too, so I shrugged, thinking why the hell not. From there, my friendships with guys spiraled out of control. I'd gotten close to Pick, and Hamilton, even Lowe, and kind-of-sort-of Hart. But I'd always been careful not to get close to the feminine persuasion. Use them for booty calls and move on, that was my motto.

Women gutted you. They either said shit that tore out your self-confidence, or they got hurt when you should've been able to protect them, which left you so broken you wished you were dead. I tried to stay away from all of that "feelings" shit when it came to women. Sometimes I was downright rude to them.

Okay, fine. *Most* of the time I was rude...and offensive...and overall annoying. But a guy had to protect himself somehow, because women fucking gutted you.

I wasn't expecting what happened to me to happen when Gamble carried Caroline into my life. I didn't welcome it either. And I wasn't very happy about the fact that Hamilton's woman managed to crawl under my defenses and make me feel things, either. But Midnight Visitor? No. No fucking way. This shit had to stop. Except it was already happening. Texting my hot little bed companion had been fun. And that made me damn nervous.

I was getting too happy and sappy around too many women.

I'd seen Caroline earlier today, walking with Lowe and Lowe's woman toward the science department. I'd been heading toward them, but I'd ducked out of sight before they could see me. I'd worked with Lowe just last night, and I always loved to say something to piss off his woman—whom I'd dubbed Buttercup. But I couldn't go anywhere near them just then. Not with Caroline around.

After making my plans with Midnight Visitor two nights ago, I'd been worried about seeing Caroline again. It was as if I was too guilty to face her or something, which was whack. I'd had numerous women since meeting her almost a year ago. I'd never had a problem facing her after a night of debauchery before. But this just felt... different, which is probably what prompted another session of stress drawing.

I was trying to scribble my stupid feelings away when someone jumped me from behind, grabbing my shoulders and shaking me.

"What up, loser," Gamble called, making me leap out of my fucking skin. "Doodling again, as usual?"

I looked up and tried to cover my drawing pad before he could see what I was making, because I honestly wasn't all that sure what I'd been drawing; I hoped to God it wasn't another picture of Caroline. But his eyes were already widening.

I gritted my teeth and hesitantly glanced down. It wasn't a perfect depiction of his sister's face, however. Thank God. But to me, it was something so much worse. A sick dread pitched in my stomach as I stared at the four letters I'd drawn and decorated with flames.

Gamble glanced at Ham, who was with him and seeing my notepad, too. Then he turned back to me. "Why are you drawing the name Zoey?"

All warmth and sensation drained from my face. I didn't know what to tell him. I glanced at Ham, but instead of anger or confusion, a sad kind of sympathy filled his face. I gritted my teeth. "I...I'm designing a tattoo for Ham here."

There. Yeah. Shit, that actually sounded good.

Gamble lifted his eyebrows to Ham. "You're getting another tattoo?"

Ham blinked, but returned his attention to the page where his woman's name was stenciled. Temptation flickered in his gaze. "Yeah," he murmured. "Yeah, I've been thinking about it."

I almost groaned, certain he hadn't thought about it until just now. But now that I'd put the idea in his head, he was actually considering it. Stupid ass. Didn't he know you didn't tattoo a woman's name on you? Even if I did have a feeling he and Blondie would be the lasting kind who stayed together forever, it was just dumb to tempt fate that way. What if Blondie died on him? Where the fuck would he be then?

I slapped the notepad closed. It was about time for me to start toward my next class, plus Gam was sending me the oddest look, giving me the willies, so I stood up and tucked the notebook away.

I was about to bid these two losers farewell when Gamble glanced past me and shook his head. "Great. Here comes trouble."

I looked over to see Caroline and Blondie headed our way. "Fuck," I muttered under my breath, knowing I couldn't escape unnoticed, except Gam heard me.

He sent me a startled glance before a knowing gleam entered his eyes. The blood drained from my face. Shit, what the hell had he just figured out?

Instead of letting me in on his little revelation, he turned to his sister as soon as they were within speaking distance. "Hey, shorty. Have you been behaving?"

She smirked back and fluttered her lashes. "Never."

Damn, I loved the snarky little responses she gave. They always made me want to kiss the fuck out of her.

But today, it kind of hurt to look at her. I mean, glimpses of her wispy corn silk hair, her sparkling blue eyes and stubborn chin always left an ache in my chest. But today felt worse than usual. Damn females making me feel way too damn much.

I'd gone through I-don't-know-how-many girls to flush my want for her out of my system, and it'd never bothered me to look her in the eye the next morning before. But something about my encounters with Midnight Visitor was making me feel guilty as shit. It felt as if I'd betrayed her, when she wasn't even mine...and she never would be.

That didn't feel wonderful to think about either, so I turned my attention to Zoey and Ham as they came together for a heated little greeting. Tongue and everything.

From the corner of my eye, I saw Gamble wrap his arm around his sister's shoulder and say something into her ear. She laughed and jabbed him in the side with her pointer finger before saying something back. The curiosity killed me, wondering what the fuck they were discussing. It was times like these I hated how close they were. Freaking messed with my head.

Brother and sister getting along, hanging out, just shooting the shit.

God, I missed that.

Gam kissed the side of Caroline's head and pulled away, relieving some of the pressure that had been building in my chest. "Well, I'm headed to class. See you later. Ham. Zoey," he called in farewell.

I was technically still watching the lovebirds grope, so I saw them break apart to wave at Gamble. And then Gamble said, "Ten."

Risking my sanity, I turned my attention to him. He had that look again, like he knew something about me that no one else knew. I didn't like that look. I tipped my chin at him and mumbled, "Later," and promptly ripped my gaze away again.

As he strolled away and Ham went back to kissing his girl, I decided to take off too.

But Caroline's voice just had to go and waylay me. "What's wrong with you?"

I frowned her way, and shit. What was it about her that always reeled me in? Just because her eyes were a pale, compelling shade of cornflower blue, her cute, pert little nose turned up at the end in the most adorable way, and a handful of barely discernible freckles dotted her cheeks, didn't mean she was movie-star hot. And yet I could look at her all day and still want more, because she was the most beautiful thing I'd ever wanted.

"What're you talking about?" I asked with a confused shrug at her accusing stare. "I didn't say anything."

"I know. And it's suspicious as hell." She set her hands on her hips. Hips I wanted to put *my* hands on. "Why're you being so quiet?"

Unable to look her in the eye, I lowered my gaze, only to be met with an eyeful of perfect breasts. And I mean *perfect*. Perfect shape, perfect size, perfect lift. I just wanted to stick my face in between them and die a happy man in motorboating heaven.

Shaking my head slightly, I opened my mouth to tell her I didn't know what the hell she was talking about. But instead, I said, "I gotta go."

Turning, I half sprinted, half walked away.

Maybe agreeing to meet with Midnight Visitor again wasn't such a great idea after all. It'd been hot the first night because I'd let myself pretend she was Caroline, but now that I knew they weren't one and the same, I just felt shitty, because I wasn't sure if I could let go of my fixation on either woman now.

God, I was so fucked up.

Caroline

I GAZED AFTER Oren as he fled the courtyard, and yes, fleeing was exactly what it looked like he was doing. He'd just lit out of here as if his ass were on fire.

Glancing at Zwinn, I pointed after him. "Seriously, what's wrong with him?" He'd seemed...moody, distant, quiet: all adjectives I had never associated with Oren before. Concern flickered inside me.

"Maybe he figured out your trickery," Quinn said, arching a censorious eyebrow as he wrapped an arm around Zoey's waist and tugged her close.

Damn, he really didn't approve of what I'd done, did he?

I gulped and glanced away. "Did you tell him?"

"No. But he's not stupid, Caroline. If you keep this up, he will figure it out."

Not sure how to answer that, I drew in a deep breath.

"What you're doing can't lead anywhere good." Quinn sent me a steady look that shot a shiver up my spine and made me feel worse about what I'd already done.

But even as Zoey softly admonished, "Quinn. You didn't have to tell her that," I nodded, agreeing with him. I knew he was right. I really should stop the insanity. It was already affecting Oren, and the last thing I wanted to do was hurt him. I couldn't think of anything *else* that might be bothering him, and Zwinn, hadn't come up with alternate reasons for why he might be moody, distant or quiet. Maybe this *was* about Midnight Visitor.

I moved away from them, waving a goodbye as my mind stayed on Oren.

Before I could stop myself, I dug my phone from my backpack, brought up my new Google number and tapped out a message.

Maybe we should call off tomorrow night, I wrote and pushed *send* before I could stop myself. A pinch formed in my chest, and suddenly I wanted to cry. Was I really never going to share another intimacy with him again?

My phone dinged, and I drew in a shuddered breath. Half praying he was going to beg me to meet him anyway, I opened the message and stared blankly at his response.

Maybe, was all he said.

Maybe? Wait, what? He was supposed to want me no matter what. Why didn't he want me? Something was definitely wrong with him. Or maybe I was destined to be rejected by him in whichever identity I used.

I didn't like that. Ire rose inside me. *So why don't YOU want to meet?* I demanded to know.

Why don't YOU? he shot back.

I asked first.

Well, you started this entire fucking discussion, so you have to answer first.

Damn it. I gritted my teeth. *I don't know. Where do you want me to start? I feel cheated, I guess. They say you only do it in the dark and from behind. But what if I want more? What if I want to run my hands up your chest and into your hair? Or dig my nails into your ass while you pound into me. I want your breath, hot and heavy, in my ear whispering all these dirty things while our chests bump together.*

Oh my God. Why did I keep typing this shit to him? Probably because I just couldn't help myself. My fingers suddenly had word vomit.

I want to roll you onto your back and crawl onto your lap, and just...ride you until you come inside me. But I'll never be able to do that, will I? If you only do it from behind, I mean. I'll never get to face you and kiss you senseless when you're inside me. I'll never get to go down on you. I'll never get to do ALL KINDS of things I'm craving to do to you.

What I told him was all true, but it was just a smoke-screen for what I really craved. Most of all, I was upset because I'd never get to have a real relationship with him.

My phone dinged, causing my pulse to lurch. I was

almost afraid to read his message. *I hate to break it to you, sweetheart. But whichever THEY you've been talking to are wrong. I do it in ALL kinds of positions. Your worries of NEVER are completely unfounded.*

Fudge nuggets. Now I was picturing him in...all kinds of positions, especially the ones I'd named. My breathing picked up. I was once again tempted to tell him tomorrow night was back on.

I sank down onto the first bench I passed and clamped my thighs together because I was wet and pulsing.

What about the dark? I hedged in my next text. *Do you do it with the lights on too, then?*

As I recall, it was YOUR idea to keep the lights off for this next round. Do you want them on?

No. I don't.

Well then, princess, maybe now I'M feeling cheated. Maybe I want to watch your titties bounce or your pussy all wet and stretched while it's holding on to my cock. Maybe I want to know what color your eyes are, or your hair, or if your cheeks get flushed when you're aroused, if you have pink nipples or brown.

I groaned and bent at the waist, my thighs clamped so hard together I was a little afraid I might not get them pulled apart again.

You can never see me, I told him.

Why not? he instantly flipped back.

I swallowed and glanced up at the trees overhead. For some reason the buds of newly blooming leaves gave me the courage to answer honestly. *I'm afraid you won't like what you see.*

Impossible. You felt beautiful to me.

A lump formed in my throat, and I couldn't swallow it down. I loved what he said, and yet, I didn't love knowing he would write something so sweet and pure...to another woman. A hard laugh blurted from my chest because I realized I was freaking jealous of myself.

This was getting more and more ridiculous by the moment.

Needing to keep him from saying anything else that might make me jealous of myself, I said, *So your turn. Why don't you want to meet? Did I cause a trigger last time?*

Trigger? He was obviously clueless, which made me smile and instantly loosen my tense stomach muscles.

You told me about your sister's death, I reminded him. *Maybe you didn't like exposing so much of yourself to me. Or maybe you didn't like how I kept calling you Oren. Maybe you let me get too emotionally close and that made you uncomfortable.*

I don't know why I said any of that. Anything he responded with would probably hurt. If he told me he hadn't felt anything for me during our encounter, I'd die. If he said he'd liked how he'd opened up to me, I'd get jealous of myself...again.

But instead of either of those responses, he said, *You're totally whack.*

As I laughed and shook my head, he added, *But that's okay. I dig crazy chicks. I don't mind that you're a complete stalker or that you probably even know what color my panties are right now. I think your obsession with me is hot.*

I laughed again, this one bordering on an outright giggle. *You're not wearing panties,* I wrote, because they were probably boxers or briefs, or oh yum, my favorite: boxer briefs.

Damn, you're good.

Reading his response made my grin widen, but a second later, I sobered. *So if my creeper traits aren't scaring you off, you don't mind that I want our meeting in total darkness, and I didn't hit any triggers, then why were you so quick to call tomorrow night off?*

Baby, you're the one who called it off.

I rolled my eyes. Was he really that dense? *But you agreed IMMEDIATELY.*

Oh I'm SO sorry, was I supposed to beg you to let me back into your pussy again?

With a frown, I pounded out my response. *YES, DAMN IT!*

Jesus, fine, he shot back. *Please, my mysterious midnight visitor who feels like heaven around my cock, would you be so kind as to let me back into your pussy again?*

Oh my God. What a douche. *Fuck you.*

That's the plan, sweetheart. I want to fuck you until you can't walk straight the next day. So are we on or not?

That would be a hell no. You don't want me.

You are definitely a confusing fucking woman. FUCK! I

do want you. Okay? I want you, and THAT'S the problem. I want you, but I want someone else, and I'm all fucked up in the head, feeling like I'm cheating on you both, when honestly I don't really have either of you, do I? So any kind of cheating would be literally impossible, wouldn't it?

I pulled back, staring at his words in a strange kind of shock. But he'd just admitted to wanting...someone. Was it me? Immediately, I wondered if it could be. Zoey seemed to think he cared about me. Occasionally between all his foulmouthed sluttiness, I caught a flicker of interest, but...I'd never been completely certain.

My mind raced. Could I actually make him feel guilty about sleeping with me because he thought he was betraying...well, *me*? Damn, that was as messed up as me feeling jealous of myself.

Are you saying you're currently sleeping with another woman? I asked, purposely misunderstanding him, because I needed to gain more intel here. But I think the question irritated him a little.

Jesus! No. I just TOLD you, you're the only person I'm fucking right now. I've never fucked the girl I want. I will never fuck her. I can't.

My breath caught in my chest, but holy shit. It was me. He was talking about *me*. He had to be!

She's forbidden to you? I pressed.

Bingo. And when you came along, in the dark with no name, no face, it was easy to picture HER.

And...here came more jealousy of myself. Or—if I was wrong, and he was as crazy for another woman as I was for him—then here came a load of jealousy for that fucking bitch who stole his heart, whoever she was.

YOU DICK! You imagined you were with ANOTHER woman when you were with me? I bit my lip, not really as upset as I made the message sound, but I had to know how he would answer that.

Fuck. I really am losing it. I cannot believe I admitted that to you. Can you pretend you never read that? Please.

Okay, that wasn't exactly an apology, but he did sound contrite. I wasn't sure what to make of it all, so I asked, *What's her name?*

That would be a hell to the big fucking no, I will never tell you her name.

Again, I wasn't sure how to feel. If he was talking about

me, I was pretty smug that he felt so protective. But if he was referring to someone else, I wanted to bawl. *"Bet I can make you cry it out when you come inside me tomorrow night."*

Holy Christ. Why had I said *that*?

Maybe because I was more certain that he'd cry out my name than someone else's, and oh...my poor ovaries. The idea of him saying my name when he came was more than I could take.

So we're back on for tomorrow night? Oren asked with his next message. *Even after everything I just confessed to you?*

I bit my lip. *Was* I saying that? Oh, hell. Yes, I was. Thinking he might want me that much was impossible to resist. So I answered, *I can handle knowing you're picturing me as someone else if you can handle always taking me in the dark.*

That's messed up.

Thought you just said you liked crazy. Truth is—though it was completely a lie—*I want you again, and I'm willing to listen to you cry out another woman's name to get you to fuck me like you did on Friday.*

Damn it, now I'm hard.

Well I've been soaking wet for a while, so I have no sympathy.

Tomorrow night can't come soon enough. Are we really doing this again?

We're both fully aware of what we're walking into now, so sure, why not?

Sweet. Lick you later, baby.

I shook my head and slipped my phone back into my bag. I loved talking to him, whether it was arguing, our strange version of flirting, or just commenting about the weather. Any byplay with Oren Tenning left me exhilarated. I swear it was *his* presence in my life that had brought me back to life after Sander had left me pregnant and alone. And quite frankly, I was going to gobble up any chance to be with him that I could steal. I craved the vivacity he put in me *that much*.

CHAPTER 9

Ten

Someone stick a fork in me. I was crispy-fried and well done. Lounging on the mattress beside my midnight visitor, I blew out a breath and flopped my arm over my forehead as my breathing finally settled and evened out. But... "Fuck," I breathed out. That had been...yeah. Mind officially blown.

She'd remembered her threat to sniff test my dick, because she'd attacked me first thing after she'd walked into my room and shoved me against the door before yanking at my pants and going down on me. I guess I must've passed muster, because the blowjob that followed left me so weak-kneed I almost couldn't carry her to the bed after that to perform my own sniff test.

God, I loved the scent of a woman's arousal. And the taste. And the softness of her inner thigh against my cheek.

Now she lay snuggled against my side in the dark. I closed my eyes and kept my lashes fused together, because it wasn't like I could see anything anyway in this pitch black darkness. Then I just enjoyed the quiet contentment of the moment.

Curling against my side, she rested her head on my shoulder. Her breathing had also slowed, but her leg sliding over my thigh was still warm and damp. Just the way I liked to leave my woman: hot and sweaty and well ridden.

A triumphant smile curved up my lips as I palmed her hip to keep her attached to me. Damn, we were good at this together. Everything that had been bugging me yesterday and forcing me to stress draw cowered off into a distant part of my brain. All I could focus on was how amazing my post-coital glow was.

I expected her to start praising me any second. But what I heard sounded a lot more like, "Yuck. Eww. What *is* that?"

Wasn't quite the, *Wow, you're the best I've ever had*, I'd been expecting.

"Huh?" My cocky grin died a tragic, disappointed death. Stunned by any kind of negative review, I whipped onto my side so I could face her, even though I couldn't read her expression in the dark. "What the hell are you talking about? That was fucking awesome."

When I reached her, she was arching her back off the mattress and wiggling as if trying to escape something under her.

"Wha...*eww*. Oren Michael Tenning, have you been eating *crackers* in bed?"

"What? No." She knew my middle name too? I wasn't surprised. "What kind of dork eats *crackers* in bed?" I sniffed at her nerve for even suggesting such a pathetic idea. "They were potato chips. Cool Ranch Doritos." Because I was a cool guy.

She let out a big, disappointed sigh as if she thought I was hopeless. "Lovely. I have cool ranch crumbs coating my butt right now."

"Mmm." That actually sounded hot. "The better to lick off you, my dear."

I reached for her to do just that, but she swatted my hand away, grumbling about the crumbs. As she sat up, I could hear her dusting herself clean, so I reached over to blindly slap some of the crumbs off the mattress.

"There," I offered as valiantly as possible. "All gone now."

Her answer was a disbelieving sniff. "You need to clean these sheets before I visit you again."

I was so busy drifting off into a daze, thinking about the phrase, "*visit you again*," and liking the idea of more encounters with her, I rattled off one of my habitual Ten answers. "What? And give up all the slut cooties I've accumulated over the years?" I even gave an audible gasp and set my hand against my heart, because fuck, that's just how I rolled.

She stilled. When I actually felt a cool draft waft off her, I realized, shit, I'd just fucked up big time.

"Please do not tell me you've had other women on this bed since the last time you *cleaned your sheets*."

Double, triple and quadruple fuck.

"Um...sure."

"Oh, sick. *Oren!*" She started to climb off the side. I knew if she left now, there was a good chance she wouldn't be coming back, so I dove after her and tackled her under me.

"No. Wait."

She growled as I rolled her onto her back. Then she shoved at my shoulders. "Get off me. Now! I can't believe you—"

I kissed her silent.

I have no idea how I knew that would work, but shit, it actually did. She accepted the thrust of my tongue and even kissed me back. Then she went and wrapped her legs around my waist and dug the heels of her feet into the base of my back as her nails sank into my shoulders.

I broke off the kiss, panting hard, and pressed my forehead to hers. "Don't go. Not yet."

Her answer was just as breathless. "Why not?"

"Well..." Shit. I had nothing. Talking from the top of my head, I said, "One. You know I'm an asshole. I don't... I mean, I'm not ever going to think of shit like...like cleaning sheets and wiping away all the past women. I'll probably always be inconsiderate and...and...*you know me!* You're my stalker. You know my work schedule, how to get into my cell phone, my middle name, what kind of fucking soap I use. Don't tell me you don't know what an ass I am, too."

She seemed reluctant at first, but she finally said, "Okay, you have a point."

"Damn right, I do. And two..."

"Two?" she prompted when I didn't come up with a two fast enough.

"Shit. You *know* me. I'm an asshole." Really, why did I need a two when one seemed to cover it all?

She laughed, and my pulse settled some. "Don't go," I

said more softly and reached out to find her cheek. Her breath caught and it caused something massive to shift in my chest. "Stay." I leaned in to nuzzle my nose up the side of her neck. "Just a little longer."

"Why?" Her voice was raspy and soft; it caused my thoroughly exhausted dick to stir. "You've already had your way with me."

I didn't tell her I was ready to have it again. There was a vulnerable little hitch in her voice, as if she thought sex was the only thing we had going, when actually it was supposed to be. But I didn't like thinking my soft-skinned, dirty-minded midnight visitor was hurt.

I took my mouth off her delectable throat. Turning onto my side, I faced her, resting an elbow on my pillow and my cheek on my hand. With my free hand, I found her hip and began to crawl my fingers up her side. "Let's do something, then. What do you want to do?"

"I don't know." The question seemed to take her by surprise. "We could maybe...talk, I guess."

"We're talking right now," I reminded her. When I leaned in and tried to skim my mouth up her jawline, because I just couldn't stay away, she turned her face to the side and evaded me.

With a groan-like growl, I buried my nose in her shoulder. "What do you want to talk about?" I asked, my voice muffled against her amazing-smelling skin.

"I don't know."

I laughed a little derisively. Of course, she wouldn't know. "Okay, fine." I lifted my face and stared through the dark in her direction for a good five seconds, my mind completely blank of anything to say.

My wandering hand finally found her breasts. When her nipples hardened under my touch, my cock went from half hard to full-on ready for deep penetration.

I swallowed a moan and shifted my hips back so she wouldn't know how aroused I was. But I couldn't stop myself from circling her nipple with my finger, because the damn thing kept taunting me with its erectness, making my mouth water and my tongue tingle until it wanted to do nothing else but lick, and lick, and lick...

She drew in a breath and arched her breasts out to me, loving the attention. I knew she was getting wet, and it made my erection throb for release.

"How old were you when your breasts started to grow?" I asked.

She let out a couple pants before she hauled off and slugged me in the shoulder. "Damn it, Oren." She jerked up into a sitting position. "That's not the kind of conversation I was talking about, and you know it."

"Well, then you better pick the topic," I snapped back, sitting up too, "because all I can think about is sucking those hard, succulent berries into my mouth and rolling my tongue across them, and then jerking your legs up and diving that same tongue as deep into your pussy as it'll go."

She shuddered and started to breathe harder. "You're fucking hard right now, aren't you?"

Um, *duh*. "As a steel fucking pipe."

"Damn it." She growled again. "We just did it, like, *five* minutes ago." Even as she complained, she pushed me back onto my spine and crawled on top of me to straddle my waist. Then she hovered above me and tucked her thighs warm and tight around my waist. I listened to her fumble and find a condom on my nightstand.

The sound of her ripping it open made my stomach muscles tense in anticipation. Then she gripped me with her free hand and felt her way into slipping on the latex. Once she had me sheathed and she'd positioned herself in place above me, I lifted as soon as her warm wetness settled against the head of my cock. But Midnight Visitor caught my hip, keeping me from plunging into her.

I arched an eyebrow in the dark. "I guess you want to be totally in charge this round, huh?"

She answered me by grasping both my wrists and pinning them to the bed on either side of my head. With a roll of her hips, she guided me inside her. I could've broken free; she wasn't holding me all that tight. But she seemed to like what she was doing, and I sure as hell didn't mind it.

She began to ride me, and I groaned, arching my back. "Fuck...me." This was awesome.

Above me, she let out a husky chuckle. Fingernails lightly scraped up my chest to play with my nipples. "What're the odds that I can make you cry out that other woman's name when you come?"

"Wha...?" She about made me go cross-eyed by how tight and fast she moved. I couldn't think about anything else at the moment.

"Are you imagining I'm her right now?"

The woman was killing me. I was getting carried away with how good she felt, and here she had to go and remind me of *Caroline*? "Shh," I hissed, reaching up to grip her breasts. "Don't be weird."

"It's okay," she murmured, as if coaxing a frightened animal. "You can say it. Say her name."

I gritted my teeth. "I'm not going to fucking say her name."

"But I don't mind if you—"

"That's fucked up. You *have* to mind. Why wouldn't you mind?" Hell, I wanted her to mind. If she didn't care, then this couldn't mean as much to her as it did to me. And I couldn't accept the idea that she wasn't as into me as I was into her.

She slid her hand down my chest, over my belly and below my navel to where, oh Holy God, I think she touched herself. "Because what if...what if it's *my* name you say?"

"It's not...it can't be." I shook my head, denying it, even as I reached for her hand, because I had to know what she was—fuck me, she *was* rubbing her clit.

"But what if it is?" she pressed, drawing me back to that damn annoying conversation. Her voice grew breathier. She had to be getting closer to her release, an idea which made me closer to mine.

"You better not fucking be her," I gritted out, arching up into her.

"Why not?"

"Because I can't...shit, fuck, that feels good. I can't feel this with her. I can't *do* this with her."

"And yet that's exactly what you might be doing."

Just the idea that she could be Caroline had me so close, I bucked my hips again, harder this time, driving into her as deep as I could go. She cried out and dug her fingers into my shoulders. "*Oren.*"

"Damn," I panted. "I want to see you so bad right now."

She leaned down so I could feel her legs shift with each plunge that she wrought down on me. Something that had been hanging around her neck thumped against my chest right before she whispered into my ear. "Sorry, but you'll just have to use your imagination. Because you'll never see me during these visits."

"Oh, yeah?" I was tempted to just put her in her place. "I

could reach over and flip on my nightlight...right now."

She sucked in a breath and clamped her hands back around my wrists, pinning them to the mattress again. But then she went and challenged me. "Then why aren't you?"

I tugged my hands free, which made her suck in a startled breath. But instead of going for the light switch, my fingers attacked her hair, burying themselves deep and giving a tug, which she'd seemed to like as much as last time.

"Because I like this game," I hissed in her ear.

"Ohmigod, ohmigod, ohmigod," she chanted her orgasm mantra, telling me she was right there. Then the walls of her sex collapsed around my dick, squeezing tight as she came. "*Oren.*"

Her use of my first name was what tipped me over the edge. I'd wanted to wait until she was done, then try to build her up again, but her orgasm seemed to clutch me by the balls and had me releasing deep inside her.

"Damn it, damn it." I clenched my teeth and bucked my hips wildly, lifting her from the bed as I tried to hold it back. And failed. "*Caroline.*"

It felt so good, I couldn't even think as I pulled her hair and slammed up into her again and again.

When she collapsed on top of me, that thing she was wearing thunked against my chest again. A cool metal chain was connected to it, so I figured it was a necklace.

Silken hair fluttered over my arm as she nestled her cheek on my shoulder. It felt nice. I knew I could keep her there just like that forever and be completely content. But that thing still resting on my chest piqued my curiosity.

"What is this?" I asked as I dipped my face to feather my lips down her neck until I had a mouthful of the chain and gave it a small tug. I picked up the amulet with my fingers and felt out its shape. Sadness rocked through me because I couldn't remember Caroline ever wearing anything so large.

I didn't like proof that Midnight Visitor wasn't her, even though they were beginning to separate in my mind and become two different people.

"It's a necklace," she murmured, her voice amused.

"Hmm." Maybe Caroline just wore it under her shirt. That wasn't completely unrealistic. It was about as realistic as me admitting Midnight Visitor was her. I continued to trace the rounded oval shape before I pressed it back to her chest and outlined it with my tongue. She let out a hum of pleasure.

"Does it mean anything special to you?"

Her fingers drifted into my hair, making my scalp tingle. "Of course."

I chuckled and lifted my face when she didn't elaborate. "But you're not going to tell me?"

"Do you really want to know?"

I shrugged. Kind of, yeah. I was beginning to grow very curious about my midnight visitor. I wanted to know all kinds of things, including, apparently, the importance of her necklace.

The more time I spent with this woman, the more confused I grew. Whoever I was with now was getting under my skin. She knew how to draw me out. Or maybe I'd allowed myself to grow closer to her because I secretly wanted her to be Caroline. Either way, what we had here between us was pretty sweet, yet I felt like shit because she was a true, live person that I was using.

Then again, this wasn't Caroline. This was someone I could actually be with, so why couldn't I stop imagining she was someone else and just...be with her?

Unease stirred within me. There were reasons why I hadn't had a steady girlfriend in four years, why I didn't let myself stay long with one chick, why I refused to let myself open up and let anyone in. But meeting Caroline a year ago had changed all that.

And now that I'd loosened my ways for her, this woman here was trying to squeeze in too. That panicked me. I had no clue what she looked like or what her name was, but the girl with me right now had a hold on me.

I had thought I liked the mystery of not knowing who she was. But now I was curious. Tracing my finger down the middle of her chest between her breasts, I kissed her cheek. My gut clenched, because I knew a small part of me would be disappointed. I'd been having fun day-dreaming she was Caroline, but I was going to have to get over my obsession with her. And this woman was the closest I'd ever come to what I felt for Gamble's little sister.

I buried my face in her neck. With our arms and legs wrapped up in each other, I felt as close to her as I'd ever felt to another living human, and yet I also felt worlds apart.

I knew what I was hiding. But what the hell was *she*

hiding? Why didn't she want me to see who she was?

"I've been working on my portfolio," I said, hoping if I shared something about me, she'd share something about herself.

"Hmm?" Her voice was drowsy and pretty much disinterested in whatever I had to say. "What?"

"Jesus, woman." I sighed. "First you tell me to talk to you, and when I finally start to, you fall asleep on me. What's up with that?"

She yawned and sat upright. "No, I'm awake. I'm awake. Sorry. Now, what were you saying about a portfolio? As in...your architecture portfolio? Oh my God, are you already looking for a job?"

"Yeah." I should've known she'd be fully aware I was an architecture major, even though I told most everyone I was getting a construction degree. My stalker was just that good. "All my teachers and my counselor are telling me it's smart to get a head start and apply to places now, before I graduate."

"Wow." She sounded shell-shocked. "But your graduation is just—"

"Less than a month away," I finished softly, moving closer to her without meaning to.

"Yeah," she whispered and nestled back down beside me to burrow close and kiss my shoulder. "So...have you found any places looking for new architects?"

Again, I nodded. "A couple."

"Oh my God. Wow. W-where?"

"There are a few in-state firms I'm checking out. Some in Missouri and Ohio. One as far away as Lake Tahoe."

"Lake Tahoe? As in *California*, Lake Tahoe?"

"Mmm hmm." I drew the scent of her hair deeply into my lungs and grew drowsy.

"Wow." I swore I heard disappointment in her voice and wondered, what that was about?

"I'd show you some of the designs I was putting into it, but that would take turning on a light." Plus I was just too tried to move off this bed and fetch much of anything right now.

"That's okay," she told me as she began to pet my hair. "I'm sure they're amazing. You're such a talented artist."

A muscle jerked in my cheek. It'd been four years since anyone had used that very term on me. Talented artist. My sister used to demand that I draw pictures of her. She'd even posed in the strangest ways and screwed her face up into some comical expression. And she'd said I nailed her portrait every time.

I closed my eyes, pushing those memories away.

"I can't believe you might seriously move all the way to California." Midnight Visitor scraped her nails gently across my scalp, and they were doing a serious number on my consciousness.

Sleep soaked into my veins as I relaxed into her soft breasts. "I don't know what I'm going to do yet," I mumbled, and then I remembered no more.

CHAPTER 10

Caroline

As Oren went limp against me and I knew he'd fallen asleep, I released a deep breath and slowed the progress of my fingers that were skimming through his hair.

There was so much to swallow all of a sudden. But he was *leaving*? I knew it was the next logical step for someone who was graduating from college, but shit...I hadn't even considered the possibility. Because I was obviously an idiot.

Or maybe because Oren never acted like someone who was itching to grow up and move away.

But what was even more unnerving was the fact he'd said my name when he'd come. I don't think he even realized what he'd done. He hadn't *said* anything about it afterward, and he hadn't *acted* strange. I grew more certain with every passing second that he didn't have a clue what he'd done.

My hands began to shake and tears welled in my eyes. Well, it had happened. My dream for him to want me as much as I wanted him had come true, but I just wanted to bawl because it was too much to take. It was too beautiful, too surreal, too...God! And two seconds later, he drops that bomb about maybe moving away, as far as *California*?

What the hell was I getting myself into? I was risking the

wrath and trust of my brother for an immature, man-whore jerk who was probably going to leave and break my heart. And I was doing it with my eyes wide open, because no matter how hard I told myself to run, I just couldn't leave him, not yet. I dropped my cheek to his shoulder and ran my fingers up and down his hard chest.

"I love you," I whispered, glad I at least had this peaceful moment with him, a memory to carry away with me long after he was gone. But still, I had to add the quiet plea. "Please don't go."

When he didn't answer, didn't even stir, I gave a sad sigh and crawled out of his warm embrace. As I left the bed, he rolled my way as if seeking me in his sleep. Pain knifed through me, but I kept going and found my clothes in the dark.

I was tempted to flip on the night lamp so I could have one glimpse of him asleep and naked on his bed, but I didn't want to risk waking him and letting him see me, so I felt my way to the door and hurried down the dark hall toward the front room.

As I walked along the sidewalk toward home, eighteen blocks from Aspen's house, I decided it would be best if Midnight Visitor had just made her last foray to Oren's bedroom.

TEN

WHEN I WOKE IN the morning, I was alone. I instantly missed her and swiped out my hand to her side of the bed. The head-shaped indention in the pillow next to mine made me smile. At least I had proof she was real.

The stinging on my back as I showered was more proof.

"What the hell?" I muttered, twisting and trying to feel around back there to figure out what was wrong with me. It wasn't until I'd stepped out and was drying myself off that I caught a glimpse of the scratch marks on my shoulder blades and realized what the sting was. She must've left her mark when I'd gone down on her last night. She had gripped me pretty hard.

Damn, I liked that. Grinning, I whistled as I strolled back to my room in nothing but a towel. I started to make my bed, feeling like a dork when I had to pause and lean down to smell her on my sheets. When I caught a whiff of her unique perfume, I sighed and sucked in an even deeper inhale. God, she smelled so good. I was about to crawl onto the bed and jack off to thoughts of her when I stopped myself.

What the hell was I doing? Was I really this far gone for some chick I knew nothing about except how she felt, and smelled, and tasted...oh, and that she had an unnatural obsession for me? I must've lost my frigging mind. I was already fixated on someone, damn it; I didn't need to add another woman to the list.

I'd let her in way too easily last night and given her some of that talking crap she'd wanted. Why had I done that? We didn't need to talk. We were all about the physical. And that's *all* it was, I commanded myself a little more firmly. In fact, next time she texted, I was just going to ignore her. I should find some chick that I had no problem just being physical with, and my life would return to normal. No more stress drawing, no more disturbing dreams like that one I'd had last night of my sister, and no more of this "feelings" bullshit. Not for me.

With a fistful of sheets, I ripped the covers off my bed, meaning to wash her scent off them, but then I realized I was actually following her orders to wash my bedding.

Damn it.

Fuck. They needed to be washed anyway. I kept tearing them from my mattress, a little more aggressively, pissed that some unnamed, faceless woman had me changing my mind so much in the past week. Dudes weren't supposed to be such mind-changers. Before I knew it, I'd be growing ovaries.

"Pfft." I snorted. "Not likely."

When one corner of the fitted sheet wouldn't come free of the mattress after one tug, I growled and jerked it with so much pressure that I stumbled backward when it finally came free. I ended up landing on my ass with the towel I had wrapped around my waist coming free and falling by the wayside.

But the most painful part was the hard, rock-like thing I landed on as it dug into my right butt cheek.

"Ouch. *Fuck!*"

Bare-ass naked, I scrambled off it and spun around to notice a necklace with the gold chain bunched around a bright oval stone.

Blinking, I sucked in a breath. "Oh, hell." Remembering how I'd asked Midnight Visitor about her necklace last night, I swiped my thumb over the glittery green amulet. The clasp was broken, telling me it had accidently fallen off its owner.

This was the only link I had to her. Whoever she was, emeralds were somehow important to her. It made my chest fill with accomplishment to know that, and then irritation for even wanting to know it.

Caroline's birthday was in May, so I instantly wandered what the birthstone for May was. No, fuck. I wasn't going to associate her with Caroline any more. This woman should have her own identity, an identity I needed to dissociate myself from.

I debated what to do. Yesterday, I would've pulled out my phone and sent her a little message, holding her necklace for ransom until she agreed to give me what I wanted. Hell, I was still itching to do that. But I needed to get my head on straight here.

After tossing the amulet onto my bureau, I dressed for the day. I jammed a sketchpad and a few textbooks that I might need into my backpack, and I started for the door of my bedroom, only to pause and glance down at that damn necklace.

A split second decision later, I snatched it up and tucked it into my pocket before hightailing it out the door.

The Blondie-Ham combo were already gone for the day; they had early-ass classes, so I took my time, raiding the kitchen. I snagged a donut and Sunny D, then headed toward campus. My first class of the day was some boring business ethics thing I tried not to sleep (too heavily) through. Next was an architectural design class and then a lunch break before architectural history.

I hunted up some food at the campus deli during my free hour and then sprawled out in a big, comfy chair in the student union. I was polishing off a sub sandwich when I pulled the necklace from my pocket and fiddled with the broken clasp. Maybe I'd fix it, get it back to her and then I'd call it good between us. I mean, she'd sounded as if it meant something important to her; I'm sure she'd want it back. And one last goodbye fuck couldn't hurt—

"Hey, fucktard, what're you doing hanging out in here?" Gamble's voice made me jump right before his palm slapped me across the back of the head.

"Hey, fuck you, man," I muttered, dodging my face to the side, in case he went after me again. "I'm eating my lunch, what does it look like I'm doing?"

Gam slumped into a matching chair across from me and instantly groaned, throwing his head back as if in the throes of ecstasy. "Damn, these things are comfortable."

I screwed my face into a grimace. "Dude, stop molesting the poor chair. Seriously." Not really realizing what I was doing until it was too late, I wound back my arm and threw whatever was in my hand at him, nailing him in the center of the chest. Perfect shot.

"Ouch. What the hell?" He rubbed the spot and picked up the necklace.

I froze and silently hissed every curse word I knew in my head. But what the fuck had I just done?

Gamble stared at the emerald in his palm before he blinked and lifted his face. "What're you doing with Caroline's necklace?"

I stared at him.

"What?" I somehow found the voice to ask. I shook my head, confused. But Caroline's necklace?

Caroline's necklace?

Gamble narrowed his eyes suspiciously and wrapped his fingers slowly around the amulet. "Why the fuck do you have my sister's necklace?"

I didn't know what to say. Fuck, I didn't even know what to think.

My gaze dropped to his fisted hand and blood rushed to my head. Finally, I pointed. "No. No, that's not..." I had to shake my head again, unable to even fathom it. "That's not hers." It *couldn't* be. "I... I..." I looked at my best friend blindly, but all I saw was his sister's face. Her blue eyes. Her nose. Fuck, they even had similar lips. My hands began to shake. "Are you sure that's *hers*?"

There had to be a mistake. Caroline was not Midnight Visitor, no matter how much I'd initially thought she could be.

But then, Jesus, I sprang instant wood over the very

idea. Shaking my head some more, I gaped at her brother, waiting for him to change his mind.

"Hell, yes it's hers," he said. "I know the only piece of jewelry she ever wears. I even had her birthday engraved on the back before I gave it to her." He flipped it over to show me, and I had to crawl out of my cushiony seat to step forward and take it from his hand.

I flipped the emerald over. "Fuck me," I blurted out. I hadn't even noticed the day *May 24th* engraved on the back. I looked up blindly at my best friend. "You gave this to her," I then stupidly repeated.

But oh, holy, holy shit. This was bad. This was incredibly bad.

I'm sure he could see all the guilt on my face because he scowled and yanked it out of my hand. "Of course, I gave it to her. It was for her sixteenth birthday. Emeralds are her birthstone."

My head must've turned into a pendulum because it kept shaking back and forth in total denial. But this was insane. Totally unreal. Caroline really *was* my midnight visitor? Impossible. In no realm of reality would all my dreams coming true like this even be feasible. "But I've never seen her wear it," I argued, because...shit. I could not let myself believe it was truly true.

Gamble turned the stone in his hand to run his thumb over the emerald. "That's because she wears it under her shirt. She's always been worried about losing it."

My throat felt like it sank into my stomach because I suddenly couldn't talk. I sat back in my chair, feeling... shit, I don't even know what I felt.

Feelings sucked ass.

Gamble seared me with an accusing glare. "Care to explain why you have this?"

No. I shook my head. "I thought it was..." Crap. Think. "Hamilton's woman's. I...I found it on the couch... in our apartment. I saw it was broken, so I was going to fix it and get it back to Zo—Blondie."

Fuck, I really was losing it. I'd almost called Blondie by her real name. Panic and shock were making me undoubtedly loopy.

I shrugged what hopefully looked like a careless signal and motioned to the necklace. "But if you're sure it's Caroline's, she must've dropped it there some time or other when she was over visiting Ham's woman."

Gamble nodded, and a knowing look entered his eyes. "You really have a thing for her, don't you?"

I couldn't breathe. I didn't know what to say. Shit, I was a split second from passing out.

Instead of leaping across the rug between us to strangle me with his bare hands, though, Gamble let a sly smirk spread across his face and he shook his finger. "I knew it! I knew the moment I caught you drawing her name the other day. Designing a tattoo for Quinn, my ass. You want his woman."

I pulled back in surprise, not expecting him to say *that*. "Excuse me?"

He just kept nodding as if he was so sure he was right. "Yeah, I knew something was up when you let her move in with you guys after you wouldn't even let Cora stay overnight."

Growling, I muttered, "I didn't let that whore stay overnight with Hamilton because I hated her fucking bitch guts and I was afraid she'd try to crawl out of his bed one night and right into mine. I don't have to worry about that with Blondie. *She* actually has morals."

"Wow, you've fallen *hard* for her, haven't you?" Gamble shook his head as if amazed. "I never thought I'd see the day. Ten's in love."

"I am not!" I snorted and shook my head. "You're fucking crazy."

"Don't worry." The bastard's grin just wouldn't die. "I won't tell Quinn."

"Whatever." I rolled my eyes and decided to just ignore him. Except that didn't work, so I exploded. "You won't tell him because there's nothing to tell. You're completely fucking wrong. I am *not* into Blondie." My gaze slid to his hand still holding that necklace captive, and I had to curl my fingers into fists to keep from diving at him and taking it back.

It belonged to my midnight visitor, to *Caroline*. I didn't want him touching it.

"I knew something was off about you lately," he murmured, nodded his head. "You haven't been as annoying and crude as your usual self. I should've known a woman was involved."

Well, he was close. Just not close enough. "You're

delusional, man." Pissed that I wasn't getting her necklace back, I stood and slung one strap of my book bag over my shoulder. Then I tossed the last of my sandwich in a nearby trash can. "I'm not going to sit here and listen to this shit. I don't want Blondie. I have no plans of stealing Ham's woman. And I have been as perfectly crude and annoying as usual." To prove that last part true, I kicked his foot as I passed him and leaned in to call him the dirtiest, most offensive thing I could think of.

And then I was out of there.

But as soon as I stepped into the April air, I felt even more claustrophobic than I had inside. The panic crowding my chest sucked the oxygen straight from my lungs, until I was nearly gasping for breath. I turned in a slow circle, trying to focus on the blurry images of buildings and trees around me. But I just felt like passing out.

Blindly, I pulled my phone from my pocket, and then I drew in a few deep breaths before I could concentrate enough to focus. After scrolling through the contact list, I shook my head, mystified. I still had Caroline's number in my address book, and it was a different number than Midnight Visitor's.

See, they *couldn't* be the same person.

Caroline had just gone into my room at some point and dropped her necklace, and that was all. Not that I knew what the hell she would've been doing in my room in the first place, but it was plausible...except I'd felt it on Midnight Visitor last night and even asked her about it. And she hadn't told me about its importance because, Jesus, it'd been a gift from her brother, my best goddamn friend on earth.

Oh, fuck. My vision went black around the edges as I took in the possibility that it really had been Caroline. Stone hard, my dick twitched in my pants, and my skin buzzed with awareness.

Had I fucked Caroline?

The best sex of my life. The way she'd called me Oren. The way she'd sparred with me and gotten into my head.

Jesus, I was so stupid. No one got under my skin the way she did. Why had I even entertained the notion that two different women could affect me the same exact way?

Probably because I'd wanted to believe she was someone else, someone I could actually be with.

I buried my face into my hands and concentrated on breathing. But my body was on fire, I was afraid I might come in my pants. I needed answers, more answers, good solid answers, or I was going to drive myself insane.

Logging into my phone again, I texted Midnight Visitor. *Tonight.*

She replied almost immediately, which made my blood race to watch a message from her pop up. *What? No 'please'? I don't feel very inspired to say yes.*

Damn, that was such a smart-ass Caroline retort. Why had I not let myself realize that?

My cock pulsed hard. I wanted it to be her so bad, and then again, I didn't. Everything would change if she was Caroline. It'd no longer be fun, meaningless hot sex. But then, it was already more than that, wasn't it? This woman had captured my complete attention without me even realizing what was going on. And I still wanted more from her.

Gritting my teeth, I began to type.

I'm already throbbing for you. Don't wear panties unless you want me to rip them off in inventive new ways, because I'm going to take you HARD as soon as you step into my room. You wanted it dark. Well, prepare for the darkest, grittiest, most sinful sex of your life.

After I shot that note off, I waited, chewing on my bottom lip. When she answered, I blew out a relieved breath.

Okay, I'm inspired.

I grinned. *Prepare to be sore tomorrow. Lick you later, baby.*

She didn't respond, and I didn't want her to. I was too busy scrolling back up to the C's in my contact list. When I pulled up Caroline's information, I typed in a new message. *What're you wearing...I mean, doing?*

If she was Midnight Visitor, she'd already have her phone open, unless she had two phones. I shook my head. Nah. She'd probably just gotten one of those Google Voice numbers.

And, shit, why the hell hadn't I thought up that idea before?

Twenty seconds passed and disappointment filled me. Maybe Caroline *wasn't* Midnight Visitor after all.

Shit. I'd just been getting into the idea, too.

But then my phone dinged, and my heart lurched.

Why? she said.

"Because I'm about to figure out all your secrets, woman." A smile slipped onto my face. But instead of telling her that, I wrote, *I'm bored.*

I envisioned her reading this and giving an irritated sigh. My delight grew.

I'm at the library with Zwinn.

Zwinn?

Quinn and Zoey. You know...Zwinn.

Hmm. I liked that name shipped for them. Jealous I hadn't thought it up myself, I started toward the library even as I keyed in a reply. *A threesome? Kinky.*

A typical smutty Oren answer? Unimpressed.

I laughed. Damn, I loved her smart-ass wit. *Give me twenty-four hours, and I'll find a way to impress you. Guaranteed.*

Not interested, she wrote back.

"Oh, but you will be," I murmured. Pocketing my phone, I bounded up the steps to the front door and pulled it open. I'd never been in the campus library before, so I wandered aimlessly for a minute before I found her and the two love doves cozied up at a study table together. After approaching her from behind, I leaned in and whispered into her ear. "Too late, little girl. Prepare to have your mind blown."

Caroline jumped and whirled around to gape up at me. "What? What the hell are you talking about?"

"Our phone conversation just now." When her eyes flickered, I wondered which conversation she was thinking about. I blinked innocently and added, "I believe you issued me a challenge to impress you. And I've accepted it. I am going to amaze you...probably before you even get to sleep tonight."

"Oh." She rolled her eyes. "I thought you were talking in your usual, uncouth sexual innuendo speak."

I winked at her. "Wow, you have a dirty mind today." I watched her face as I uttered those carefully chosen words. No memory of our other phone conversation flickered across her expression, though. She merely blinked at me.

Unfazed by her refusal to react, I unzipped my bag and instead of pulling out textbooks to study from, I found a banana and bottle of Powerade. The appetite Gamble had killed minutes ago suddenly roared back to life. Not surprising; I always felt vividly alert around Caroline.

"You know, not everything I do or say revolves around sex," I told her, picking our conversation back up.

Her gaze tracked the banana's progress as I unpeeled it and stuck the end into my mouth. Her eyebrows lifted as she watched. "Really?"

I almost choked as I chewed. "Jesus, are you sure everything's not a sexual innuendo with *you*? Wow, I was just eating a snack, not giving some imaginary guy head. And FYI, I only get, not *give* blow jobs."

Grinding her teeth, she slapped her book closed and glared. "Why the hell are you here, bothering us?"

I turned to *Zwinn* for the first time since arriving. They were staring at me quite openly, probably wondering why I was being even more annoying than usual. "Am I bothering you two?"

Blondie instantly nodded. "A little bit, yeah."

"Big time," Quinn answered right behind her.

I turned away from them. They were no help. But Caroline had already eased her book open again and had her head tipped down as she studied the text. Her pale tresses had a slight wave today that flowed over her shoulder to obstruct her face. I had to shift in my seat to readjust the pinching constraints of my jeans because I was growing so aroused. But staring at that hair only reminded me of how much she liked having it pulled.

Had my fingers really been buried in all that gorgeous blonde as I'd pounded into her?

A moan tried to crawl up my throat. I quickly covered it with a cough. She continued to ignore me. So I openly stared. She picked up a pen and jotted down some notes on the notebook beside her text. My gaze fell to her slim fingers. Had they been wrapped around the base of me last night, tugging until I'd come in her mouth? They could've been. And thinking they *had been* only shot a throb of pure longing through me.

I couldn't wait until tonight. Tonight, both her life and mine would change forever.

Finishing my banana, I played with the peel as I glanced around for a nearby trash can. My fingers came across the produce label sticker on it. After peeling the sticker away from the yellow skin, I leaned in and pressed it to the back of Caroline's hand where she was still busy writing.

It totally messed up whatever word she was trying to spell. "What the hell?" She jerked her hand away. "I'm writing here."

I winked. "Now you can't say I never gave you anything."

"Oh, gee. Thank you. I'll treasure it always." The dry sarcasm in her voice and plastered across her face told me I hadn't managed to impress her yet. But the day was still young.

"Really?" I arched an eyebrow. "Twenty bucks says you won't even be wearing it tomorrow."

"Oh my God. You really are bored, aren't you?"

Not even a little bit. I merely smiled at my fly as I finished weaving the web I was going to use to trap her. "What? Twenty bucks, Caroline. Sounds like an easy bet to me. Or does my gift just not mean that much to you?" I pressed a hand to my heart and pretended to look hurt.

She rolled her eyes.

One of these days I was going to count how many times I could make her roll her eyes in a single conversation. There had to be a world record for that shit, didn't there?

"Fine," she muttered. "But you better pay up."

"Oh, I will."

CHAPTER 11

Caroline

As Oren slid out of his chair and strolled away, I stared after him, wondering what had just happened. His cheerful whistle echoed back to me before he turned a corner and disappeared out of sight.

I spun toward Zwinn as I pointed after him. "What was that about?"

While Zoey shrugged, Quinn said, "He must know."

I flashed my teeth. "He doesn't know."

He couldn't know, though it probably wouldn't take a genius to figure out who I was. All he'd have to do was flip on a light. Maybe he'd followed me last night after I'd left. Maybe he'd finally recognized my voice. Or maybe Quinn was putting thoughts into my head.

Oren hadn't let on to Midnight Visitor that he knew anything when he'd just texted her. And what was up with that, anyway, texting and coming to see me right after he'd texted *her*? Unless...no, I don't think he knew.

Unless he did.

Crap, I didn't know what to think anymore. I hated being this confused.

I hated how easily I'd let Midnight Visitor accept that invitation from him too. But that probably had something more to do with the dirty, dark, sinful way he promised to take me. God, I was way too easy for letting sex get in the way of my common sense. But it wasn't just my hormones moaning for him; my silly, stupid heart was also pro-Oren. Denying him was frankly impossible, no matter how much I tried to encourage myself that a good, healthy *no* was the way to go.

"I gotta go," I told Zwinn as I slapped my textbook closed. No way could I study now. I had a night with Oren to look forward to.

A night of dark delights.

Dark. Hmm, I suddenly wondered why he so easily let me keep the lights out when I came to him. I know he'd said he liked the game of not knowing who I was, but it'd been his idea to keep it dark the first night I'd come to him, butting into his plans with Kelly. Maybe that rumor was actually true. He only did it that way.

But...why?

You'd think he was trying to hide something; a deformity or scar or something. Except Oren Tenning was not a modest guy. I'd seen him whip off his shirt numerous times...all glorious, breath taking moments too. I'd seen him in shorts—really short shorts that showed off the muscle and golden tan of his toned thighs. He had no problem exposing his sculpted, athletic body. The only things I hadn't seen was his cock...or his tush. I doubted he had anything wrong with his tush, though; I'd seen it molded too perfectly to the back of his snug football tights. There was definitely no deformity there.

That only left his junk. Frowning, I shook my head. No. That part of him hadn't felt strange or deformed. And it sure as hell hadn't felt too small, in case he was worried that his size didn't measure up to his huge ego. The way he had to stretch me to get inside, I knew he easily had to be twice as big as Sander.

I flushed and glanced around me, hoping no one knew just how wet I was, or how hard my nipples were. But, geesh, this was so embarrassing. How could Oren Tenning turn me on so fully without even being around?

I cleared my throat and started toward my next class, even though I was too early for it. I needed some kind of destination because my mind was wandering way too much.

Seriously, though. What was he hiding? If his dick was

perfectly formed and sized, then was it a strange color, covered in spots, zebra stripes?

I snorted. I had to stop daydreaming about Oren's cock. I'm sure his preference for lights-off sex had more to do with emotional reasons than physical ones—like a spotted dick—anyway.

Maybe...ooh, maybe he liked to pretend he was with someone else—like, ahem, *me*—so he took pains not to see his partner's face. He'd already admitted that he liked not knowing who I was so that scenario actually made sense.

I grinned, liking that idea. Yeah, *I* was the reason behind his strange darkness fetish. Sure.

TEN

SHE WORE PANTIES.

I had to rip them off her with my teeth. She gasped, but even as the cotton tore, her hips surged up to meet the first dip of my tongue between her pussy lips.

"Oh God." She gripped my hair as she groaned.

I ate her without mercy, not even pausing between licks as I went straight to the little nub of muscle that had her immediately squirming, and straining, and panting. Her fingers fisted in my hair and she pulled my mouth harder against her. Her smell and taste flooded my senses. I was so hyperaware of every fucking detail, knowing I was going down on Caroline.

My cock pulsed as I thrust two fingers in her. She started coming almost immediately, her body bowing up, her breath catching, her tight little channel pulsing around my digits. I nearly jizzed in my shorts as she cried out. It seemed to last forever too. My tongue kept massaging just one more shudder out of her. I couldn't seem to stop licking. But then her hands lost their grip in my hair and her thighs loosened around my ears.

Phase one complete. Phase two ready to begin.

"Damn, you taste good. Remind me to come back for dessert in a minute here."

Picking up her legs as I crawled up her body, I pinned

her knees up by her ears so she had no control of those long, luscious limbs.

Tonight, I held all the control.

"You're going to need to hold on to me for this next part," I told her, keeping her legs in place with my torso as I found her hands and interlaced our fingers. Then I kissed her. Our tongues mated; I wondered what she thought of her own taste. She moaned with approval, so I ran my thumbs along the backs of her hands as I kicked my way out of my shorts. I already had my condom on, ready to go.

When the pad of my thumb encountered the banana sticker I'd put on her earlier in the library, I groaned and had to let go of the kiss to press my forehead to hers.

But fuck. I really was with Caroline. There was no way to dispute it now. My body became a live wire. I was so ready to explode inside her I feared I might come before I even slid in.

Still playing with the sticker, I let my thumb begin to peel it away.

"Hey." She struggled against me, trying to stop me. But I had her neatly pinned into place.

"Oh, whatever," I said into her ear. "You and I both know I was never going to pay you that twenty dollars."

She gasped and tensed under me. "Oh my God."

I thrust into her, absorbing her shock and relishing it, taking advantage of it to kiss her again. Clamping my fingers around her wrists, I trapped her to the bed. My torso still held her thighs up and immobile, stretching her until she felt extra tight around me while I had deeper access.

"*Fuuuuuck.*" I groaned and pressed my forehead back to hers, pumping my hips hard and fast. "I love being inside you. Damn, you feel so good."

"Oren," she sobbed, her breath catching as her muscles contracted around me. "Ohmigod, ohmigod, ohmigod."

"Already?" I taunted. "So soon? But didn't you just come, like, thirty seconds ago?"

"Shut up." She tried to buck me off, but not very effectively because she was too busy trying to keep herself from coming again. "I...hate...you." Then she gave a long, strained moan as her orgasm took over.

My eyes about rolled into the back of my head. It robbed me of everything I had not to explode with her. But I wanted to torture her for as long as possible. When the best of her quakes were over and she was panting and limp under me, I sat up enough to let her legs go. She immediately stretched them out. But I kept moving in and out of her until she sobbed out a sound.

"I can't. Please."

Poor girl. She was already worn out. Didn't think she could possibly come again. Well, it was time to show her how wrong she was.

Grasping her hips, I rolled us across the bed until she was on top. When I urged her to sit up, she gave a little groan of protest. "Oren, I can't."

Gripping her face between my hands, I whispered a harsh hiss. "Damn it, Caroline. *You* started this. *You* came to me and tricked me into playing with you. Now you have me. Your brother is going to kill us both for this, so you better make it worth our while. You better sit up there and fuck me like you meant to the first night you came into this room, wearing no panties."

"Oh God." She groaned a microsecond before her mouth crashed against mine. Her fingers caged my face and her pelvis ground down against mine. She went crazy, kissing me hard and dirty, pawing at my skin, bouncing up and down on my lap. It sent me right over the edge, losing my shit and exploding deep inside her. She followed me into oblivion, grinding down as if to eek every last ounce of orgasm out of both of us. We kissed open-mouthed and clutched each other hard.

Once my cock released its last drop, I rolled us again until I was back on top. Staying inside her, I kept kissing her, thrusting my tongue and cupping her face, mating my mouth with Caroline's.

Caroline's mouth.

I groaned and deepened the kiss with slow, wet, lazy strokes, connecting with her in ways I'd never connected with anyone. Tonight was technically our first official kiss. I couldn't remember if we'd had any mouth-to-mouth action our first two nights together. But then, now I knew without a doubt it was her, and she knew that I knew it was her, and that changed everything.

We didn't come up for air. We breathed each other in, lips locked until she finally pulled her face away, gasping for breath.

"Oren," she panted and pressed her brow to my

shoulder. "I can't believe you know—"

"Shut up." With a savage snarl, I kissed her again, pushing my tongue in ruthlessly, and making her whimper before she eagerly latched back around it and sucked it into her mouth.

We seemed to duel then, fighting each other for more passion, for...hell, I didn't even know what.

"Fuck," I muttered, breaking away to slap the mattress beside us. "Fuck, fuck, fuck. I can't believe it's really you."

I sat up, needing space to clear my head, but as I ran my fingers through my hair, I could still taste her.

I reached out and flipped on the light, making her gasp and blink, then lift her hand to shade her sensitive eyes.

"Oh, Jesus." A strange sob tore from my chest. She was so infuriatingly gorgeous. Her hair was a snarled mess from my hands, but it'd never looked better. Her breasts that seemed perfect when they were tucked away inside a shirt, were even better bare and marred with beard burn. Damn, her entire body was just...I started to grow hard again. She was flawless.

I clutched my hair with both hands. "Fucking goddamn shit motherfucker. It really *is* you."

Scowling at me, she yanked my newly clean sheets up to cover her amazing tits. "Well, I am so sorry to disappoint you."

Her chin lifted regally and I wanted to kiss her so bad, but I was rocking my anger—or more aptly, my *fear*—too strongly to give into that urge.

"I'm not *disappointed*," I bit out, frankly incredulous that she could even think that. "I'm pissed as hell. I promised—I fucking *promised*—your brother that I would never touch you."

I swear, a microsecond of guilt flashed across her face before her eyes narrowed. "Well, you can relax. You didn't touch me. *I* touched *you*, remember? I tricked you and came to you; you had no idea—"

I snorted, cutting her off as I shook my head. "Yeah...I have a feeling Gamble won't see it that way."

Flopping back against my pillow, I stared up at the ceiling and wondered how the hell I was going to come out of this unscathed. "I'm dead," I said more to myself than her. "I'm so fucking dead." Moaning out my predicament, I ran my hands over my face. "Christ, Caroline. He's going to fucking kill me."

Caroline

ASHAMED, I BIT my lip and turned my attention away from Oren, who was slaughtering me with his perfectly logical accusations.

But really, how could I have done this to him? I'd put him in the worst situation ever. He loved and respected Noel; he'd never want to betray my brother this way. But I'd ignored all that for my own selfish needs. I couldn't believe what a bitch I was.

Biting my lip, I fought off tears and tried to think up a good enough apology when I noticed the banana sticker he'd put on my hand earlier.

I blinked, staring hard. He'd known who I was when he'd put that there, hadn't he? He'd known who I was when he'd called Midnight Visitor and arranged tonight's rendezvous. He'd known who I was when I'd walked into his room tonight, and he'd grabbed me around the waist from behind and carried me to his bed where he'd tossed me onto the mattress. He'd known the entire time he'd ripped off my clothes and put his mouth and hands on me.

That bastard had *known*, and he was sitting there casting judgment on *me*?

I clenched my teeth. "If you're so mad at me for tricking you, then why did you wait until you were *inside* me to tell me you knew?"

The question threw him off his game. His hands fell away from his head as he blinked up at me. "Because I'm a guy?" He phrased it more as a question than an answer.

I snorted. "Bullshit. Bull freaking shit. You've wanted me just as much as I've wanted you, and for just as long as I've wanted you, too, I bet."

Growling as he sat upright, he scowled back at me. "Well, *obviously* I have more impulse control than you do, because I was planning on never *acting* on those urges. Gamble is one of the best friends I ever had. And the only thing he ever asked me not to do was *you*. I fully planned on respecting his wishes, damn it. I do *not* want to betray my best friend."

I lost my grip on the sheet I was holding up to cover my chest when I set my hands on my hips. "Oh, don't even pretend to act all holier than thou to me. I will take culpability for the first two nights, but not tonight. And no, you obviously *don't* have any more impulse control than I do, because you *still* slept with me again after finding out who I was."

When I realized his attention had dropped to my bare chest, I lifted the sheet again. He grabbed them as well, and used the cloth between us to yank me close until we were only inches apart. His eyes flared with anger and heat and his teeth gritted in outrage, right before he said, "Only because two nights with you is not fucking enough."

Then his mouth attacked mine. I opened for him and kissed him back, hard and hot. He kneaded my breasts, his grip slightly rough, reminding me of the times he'd pulled my hair. I liked it when he wasn't so gentle. When he was consumed with a mindless, ravenous passion.

I started to wind my legs around his waist when he jumped back, cursing and wiping the back of his hand across his mouth.

"Damn it," he muttered. His face was flushed and eyes were wild and glassy. "Damn it, we can't do this again."

The metaphorical slap of cold water did not feel good. "Oh my God, will you stop going from hot to cold and just make up your damn mind already? Do you want me or not?"

His eyes flared as he looked into my face. "You know I want you. That's the problem. I want you but I can't *have* you."

I set my hands on my hips. "Well, you already *have* had me. Repeatedly. And you've had me when you knew good and well who I was. We've already established how thoroughly you can have me. The question is...are you going to *keep* me?"

His Adam's apple bobbed nervously as he swallowed. His eyes grew haunted and tempted as he gazed over my body. Then he squeezed his eyes closed and gritted out, "No."

My eyes filled with tears. I gulped in air, trying to dry them before he opened his lashes, when they flashed up as if he could hear my agony.

Immediate regret clouded his face. "Caroline." He started to reach for me, but I held up a hand.

"No. Just stop right now. I'm done. I'm out. You and your stupid spotted dick can just go to hell."

He froze. "My spotted...*what*? Shit." He glanced wildly around the room before hissing, "I'm going to kill her."

When his face drained of color, I frowned. "Huh?"

He didn't even hear my question as he ranted on to himself. "I cannot believe Blondie told you about that." His gaze seared into mine, suddenly intense and desperate. "And it's not *spotted* like there's a bunch of dots. It's one fucking birthmark. *That's it.*"

I shook my head. "What the hell are you talking about?"

"Wait." His eyes flared with shock. "You mean...ah, fuck. She *didn't* tell you, did she?"

CHAPTER 12

Caroline

"TELL ME *WHAT*?" I let out a strange laugh. "You don't really have a spotted dick, do you? I mean, I thought up that scenario because you'll only do it in the dark and that's really the only part of your body you haven't shown off in public to, like, everyone. It was just a...theory." My eyes began to grow wide as I realized how strangely he was watching me. "But, wow..." I blew out a long breath. "It's true, isn't it? You honestly have a spotted—"

"Birthmark," he growled. "One fucking birthmark." When he glanced away, I noticed how pale he was. "One...really big birthmark."

"So I was right?" I laughed out loud. "That's incredible. I am so awesome."

His scowl totally disagreed with me.

I cleared my throat and calmed down because the topic clearly unsettled him. "Sorry. I just...I knew there had to be a reason you'd only do it in the dark, and..." I shook my head. "Does that actually work? I mean, none of the girls I overheard gossiping about you in the bathroom mentioned it, and they mentioned *everything* else, so I'm sure they would've. I can't believe no one you've been with before has ever seen it."

He shrugged one of those uncomfortable, I-don't-want-to-talk-about-it shrugs and wouldn't meet my gaze. "Two other girls have seen it...besides Blondie."

My back straightened. "And why has *Zoey* seen your penis?"

He opened his mouth to answer but paused when he saw my face. His lips quirked into a smirk. "Are you jealous? Of *Blondie*?"

I sniffed and sent him a glower. "No."

Yes, totally.

His grin only grew. "She walked in on me in the shower once; thought I was Hamilton." Smile suddenly dimming, he glanced away. "To say the least, she totally flipped out. So did the other two."

I don't know why it bothered me that three women had seen his penis, but it really, really did. I pulled back, my chest tight with pain, even as I forced casualness into my voice. "Oh, yeah? How'd they freak out?"

"How do you think?" His gaze was hard and penetrating. Then he gave a hard, sniff-like, self-derisive laugh and shrugged. "The first time was...well, *my* first time. I didn't even think about hiding it or being ashamed. I didn't know it was a fucking abnormality. Everyone in my family knew about it and had seen me run around naked when I was younger. No one ever told me, 'Hey, this could totally freak out some girl later on in your life.'"

"So, she didn't see it until after you two had...?" I motioned with my hands, wondering why I was talking about this with him while we were naked and in bed together, arguing about completely unrelated, more-important things...like our possible future together.

"Right," he said.

"What'd she do?" I think the only reason I could ask was because I knew it had ended badly for him. If I had known he'd had a good time with her, I wouldn't have been able to ask at all.

"She screamed. Then she demanded to know what the hell was wrong with me and if it was contagious and...you know." He glanced away, pale and serious. "All that shit."

I snorted. "What a bitch."

His gaze zipped back to me. "She was only sixteen."

That still didn't excuse her in my book. She'd traumatized my Oren. The bitch must die...in my head anyway. I pictured myself pushing her off the side of a bridge and listening to her scream all the way down until...oops, she wasn't screaming anymore.

And yikes, I really did have issues, didn't I?

"And the next girl?"

"Tianna," he said.

I seized up inside, not liking that I knew one of his past sluts' names.

Tianna, Tianna. The big, fat bitch-anna, I sang in my head.

"She gave good head," he went on, and yep, I *really* didn't like knowing that. But he didn't seem to know I was in the room anymore; he was trapped in a memory. "And she seemed okay with doing it in the dark until one night she pulled her cell phone out and turned on the light so she could see what she was doing."

"And she flipped out, too," I guessed.

Oren nodded. "Oh, yeah. Big time. Called me a freak and threatened to cut off my pecker if I'd given her an STD. All kinds of lovely shit. I actually had to blackmail that one to keep her trap shut about it." He let out a small, depressed sigh. "She still really hates me."

In a split second, I went from crazy jealous to heart-broken with sympathy. But seriously, what was wrong with all the whores who'd seen him? How could they treat such a sensitive area so callously?

"I want to see it," I blurted out.

"*What*?" He sent me an incredulous glance. "No. Besides, you're not supposed to see me like this ever again." As if suddenly remembering that part of his vow he'd made himself only minutes ago, he grabbed the sheets and lifted them to cover himself to his chin.

I rolled my eyes, but then grinned and crawled toward him. "Oh, come on. *Please.* I promise I won't upset you with my reaction."

He crab crawled away from me, shaking his head vigorously. "No fucking way on earth. Even Blondie freaked out when she saw it. And she's like the last person ever who'd hurt someone with her reaction to their... differences."

"Well, I already know to expect something different, so it's not going to take me by surprise."

He glanced away, and the panic on his face almost killed

me. "It's really bright purplish red and looks like a blood vein popped or something. And it looks worse when I'm soft."

I lifted my eyebrows, intrigued. "Really? Then I guess we should make it hard before I see it at its best, huh?" Reaching down, I found him through the sheet and wrapped my hand around his cock. When he jerked in my palm, I tsked at him to behave. "And bright purplish red is actually one of my favorite colors."

He looked at me, his expression full of so much uncertainty, but I swear I also saw an ache as if he wanted to believe me, as if he wanted to trust me with the most vulnerable part of himself. "Caroline." The way he rasped my name and hardened even more under my touch made me hum with delight.

I leaned in to kiss him, my hand working up and down his steadily growing length through the sheet. He kissed me back, spiking his tongue deep in my mouth. When he groaned and cupped my face in his fingers and the sheet dropped from between us, I knew my distraction had worked.

I ripped the covers off him at the same moment I tore my mouth from his and looked down.

"Damn it." He sucked in a breath and fisted his hand over his mouth before turning his face aside.

"Oh!" Genuine surprise littered my voice. "It's bigger than I thought it'd be." Then I smoothed my thumb over the mark that had caused him so much grief and added, "So's the birthmark."

He turned and looked at me. I grinned at him as innocently as I could. Reluctant amusement finally entered his eyes. Then he let out a short laugh and glanced away. His cheeks were a little flushed though, so I knew he was still embarrassed. Wanting to put him at absolute ease, I leaned down until I was lying on my belly and eye level with his lap.

"It kind of reminds me of one of those Rorschach test things. Which image do you see in the inkblot. Hmm..." I pulled my bottom lip in between my teeth as I examined him fully. "I see...West Virginia. Or a really strange, misshapen sperm. No. I like West Virginia better."

When I glanced up at him, he just blinked at me as if he couldn't figure me out at all. "What?" I asked.

He slowly buried his fingers in my hair. "You don't have to pretend it's okay if you don't want to. If it wigs you out, just say so."

I crinkled my face with confusion. "Why would a birthmark wig me out? Seriously, Oren." I went back to examining my Rorschach test. But, nope, all I could see was the state of West Virginia...on a really big, yummy-looking cock. "You know, this is probably the only time I'd be able to fit an entire state into my mouth."

When all of Oren's stomach muscles tensed, I smiled smugly. Then I leaned in and licked him from base to tip, lingering at the tip until I lapped up the droplet beading from the slit at the end. "Mmm." I closed my eyes, relishing the salty flavor of him on my tongue. "West Virginia tastes good."

I opened my lashes and glanced up to meet his gaze. We kept the intense eye contact as my mouth opened and I leaned forward to take him between my eager lips. His eyes flared wide and his fingers clamped down harder in my hair.

"Christ," he hissed as he watched me take in as much as I could. His neck arched back and he panted a few times. Then he smacked the heel of his foot against the mattress beside me as if he needed to relieve some of the pleasure before he looked back down, his gaze darting between my eyes and the place where my lips slid up and down on him. "God, Caroline."

I cupped his balls, and he blurted out a sound I'm sure he didn't mean to.

"Fuck, this is..." He arched up his hips and simultaneously pushed down on my head with the grip he had on my hair. When I started to gag, he instantly let up pressure. "Shit. Sorry. I didn't mean to...Jesus. It's just so fucking good. Who knew actually *seeing* someone go down on me makes it so much hotter. Or maybe it's just you. Watching *you*."

I sucked on him a little harder and took him deep into my throat. He shouted out another unintentional sound. Gripping the sheets beside us with his hand that wasn't buried in my hair, he seemed to be bracing for the grand finale. "I'm coming." His voice was strained and his fingers were like iron, clamped in my hair. "Caroline, I'm—*shit*."

He tried to tug me off him, giving me plenty of fair

warning, but I didn't want to go anywhere. I wanted all of him. I moaned at the pressure on my locks and applied more suction as I stroked him faster.

The stream of curses that left him when he flooded my mouth was so filthy and delicious, I reached down and touched myself as he came.

For a moment, he was too shocked and sated to realize what I was doing. But when he noticed I was trying to get myself off too, his eyes flared.

"Oh, I don't fucking think so." Grasping my wrist, he ripped my fingers away from the throbbing wet spot between my legs. Then he flipped me onto my back and climbed on top of me. "Last night, it was hot when I knew you were touching yourself, but two nights in a row just makes me think I'm not doing my job. This is *my* pussy, woman. No fingers touch this clit but mine."

His thumb instantly found me and began to massage without mercy, sending me to an immediate peak. I cried out and arched under him. "No tongue laps up this cream but mine."

He leaned in, and I couldn't help it, I gripped his hair in my hands, so eager to feel his mouth on me, I almost couldn't take it. "Oren."

He paused right before contact and glanced up. "And no one calls me that but you."

I loved the way he claimed ownership of me, but more than that, I loved the way he gave ownership right back to me. As soon as his warm, wet tongue touched me, I came.

I DON'T KNOW how much time passed. I think I drifted in and out of sleep for a while as I lay limp and satiated against him. The sweat from our bodies was still drying as we clung together, but I knew he was awake because his fingers kept stroking up and down my spine. Occasionally, they dipped down farther than usual on his descent until he reached my ass and he'd cup a globe in one of his warm palms, but then a second later, he was on the move again, caressing his way back up the center of my vertebrae.

"I should probably go before I fall asleep," I murmured, too liquid limp to move. He didn't answer, didn't try to get me to stay, so I blew out a disappointed breath and sat up.

But when I tried to crawl off the mattress, he grasped my wrist. I glanced down at him, my heart thumping hard in my chest.

Instead of asking me to stay, though, he said, "You don't have a car."

I blinked. "Huh?" I knew I didn't have a car.

He shot upright, his face flaring with anger. "Are you fucking insane? How the hell have you been getting here and home each night? Don't tell me you've been walking, because what is that, *twenty blocks*, between your place and mine?"

I cleared my throat discreetly. "Okay," I said. "I won't tell you that, then."

He closed his eyes and growled. "*Caroline*. What the fuck?"

"The first night, I had Aspen's car. And besides, it's only eighteen blocks, not twenty."

"Oh. Well, thank God," he muttered, not sounding relieved at all. "Because those two less blocks make it sound *so* much safer. I cannot freaking believe you. Don't you ever—ever—put yourself in that kind of danger again just to see me."

"Excuse me?" My back straightened self-righteously at his demanding tone. "Don't tell me what to do. I can take care of myself." I set my hands on my hips and glared at him as he jumped from the bed and began viciously ripping clothes off the floor and jerking them on. "I took a credit hour of self-defense training last semester, plus I'm always armed with mace, a whistle, *and* Noel set me up with one of those nifty Taser things."

Fully dressed, he slapped a ball cap onto his head and grabbed his wallet and cell phone off his dresser. "Well, that makes me feel half a percent better." He frowned at me where I was still sitting in nothing but his sheet. Then he clapped his hands. "Let's get going already."

I shook my head. "Where exactly are we going?"

He tipped his chin down toward his chest but kept eye contact as he sent me a dry glance. "I'm driving you home."

Immediately, I started to shake my head. "But you can't do that. What if Noel sees your truck pulling into our driveway and me climbing out of it, and he kills you?"

He stepped closer. "And what if some psycho douchebag

spots you on your eighteen-block *jaunt* and rapes you and kills *you*?" With a snort, he added, "I'd rather face your brother."

Aww, he really was so concerned about me that he was willing to take on Noel to keep me safe. That was just incredibly sweet. I was about to tell him how considerate he was when he said, "Besides, we'll just borrow Blondie's car. She leaves the key to it hanging right by the front door. If he happens to be looking out his window when you get home, he'll think she's dropping you off. Problem solved."

My lips parted as a bit of disappointment filled me. "Oh," I said. "Good idea. Are you sure she won't mind?"

He snorted. "Blondie? Of course not. She loves me."

TEN MINUTES LATER, we approached my place, only two blocks away when I shifted uncomfortably in my seat. Zoey's car was probably the most comfortable thing I'd ever ridden in, but it felt different in here tonight, with Oren behind the wheel. Plus there was the fact that nothing between us was even remotely resolved.

"You can pull over here," I said quietly.

Oren sent me a hard glance. "I don't think so. We stole Blondie's ride so I can see you right to your front door."

"Yeah." I shrugged. "But if you stop here, I can give you a proper goodbye, and Noel wouldn't have to wonder why Zoey's windows steamed up before I got out."

Stomping on the brake, Oren veered the car toward the curb and jerked us to a halt. But he didn't reach for me. He didn't even look at me. He wrapped his hands around the steering wheel and stared out the front window. His jaw looked hard in the glowing reflection from the dashboard lights, and his expression was tense.

I pushed my hair behind my ear and licked my dry lips as I realized what this meant. "You're never going to touch me again, are you?"

He let out a breath and quietly said, "I don't know." Then he groaned and let go of the steering wheel to clutch his head. "I don't know. I don't know. I don't *know*."

I hugged myself, feeling like shit for putting him through this. "I'm sorry," I whispered.

LINDA KAGE

He looked at me but said nothing.

I shook my head, defeated. "I know what kind of position I put you in. With Noel. With yourself. And I'm... I'm so sorry for making you go through this. I'm sorry I tricked you. I'm sorry...I'm just sorry for everything. But most of all I'm sorry that I don't...I don't regret it." I winced. "I know that's really awful and selfish of me, but I don't regret it. I loved it. I loved every moment, and I just...it was the best time of my life. So, thank you—"

"Come here," he murmured quietly, stretching his hand my way.

I went to him, and he pulled me into his lap. One hand went to the back of my neck, tangling in my hair, while the other rested on the side of my face. He gazed into my eyes a moment, the temptation on his face so acute that it filled me with a need to soothe him. Then he pulled me in close until my cheek was against his heartbeat and his arms were around me.

"You know I'm not mad, right?" he said softly. "When I blew up earlier, I wasn't even really mad then. I was...I don't know, having a freak-out moment because the reality of it all just overwhelmed me, I guess. I shouldn't have directed it at you, though."

I sniffed and wiped at my dry face, feeling shitty anyway for putting him into such a situation. Pulling away from his warm chest, I looked up into his eyes and whispered, "I'll go."

But he said, "No," and kissed me. His hands held my face captive as he tortured my mouth, softly stroking his tongue between my lips and claiming a piece of my soul.

I gripped the front of his shirt and pulled him closer, sliding across his lap until I was straddling him and rubbing my heat against his hardness. He arched up and groaned into my mouth. I thought he was going to take me, right there in the driver's seat of Zoey's car, two blocks away from my brother, but he broke away, heaving and gasping.

He pressed his forehead to mine. "One week."

I blinked, confused. "One week what?"

"This. You, me, us. We give it one week to explore... whatever we want, and then—out of respect for...your brother—that's it. The end. We never speak of it again. Okay?"

He didn't even want to give me a week. I could see it in

the swirling torment in his gaze, the tautness of his jaw, could hear it in his harsh, whispered words. Betraying Noel honestly killed him. But he was as tempted as I was.

I nodded immediately, realizing I was getting more from him than I should be. "I'll take it," I said. I was as elated as I was sad to know I had seven more days with him.

CHAPTER 13

Ten

I TOTALLY DIDN'T mean to let the temptation win. I was supposed to be stronger than a silly little craving. But then I underestimated the power of Caroline Gamble.

She'd wanted me, so she'd gotten me.

I knew I should be pissed. Because of her underhanded sneakery, I'd betrayed my best friend and done the one thing he absolutely did not want me to do to him. But knowing she'd wanted me that much, that she'd gone to such extremes, became my own personal stalker, it really turned me on. And so the anger just kind of disappeared somewhere in between all the awe and flattery and desire.

That didn't mean I was ready to play full-out liar and deceiver the very day after stabbing Gamble in the back, though. Except, yeah, that's how it went down, anyway.

"I call bartender tonight," he said as we strolled across campus together.

He'd texted me after my last class of the day, demanding we meet at the student union for a drink. Hamilton had met up with us too, and after we'd had a coffee break, we decided to head our separate ways before we met again later that night for our shift.

Since it was Thursday—ladies' night—that meant all of

us guys had to work. Two manned the bar while the other three waited tables out on the floor. And like every other week before, it turned out that Gamble and Lowe worked the bar every Thursday.

I usually had no problem waiting tables, since it brought me more tips and I met more chicks that way, but today, I kind of wanted to stick behind the safety of a counter. I was no longer a free agent; I couldn't just let random women slip me their phone numbers or—

"Holy shit." I slowed to a stop and blinked dazedly at the world around me. But had I really just thought of myself as *taken*? No longer available to the ladies? Committed?

Whoa. Where had that shit come from?

Since I'd stopped dead in my tracks to absorb the shock, both Gamble and Ham stopped walking too, and glanced back.

"Ten?" Gam asked, his brow wrinkled with concern. "What's up?"

I shook my head. I was about to tell him it was nothing, but there was no way he'd buy that. So I settled for scowling at him. "You hog the fucking bar every week. Why don't you give it up once in a while so the rest of us can get a break from all the handsy chicks grabbing at our junk?"

Gamble stared at me as if I was insane. Then he shook his head and snorted. "As if you mind that part? Besides, *I'm* married, you're single. I have no business being on the floor, working my way around a bunch of single, drunk women."

I made a face. The urge to tell him I was no longer all that single myself itched at my throat until I had to say *something* or I was afraid I'd blurt out everything. So I pointed toward Hamilton. "Well, Ham's no longer single, and you have no problem making *him* wait tables every fucking week."

"You're right." Gam glanced at Ham. "Sorry about that, Quinn. You can take the bar tonight if you want it."

Hamilton perked up and immediate pleasure clouded his face. But then he frowned slightly as he glanced toward me and then back at Gam. "Are you sure? I don't want to cause any strife."

"Oh, go ahead and fucking take it," I groused, waving my hand and storming away from both of them.

It'd felt weird being around Gam all day. But strangely,

guilt wasn't the only thing afflicting me. I was suddenly so very irritated with him. Everything he said seemed to get under my skin. I needed to escape.

But instead of letting me go off on my own, he called after me. "Hey." A second later, he jogged up and appeared at my side, keeping pace with me. "What's up with you today? You okay?"

I sniffed but didn't answer.

"How are your classes?"

"Fine."

"So, you still get to graduate?"

Sending him an odd look, I nodded. "Yeah. Why?"

With a frustrated laugh, he jerked his hands into the air. "I don't know, man. You tell me. Something is definitely bothering you. You haven't been typical annoying Ten since...fuck, I almost can't remember when."

"Well, I'm sorry to disappoint you," I snapped. "Nothing's fucking wrong. I'm not fucking sick. And the world's not fucking ending. But I *am* beat. I'm going home to take a nap before I have to put up with you losers for the rest of the night."

A sudden smile lit his face. "Oh, so that's what this is about. Your midnight visitor been keeping you up too late lately?"

I almost choked on my own oxygen. "What? No. Fuck, that's over. She's not...she's not coming back again." I had to glance away when I said that. My face felt hot and shit. But when I did look away from Gam, I accidently met Ham's gaze.

When my roommate narrowed his eyes and frowned sternly, I blinked in confusion. What was up with *him*?

"As I live and breathe," Gamble murmured beside him. "I never thought I'd see the day a woman could tie you into knots." His grin died as he studied me longer. "So what'd you do to piss her off and send her running?"

"Nothing," I muttered, pissed he instantly thought *I* had to be the reason for my imaginary break-up with my imaginary midnight visitor. "And for your information, I am not tied in—"

I kind of forgot the next thing I wanted to say when I spotted Caroline and Blondie strolling our way. The knots in my stomach expanded, letting me know just how securely they were indeed tied.

Jesus, this girl owned me completely, and she probably had no clue.

Heat raced across my skin. The urge to go to her swept over me, and it took everything I had not to just... go. But Hamilton bumped me—hard—in the arm, making me stumble off balance and break my gaze from her.

I scowled at him, but he only mouthed two words my way, which looked like *Stop staring*.

Fuck, I *had* been staring at Caroline right in front of her brother, and getting turned on, unable to forget last night, or the night before that, or the fucking Friday before *that*.

"Hey, kiddo," Gamble called when he noticed her. "You ready to get home? Aspen said she was cooking lasagna for supper."

"Mmm." The unintentional seduction in Caroline's voice about made me go crosseyed. I kept myself from looking at her directly, but I could tell by watching her from the corner of my eye that she was rubbing her belly. "I could die fat and happy from Aspen's lasagna."

And I could die fat and happy from her little moans.

Gamble's woman really did make a kick-ass lasagna, though. In fact, if I'd been acting as my usual self, I'd step in right about now and finagle my way into getting an invite to supper, or fuck, I'd resort to outright begging for one and end up inviting myself over whether Gam said yes or no.

But I had this sense that if I opened my mouth right then, I'd say the first thing on my mind, which would be to tell Caroline how good she looked, or ask her when I'd get to see her again...alone, in my bedroom.

So I kept my lips clamped firmly and my attention on a fucking tree next to us as the other four members of the group chatted a few minutes before Gamble slung his arm around his sister's shoulders, called a goodbye to us and steered her away.

She had to walk right past me to leave, though, and I just couldn't handle it. As soon as she passed, I shifted out my arm that had been hanging down at my side and flexed the backs of my fingers so that they brushed across hers. I kept my attention on Gamble, making sure he saw none of this. Caroline responded by weaving her fingers through mine so they interlaced for the fraction of a moment before she pulled them away and was gone.

I stared after her, pulverized. She'd been right fucking

there, and the only thing I'd gotten to do was barely brush my hand against hers?

Not fucking right. That had sucked ass. Majorly.

Turning away, edgy and cantankerous, I jerked to a stop when I found both Blondie and Ham watching me quite openly, and sternly.

Shit. I'd forgotten about them.

Ham lifted a disappointed eyebrow. "Really? Do you think you could've been any more obvious?"

I blinked, confused but worried what he might suspect. "Huh?"

"You're going to get yourself caught if you keep staring at her like that. And what was up with that hand thing? Noel's definitely going to figure out she was Midnight Visitor if he catches you sneaking in crap like that."

My mouth fell open as I stared at him, unable to say anything. But, yeah...mind blown.

"You...*know*?" I finally found the words to rasp. I glanced from between him to a flushing, guiltily cringing Blondie. Well, shit. They *both* knew. "How long have you guys known?"

Ham sighed and rubbed a spot on the center of his forehead. "Since Saturday," he admitted.

Again, I could only stare. Unable to believe him, I glanced at his woman for confirmation. She gulped and nodded.

"What the hell?" I exploded. "How could you two know before *I* knew?"

Blondie shifted closer to Ham and began to wring her hands as she confessed. "Caroline. She, uh, she confided in me."

"Well...fuck." I set my hands on my hips and stared up at the sky where oddshaped clouds drifted overhead. For a moment, I was transported to my childhood when my sister and I would lie on our backs in the grass and think up dirty images we saw in the clouds. Yeah, I was troubled enough that I almost settled for memories of her rather than dealing with my two know-everything roommates. But shit, the pain that came with those memories chased me back to the present.

I shook my head and glared at Ham. "And you never thought to tell me who was sneaking into my room? Jesus, man. I was fucking *betraying* Gamble, and I had no idea."

Saying that felt like a lie though, because okay, I'd had an idea, but I hadn't *known*.

Had I?

Fuck. The sudden taste of bile at the back of my throat made me swallow hard.

"It'd already happened by the time I found out," Hamilton told me. "What would telling you have accomplished?"

Was he freaking serious? "It would've kept me from doing it *again*, maybe."

"Are you sure?" He lifted an eyebrow. "You know now, and it's...not going to keep you from going back for more, now is it?"

"Shut up." I scowled at both him and his woman. "It's too late now. We've already..." Shit, I didn't know what we'd already done. But there was no way we could just...stop it just because it was wrong to keep it from Gamble. That point had passed too many kisses and orgasms ago. We were already set and aimed straight toward our collision course with fate.

"Do you remember when Noel thought I was doing something with Caroline and he went for my throat?" Ham asked out of the blue, his voice soft and almost apologetic.

I snorted. "How could I forget?" It had proved to me that Gam would never think I was good enough for her if he didn't even think my flawless roommate was worthy of her.

"Yeah, well, when he apologized to me for overreacting, he said it wasn't because he thought I wasn't good enough for her but because he thought I was sneaking around with her. He said someone else had done that to her, had treated her like she wasn't the type to date openly, and Noel thought she deserved better than that. He was mad because he thought I'd been keeping her a secret."

Ouch.

Shame bore down on me with a vengeance. My roommate was standing there telling me I was no better than that fucker from Caroline's hometown who'd used her and left her pregnant and alone, and I had to agree with him.

"Well, she *does* deserve better than becoming someone's secret," I said, my voice all raspy with regret. But shit. I hissed, "Why didn't you tell me about this *conversation* before?"

"Would it have made a difference?"

I shrugged. "I don't know. Maybe." But it was too fucking late now. He'd already think I'd been sneaking her around if I told him now, because I'd already been fucking sneaking her around.

Damn...it.

I wiped my quivering hands over my face. "Doesn't matter. Like I said, it's too late. Thanks so much for your fucking help."

I strode away from them in a bundle of broiling nerves. It was then I fully realized just how badly this was going to end. And I started to panic.

I know what you're thinking. Why didn't I just cut ties with her then if I was so worried about Gamble? Well, why don't you ask a smoker why they don't just stop smoking, an alcoholic why they don't just stop drinking, a book lover why they don't just stop reading? And fuck you for thinking an addiction was even remotely easy to quit. I was addicted to this girl. I wasn't anywhere near ready to give her up.

And thus started the true turmoil.

So, STABBING MY best friend in the back sucked ass, but finally having Caroline after months of wanting her...that was fucking heaven.

On day six of our week-long agreement, she rested her cheek against my shoulder, pressed her damp breasts to my side and started drawing patterns on my chest before saying, "So tomorrow's our last night together, huh?"

My brow furrowed. Not even wanting to think about it, I took her hand and concentrated on weaving our fingers together. "No," I said slowly. "I think your math's off. We've still got, like, four or five more days left."

"Yeah," she finally murmured. "Yeah, I think you're right."

And that was that.

The next day, our one-week time limit came. The day after that, it passed. I kept picking my midnight visitor up at the curb a block from her house damn near every night and then dropping her back off hours later. And I kept doing naughty, unspeakable things to her. And yeah, I loved every second of it. But then, so did she.

So, not on day eight—hell, not even on day twelve—did either of us mention the fact that we'd gone over our affair's deadline. I'm pretty sure neither of us cared that we totally broke the rules. In those first few weeks, nothing mattered but the next time I could be inside her. Not even the fact that I was completely betraying my best friend on earth.

I still hated it when she brought up his name though, especially when we were wrapped up together and relaxed into a near coma after a really vigorous round of sex.

"Is it immature to hide this from Noel?" she asked, her cheek resting on my arm and her perfect ass tucked in my lap as my arms remained banded around her.

A tick formed in my jaw, but she didn't see it, so I shrugged. "We're still young. Aren't we allowed some immaturity?"

She sighed. I hated that sigh because it told me keeping this from him bothered her as much as it bothered me. "I know you hate lying to him, but I...I want to wait to tell him, if that's okay with you. This is just..."

"None of his damn business." I growled, irritated because he was even an issue.

"Well, that and...it's new and fun, and he'll make it—"

"Trust me." I stroked her hip to relax her. "I'm not exactly thrilled about the idea of having my best friend go all disapproving dad on me. And we know he will. I don't mind waiting. Maybe if he sees me settling down for a while and not chasing every woman who crosses my path, he'll grow a little more...open to the idea."

He wouldn't. She probably knew that as well as I did. Gamble had gotten drunk with me too many times, he'd seen me hook up with scores of women too many times, hell, he'd *shared* women with me too many times to ever let me chase after someone important to him.

"Yeah." Caroline blew out a breath and sent me a blinding smile, letting me know I'd said the right thing. "Maybe a little time will help him...adjust to the idea."

Her smile did things to me, so I rolled her until she was on her stomach. Needing to distract her from the sadness, guilt and unease that always followed a "Noel" conversation, I rubbed her back and kissed my way down her spine. A grin lit my face as she gave a dreamy sigh.

"Damn, I love your mouth and hands on me."

Her voice was languid yet husky, so I leaned in to whisper in her ear. "And I love your after-sex voice. Just listening to it makes me want to..." Instead of describing my fantasies, I pressed my hips up against her perfect bare ass and rubbed my growing cock against her sweet tush.

She sucked in a breath and arched back. "Again? Already?"

"With you? Always." After suiting up, I took one of her legs and shifted it out of my way so I could slot myself between her thighs. "Excuse me. Pardon me, ma'am. I just need through here. Thanks."

She giggled just as I entered her from behind. And then... "Oh," She gasped in surprise. "Wow. I love how full you always make me feel, how perfectly you slide in and out, how warm and stimulating your fingers are when they cup my breasts and...yeah. *That.*"

I grinned as I lightly pinched her nipples. She arched and moaned out her need. "Oh God. *Oren.*"

I wanted to tell her I loved it when she said my name like that. But I just sighed. "I know, right? I'm really good at this."

Another laugh blurted from her. "And so modest, too."

"Modest, schmodest." I rolled onto my back so she was on top of me but still facing away. The new exposing angle made her gasp, but I took advantage of it by cupping a breast in one hand and her clit in the other. "Who wants modesty when you can have the best sex of your life?"

"Not...not me, I guess," she panted out, turning her face to the side until our cheeks brushed. "I...ooohhhh."

I slowed the movement of my fingers, really getting into the playfulness of the moment. "What was that?" I asked as I nibbled at her earlobe.

"Oh, shut up." Panting and straining on top of me, she caught my hip and buried her fingers into my flesh. "Just finish it already."

Slowing the progress of my fingers even more, I applied more pressure to her pussy lips. "Haven't you ever heard of patience, Miss Gamble?"

"Damn you," she muttered. Then she arched her back, pressed her cheek alongside mine, and lifted her hips before coming down on me and sending an electric jolt through my dick. But the girl wasn't finished yet. She squeezed her inner muscles at the same moment she reached behind her and grasped two fistfuls of my hair. And holy hell, okay, so maybe I liked my hair being pulled too.

"Not fair." I growled and went off, unable to stop the orgasm that gripped me by the balls.

Caroline laughed as I came inside her. Then she cried out as she followed me into oblivion.

IF WE MADE IT to a second round in one night, I usually took her home directly afterward, because otherwise we knew we'd fall asleep and accidently spend the entire night together.

But neither of us had moved yet. I was even too exhausted to run my hand over her like I always liked to do. We kind of just lay slumped there, limp against each other. I didn't want the moment to end, though I knew we'd have to go soon.

The worst part of each night was sneaking her back home.

"I'm thinking about getting set up on birth control," she said out of the blue.

Every muscle in my body tightened. I knew she felt my reaction. But shit. This was the first reference to a future between us that she'd ever mentioned. This meant she actually *wanted* a future between us. The idea scared me as much as it thrilled me. I'd avoided relationships for four years for a reason, but here I was ready to dive into the most dangerous one ever without even batting an eyelash. This wasn't me, and that was the terrifying part.

But, God, a future with Caroline. That thought was fucking nirvana.

I cleared my throat and pushed all the casualness into my voice that I possessed. "Sounds good to me."

"Good," she echoed.

I didn't answer, a little dizzy from what had just happened. We'd just made an agreement. We were now a couple.

Minutes of silence filled the room. I was too petrified to say anything, even offer to take her home now.

Caroline drew in a breath and asked, "How's your portfolio and resume writing coming along?"

Ready to discuss anything but our new relationship status, I sat up and started to climb off the bed. "I'll show you if you want to see."

"Of course."

As I gathered the bag full of shit I'd collected with my portfolio and resume kit, she sat up naked and crossed her legs, eagerly waiting for me to show her what I had. I paused, freshly startled by just how good she looked sitting that way, prim yet naughty.

Having her here, naked in my bed, was a wet dream come true.

Shaking my head free of such thoughts, I dragged my crap to her and flopped onto the mattress next to her. "This one's my portfolio." I handed it over. "Here's the list of places seeking new partners. Here's the resume I keep scrapping and starting over again. And this—"

She looked up from the shit I was piling into her arms. "So you haven't applied to any of these places yet?" She dug out the folders full of job listings.

I shook my head. Of course, I hadn't applied. I was scared shitless of growing up and finding a real job. I liked my life as it was. I supported myself and was surrounded by my friends, and Caroline was in my bed now. If I found a good job, I'd most likely have to move, and I didn't want to leave this yet, not when I was as satisfied right where I was and as happy as I'd ever been.

"My resume looks like shit," I said instead, using that excuse. "I can't send it out looking like this."

Caroline chewed on her lip as she glanced over my resume. "You know," she said. I thought she was going to offer to read it for me, but she surprised me when she said, "Aspen just went over her own resume when she applied for that position at the high school. I'm sure she'd be happy to help you make yours shine."

I hadn't even thought of going to *her,* of all people, for help. I usually avoided Gamble's wife at all cost. Not because I didn't like her. She seemed nice enough, and she made my best friend insanely happy. But it was hard not to think of her as my professor instead of my buddy's wife, because that's what she'd been when I'd first met her. Plus, I'd kind of cussed her out one night when she and Gam had been dating—or more actually, when they'd had a mini split. But she'd used me to keep him away from her so he couldn't become embroiled in some dirty student-teacher affair scandal. She'd been trying to protect him, sure, but I hadn't liked getting dragged into the middle of anything that involved upsetting him like that had.

And though we'd all moved past that and everything had miraculously turned out okay for them, I still hadn't apologized to her for yelling at her that night...or other things I'd done that weren't quite respectful to her.

I glanced at Caroline and wrinkled my face, letting her know how uncertain of her idea I was. "I don't know. You think she'd be willing to help me?"

She just laughed. "Um...it's Aspen. The engrained English teacher. She lives for this kind of stuff."

"Well, okay. I guess...I'll ask her, then."

Caroline glowed with approval and kissed my nose. Then she returned her attention to the listing of job openings. "Wow, there sure are a lot of opportunities for you..." Her gaze froze on one detail. "And they sure are far away."

When she tucked a piece of hair behind her ear—her nervous hair fiddling—I knew she didn't like the distance aspect. I wanted to reassure her and tell her I'd never leave if she didn't want me to go. But shit, we'd officially been an "us" for all of two minutes now. It was probably a little premature to go making any such promises.

"From the way you marked this one, I can tell it's your favorite." She turned to show me which job opening she was talking about. The one I'd circled five times and underlined. The one located in Lake Tahoe. When her fingers went to her hair again, I clenched my teeth.

"Yeah," I said. It sounded like there was a ton of gravel in my throat. "It's got the best pay and benefits and is exactly the kind of work I want to do."

Caroline nodded. "You should definitely apply there, then."

"I don't know what I'm going to do yet." I stared at the sheet that was starting to tremble slightly in her hand.

She sniffed as if my indecision was ridiculous. "You should. I mean, it sounds like the opportunity of a lifetime."

When her hand lifted for her hair a third time, I couldn't handle it. I caught her wrist to keep her from touching a single lock. Then I brought her fingers to my mouth and kissed them. Her blue eyes looked watery when she looked up at me.

"I don't know what I'm going to do," I repeated.

But I did know what I wasn't going to do. I wasn't going to let her stress about this.

"It's late. I should be getting you home."

She groaned and dropped my mock-up resume into her lap. "I hate the going home part of our nights."

"Me too." I kissed her hair and slowly removed my portfolio from her lap. "I don't have to work tomorrow night. How about you tell Gamble you're doing something with Blondie and come see me instead."

She hummed and melted into me before saying, "I'm working until nine."

I growled back. Work, school, brothers. I was tired of everything constantly coming between us. I nipped at her ear, then moved my mouth down to her neck. "Tell him Blondie's picking you up from work then, and *I'll* pick you up instead."

Her head fell back as I feasted on her neck. With a whimpered moan, she gave in. "Okay."

CHAPTER 14

Caroline

NEARLY THREE weeks after starting an affair with Oren, I visited the doctor late on a Friday afternoon. I'd been lucky and gotten in a checkup as one of his last patients of the day so I could go after my classes.

I kind of thought I'd just tell him what I needed and he'd hand me a prescription and maybe a couple free sample packs of birth control. But apparently, that was delusional thinking. Before I quite knew what was happening, I was peeing into a cup, changing into a skimpy sheet thing that opened in the front, and being asked to put my feet into the stirrups of horror. God, I hated gynecologist visits.

I started to think it'd be over and done after a quick pelvis exam, and then I'd finally get my nifty pills to go off and have dirty, amazing sex with Oren. But there was nothing quick about what happened next. In fact, it felt as if time slowed down and every second clicked by at a day's pace.

The sensation of years had passed an hour later when I walked into the back door of Noel and Aspen's house, numb and stupefied. Absolutely bone-crushingly numb. I wasn't even sure how to process what I'd just learned. I sank into the first kitchen chair I encountered.

Aspen found me just like that a few minutes later as I stared in dazed, dull shock at all the pictures Colton had drawn for Aspen tacked to the refrigerator with little fruit magnets.

"Caroline?" Aspen paused and tipped her face to the side. "Are you okay?"

I nodded without thought, but then I said, "No."

She started forward and pulled out the chair next to me. "What's wrong?" When she sat, she grasped my limp fingers that'd been resting in my lap and sucked in a shocked breath. "Your hands are freezing."

"Are they?" I looked down at them. I didn't really feel them, but they looked pale and rubbery in Aspen's grip. She tried to rub some life into them, but that only made me want to yank them away.

So I did pull them back to me. I cradled them to my chest, wanting them to remain cold. Lifeless. Dead. Exactly how I felt, how I deserved to feel.

Aspen lifted her face in shock. She opened her mouth and then wisely shut it.

I couldn't handle hurting her and I knew pulling away had, so I cleared my throat. "I..." Then I shook my head. I just couldn't say it. "I...I went to the doctor today, to get set up on birth control. And—"

"Oh!" Her eyes grew wide as she pressed a hand to her chest. "I...I'm sorry. I didn't realize you were...seeing anyone."

I blinked. Crap. Had I just blurted that out? Face flaming red, I began to shake my head but Aspen lifted her hands. "Ignore me. I'm sorry. It's none of my business. What were you saying...about the doctor's visit?"

I continued to gape at her. "Are you going to tell Noel?" I held my breath for the answer.

"Um..." She glanced away, her expression giving away all her uncertainties. Loyalty to her husband battled with loyalty to me. "I don't—That is...no, if you'd prefer I not... I'm sure it's no more his business than it is mine what you do in your...private time, but...as a friend, and new sister, I know I'd very much like to meet your... young man." Then her eyes flashed wide as if a new thought had just struck her. Leaning closer, she lowered her voice. "There is just *one* young man, right?"

I smiled. Actually, I blurted out a short laugh. She was

just so cute when she was attempting to be appropriate and not cross any of my boundaries all while trying to tell me what she thought. "Yes," I told her. "There's just one..." I smiled wider as I stole her term, "young man."

She flushed and tucked a piece of hair behind her ear. "Sorry, I didn't know what to call him."

My shoulders slumped, and suddenly everything awful flooded back to the surface. Feeling like shit, I confessed, "Yeah. Neither do I."

Aspen reached for my hands again, but stopped herself as if remembering how I'd just pulled away from her. "You know," she started slowly. "If you ever need to talk about anything, I'm here. I'll even promise not to report every detail back to Noel. But sometimes, people just...they need someone to talk to."

I smiled softly and took one of the hands she was wringing in her lap. The muscles in her face immediately loosened, and she squeezed back on my fingers. I was about to tell her I had Zoey to confide in, but then I wondered if she wanted a friend as much as she seemed to want me to have one. So I blurted, "The doctor doesn't think I'll ever be able to have children."

Her eyes immediately filled with horror as her hands clamped around mine. "Oh my God, Caroline."

I stared down at our connected fingers. "I...this was the first time I'd been back to a gynecologist since last year. I had no idea I'd messed so much up when I—" I lifted my face and tears filled my eyes. "I've completely ruined my future, haven't I?"

"No! No, sweetheart. You can still have a full, happy life. You—"

"If I'd known that would've been my one and only chance to ever have a baby—"

"Please don't think about that. I don't want this to distress you."

I shook my head. "What else am I supposed to think about, Aspen? I may never be able to hold my own child in my arms. Never watch him or her grow up. Never..." I shook my head when my voice wavered. "How can I not think about that? How can I not regret falling for some stupid, rich boy whose stupid rich parents talked me into doing something I didn't want to do?"

Tears filled Aspen's eyes as well. "You're right," she

admitted. "It would devastate me too." When she leaned in to hug me, I hugged her back hard and buried my face in her shoulder. She was petting my hair and murmuring soothing words of comfort when a fist banged against the back screen door.

"Yoo hoo." The door came open. "Damn handsome hunk calling."

I jerked away from Aspen and frantically dabbed my wet eyes. But Oren already stood frozen in the doorway, seeing everything. The ornery grin on his face instantly dissolving, he glanced from me, to Aspen, and back to me.

Shit. I'd forgotten he was coming over tonight to get help from Aspen for his job applications.

"What's going on?" he demanded.

"Oh, nothing." A sudden flurry of motion, Aspen popped from her chair, waving her hands. "You know us girls. We cry at happy greeting cards."

Oren arched her a disbelieving glance before he turned back to me. His gaze tracked every tear that had slipped down my cheek. "I don't see any greeting cards."

Aspen cleared her throat and sent him a tense smile. "To what do we owe the pleasure of your visit, Mr. Tenning?"

It took a few more seconds for Oren to drag his attention from me, but when he did, he still looked distracted as he turned to Aspen.

Lifting a folder in his hand, he reminded her, "Resume. Proofreading. Your red pen once again slashing its way across one of my papers."

"Oh, right. Sorry." Pressing her hand to her forehead, Aspen blew out a frazzled breath. "I forgot." Then she frowned slightly and set her hands on her hips. "And for your information, I no longer use red ink." Then she cleared her throat discreetly. "It's green now."

One corner of his lips hitched up at her joke, but his gaze strayed back to me and his smile fell. I knew as soon as he opened his mouth, he was going to ask all over again what was wrong. But thank God, the ringing of Aspen's cell phone in the charging station on the counter interrupted him.

Aspen hurried to it and checked the screen before a soft smile lit her face. "There's Noel. He's at the grocery store and probably has a question. Excuse me a moment."

As she walked stiff-backed from the room, Oren shook

his head, staring after her. "She's still so formal and teacher-ish sometimes; it freaks me the fuck out." Then he turned to me and lowered his voice, "Now, seriously. What the hell is wrong?"

No way could I put any of this on Oren. It was way too personal and distressing and...and *deep* for whatever we had going on between us. I stood up so quickly I almost knocked the chair over backwards behind me. Rushing to catch it, I fumbled awkwardly. "Oh, it's just—shit, sorry— you know, girl stuff," I answered vaguely, mimicking Aspen's term.

Oren caught my hands, trapping them on the back of the chair. "Don't pull that bullshit on me, Caroline. What the fuck happened?"

I met his near-angry gaze. "I said it was *girl* stuff. Do you really want the grisly details?"

"Like a heavy fucking menstrual cycle is going to scare me off. Besides, I know that's not what this is about. You're crying, and I want to know why."

"Fine," I snapped. I tried to pull my hands from his, but he locked his grip around my wrists. "I went to the doctor today for...for birth control." I could feel the challenge in my stare when I lifted my face to meet his gaze, and I don't know why I put it there. Maybe I was daring him to back down and leave the issue alone. Sharing distressing doctor's news meant we weren't just bed buddies. It meant there was more to us than just sex.

But he didn't back down. "And.?"

"And he had to do an exam first."

Instant understanding lit his gaze, and I was once again overwhelmed with the need to cry. "Shit." He closed his eyes briefly. When he opened up, his hazel eyes were full of misery. "The abortion messed you up down there, didn't it?"

"Yeah." My shoulders curled in around my chest as I bowed my head and squeezed my eyes closed. "He doesn't think I'll ever be able to get pregnant again."

"Damn," he breathed out softly, his warmth soaking into my cold, numb bones as he shifted closer. Then his breath was in my hair. "I'm sorry."

When his fingers gently touched my shoulder, I stepped back and turned my face away. "Seriously, you don't have to—"

"Will you just shut up and come here." He grabbed me

with more force and yanked me against him. His large hand cradled the back of my head, guiding it into place against his shoulder. Then his arms enfolded me, and he just held me like that.

I shuddered the moment his lips touched my temple. Burrowing deeper into him, I grabbed handfuls of the back of his shirt and held on for dear life.

My sorrow erupted, and I started crying again, in great sobbing heaves.

He rocked me back and forth, the warmth from his body soaking into mine. "Shh, baby," he crooned quietly. "It'll be okay."

I had no idea how this could ever be okay. I lifted my face to look up at him. "Is it okay if I regret it? I know I was only seventeen and had no place being a mom. There was no money. It would've probably buckled Noel under completely with responsibilities. But I wish...I just...even from the moment it was done, I never felt relieved. I've only ever felt sick with regret."

Oren leaned down and kissed away the tears on my cheeks. "You can regret whatever the hell you want to regret. I regret plenty. Just don't let this suck you down and take over your life."

What surprised me more than the fact that Oren Tenning was full of good advice was the fact that he looked completely serious and genuine when he gave it.

"How do I do that?" I asked. "How do I not let it take over?"

His lips softened and then spread into an encouraging smile. "Just keep going forward, I guess. Fuck, I don't know."

I laughed, and he leaned in to nuzzle his nose against my hairline.

"Keep smelling this good every day is a good start." His voice rumbled into my ear and made me shiver...the good kind of shiver.

Then his hands slipped up my back in a sensual caress as he kissed my temple. "You could also keep driving me crazy with every breath you take, or—"

"Oren," I said, my voice breathless as my arousal kicked into gear. "Shut up or you're going to turn me on."

He chuckled. "Going to? Woman, I know you're already soaking wet for me." His nose batted playfully against my ear before he whispered into it. "Aren't you?" And then his teeth nipped the lobe.

My fingers curled into his shoulders as my neck arched back and my body crawled up his and pressed hot against his hard chest. "Nobody likes a braggart," I panted, aching for him to kiss me already.

"Yeah, you do." The rasp in his voice caused an electric spark to shock through me. I shivered against it and curled even closer into him. "You like every fucking detail about me, from all the stupid, annoying lines I spew to how it feels when I'm buried so deep inside you, all you can think about is screaming my name."

He was right. Shame on me, but I did love every aggravatingly flawed detail about him. "Damn it," I muttered. He was going to make me be the one to kiss him, wasn't he?

I grabbed fistfuls of his hair and slammed my mouth against his. His cocky, victorious laugh was cut short when my tongue spiked into his mouth. The groan that rumbled from his throat filled me with accomplishment a split second before he cupped my ass hard and lifted me off the floor.

Embedding myself in the distraction he offered, I relished the friction of our chests rubbing past each other as I rose above him. I wound a leg around his waist and he thrust his hips against my hip, letting me feel how aroused he was.

It totally didn't occur to me how this was absolutely the worst time and place to kiss Oren Tenning until the back door swung open and two voices filled the kitchen.

Just as abruptly, they shut off.

Oren and I leapt apart. "Oh my God." I pressed my hand against my chest as I gaped at Colton and Brandt. "What're you two doing here?"

They stood frozen in the back entrance of the house, gawking between me and Oren, who'd turned his back to us and was breathing hard as he latched on to the edge of the counter, trying to calm his breathing and no doubt his libido too.

"We live here," Brandt finally answered. Then the twerp glanced away from Oren's back to send me a little smirk. "What're *you* doing here, Caroline?"

"Why were you kissing Ten?" Colton asked.

Mortified heat washed over my entire face. "I...I wasn't."

Both brothers sent me a get-real glance. Finally, Brandt asked, "So, then he was...*choking,* and you were...trying to resuscitate him...with your tongue?"

When Oren laughed and finally turned around, I cast him a killer glare. "Why are you laughing?"

Oren sent me an innocent, *What? What'd-I-do?* shrug. "Because it was funny," he answered. "Sounds like something I'd say." Then he grinned at Brandt and offered him a congratulatory fist bump, to which my brother grinned back and accepted.

Oh my God. I totally did not understand guys.

Rolling my eyes, I threw my hands into the air, feeling clueless.

"Does Noel know you guys are...?" Colton waved a hand between Oren and me. Even he wasn't sure what was going on between us.

I folded my arms over my chest and lifted my chin. "Of course."

Brandt snickered, knowing better. "So if we mention it to him tonight...?"

Damn it. "Don't you even dare."

The fourteen-year-old chuckled, telling me just how doomed I was right before he said, "I don't know, Caroline. I really don't think he'd like you dating his best friend...the very friend he warns to stay away from you, like, every time Ten visits."

Oren groaned and looked up at the ceiling. "Damn... he's even going to blackmail us for his silence just like I would."

I sighed out my acceptance and glared at Brandt. "Fine. Whatever. Twenty bucks."

"Gee, big sister." Brandt scratched his cheek thoughtfully as he glanced from between me and Oren. "This is kind of a big deal. Noel would be *really* mad if he knew."

"Twenty-five?" I hedged, hopefully.

He snorted. "Try fifty."

"Fifty *dollars*? Are you insane? I'd go tell Noel about it myself for fifty dollars."

"Hmm," Brandt answered mildly, totally not buying my bluff. "It just went up to a hundred."

"Oh my God. Seriously, I don't have that much money."

I did, but it was tied up in a banking account with Noel's name on it too. He was alerted to every withdrawal I made.

"Fine. Okay." Oren waved his hands and stepped between me and my brothers. "I have fifty. You chip in fifty," he told me before he turned to Brandt, "And you keep your damn mouth shut? *Capiche*?"

Brandt nodded, the happy gleam in his eyes telling me he was satisfied with Oren's offer. "*Capiche*," he answered.

Shoulders slumping as he blew out a relieved breath, Oren turned to me. "Your haggling skills seriously suck."

"What?" I said just as Colton cried, "Hey, I want a hundred dollars too."

"The hundred dollars covers *both* of you," I said through gritted teeth

Brandt snorted. "The hell it does. I'm not sharing with him."

"Watch your mouth, you little smart ass."

The fourteen-year-old batted his lashes at me. "I'd tell you to watch yours, but it seems Ten's already got that job covered."

"Jesus," Oren groaned, shaking his head. "He's a freaking mini me."

Unfortunately, yes, he was.

Just then, approaching footsteps outside alerted us to someone new approaching. All of us in the kitchen exchanged wide-eyed glances, knowing it had to be Noel.

"A hundred each," was Brandt's hushed final offer.

I began to sweat as I glanced at Oren for help. His eyebrows lifted as if letting me decide our fate. Scowling, I hissed at Brandt. "No way."

He shrugged. "Suit yourself." Then he turned toward the doorway, and as if reading his mind, Colton followed.

"Noel," they called together.

My eyes bugged open. "No!" I screeched just as Oren muttered, "Shit," and grabbed both boys by the scruff of the neck and hauled them backward so he could growl into their ears. "One fifty each, and you both better be dead fucking silent."

Colton and Brandt nodded. Then they stared up at Noel with overly innocent smiles when he opened the back door and stepped inside with an armful of grocery bags.

Noel paused when he saw them. He glanced from Brandt to Colton and then frowned a little before turning his attention to Oren.

"Hey. You here to work on your resume with Aspen?"

As Oren nodded and murmured, "Yep," Brandt let out a small snort, which caused Noel to slice his attention back to the two boys, who were still standing frozen in front of him and watching him attentively.

Crinkling his eyebrows in confusion, Noel lifted a finger to waggle between Brandt and Colton after he slowly set the bags on the kitchen table. "Okay, that's creepy. What's wrong with you two?"

"Nothing," they chorused in tandem.

I groaned and rolled my eyes. I was going to kill both of my younger brothers, silently, at night with pillows over their faces. Really, it would do the world a service.

"Seriously," Noel pressed, still staring at them before his curious gaze moved to me. "What's wrong with them?"

"We can't say," Colton chimed up. "We're being paid to stay silent."

I slapped my hand to my forehead and groaned. Scratch the pillows. That was way too humane of a way to take them out.

Noel's gaze zipped back to me. "Really?" he said slowly. "So what is *Caroline* trying to hide? Hmm, Caroline?" Then he crinkled his eyebrows with concern. "Have you been crying?"

When he instantly turned to Oren as if it was his fault, I stepped between the two guys and held up my hands, facing off with my brother. "You know, just because you're the legal guardian to those two, doesn't mean you're one to me any longer. I don't have to tell you anything that's going on in my life."

Ripping his narrowed gaze away from Oren, Noel shot me a surprised blink. "I may not be your legal guardian, no, but you do still live under my roof. And I don't appreciate my own sister keeping secrets from me, or paying off Brandt and Colton to keep them from me either."

"Well, then I guess it's time for me to move out." I straightened my spine and sent him a little *ha, take that!* smirk.

He lifted his eyebrows. "Wow. So, this secret is so important that you're willing to move out just to keep it from me. Thanks, sis. Really, I'm feeling the love here."

"Good Lord, Noel. I'm not saying I don't love you. I'm just saying maybe it's time I leave the nest and get a little independence. I'm sure Zoey and I could rent a place together."

"Whoa, hey. No." Oren lifted his hands, stepping forward to interrupt. "Blondie's fine where she is."

When I sent him an incredulous glance, he shrugged guiltily. "What? She cooks, and cleans, and keeps Hamilton perpetually happy and off my back. She ain't going anywhere."

"Oh God," Noel blurted out, horror dawning on his face as he spun to me. "Please don't tell me you're pregnant again."

"Hey!" Oren boomed and shoved him back hard enough that he stumbled in reverse, just as Aspen gasped, "Noel!" from the doorway.

As Oren demanded to know what Noel's problem was, and Noel wanted to know why Oren had shoved him, I reached for the counter to support myself as all feeling once again drained from my body, leaving me cold and exposed.

Everything I'd learned at the doctor's office came rushing back, all the words I'd heard, the feelings I'd experienced, the absolute, crushing regret. My chest heaved as I tried to pull in a steady breath, while Oren stepped into Noel's face, looking livid.

"I fucking shoved you because that was a douchebag thing to say to your own sister."

I wanted to call him off; he was going to get us exposed if he kept acting like an enraged boyfriend standing up for his girl who'd just been insulted. But everything else just hurt so bad.

"Who the hell do you think you are, telling me how to treat my family?" Noel snarled. "And given her past, it was a completely legitimate question."

"Noel!" Aspen stormed forward to poke him in the chest

But before she could berate him as well, I said, "You know what, it *was* a legitimate question. Who knows when Caroline will get herself *knocked up* again? But you'll be happy to know, big brother, that I can never bother you with another pregnancy scare ever again. The doctor just informed me today that my baby-making equipment is permanently *out of commission*."

His mouth dropped open. "What?"

I couldn't explain any more to him. Whirling away, I raced from the room.

CHAPTER 15

TEN

WATCHING TEARS fill Caroline's eyes right before she rushed from the kitchen and not being able to chase after her had to be one the hardest things I'd ever fucking done—or *not* done, in this case. Or maybe restraining myself from knocking Noel's teeth down his throat was the hardest. I couldn't quite decide. But I'll tell you one thing; standing there like a dumbass and doing nothing slaughtered me.

I shook—literally vibrated—with the need to react, while Gamble lifted his hand and spun in a circle, looking to all of us for answers. "Will someone please clue me in on what the fuck just happened?"

I turned away from him and grabbed the edge of the counter, squeezing as hard as I could to keep from choking him and telling him how much he'd just hurt Caroline.

"I don't know about the baby-making equipment thing," Brandt insisted, lifting his hands in innocence.

"Ten?" Gamble said, his voice hard.

Still facing the cabinets, I clenched my teeth. "I just know what I overheard her telling your wife."

Gamble sighed. "Aspen?"

Her voice sounded irritated when she answered. "Like she told you, she just got back from the doctor."

I glanced toward Gam in time to see his face pale. Even his freaking lips bleached of color. "And?"

"And...there was...damage." Her gaze strayed toward the two younger Gamble boys. But Noel didn't seem to care about them. He rolled out his hand, asking to hear everything. "That procedure she had last year," she started tactfully. "I guess she didn't heal right from it."

Gam sucked in a breath and then lowered his face. "Fuck," he whispered. Covering his face with both hands, he groaned. "Now I feel like total shit."

"Well, you should," I snapped before I could stop myself. "Because you are."

Dropping his hands, he turned a glare my way. "Excuse me?"

"You knew how all that shit affected her. You mentioned how worried about her you were every fucking day. You'd have to be a complete idiot not to realize how sensitive she'd be about the entire topic. And yet you bandied it around tonight like it was some...*joke*."

"Great." Gam shook his head and glanced up at the ceiling. "I'm getting a lecture about my behavior from Mr. King of Insensitive himself."

I sniffed. "Guess that should tell you how fucking wrong you were."

He nodded. "You're right. You're absolutely right." With a glance at his wife and two brothers, he announced, "I'm going to go find her. I need to apologize."

As he left the room, I rubbed my hands over my face and slumped against the counter.

"Well, I'm glad you said that to him so I didn't have to," Aspen murmured.

Dropping my arms to my sides, I forced a smile. "Happy to be of service."

She sent me a gracious nod. "And in return, I'm happy to glance over your resume."

AN HOUR LATER, my mind was straying. Oh, who the fuck was I kidding? It'd been impossible to concentrate from the moment I'd sat down with Gamble's woman in the dining room. Overall, she seemed impressed with my format, but she'd definitely used her green pen.

"I think if you employ the suggestions I made, you'll get some amazing results."

When she glanced at me, I nodded. "Yeah. Thanks."

She nodded too and drew in a breath. "So...do you have any places in mind that you'd like to apply to?"

"Actually, yes. I have a list." I checked the front door, for like the millionth time in the last sixty minutes, but no one opened it. No Gamble. No Caroline. No boogie man. Where the hell were they? Was she okay?

"Really?" Aspen sounded surprised by my answer. "That's...wow, that's great. I knew Noel was worried you wouldn't—"

I cocked her a look, and her eyes flared before she slapped her mouth shut. I sniffed. "He was worried I wouldn't grow up and look for a real job after I graduated?"

"I..." She shook her head, completely flustered. "He just..."

"Takes on the responsibility of the world," I said for her, "and worries about everyone and everything they do."

She smiled softly. "Just everyone important to him."

Realizing I was included in that group, I glanced down at my hands, the very hands I'd used to lay claim to his sister.

I was such a bastard.

"Well..." Aspen sounded suddenly uncomfortable.

I looked up. "I'm sorry," I blurted.

Her eyes widened and she pulled back in shock. "You're...I'm...sorry, I'm confused."

"I wasn't very...respectful," I told her, "when you and Gam were, you know, first hooking up."

She swallowed noisily. "Well, it was pretty scandalous and...illicit." She shrugged and let out a nervous laugh. "Really? What were you to think?"

"I should've thought I had my friend's back, no matter what."

"But, you did," she started in my defense. "I explicitly remember you coming to my house to cuss me out after I broke up with him. And then you—"

"I got rip-roaring drunk and hollered at him from across a room full of people asking how you guys did it," I confessed in a rush.

Aspen sat up straighter and worked her jaw before

exhaling. "Oh," she finally said. "I...did not know about that."

I looked down at my hands. "At the time, I didn't think anyone would believe me. I mean, I was drunk, and I always spouted off crazy shit. But I bet you anything Marci Bennett was there, in that room, and heard everything."

Aspen shivered and hugged herself.

"All it took was for one person to believe me and do a little investigating, and knowing that has bothered me for a full fucking year." When she glanced at me, I almost felt the urge to tear up. "It's my fault you got fired."

Her shoulders fell. "No. No, it's not. It's *my* fault I was fired. I'm the one who started a relationship with a student. I knew the rules. I knew the consequences, and I did it anyway."

"But—"

"No. If anything, your actions merely accelerated the inevitable. What happened was going to happen, Ten. And you know what? I'm glad. I ended up with the man of my dreams. I wouldn't have been able to do that if I'd stayed there. But here I am now, and I'm happier than I've ever been, happier than I ever thought I could be. I feel fulfilled in every way, because I'm going to get that goddamn teaching job at that high school, and Noel is going to stop stressing that he somehow ruined my life, and then everything is going to be perfect. So, honestly, I would like to *thank you* for whatever part you played in all that."

I shook my head. Instead of getting mad at me, the woman had ended up thanking me. "That's messed up," I said.

She smiled. "Well, take it or leave it. I'm still grateful for everything you've done for us." This time it was her turn to eye the front door. "It's been over an hour since they left."

"An hour and eighteen minutes."

Aspen shot me a knowing glance. I pulled back, hoping I hadn't given anything away.

"Caroline's been so much happier lately," she said.

My pulse thundered through my ears. I had no idea how to respond. Was this her way of telling me she knew about us? Or was she just rattling out stray conversation topics?

"I'm sorry, what?" I asked, my mouth incredibly dry.

Her eyes flashed wide. "Nothing."

I nodded. "Well." I pushed to my feet. "I'm probably

going to shove off. This conversation's filled my quota of touchy-feely for the next few months, so I'm getting the itching need to go do something really manly like go home, watch some sports in my underwear, and scratch my balls for an entire hour."

"Oh, good." Her shoulders released all the tension in them. "Because I was running out of things to say."

I chuckled and gathered my things. "You're all right, Dr. Kavanagh. I mean...shit." I flashed her an apologetic cringe. She hadn't been Dr. Kavanagh for months. She was Mrs. Gamble now. Or was it *Dr.* Gamble?

"It's just Aspen," she told me.

I slipped the strap of my messenger bag over my shoulder. "See you around."

As soon as I escaped the house, I pulled out my phone and started for my truck.

Where are you? I wrote to Caroline. *Meet me. Now.*

I didn't even have to wait thirty seconds for her reply. *I'm not really in the mood for sex tonight.*

"Jesus, woman," I muttered, and punched in my reply. *Wow, you honestly think that lowly of me, don't you? This isn't a booty call. I just need you.*

I waited another minute. When she didn't respond, I growled under my breath and started my truck. Once I made it home, I restrained myself from sending another message until I was in my room with the door shut. Zwinn had been cuddled on the couch, watching one of their shows together, but I'd just grumbled something at them as I passed.

As soon as I flopped myself onto my bed, I pounded out a new text. *Do you even realize how fucking hard it was for me not to race after you when you left the kitchen crying? I just got out of my session with your sister-in-law, and I'm not holding back any longer. If I don't get you into my arms before the end of the night, I might lose my fucking mind. COME OVER NOW.*

Wow. You have the sweetest way with words, she wrote back.

I snorted. *If you wanted sweet, you would've gone after Hamilton. But you wanted me, so this is what you get. If your ass isn't in my bedroom in twenty, I'm coming for you. I don't care if I have to break into Gam's house, push him out of my way, and storm the halls to find you.*

Fine. I'll be there in five.
Tell me where you are. I'll come get you.
I SAID I WOULD BE THERE IN FIVE.
Okay. Fine. Damn. I let her win that one and come to me.

Caroline

I WASN'T SURE what I was doing here. Oren had been downright pushy in his texts. I wasn't in the mood for pushy. I wanted to be mad at him, at the entire world. I didn't feel stable enough to be around anyone, but I found a sense of relief as I tromped up the steps to his apartment building and to his front door. No matter how I felt or what mood I was in, I still wanted to be near him.

I knocked once on the door before trying it to find it unlocked. So I let myself in.

Zwinn sent me a sympathetic smile as if they knew everything. Then they pointed down the hall. "He's in his room."

I headed that way. As soon as I stepped through the doorway, hungry hands pulled me against a hard, hot chest. He kissed my forehead before grasping the hem of my shirt and yanking it up, over my head.

"I thought this wasn't a booty call," I said as I lifted my arms to help him along.

He reached around for the back clasp of my bra. "It's not. No talking."

After discarding the bra, he leaned in and kissed the topmost swell of my breasts. Then he removed my pants. Yeah, this sure as hell felt like a booty call to me. I expected him to go for my panties next, but he shocked me senseless when he urged one of his huge T-shirts over my head instead. It smelled like him, and I couldn't help but to inhale the heady scent.

Then he took my hand and led me to the bed. Once we'd crawled under the covers and he'd positioned my head to rest on his shoulder as he wrapped his arms around my waist, he finally released a sigh and all his muscles loosened under me. "There," he said, sounding satisfied. "That's better."

I smiled and closed my eyes, letting his strong, solid heartbeat echo into my ear. It really was better. But he made it even more amazing by threading his fingers through my hair and rhythmically stroking my long locks.

"Mmm. That feels good."

I could fall asleep to this, no problem. I could just forget everything and let him take care of me.

And in the morning, my womb would still be barren. My brother would still be in the dark about the greatest relationship of my life, and Oren...Oren still wouldn't know just how strongly or how long I'd loved him.

"Tell me about your childhood."

His soft question had me fluttering my eyes open. "Why?"

"Because I want to know. Gamble never talked about it. I knew next to nothing about you, except that you existed, until the day I met you."

"It's not very glamorous."

"I don't care. I just...I want to know what it was like for you. Had you lived in that trailer house your entire life?"

"No. I mean, yes, we'd always lived in trailer houses, but not that one specifically. We stayed in a little bit nicer, three-bedroom place until Noel left for college. My mom couldn't keep up with the bills, though, so we downgraded to the one you met us in."

I felt him nod, but he kept petting my hair as I described my life to him. "Noel basically raised us. My mother was gone a lot, and when she was home, she didn't pay a lot of attention to us. I remember her snapping at me when Brandt and Colton were little, telling me to keep them quiet because she had a headache or something. Noel buffered a lot. He's such a natural leader." I smiled. "Still is, kind of bossy sometimes, but I wouldn't trade him for the world. He always made sure we were fed and clothed and entertained. Looking back now, I'm amazed by how much work he went through to keep the three of us happy. I mean, he couldn't do much, but he...he tried, you know. He really tried."

"He's a good brother," Oren murmured.

"The best," I agreed.

"Were you mad at him when he left for college?"

"No. Not at all." I remembered how petulant Brandt had

been, but I'd known Noel needed to go. I'd been ready to take over and do whatever I had to so he could make something of himself. I'd been so proud my big brother was going to get a college degree with his football scholarship. "I didn't realize quite how much stuff he took care of until he was gone, though." Until I'd had to step in and try to do what he'd always done.

"How old were you?"

"Fifteen. And I really tried to use the money he sent home wisely. I paid the bills he told me were the most important first, and I got the groceries we needed, but sometimes...I don't know. I'd splurge when I shouldn't have, and I'd get Brandt and Colton some toy they really didn't need or me a cute outfit that cost way too much. But I kept trying to fix every mistake I made, except each one seemed to set us back just a little bit further."

"You did the best you could."

"And yet I never achieved the Noel Gamble level of perfection."

Against me, Oren snorted. "Who could? Trust me, I played ball with the guy for four years. *No one* can be as great as ESU's almighty football star."

Arching my eyebrows, I rolled around to face him. "Do I detect a bit of jealousy in your voice, sir?"

He shrugged and leaned in to lightly kiss my nose. "Not really, but he did steal all the glory, despite the fact I had to catch most of his damn passes. I'll tell you now, not all of them were that perfect."

I moved my hand up his beard stubble. "Well, thank God I'm not the only one put out about the fact he's so perfect, and I'm not."

"Hey, I never said I wasn't perfect. He just has to be...perfecter?"

"You mean, more perfect?"

He shrugged. "I like perfecter better."

I grinned and snuggled against him.

"Keep talking," he instructed softly as his hand strummed along my back. "I like learning about you."

"Well, there's not much else to say. After Noel left, I progressively started to slip. I grew lonely, stressed, perpetually worried. When Sander Scotini said hi to me one day in school, I was so starved for something to just...take me away from it all, I latched on to his attention like the...the stupid idiot I was."

Oren tensed under me and his hand stopped moving. "You weren't stupid. The fucker just knew to strike when you were the most vulnerable."

I sighed. "Yeah, I guess. But I really should've known better. I should've known I didn't mean anything to someone like him. I should've—"

"What the hell ever," Oren snapped. He rolled me onto my back and rose up to send me a piercing scowl. "You meant to say you should've known you were too good for a pansy-ass rich prick like *him*, right?"

I smiled softly, but glanced away. "I know I'm not too good for anyone—"

"The fuck you're not." Grasping my chin, Oren turned my face until I was looking up into his eyes. "You are...amazing. And the only thing that douche did right was fuck everything up for you, because it landed you here. With me."

I drew in a breath, unexplainably touched by the intensity in his gaze and the fever behind his words. He meant what he said. Tears prickled my eyes, but I blinked them away.

Setting my hand on Oren's bare chest, I felt the steady thump of his heart under my fingers and marveled at what an amazing heart it could be. "So, you really don't expect sex right now?" I asked.

He blinked at the question, obviously not expecting it, and maybe not even thinking about it. Then he scowled. "I told you I didn't in the text, didn't I? Did you think I was lying?" He sounded a little insulted.

"Well, no." Hmm, this was strange. "I knew you weren't lying...when you said it. But now that I'm here..."

He huffed out a breath, definitely insulted. "I know this might sound crazy, but I actually can survive without it for one night."

"Yeah, but..." I shrugged self-consciously. "Since you're being all nice, and snuggly, and understanding, I kind of...want it now."

"Oh, Jesus," he groaned, tightening his arms around me. "I think my dick just went instantly hard. Like, all the blood rushed south so fast my head is woozy."

A smile lit my face. "Is it, now?" Instead of reaching up to massage his woozy head, my hand went south to massage...well, his other head.

The boy was definitely not lying. He was as hard as a rock under my fingers. He groaned as I wrapped my palm around him through his boxer shorts and pumped.

"Goddamn." He arched under my touch, pushing his hips up against me. "I was prepared to be a noble gentleman and everything. But fuck that."

"I'd rather you fuck me instead," I said as I pushed him onto his back and crawled on top of him.

CHAPTER 16

Caroline

I KNEW I HAD to go home eventually and face Noel again, but I avoided it for as long as possible. After I fell asleep in Oren's arms, I didn't stir for the rest of the night. I woke to light streaming through the window and his palm cupped possessively around my breast.

He was warm at my back and I just lay there a second, reveling in the feeling of waking up in his bed, with his hands on me. When I drew in a deep, invigorated breath, loving this moment, he stirred behind me, shifting until he was spooned up against me, his morning wood nudging my bare bottom and his fingers reflexively tightening on my breast.

"Damn," he said on a groan. "I could wake up like this every day. My cock really likes snuggling with your ass."

I grinned. "Oh, does it? Or does it like this better?" Sitting up, I twisted around to face him, and then I rolled him onto his back so I could kiss my way down his chest and take his erection in my hand. His purple birthmark in the shape of West Virginia looked particularly bright this morning. I loved how he never bothered to hide it from me anymore. We hadn't been together with the lights off since the demise of Midnight Visitor, and I loved that too. We were open about everything with each other, kept no secrets, and we shared all kinds of things I'd never shared with anyone else in my life.

Wanting to show him just how much he meant to me, I paid his birthmark a little extra attention and licked my way up the side of it before taking the head of his cock into my mouth.

He grasped my hair tight, just the way I liked, and I groaned as I sucked him to the back of my throat.

"Okay, you're right," he rasped. "I like waking up this way better."

I chuckled around a mouthful and proceeded to give him the best head of my life, except he tugged me off him just before he came. Then he rolled me onto my back and gazed in awe at me before picking up one of my legs. Starting at my ankle, he kissed and licked and nibbled his way down until his mouth was on my pussy and his tongue was inside me.

"Oh my God, Oren." I panted and squeezed handfuls of the sheets under me. "You feel so good. That feels so good."

He glanced up to ask, "You gonna come?"

"Yes!" I snapped, wishing he'd return his mouth to me, but instead he reared up into a sitting position.

Gazing down at me where I was still lying on my back with my legs, splayed open, he smiled slowly. "You are so fucking gorgeous."

He grasped one of my legs and then the other. "The first moment I saw you, in nothing but a T-shirt, I looked at these beautiful toned thighs right here," he lifted them as he spoke, "and I wanted to know what they'd feel like wrapped around me."

I helped him curl my legs around him. He pushed up onto his knees and then hovered himself above me, aligning us until I felt his heat and hardness against me, ready to enter.

"I saw this mouth," he went on, "chapped and pale. And I wanted to taste it." Leaning down, he pressed his lips gently to mine. We breathed each other in until he murmured, "then I looked into your eyes, and...Jesus."

He pressed his forehead to mine and gazed into my eyes. "What the fuck have you done to me, Caroline?"

He thrust into me, and I gasped out my shock from the initial stretch, so full, so big. Always so big.

"Why couldn't I stay away from you?" he demanded with another long, slow thrust. "Why can't I get enough of you?" Thrust. "Why do I want to own every fucking piece of you?" *Thrust.*

"B-because turnabout's fair play, I guess." I grasped his hair to help me absorb the delicious impact of each plunge, but that only seemed to make him pump harder and faster.

With a disbelievingly little laugh, he shook his head. "What're you saying? That I *deserve* this because you want me as much as I want you? Impossible. No one could want someone else this much. No one could fucking crave another this much."

Leaning up, I whispered into his ear. "I do."

With a tortured groan, he went crazy, fucking me to the mattress with a fervor I loved. I tightened my legs around him, tightened my grip in his hair and kissed him hard.

We attacked each other so savagely that when I came, I bit his tongue. And I think he liked that too.

"Damn." He panted against my throat as sweat dripped off his temple and onto my shoulder. "That was...that..."

"Fucking awesome," I breathed.

He lifted his face and grinned down at me. "Yeah." Then he blinked, and his brow furrowed. "Do I *have* to take you home today?"

I shook my head, gladly willing to let him keep me forever. But then I frowned and nodded, realizing reality still awaited us, no matter how long we stayed holed up in his room.

He groaned. "That's what I was afraid of." Then he rolled off me and sat up. I wasn't ready for the absence of his warmth yet, but I hugged myself and sat up too.

We dressed quietly. Oren glanced at me with a wrinkle of concern between his eyes as I slid on my shoes and he grabbed his wallet off his dresser. "You okay?"

I knew he was asking about last night and what I'd learned at the doctor's office, but I rolled my eyes. "After what just happened, I'm fabulous."

He chuckled, but not for long. "I'm serious, baby." Slipping his arms around my waist when I straightened, he pressed his forehead to mine. "I know what the doctor told you wasn't what you wanted to hear, but..." He sighed. I don't think he knew what to say next, so he just shrugged. "Fuck, you got me, and I'm probably more to handle than any kid you could have."

His attempt to cheer me up made me smile. I was so tempted to tell him I loved him, that I'd loved him for months, before I'd ever snuck into his bedroom posing as someone else. But I settled for setting my mouth against his and murmuring, "I'll take it. Thank you."

He kissed me back just as lightly before drawing away. "Let's get you home."

I followed him from the bedroom, only to smell something really, really good coming from the kitchen. "Oh my God." I squeezed his arm. "What is that smell?"

He winked back at me. "Saturday mornings with Zwinn. Come and see."

After drawing me to the opening of the kitchen, he paused beside me and looped an arm around my shoulder. "They cook pancakes and bacon together every week. It's kind of cute."

Cute? It was freaking adorable. Quinn and Zoey had their backs to us as they stood at the griddle, one pouring batter in, one flipping pancakes. They talked in hushed tones, and their heads were intimately close. Every couple of seconds, one would touch the other.

I could see them in fifty years still doing this very thing, cooking together and just...reveling in ordinary things, as long as they did them with one another.

"It's like greeting card precious," I whispered up to Oren. "I think I'm going to cry." He snickered and passed me an imaginary tissue. I pretended to accept and wipe my face. "Thank you."

Zoey turned then. "Oh." She jumped, and Quinn glanced over. "Caroline! You're still here."

"We slept in," I confessed, though neither of us had once mentioned taking me home last night. I think we both knew I wasn't going anywhere until morning.

"Since you're already this late, why don't you stay for breakfast? We always make plenty."

I glanced up at Oren, and he answered for me as he stepped into the kitchen. "Sure. She needs to understand why I'm not willing to let either of you move out of this apartment."

Zoey crinkled him a confused look. "O...kay."

So we ate breakfast with Zwinn, and it was nice. Oren cracked his usual off-color jokes, and Zoey updated me on her life since I hadn't seen much of her lately.

"My biological father keeps asking me to visit him in California where he's staying this summer. But...I don't know."

"I say fuck him," Oren spoke through a mouthful. "The asshole did nothing while he knew you were being raised by an abusive douchebag. You don't owe that dick shit."

I glanced at Quinn, who remained quiet. I had a feeling he probably agreed with Oren, but he would loyally back any decision Zoey made.

"I don't know," I murmured thoughtfully. "If I ever had the opportunity to meet my sperm donor, I'd want to, if nothing but for curiosity's sake. Find out where my chin and eyes and stubborn personality came from."

"I'll tell you where your stubborn personality came from." Oren stood and not only gathered his cleaned plate, but mine too. "That's all from your brother."

I watched him load the dishwasher. Not only did his sweetness in taking care of my dish impress me, but I liked how he reminded me that I didn't need to know how far back my roots went; I knew where I'd come from and who my real family was. Noel. No matter how much his thoughtless words had hurt me yesterday, I loved my big brother and he loved me.

I needed to go home and talk to him.

Once Oren was finished, he dusted his hands on his thighs and turned to me. "Ready to get back?"

Zoey spoke up before I could answer. "Oh, I could take her home, if you want."

Oren instantly scowled. I liked that he wanted to be the one to drive me home. But then he sighed in defeat and mumbled, "Yeah. That'd probably be best."

So Zoey ended up driving me home, but not until Oren had yanked me into the hall for a goodbye kiss. "If Gam gives you any shit for staying out all night, call me."

I grinned up at him and slid my fingers over his sexy scruff. "And what're you going to do if he does?"

He shrugged and grinned back, rubbing his nose against mine. "I'll come over and run interference, make him hang out with me or something so he can't rag on you."

"That's sweet." I lifted my mouth to his, but didn't kiss him. "You're so sweet."

"Oh, yeah? How sweet?"

"Sweet enough that I may want to see you again."

"You better, woman." To stake his claim, he kissed me hard and long. Zoey finally had to clear her throat to break us apart. Still, Oren had to pat my butt and nuzzle my neck a second longer before stepping back and letting me go.

I couldn't stop glowing all the way home.

"You're still smiling," Zoey said, glancing across her car at me.

With a sigh, I nodded. "I just can't stop."

"He makes you happy."

I glanced at her, scowling slightly. "Well, yeah. Did you think he'd make me miserable?"

"No, but I thought you guys would...I don't know, argue more, I guess."

I shrugged, thinking it through. "We do...kind of. But we seem to be just as quick to make up. Disagreeing with him is like...foreplay."

Zoey sputtered out a laugh. "Okay, that's more than I wanted to know, but still, I'm glad for you. I hope it all comes out okay."

"So do I." I leaned over and slapped a quick kiss to her cheek as she pulled into my driveway. "Thank you for being the best friend ever."

"Just take care of yourself," she warned as I opened the door. "And call if Noel gets mad. I'll tell him you stayed on our couch."

I felt bad for making her lie as much as I already had, so I blew her a kiss after I slid out of the car. Then I jogged to the back door, thinking I'd be less likely to run into anyone in the kitchen than the living room.

But there Noel sat at the kitchen table, reading something on the laptop in front of him. He looked up as I eased open the door. When our gazes met, I froze.

"You're home," was all he said.

I came the rest of the way inside and shut the door quietly behind me. "Yep," I answered the obvious.

"I left you about a dozen messages."

"And I answered you."

"All you said was, '*I'm fine.*'"

I shrugged and glanced away. "Well...I was."

"No, you weren't." Clasping his hands together, he set his elbows on the table and kept watching me. The fact that he wasn't shouting was a small miracle, but still...I didn't really want to talk to him just yet. I needed time to prepare my words.

"Where were you?" he asked.

I snorted and shook my head. When I started for the doorway to leave the kitchen, he hopped from his chair and darted into my path.

"Caroline, I'm sorry."

I stopped abruptly and gaped up at him, not at all expecting an apology.

He blew out a breath and spiked a hand through his hair. "Aspen told me not to ask where you stayed all night, and fuck. Here, it's the first thing I ask. What I really want to know is, are you okay?"

Now *that* was completely unexpected. "What?" I had to ask, sure I'd misheard him.

He flushed. "I was way out of line last night. And I'm...you know I never meant to hurt you, right?"

I blew out a breath, realizing he was talking about my doctor's visit. Oren had successfully made me forget it for a while. I'd even forgotten to tell Zoey about it.

Lifting my chin, I glanced into his concerned blue eyes, the same color as my own. "You didn't hurt me, Noel. I hurt myself. I did this to myself."

When my chin trembled, he muttered, "Shit," under his breath and yanked me to him for a hard hug. "But I didn't have to be an inconsiderate ass about it, and I...I'm so damn sorry, kiddo. I can't even imagine what you're going through."

Well, not thinking about it had been working the best so far. But now that he was talking about it again, my eyes stung. "I just wish..." I choked out. "I wish I'd done so many things differently. I wish..."

"I know." He stroked my hair slowly. "I feel like shit because I wasn't there for you when you went through all that. If only I'd been there, if only I hadn't made you feel as if you couldn't come to me for help—"

"You didn't do anything wrong," I started, but he shushed me.

"Yeah, I did. I was supposed to protect you and take care of you. Instead, I yelled at you when you told me you were pregnant. I made you—"

"Noel, you can't take credit for everything I did wrong. I made my own decisions, and I've had to live with them. I've had to—" My voice choked up. "I deserve this, you know. I killed my first baby, I kept it from even starting its life, from taking its first breath, I don't deserve another chance—"

"Care, don't talk that way. Don't—" He grasped my arms and looked deep into my eyes. "You were a scared, seventeen-year-old girl alone with no one around to hold your hand. And you'd already told me about it. That meant you were ready and willing to have that baby. I don't think you ever planned on getting an abortion. I think that little dick's mommy and daddy got a hold of you and intimidated you into it. They flashed a fuck load of money into your face and—"

"It wasn't about the money. I didn't do it for the money." Noel nodded, believing me, so I added, "They threatened you. They said they'd hurt you, and Colton and Brandt too. You were doing so well with football, headed for the pros. And Colton and Brandt... Why should you or they have to pay for something stupid I had done?"

He snorted and shook his head. "And just how in the hell did they think they were going to hurt *us*?"

I shrugged. "They didn't say, but they were rich and powerful. I knew they could if they wanted to."

"Bastards," he hissed.

I nodded. "Yeah. They were, but I still didn't have to..." When my voice failed me, Noel kissed my temple.

"It's over and passed," he assured me. "I know it's going to keep haunting you for quite a while, but I want you to know, from here on out, you'll always have my support...no matter what."

I nodded and swallowed hard. "Thank you," I whispered. But now I felt like crap. I think I would've preferred it if he'd just yelled at me. Nice Noel knew how to pile on the guilt without even trying.

I hugged him because I just couldn't look him in the eye, knowing I was keeping so much stuff from him, knowing he still wouldn't support me if only he knew where I'd spent the night.

"Well," I started. "I have finals to study for, so..."

"Oh, before you go." He grabbed a slip of paper off the table. "Tad called."

I paused and whirled back, snagging the sheet from him. "Did he? Oh, thank God." Then I scowled thoughtfully, wondering why he'd called the house phone. "Hmm. I must've given him the landline number instead of my cell."

Noel lifted an eyebrow. "Is he who you were with last night?"

The question made me stumble to a stop. "What? Good God, *no*." I wrinkled my nose into a frown. "He's in my film class. Our final is a group project, and I had to be the group leader. He was supposed to do the sound effects, and I was starting to worry I'd have to take care of it myself."

I'd already had to take over Blaze's job to write up the dialogue for the short skit we'd had to film. She was still pissed at me for calling her a loser at Forbidden, but it boggled my mind why she'd shoot herself in the foot and not even participate in the group project. Not only did the professor grade us, but we had to turn in reports on all the other group members too. No one was going to give her a good grade.

"So, this Tad guy isn't who—" When I glanced at Noel and lifted an eyebrow, he paused and cleared his throat. "It's just that you've been gone a lot more lately. I figured you might be...seeing someone."

"Oh, you did, did you?"

"If you are," he went on, emphasizing his words through gritted teeth, "then I want to meet him."

It was obvious that Aspen had gotten to him and strongly advised him as to what he should and shouldn't say to me. It was kind of funny to see him hold back and not blurt out what I knew he wanted to say, but it only made me feel worse because he was being this considerate.

Still. "If I *was* seeing someone," I smiled and patted his cheek, "I'd wait a good long while before letting the poor guy meet you."

He snorted. "Yeah, probably after you're married and pregnant with your second—"

When my face paled, he realized what he'd done. Gnashing his teeth, he closed his eyes and cursed softly. "Shit, Caroline. I'm sorry. I forgot."

"It's okay." But honestly, it hurt. It hurt like hell. "I think the whole idea is going to take us all a while to get used to." I just had to concentrate on everything else—school, my family, Oren—and I could survive this.

Noel didn't seem to believe my forgiveness, so I hugged him tight.

"We'll make it through this. One way or another."

CHAPTER 17

TEN

I WAS GOING through Caroline withdrawals.

After she'd stayed all night with me on Friday, I woke up every morning after that reaching for her. It sucked ass that she was never there. We hadn't even been able to sneak her over for the next four nights because of her work, my work, and fucking school assignments coming due. So, not only did I just want her around, I was starting to get horny, too.

When I spotted her sitting under a tree on campus on Wednesday, wiping her hair out of her face as she read something on her phone, no way was I staying away.

"Just the woman I was thinking about," I said as soon as I approached.

Her head jerked up, her eyes wide with surprise. After glancing around at all the passing people heading off to classes, she turned back to stare up at me. "People can see us."

"Damn." I snapped my fingers and winced as I plopped down next to her. "And here I thought my invisibility cloak was working today."

She rolled her eyes. "Hardy har har. But seriously, what are you doing talking to me in public?"

I scowled. "Is talking to you in public not allowed?" To

keep from reaching for her like I was aching to, I opened my book bag and dug around before pulling up a box full of Junior Mints.

"I just...I guess I didn't expect for you to...you know...talk to me in public."

After I opened the top of my Junior Mints, I silently offered her a handful.

A smile lit her face before she held out her palm. "Thank you." I sprinkled a pile into her hand and then dumped some straight into my mouth.

"I talk to you in public all the time," I told her around a mouthful.

She seemed to consider that a moment before shrugging and chewing. "I guess you have a point."

"I know I do." I swallowed and poured more mints into my mouth. "Now tell me what's bugging you?"

Her gaze zipped to mine. "Why do you think something's bugging me?"

I motioned to my own bangs. "You're doing the hair thing."

"Hair thing?" She shook her head, letting me know she had no clue what I was talking about.

"Yeah, you know." I motioned with my hand again. "You always do that thing with your hair when something's bothering you."

Blinking, she leaned in toward me. "I do...what?"

"Never mind. Just tell me whose ass I have to kick."

"You..." She set her hand over her mouth and just kind of stared at me with awe. Then she cleared her throat and dropped her hand as she shook her head. "No one's ass needs kicking. I was just checking to see if my grade was posted for my filmography final yet." She looked down at it again and pushed *refresh* on her screen. "You know the one I was telling you about? Where we had to do a group project and turn in a small skit. Since my group named me freaking director, I basically had to take responsibility for making sure *everything* got done?"

Hell, yes I remembered her telling me about it. It was the reason she hadn't been able to come over at night more times than I liked. I nodded and motioned her to continue talking.

She blew out a breath. "Well, I turned it in yesterday." With a soft growl, she went on. "And I'm worried as hell about our score. I still want to kill Blaze for flaking out on me. I ended up having to write the entire script because she was pissed at me for calling her a loser."

I held up a hand. "Wait. Did you say Blaze? Is she an Alpha Delta Pi sorority girl? Really named Jan, or something like that, but calls herself—"

"Yes," Caroline groaned out her answer with a roll of her eyes. "Do you know her?"

I bit the inside of my lip, refraining from letting it slip how well I'd once known Blaze. With a shrug, I mumbled, "You called it right. She's kind of a bitch."

"Kind of," she muttered as if that was an understatement. "She told me I should cheat on Zoey with Quinn... right in front of Zoey's face."

Oren snorted and rolled his eyes. "Sounds about right."

"Anyway," Caroline went on. "The entire project has been a nightmare. Not only did Blaze ditch out on us, but then Tad didn't get his sound effects in to me until Saturday, so I had to freaking rush to get the entire thing produced, and..."

When she looked down at her phone again, I set my hand on her wrist, stopping her. "You got an A."

She blinked and crinkled her brow. "And you know this because...?"

"Because I know how much time and effort you put into it. No way could you get something lower, and it's going to take forever for your grade to post, so I decided to just tell you what'll it be. There. Now you don't have to wait and stew."

With a reluctant grin, she bumped her shoulder into mine. "Well, look who's being all sweet and making me feel better."

I motioned with my finger to quiet her. "Just keep all that sweet shit quiet. I have an asshole reputation to uphold."

"Oh, right." She winked and set her finger over her lips. Her lips, which looked really good. I was probably about to do something like lean in and kiss the fuck out of those luscious lips when my phone rang.

With an irritated growl, I pulled it from my pocket. My parents had been trying to call all morning. I'd probably been avoiding them for too long, so I answered.

"Hey."

My mother's request was short and simple, and no way could I deny her, so I mumbled out a couple okay's, sure's, and yeah's before I said, "See you then. 'Kay. Bye."

My change in mood must've been obvious because Caroline touched my arm, making me jump from the unexpected contact. "Hey. Everything okay?"

"Hmm." I tried to send her a smile that said everything was just peachy, but as I looked into her concerned blue eyes, an idea struck.

"Yes!" I pointed. "You. I need you. Tonight. Do you think you could be my fake girlfriend for the evening?"

She blinked, the pause in her answer making me instantly itchy. "Your *what* girlfriend?" she said slowly.

With a sigh, I worked my neck around to pop it. "That was my mom. I've been *summoned* home to eat with them tonight to, you know, celebrate my graduation this weekend, or something. I really, *really* don't want the usual fucking talk. So I thought if I had you by my side, they'd not hound me about...*other* crap and just be excited I brought a real, live girl to supper."

Her lips tightened with displeasure. "Do you have a habit of bringing the blow-up kind to supper?"

"Caroline." I groaned through my teeth. "This is serious. Do you think you can *not* be a smart-ass for three freaking seconds and say, *why yes, Oren, I'd love to go with you*?"

Instead, she said, "Are you sleeping with other girls?"

"*What*?" I shook my head, utterly confused. "What in all the shit I just said prompted you to ask *that*?"

"You said you wanted me to be your *fake* girlfriend."

"Yeah?" I nodded, still clueless. "So?"

"So..." She frowned at me. "If I'm not a real girlfriend now, then what the hell am I to you?"

My mouth opened, but no words came.

Oh, shit. I hadn't even thought of labels and crap like that. "Uhhh..." I said, not sure how to answer.

Wrong fucking thing to say.

Caroline stuffed her phone into her bag. Zipping it shut, she surged to her feet. "You know that thing I just said about you being sweet? I take it all back."

If I didn't stop her, she was going to stomp off, and that would be the end of any more midnight visits for me.

"Wait." I popped to my feet after her. "Jesus, I haven't even thought about this shit. I've just been so busy enjoying what we have, I haven't exactly stopped to pin a label on it."

She paused, her eyes intent as she studied me. "Do labels scare you?"

Hell, yes!

I snorted. "Hell, no. I just..." I tossed out a hand. "I haven't had a true, honest girlfriend in over four years. I...I'm rusty at, you know, monogamy and commitment and shit."

She folded her arms over her chest and continued to stare with that *stare* of hers, the one that told me I was in deep monkey squirts.

I fidgeted under her inspection. After shifting my weight from one leg to the other, I glanced around the busy quad. "Should we really be discussing this so openly...around so many ears?"

Shaking her head sadly, she snorted out her disgust and started to stride away.

I was right on her heels. "I'm sorry, okay. Please, Caroline. You know I'm an ass."

She smiled lightly. "And yet, shame on me, I keep putting up with it."

"There's no one else but you. You *know* that. I don't know what I was thinking saying all that fake bullshit. I've been single so long it's hard to remember I'm really, honestly in a relationship now. And besides, since we have to keep it under wraps and I have to act like I'm single around *certain* people, I didn't know if the usual rules applied, anyway."

She slowed to a stop before turning around, her eyes filled with torment. "*Does* the secrecy thing negate any chance of this being a normal relationship?"

"I don't know." I shrugged, worried as hell I was going to say the wrong thing, again. "You tell me."

"No, obviously, you have your own ideas of what we *aren't*. So now I need some clarification. Are we just friends with benefits, or are we actually a couple? Have you not been with any other girls because you just haven't had the opportunity, or because you're actually being faithful to me? Because I need to know before I start thinking things."

Thinking things? That didn't sound good.

"What kind of things?"

"I don't know, Oren. *Things!* A future, love, marriage, forever. Just *things!*"

"Oh." Okay, that answer left me speechless and a little breathless. But shit, had she really been thinking about *those* things? With *me*? I'd been over here just living for each day. After our nonverbal agreement to stick together when she'd asked about birth control, I hadn't thought any further than the next time I'd get to see her and how to keep it low key.

"I take that to mean you haven't been thinking any such things." Her voice was dry and unimpressed.

She tried to turn away again, but I caught her arm and moved closer. "Damn it, Care. Just because I haven't been thinking that far ahead doesn't mean I'm *scared* of those things. I'm just..."

When I realized I didn't know what I was, she lifted an eyebrow and guessed, "Scared of those things?"

"No!" I clenched my teeth. "Christ, woman. Maybe I'm not even letting myself think that far ahead because I'm just waiting for that inevitable day when *you* realize you can do so much better and drop me flat. I'm not scared of those things. I'm scared of wanting them and then not getting them, so I don't even allow myself to *think* about them."

She stepped closer, her blue eyes suddenly full of sympathy. "Why do you think I'm going to leave you?"

I threw my hands in the air. "Probably because I'm *me*, the asshole. Why else? Do I *need* another reason?"

"Oh, Oren. You stupid, stupid man. Don't you realize how addicted I am to you?"

I shook my head and laughed nervously. "People break free of nasty addictions every day."

She stepped in closer to me, the look in her eyes telling me how much she wanted my mouth on hers. "Well, I'm not going to. This is one addiction I like."

God damn, I loved her addiction. And I loved being addicted to her right back.

"Are you going to kiss me right now?" I asked, lifting my eyebrow curiously. I was actually fine with it if she wanted to. If she wanted to come clean and let the world know about us, I could definitely deal with that.

I stepped in toward her, welcoming any kind of PDA she wanted to toss my way, but the move seemed to awaken her to reality.

Realizing we were in public, she quickly jerked back. "Crap. I forgot."

A smile bloomed across my face, even though inside, I was strangely disappointed. "Figured. I tend to have that effect on you."

She shook her head, her lips tightened from how hard she was trying not to smile back at me. Then she blew out an exhausted breath. "So, where do we go from here?"

"How about this?" I said. "My parents requested my presence tonight at this restaurant back home. I know we can't tell your brother about us, but I'd very much like to introduce you to my mom and dad. What do you say?"

"How are you going to introduce me?"

"As Caroline."

She rolled her eyes, but a reluctant smile curved up her lips. "Okay. No label. I can deal with that. At least I have a sense of where I fall with you now."

No, she didn't. She probably wasn't even close. In fact, I doubted she'd ever realize exactly where she fell with me or how crazy gone I was for her.

Caroline

WE ARRIVED AT the restaurant right on time where the Tennings were waiting to meet us for dinner. After Oren parked and killed the engine, he drew in a deep breath and glanced across the seat toward me. Then he shuddered. "Damn, you look good in that. Are you sure we don't have time for—"

I slapped my hand over his mouth to shut him up. Then I grabbed his other hand when it started to creep up my thigh and under the skirt of my dress. "I'm going to ignore the fact you just asked me to have sex with you *right before meeting your parents*, and I'm giving you one chance to behave."

Grinning, he slipped my hand off his mouth. "And how the hell do you expect me to behave when you look so fucking edible? And smell so fucking amazing?"

I had to bite back a smile because, okay, I loved how he hadn't been able to keep his eyes off me, except maybe to watch where he was driving every once in a while, since he'd picked me up. It was nice to know all my efforts to clean up nice had paid off. I hadn't dressed up since...yeah, I didn't want to think about anything that had to do with Sander Scotini right now.

"I didn't wear this for you." I smacked his hand when he resisted my efforts to keep him from going any higher on my leg. "I'm trying to impress your parents. I want to look...presentable."

His fingers paused on my thigh; his skin was so warm it almost scorched me. Eyes losing their teasing glint, he shook his head. "Presentable?" he murmured as if the word were foreign to him. "Jesus, Caroline. You didn't have to worry about that. It doesn't matter what you look like. They're going to love you because of who you are."

I drew in a deep, shuddery breath. His words meant more than he could ever know. I was thrilled he had so much faith in me, but I still had no faith in myself. Now, I was even more nervous, because I kind of sort of really wanted them to love me. "But—"

He caught my hand when I started to smooth my hair out of my face. "No buts. Everything's going to be fine. They're easy to get along with, down to earth, laid-back people, so you have nothing to worry about. Okay?"

I nodded, but my stomach continued to churn.

"I'll make you a promise." When he leaned in to kiss my temple, I immediately glanced around to make sure no one had seen when it struck me...we didn't have to hide anything here, not when we were so far away from Ellamore. Whoa. We didn't have to hide here. "If you stop worrying, I'll keep my hands respectable until after dinner with them. Deal?"

"Deal," I said, though no way was I really going to stop worrying.

It must've been the right thing to say, though, because Oren beamed at me. "Great. You ready, then?"

Hell, no. But I nodded and sent him a tense smile. "Sure."

An anxious fluttering instantly took root in my stomach as we climbed out of his truck and started up the front walk. But then Oren took my hand, and the fluttering instantly shot off fireworks through all my limbs. I glanced down at our linked fingers. His palm was so warm against mine. I felt strange, as if I was protected and cherished and desired, all due to one little squeeze from his fingers.

He was honest to God about to introduce me to his parents...while holding my hand.

Wow. This shit just got real.

As if sensing my nerves, he glanced over. His gaze moved from my face, and down to our hands, then back up to my face. "What?"

"Nothing," I was quick to answer.

So he frowned. He even slowed to a stop and turned to face me...without letting go of my fingers.

"This hand-holding thing is freaking you out, isn't it?"

"No," I blurted.

He crinkled his eyebrows, calling bullshit with a single look.

My shoulders collapsed. "Damn it," I muttered. He was getting too good at reading me. "Okay. Maybe it is. A little."

Instead of letting go, his thumb started up, tracing the back of my hand as he tugged me closer. "Why? What's wrong with holding my hand? It's perfectly *respectable*."

"I know, but it's...I don't know!" I growled as I looked away from him, feeling like a freak. "It's *public*," I hissed and chanced a glare at him, silently warning him not to make fun of me.

"Public?" he repeated slowly.

"Sander would never hold my hand."

"Sander," he hissed, his eyes narrowing as his grip tightened around mine even snugger. "The fucker who made you his dirty little secret? That jackass probably didn't even *talk* to you in public."

"No," I murmured dejectedly, realizing he was right. "He never did. Only when no one else was around." And the one time he promised to take me into public, he lied.

I wished I'd realized that before I'd fallen for his ploy and let him destroy such a fragile part of me.

"My point is..." I lifted my free hand and blindly waved it around before dropping it limply like the stupid idiot I was. "People don't go holding hands when it's just the two of them. They do it in public, as a sign to the world that they belong together, that—"

"Okay, wait." He butted in, stopping me right there. "First of all, it's not just something couples do in public. I don't know how many fucking times I've caught my parents holding hands over the years when they thought no one else was around."

"Aww." A soft sentiment flooded me. "That's so sweet."

"Yeah. Whatever." He rolled his eyes, because anything sweet and romantic that involved his mom and dad probably fell closer to an ick factor for him. "The point is, it's *not* public. And it's not some symbol to show others any such fucking thing. It's just two people who want to touch and feel closer to each other. Nothing more."

The emotion that had swamped me seconds ago returned, swirling through me with a heap of messy, emotional sop. I stepped up close to him and filled my nose with his scent, making my head dizzy with lust. "So, you want to be touching me when I meet your parents?"

His nostrils flared in return, and a tingling spread up my thighs. "I always want to touch you," he murmured in a voice that made my nipples throb. My fingers from my free hand fluttered up and over his cheek. His eyes drifted closed before he sighed. "And right now, I'd be totally fine with sticking my tongue down your throat while you met them."

I jerked my hand from his face and cleared my throat with a nervous laugh. "Well, I don't think I'm quite ready for *that*. But...I will settle for holding your hand."

"Thank God. Because I wasn't going to let go of it anyway."

I snorted even as a grin seeped out. He reached ahead of us to push open the front door of the restaurant and then held it for me to enter first. I wondered if being this close to his mother made him act so gallant, but the etiquette had me all giddy inside, nevertheless. I liked sweet, polite Oren as much as I liked naughty, playful Oren.

The hostess approached, but Oren waved her off, telling her he'd already spotted his parents.

"Where?" I murmured into his ear as we walked deeper into the restaurant.

"Right there." When he pointed them out to me, I held my breath and glanced over.

They looked like...well, like parents. I was shocked at how normal and average and parent-ly they appeared. His mother was on the plumper side with short gray hair coiled into soft curls. And his dad looked just like him...with shorter, salt and pepper locks.

I leaned up and whispered into Oren's ear. "Please tell

me you're going to look just like your dad in twenty years, because...*wow*."

He cranked his head around to send me an incredulous glance. "What the hell? You're checking out my *dad*?"

"What?" My face flushed hot, and I had to glare at him for speaking so loudly. "He looks like you...like the silver fox version of you. I mean, come on. *Meow*."

"Holy shit." He veered his gaze to the ceiling as if perplexed as to why he was having this conversation with me. "I can't believe I'm dating a girl who thinks my *dad* is hot."

I laughed, but then we moved even closer to his parents, and my smile died. Just like that. Because the nerves had set in.

I had no experience with real, live parents who actually cared about their child and wanted to be involved in his life. I instantly grew unsure and paranoid. They were going to take one look at me, see how dysfunctional of a family I'd come from, how dysfunctional *I* was, and they were going to send me away from their son forever.

What had I been thinking to *meet his parents*? Stupid Caroline.

They glanced our way, and his mom's mouth fell open when she spotted me holding her son's hand. And yep, my insecurities rose even higher.

"Oh God, Oren." I clamped my fingers around his hard. "You didn't tell them I was coming with you, did you?"

He leaned toward my ear, smirking. "I thrive on shock value."

I leaned up to hiss, "Well, I hope you also thrive on *death*, because I'm going to kill you for this."

He pinched my ass. I jumped, unable to hold in a startled yelp. When I glared up at him, he threw his head back and laughed outright, his voice decibels above everything else in the restaurant. And crap, people were staring.

Oh God, take me now.

His mother and father stood. "Well," His mother murmured, her eyes glittering with glee. "I was beginning to wonder who was walking toward us with this pretty young lady at his side because it couldn't possibly be our son bringing a *girl* to dinner, but that familiar laugh tells me I'm wrong. You really are our Oren...with a friend."

"Hey, Ma." He swept in with a huge hug and lifted her off her feet, making her squeal and slap his arm to get him to drop her back to the ground.

Then he turned to the Silver Fox version of himself. "Dad." He held out his hand. "This is Caroline. She thinks you're hot."

The floor opened up and I fell through to an alternate universe where I suddenly couldn't hear or move; I could only feel this mortified numbness freeze me into place.

"Oren," his mother scolded, reprimanding him with another tap on the arm. "Stop embarrassing the poor girl. Sorry about him, dear," she said, her voice winded, as she brushed back her hair that had fluttered out of place when Oren hugged her. But a smile had lit her eyes. She loved her son very much, even when he was inappropriate. "He's always been that way. And trying to shut him up only seems to encourage him to continue. I'm Brenda, by the way." She held out a hand to me. "Oren said you're Caroline, right?"

It was bizarre to hear someone else actually call him Oren. But I cleared my throat and nodded. "Right." My voice was stiff. My shoulders were stiff. My freaking panties felt stiff. I was afraid to breathe wrong in fear of saying or doing the wrong thing and just...shattering all the stiff parts.

It didn't even matter how gracious and polite his mother was being. I still wanted to sink through the floor in embarrassment. "Oh, what a lovely name. It's so nice to meet you." Her eyes sparkled as she beamed up at Oren. "Well done, son."

He snorted. "As if I had anything to do with catching her. She caught *me*."

I wanted to elbow him in the side and tell him to shut it, but I settled for a warning glance.

The bastard merely winked at me.

"And I'm Phil," his dad spoke up, also reaching out a hand to shake with me. "I think you're hot too."

My fingers froze in his while Oren choked on air next to me. "Jesus, Dad."

"What?" Phil dropped his palm from mine to lift his eyebrows Oren's way. "It's that slang for pretty that you youngsters use these days."

"Oh my God." Oren groaned and held up a hand. "Promise me you'll never use that slang term again."

"You got it," his dad assured before he slipped me a sly little grin, telling me he was just messing with Oren. Then he turned to his wife, murmuring loud enough for us to hear, "I guess we shouldn't let him hear what kinds of slang we use in the bedroom then."

As Oren cried out and slapped his hands over his ears, claiming, "I'm deaf. You guys have just killed my poor, innocent ears," I burst out laughing. He sent me a scowl. "It's not funny, damn it."

"Oren. *Language*," his mother scolded. "We're in public."

I lifted my eyebrows, wondering what she'd say if she heard his potty mouth while he was in Ellamore. The boy didn't know a clean word.

"Let's sit already," his dad suggested, his grin still a little smug.

As Oren dropped into a chair and slid his hands from his ears, he glanced over at me when I sat quietly beside him, my spine still stiff with nerves.

"So, Caroline..." his mother started. I gulped, tore my gaze away from Oren, and sent her an uneasy smile. "Yes?"

And so started the inquisition. Except it didn't feel as if I was being drilled for information. It felt as if they were genuinely curious and wanted to know about *me*. That was strange at first, explaining my major to a parent. But Brenda, and even Phil, were actually interested in the field of study I'd chosen. I got a little carried away and just started blurting out all kinds of things I wanted to do.

"I think sound effects are what really make a movie."

"Of course they are." Brenda nodded enthusiastically as she leaned my way and pressed a hand to her heart. "I love it when the music gets so loud it just thunders through your chest right before the hero proclaims his love to the—"

"Oh, gag me." Oren groaned and sank lower in his chair. "I swear, Mom, if you get started about *The Last of the Mohicans* again—"

"Oh my God, I love that movie." I sat up straighter. "That rasp in Daniel Day-Lewis's voice when he told Madeleine Stowe he would find her...I mean, melt my panties."

While Brenda pointed at me with wide eyes and said, "Exactly," both men started laughing. She scowled at her son. "What is so funny? You were probably conceived because of that movie."

He instantly stopped laughing and starting coughing. "Shit, Ma. I did not need to know that."

Still chuckling, Phil slapped him on the back to help him get his air back. "I just thought it was hilarious how she said *melt my panties*."

"Oh, fuck," I gasped, realizing, "I did." Then I slapped a hand over my mouth, realizing I'd just said fuck. "I mean, crap." Wait, was crap bad too? "I mean..."

I glanced wildly at Oren for help, but he still looked traumatized from learning so much about his conception.

Brenda patted my arm compassionately. "Don't worry about it, dear. We all slip every once in a while."

Oren made a sound as if to disagree with her, because I "slipped" almost as much as he did. Both his mother and I sent him a scowl.

Phil was still hooting out his amusement and wiping tears of mirth from his eyes. "Boy howdy, am I glad Oren brought you tonight, Caroline. This has been the most enjoyable family dinner since—"

He gasped when Brenda reached for her glass of iced tea and accidentally spilled it in his lap.

As he jumped to his feet, slapping the ice cubes off him, his wife followed him up with a handful of napkins, immediately pressing it against his crotch.

"Brenda!" Phil grasped her wrist and glanced around as if scandalized. "Not in public."

"Oh, dear Lord." Brenda sighed and glanced at me. "Excuse us for a minute," she told me. Taking Phil's arm, she led him away toward the bathrooms.

I stared after them in wonder. Phil reminded me so much of Oren in some ways. And Brenda...she was just awesome.

As soon as they were out of sight, I slapped Oren in the arm. Hard.

"You asshole," I hissed. "Your parents are amazing."

He glanced at me with a confused frown. "Well, yeah. I never said they *weren't*."

"But...you made it sound like it was such a hardship to see them again, as if they were terrible, but they're...they're really amazing. They love you and care about you and want to know what's happening in your life. How can you not appreciate any of that? I mean, if I'd had just *one* parent who was even *half* as interested in me as both of yours are in you, I'd—"

My voice cracked, so I settled for glaring at him. He had no idea how great he had it in the family department. I mean, I appreciated everything Noel had gone through to bring us to Ellamore and save us from the life we'd been living. And I never would've made it as far as I had without Colton and Brandt around to suffer through with me, but...I still wished I'd had a mom who'd given a shit. Or even known *who* my father was.

But no, I had nothing, while Oren had everything; and he was *complaining* about it.

Spoiled bastard.

"I didn't say they were *bad* parents. They're not, not at all. And they're supportive. Maybe too supportive. But they're just—"

He broke off when he saw them returning.

I glanced over too, prepared to ask if everything was better. But something had changed in the time since Brenda and Phil had left the table to dry Phil. They looked stoic, almost sympathetic.

"Shit," Oren muttered beside me. "Here it comes."

I glanced at him, but he was too busy scowling at his parents.

They stopped in front of our table, but instead of sitting, they remained standing, obviously ready to make some kind of big united-front announcement.

Oren tensed beside me, so I slid my hand under the table until it found his. He had balled his fingers into a tight fist, but he opened them for me so he could squeeze his around mine.

"Oren," his mother started. "I understand how much you don't like talking about her, but we thought you should know... Your father and I petitioned the town to set up a memorial for Zoey in the city park, and they've agreed. We want you to come to the grand opening next weekend."

CHAPTER 18

Ten

I HAVE NO IDEA why hearing my parents talk about her always made me physically ill. But my stomach revolted, bile rose in my throat, and my vision went wonky.

"*Really*?" Surging to my feet, I glared across the table. "You're going to bring this shit up in front of my new girlfriend?" And I'd been so sure Caroline would be the perfect buffer to keep family drama out of the conversation.

Mom glanced at Caroline, her eyes wide with alarm before she turned back to me. "This *shit* is your sister's legacy. Don't you want to honor her?"

The swirling in my gut turned into little needles of agony. I doubled slightly, setting my hands on my hips in an attempt to hide how much I hurt. "I don't even want to think about it," I hissed.

Mom sighed out a sad breath as Dad grasped her hand. I hated distressing them, but fuck, why did they always have to force this on me?

"Sweetheart, this is not healthy. Pretending she never existed isn't going to stop it from hurting."

Yeah, well, I had to disagree. It'd worked pretty damn well for me for the past four years.

When my dad tried to say something next, I held up a

hand and snapped, "Don't."

"We think you need help." Mom rushed out the words, making me jerk in shock.

"*What*?"

"Our biggest fear was that you'd never be able to move on from what happened. And for a while, we thought you had. But clearly, you're just *repressing* it. You haven't even attempted the stages of grief to work through this, and it's going to end up coming back and biting you someday when you least expect it."

"I'm fine," I exploded. "Please excuse me if I don't want to spend the rest of my life purposely being all depressed over...over someone who's never coming back."

Dad shook his head. "You still can't even say her name out loud, can you?"

I shot Caroline a sharp warning glance, telling her to keep her trap shut. Her eyes were wide as she took in my dysfunctional family scene. Fuck, she was going to have so many questions after this. What had I been thinking to bring her along?

"Mrs. Tenning," she said, turning to my mom. "I don't know if this helps ease your mind any, but Oren's been visiting a therapist."

Say what? I shot her a startled glance, but she didn't even look my way. Focusing on my parents, she clasped her hands to her chest with a genuine show of compassion. "I mean, I know it hasn't done much for him *yet*, but he's actually gone to a few sessions, which should mean something, right? He's *admitted* he needs help. Isn't that what they say is half the battle?"

My mother's eyes glistened with tears as she turned to me. "Are you really? Oh, Oren. That's amazing. I'm so proud of you."

As she hugged me, I met Caroline's gaze, widening my gaze to silently ask what the fuck she thought she was doing.

"Thanks," I muttered to my mom as I pushed out of her warm embrace that I actually kind of missed feeling. "It's my fault she's dead, but you're so *proud* of me. That makes everything so much fucking better."

Unable to handle a second more of this shit, I spun away from them and marched off. My head raced in a million different directions as I stormed blindly from the restaurant. I automatically started for my truck, but visions of my sister's bloody face covered in glass as she lay slumped against a steering wheel had me stopping in my tracks. Her scream as she shouted for me to help her echoed through my head.

I was in no shape to drive, so I pivoted right and started down the quiet sidewalk, dodging out of the way of the overhead street lamps so I could keep to the shadows.

I didn't get very far before a breathless Caroline caught up with me, jogging to reach my side. She panted as she tried to keep pace. "You weren't planning on deserting me here, were you? With your parents...whom I just *met*."

I sent her a quick, hard glare. "You want to come with me, you better keep up."

"Oh, don't think I can't." She had to half jog, but she managed to keep up, and she didn't complain.

In fact, the infuriating woman stayed absolutely, blessedly silent...which only pissed me off more. Why wasn't she yelling at me, telling me off for how rude I'd been to my "amazing" parents, demanding to know what that had been about back there? I was in the mood to fight, but how the hell was I was supposed to pick a fight with such a supportive, amazing girlfriend?

"Damn it!" I kicked a post office mailbox we passed in an attempt to vent. "How dare they fucking forgive me so easily?"

Caroline didn't answer. All she did was tuck a piece of hair behind her ear, telling me how nervous she was. I clenched my teeth, instantly contrite for putting her into such a situation.

Glancing at her, I said, "I can't believe you fucking lied for me. *Therapy*?"

I snorted. Me in therapy? What the fuck ever.

"What?" She sent me a rueful smile and a shrug. "I'm Daisy Gamble's daughter. I know all about lying."

I shook my head and finally let a smile slip free. The woman did have a fiercely conniving side, but so far, she'd always used it to my benefit, from sneaking into my room to rock my fucking world to getting my parents off my back. Frankly, I could kiss the shit out of her for the way she lied.

Glancing around the dead street of my small hometown, she asked, "Where are we going, anyway?"

I shook my head, unable to keep my temper intact. Just

being around her mellowed whatever anger I wanted to feel. Damn woman had a bad habit of making me too happy whenever she was around.

"I need to go to my place." I sent her a scowl in a last-ditch effort to hang on to my anger, but fuck, she looked really pretty with her cheeks flushed from the effort it took to keep up with me. "And since you're all about being my shadow, I guess you're coming with me."

Strangely, I actually wanted to show her my place I used to go to be alone when I was a kid. I'd never taken anyone there before, hence the alone part. Not even my sister. But it somehow felt right to take Caroline.

"You have a place?" Sending me a sidelong glance, she started to smile. "That's so neat."

I snorted. "Of course I have a place. Everyone has a place."

But she shook her head. "I don't have a place."

"Oh, whatever. I'm not buying it. There's got to be somewhere you go just to be alone, unwind, get your head out of your ass?"

"Not where I grew up. I mean, back at the trailer house, I used to camp out in my bedroom sometimes, but I had to share it with Colton and Brandt, so...it wasn't really just mine." As we passed an old, run-down theater, she gasped and glanced up at the opening where the ticket box had been boarded over. "Oh, man. This place is so awesome. It's a shame it's not still open."

With a smirk, I took her hand. "I had a feeling you'd get a kick out of it. Come on."

When I veered us down a dark alley next to the theater, she moved closer to me, touching my back as she blindly followed.

"So, your place is an *alley*?" The wariness in her voice told me she wasn't impressed. "That's kind of creepy."

I paused next to a rusty fire escape ladder. "No, smartass. My place is on the roof of the theater." Turning to pin her to the wall next to the ladder, I leaned in close. "See, I've always had a fetish for wanting to be on top of movie lovers."

With a snort, she threw her head back and laughed. "Oh God. I can't believe you. You're supposed to be having a personal meltdown here, and yet you're still cracking crude puns?"

"Admit it," I murmured, leaning into her until I could smell her hair. "That's exactly what you like best about me."

"Hmm." Her murmur of interest raced through my bloodstream and had my cock hardening. "There's something naughty and sexy about it," she finally admitted.

"Oh, yeah?" I dipped my face down to hers until our mouths aligned. But I didn't kiss her. "If I didn't know any better, Miss Gamble, I'd say you're trying to seduce me right now."

She touched my nose with a quick tap. "You almost quoted *The Graduate* right there."

"Did I?" I pressed my hips against hers so she could feel how hard I was. "I bet there isn't a quote good enough for what I want to do with you right now, though."

While her gaze screamed *fuck me*, and the sensual curving of her lips seemed to second that sentiment, she whispered into my ear. "Take me..." I started to groan in delight, but then she finished with, "...to see your place, Oren."

I shifted in closer to her, my mouth only centimeters from hers. "Then you'd better start climbing, woman. Before I *take you* against this wall."

Her gaze drifted to the ladder next to us before her eyes grew wide. "Wha...? No. Oh, no. You don't actually expect me to *climb* that rickety old thing, do you?"

With a cluck of my tongue, I grasped her waist and lifted her up, so she could reach the bottom rung. "Yep, I absolutely do. Now get going, woman."

"Oren—" She clambered and cursed before finally catching a good handhold. As she lifted herself up, she whimpered. "Oh God. I'm going to die."

"Just...climb," I murmured approvingly, enjoying the view. This was probably the second, maybe third, time I'd ever seen her in a dress, and I was getting to see it from *below*. Damn, I was a lucky son of a bitch. And bullshit she'd dressed that way for my parents. No way had she put on that lacy black thong to impress my mom.

She climbed well in heels, which impressed the fuck out of me. When I started up after her, though, the ladder swayed from our combined weight. She froze, squeaking out her fear and clutching the rungs for dear life until she grew used to the movement.

When she once again started a slow ascent, she glanced

down to ask, "Is it illegal to climb up here?"

I shrugged and sent her a grin, wondering how quickly I could get her out of that thong. "More than likely."

She faced forward again. "Oh God. What do we do if we get caught?"

"I imagine we go to jail."

She paused. "*Oren!*"

"What?" I nudged her in the ankle to keep her moving. "Why are you so worried? *I'm* the guy; I'll be the one who'll more than likely get gang raped by Bubba and friends if we're tossed in the slammer."

"Oh, you are just so funny."

"Yeah, I figured that was why you kept me around."

She snorted, but we'd reached the roof of the old cinema, so I was happy. Caroline paused as soon as she shimmied herself off the ladder.

"What now?" I have no idea why she was suddenly whispering after we'd just had a loud argument all the way up the side of the building, but I thought it was adorable.

I hooked my arm around her waist and turned her in the direction I always went when I came up here by myself. "This way." Then I kissed her hair.

After I sat down in the exact middle of the roof, I pulled her into my lap so she wouldn't have to sit on the grimy shingles and get a dirty ass. No reason to smear such perfection. Plus her lacy-wrapped tush felt really good against my junk.

Once she was settled against me, I tightened my arms around her and kissed the side of her neck. "Now lean back against me, look up at that sky, and just...enjoy," I whispered into her ear.

She followed my instructions only to let out a gasp of delight. "Wow."

"I know, right?" I looked up too, and the night seemed to swallow us whole, making me feel so insignificant and small in this moment and yet important and integral to the universe. The sensation was impossible to explain. It was one of those things you just had to feel.

Caroline seemed to get it though. She tightened her grip on my forearm and inhaled a deep breath. "The sky is so perfect from here. The stars look so close and yet so far away."

I nodded. Oh, yeah, she totally got it.

We sat in silence for a good fifteen minutes, just letting the evening take us away to that place that felt peaceful and free.

The only problem was we couldn't stay here forever. Caroline broke the lovely silence by saying, "So...your sister's name was Zoey?"

I blew out a breath and stretched out my legs under her before running my hands over her thighs. "Yep."

She turned her face in toward me to kiss my jaw. "And that's why you write her name all the time."

I scowled at the stars. "I don't write it *all* the time."

Caroline laughed softly. "I've caught you doing it more than once."

I growled out a sound but tipped my face over to rub it alongside hers.

She let out a cute hum as she caressed my scruff. "You're really uncomfortable with this discussion; it's kind of adorable."

"Thanks." I curled my arm around her waist in an effort to feel comfortable with something...even if it was just her ass in my lap. "I'm glad one of us is amused."

"I kind of thought you had a thing for her," she admitted.

I furrowed my brow. "Who? *Ham's* woman? No. Well, kind of, I guess. I mean, I *like* Blondie. But not... like *that*."

"You like her as a brother," she surmised.

Every muscle in my body tightened at that word. I'd already been a brother. That had ended badly. I didn't want to be a brother to any other poor, unsuspecting, innocent girl again.

"You know, it's okay if you have brotherly feelings for her," Caroline murmured, stroking her fingers up into my hair. "It's not going to take anything away from what you felt for the first Zoey. I have three brothers, and loving one doesn't keep me from loving the other two just as much."

I groaned. "Jesus, you didn't lie to my parents at all, did you? I really am seeing a counselor. I just didn't realize *you* were the psychiatrist."

She murmured out a quiet laugh. "And if you're an extra good boy for the rest of our hour session, Dr. Caroline might even be willing to give you a thorough physical once this is over."

"Mmm." I kissed her ear and slid my fingers from her

waist to the inside of her thigh. "Can we skip straight to that part?"

Grasping my wrist, she moved my hand up to a more respectable place on her knee. "Not until your hour's up, Mr. Tenning."

I bit her earlobe lightly. "Fun hater."

She grinned and twisted to look up at me. But her expression just as quickly fell somber. "Why'd you say it was your fault she died?"

With a groan, I closed my eyes. "Because it was."

She frowned in confusion. "So...you shot her? Stabbed her? Suffocated her with a pillow?" After a thoughtful pause, she nodded approvingly. "I've actually considered pillow suffocation for Brandt. Numerous times."

I couldn't help it, I smiled. But then the memories flooded right back up and swallowed me. "I let her drive," I finally admitted, "when I knew she was upset."

Caroline was quiet for a moment before she asked simply, "And why did you do that?"

A sigh eased from my lungs. I glanced back up at the stars and pulled the warm woman in my arms tighter against me, realizing what an honor it was to get to hold her like this. In a second, she could be stolen away from me, too...just like that.

Tucking my face into her hair and appreciating what I had right now, I said, "Because she *was* upset. She loved driving, so I thought letting her take the wheel would make her feel better."

"And did it...before the accident part, I mean?"

I shrugged. "Well, yeah. I guess. She was smiling and lecturing me when..." I broke off, remembering the headlights of the other car as they'd blared in my face right before it ran a red light and T-boned us. A shudder wracked me. Memories swirled of Zoey screaming my name, the fear in her voice as she begged for help, the utter helplessness I'd felt; it all haunted me.

"Why was she upset?" Caroline asked.

I shook my head and snorted. "Some stupid-ass guy. Thought she liked him, but then she went to a sleepover with her friends and found out one of her buddies was also hooking up with him. When she called me, crying, asking me to pick her up, I'd just—"

Fuck, I couldn't tell Caroline about *that*. But she nudged

me in the ribs with her pointer finger. "You'd just what?"

I glanced at her warily. "I guess I already told you about my first time, didn't I?"

"You mean the stupid girl who laughed at your beautiful penis?"

Appreciating the way she described my birthmark, I grinned. "Yeah. Her. Well, I was driving home from *that* when Zoey's distress call came in."

"Wait." Caroline held up a hand and twisted to look directly into my eyes. "So the same traumatic night you lost your virginity and were ridiculed by that idiot, twat girl was also the night your sister—"

Setting my hand over her mouth to keep her from saying what I couldn't handle hearing, I nodded. "Yeah."

Her eyes flared. "Wow. No wonder why you've had such an issue with your penis. It's tied to your sister."

I couldn't help it, I snorted out a laugh. "Fuck, you have no idea how wrong that sounded when you said it that way."

"What?" she asked before she must've mentally repeated what she'd just said. Then she snickered and bumped herself back against me. "Whatever. You know what I meant."

I nodded. "Yeah, but it still sounds fucking strange."

Caroline finally chuckled along with me before she cocked her head to the side. "So, was Zoey younger or older than you? I can't tell from the way you talk about her."

I cleared my throat. "She was...she was the same age. The same exact age."

Mouth falling open, Caroline gaped. "You were *twins*? Holy shit."

I nodded and closed my eyes. But the memories still attacked me. Every single detail of my childhood had involved my sister. She'd always been right there with me, almost an extension of myself until, wham, she was just...gone.

"Well, fuck." Caroline rested her cheek on my shoulder. "No wonder you're so messed up. I mean, losing a sibling has to be rough. It's got to hurt like hell and make you feel as if you failed them somehow. But a *twin*? That'd be like losing...a part of yourself."

"Yeah." In need of a distraction, I ran my fingers through her hair. "It pretty much gutted me. And I swore to myself I'd never hurt like that again. I'd never...fuck, I'd never love like that again. I don't care that it was just sibling love, it still—"

"No, I totally get it. Any kind of love—sibling, paternal, passionate, platonic—it still hurts just as painfully when you lose that person."

I nodded. "It really does. And I was keeping my promise so well for *three* years. I didn't let any chick in, not until you came along. And then *Blondie* showed up. Jesus, you guys know how to fuck my head up, you know that?"

Her fingers stroked my face again. "I'd say sorry," she murmured, her lips tipped up in pleasure. "But then I'd be lying."

I sniffed. Of course, she wasn't sorry. She'd gotten exactly what she wanted from this. I gazed at her a moment, admitting I was glad she had, though. "Are you beginning to see why I stayed away from you for so long? It wasn't *just* about your brother."

She nodded. "Yeah, I guess. You irrationally fear someone else is going to die if you actually begin to like another girl."

I snorted. "Begin to? The begin-to boat has sailed, sweetheart. I already like you. A lot. That's why this is so hard. Why our whole girlfriend-boyfriend talk today was so awkward. I don't *like* the girls I screw. I've made a point not to. I didn't date, I didn't fuck with the lights on, I never cuddled afterward." With an impatient kind of sigh, I hugged her tighter to me. "You're seriously breaking all my rules. You know that, right?"

Her smile just grew. "I'm beginning to get a clue."

Jesus, she was loving this. Why did women love it so much when you got all sappy and poured your frigging heart out to them?

"So, if the timeline in my head is right, this all happened near the end of your...last year of high school, right?"

I nodded. "Two months before graduation."

"God, that's so awful. How did you...I can't even imagine how you were able to graduate after that. How you moved on at all."

I shook my head. "I don't remember much about the last bit of high school. I just know I passed. It was moving on to college that really changed everything. I guess I looked at it as a clean slate, as if I hadn't existed until that moment. I had no past, no sister, no nothing. I was just me. Gamble..."

I paused and glanced at her.

She nodded, seemingly okay with me bringing up her brother. I swallowed. "Well, he probably helped me through everything more than anyone, without even knowing what he was doing. We were assigned as roommates in the dorms. And he just...swept me along with him and kind of forced us into being this...team." I shook my head and grinned. "It was easy not to tell him shit about me. That fucker was driven. I tell you what, he was looking so far into the future when he came to ESU, it was as if he never had a past. Like *no one* had ever had a past. So, shit, I don't know. It was easy to forget anything that had happened to me before college, too. We just lived for the present and the future. I knew about you and your brothers because he would call home, like, every fucking day, but I figured you were all really young or something. I never really thought about it. He didn't voice any concerns to me, so I didn't worry about you either. And he never worried about any of my shit I'd pushed out of my head, so...it just worked for us."

With a smile, Caroline hugged me. "I understand why he had to leave Colton and Brandt and me for a while, then. He had to be here for *you*."

I stared at her, realizing shit, she'd had to suffer so I could find a way to heal. That sucked ass. But in a way, I was kind of glad it'd worked out this way. Her suffering had brought her here, to me.

Pressing my forehead to hers, I breathed in that amazing smell that was purely my woman. Then I cupped her face in my hands. "Whatever shit happened to drag us here to this moment...I wish most of it hadn't needed to go down the way it did, but I'm still glad it ended up here, right here, with you and me together on this roof. The pain was worth it if it's what brought you to me."

Caroline sucked in a shuddery breath before murmuring, "Oren?"

"Hmm?" I closed my eyes, once again so grateful I had her.

"Your hour session's over."

I opened my eyes. She smiled up at me. Damn, I loved how horny she could get.

With a groan, I rasped, "Thank God," right before I kissed her.

CHAPTER 19

TEN

I SHOULD'VE KNOWN better than to open up to anyone about my sister. The very night I sat on top of the old theater and told Caroline about Zoey, I went home after dropping her off near her house and fell asleep in my bed, only to have a fucking nightmare.

The dream even started shitty, with Libby Lawson shrieking at the sight of my dick.

"Oh my God! What the hell is wrong with it?"

I'd just crawled off her, was still naked, and I was scouring her bedroom for my pants before her parents returned from their dinner party.

"What?" I glanced down, hoping she didn't think I was too small. Then I immediately covered myself. Shit, I wasn't smaller than Rowdy Crowner, was I? She'd dated him earlier in the year, and I'd heard they'd gone all the way. But, damn, I'd have to kill myself if she told me I was smaller than that douche.

Face molted in horror, she veered backward up the bed in an attempt to get as far away from me as possible. "Holy shit. What is that *thing* on the side? You don't have some kind of STD, do you?"

I blinked for a second before saying, "You mean my birthmark?"

"Your *what*?"

I opened my hands to show her. "It's just a birthmark. I've always had it."

She shuddered and turned her face away. "Eww. Put it away. I can't believe you had that thing inside me. How gross. Why didn't you tell me about it before we did anything? I better not catch something from you!"

"Don't worry." I couldn't get the bitterness from my voice as I scrambled to yank my clothes on. I hated how my face was heating. "Birthmarks aren't contagious."

"It better not be, or I'm telling everyone what a freak you are."

Acid churned in my stomach and bile rose in my throat. Panic clawed at me as I pictured myself walking into school on Monday with everyone laughing and pointing. Damn, I was going to have to drop out of school. Eight more weeks until high school graduation and my life was over...all because I'd finally lost it to a chick who'd obviously seen enough cocks to know mine was not average.

"Whatever," I snarled. "Thanks for the lay. Maybe you'll get better with practice."

As parting shots went, that wasn't my finest, but fuck, I wasn't on my A-game at the moment. Bowing my head, I jogged from her house and out to my car, a vintage beauty that my dad had bought for me and my sister, thinking we'd be able to share it.

Mostly, we just fought over who'd get to drive it. Tonight, I'd won the keys, and I thought my luck was sticking with me when Libby had called me over, saying her parents were away, giving us an hour to play. Who knew it'd all go to shit so quickly?

"Fuck, fuck, fuck," I muttered and pounded my fist against the steering wheel. I'd never felt so humiliated as I did in that moment. Seventeen years old and my life was officially done. If Libby followed her word—and she was probably calling all her friends right now—I'd never get laid again. My first and only time to try sex, and it hadn't even been that good.

"Damn it." I started the car and roared down the street. I

was reaching for the radio controls to find some loud, pissed-off music when my cell phone rang.

Fuck. That was probably one of my buddies who'd already heard about my freakish junk. I almost didn't check the screen, but curiosity got the best of me. When I saw Zoey's name, I groaned.

My twin already knew? Wasn't that just...great.

"What?" I muttered when I answered.

"Come get me," she demanded on a sniff, obviously crying. "Now."

"What's wrong?" Completely forgetting about myself, I slammed on the brakes and did a U-turn to speed back toward her friend's house where I knew she was staying the night with a couple other girls from school. "Who the fuck do I have to kill?"

"No one. I just...I want to go home."

"I'm four blocks away. Be right there."

"Okay. Hurry."

She came tearing out to the car, her overnight bag thrown over her shoulder and mascara streaked down her cheeks. I pushed open my door, pissed that anyone would make my sister cry. "Seriously." I slid the bag off her shoulder and shoved it over the seat into the back of the car. "Who made you cry?"

She wiped at her black-streaked cheeks. "No one. She doesn't even know what she did. It wasn't her fault anyway. Just...let's go. Please."

I turned back to scowl up at her friend's house, but the girls crowded in the doorway watching us looked worried and sympathetic, so I couldn't rightly charge up there and cuss any of them out. When I came back around, Zoey had climbed into the driver's seat.

"No," I said, motioning with my thumb for her to get out. "You're not driving. Not like this. Besides, it's *my* night, remember?"

And I didn't want to feel any more emasculated than I already felt. I'd already been told I was a freakish horror between the legs; I did not want my little sister to go driving me around. It didn't even matter than she was only a minute and a half younger than me, I was still technically the big brother.

"Damn it, Oren." She peered up at me from her tearstained eyes. "I need to...I just need to relieve some pressure right now. *Please*."

I'd never really been able to say no to her, but especially not when she was crying, so I sighed, ground my teeth and muttered, "Fine. Whatever," before I went around to the passenger side. I tugged on my seat belt as soon as I climbed in, and fucking awful brother that I was, I didn't even notice that she'd neglected to put hers on.

"So, what's the deal?" I asked as she peeled out down the road and veered around a corner.

"Corey Garboni slept with Suzanne."

I waited for her to go on, but when she didn't, I lifted my eyebrows. "Okay. So?"

"So?" She sent me an incredulous scowl. "So, I *liked* Corey. I let him go up my shirt last weekend."

"You did *what*?"

"And he was supposed to take me to the movies again tomorrow," she ranted on without even hearing me. "I had no idea he was into Suzanne too, and she had no idea about what I'd done with him."

"Bastard," I muttered under my breath. "I can't believe you even liked that guy. I've always thought he was a fucking douche."

"Oh, well I'm so sorry I couldn't like someone you approved of."

"You should be," I said. "I could probably find you a better guy than *you* could. Someone who wouldn't fucking cheat on you, anyway."

"Really?" She arched me an incredulous glance. "I would just love to hear what kind of guy *you* think I should end up with."

"Fine." I cleared my throat and resituated myself in the passenger seat, thinking it through. "He has to like football, or I wouldn't have anything in common with him, and if he's going to hang out with you, then I'll probably be stuck hanging out with him more than I want."

"Okay," she said on the nod as she slowed the car to turn a corner. "I could handle a football player."

"Right." I drew in a breath before adding, "Loyal, faithful, quiet."

"Quiet?" She sent me a mystified glance.

I nodded, sticking with my original decision. "Yeah. We're both talkers, so you'd definitely need a listener, maybe someone a little reserved but totally willing to stand up for you if need be. He'd have to be bigger than me, because I just wouldn't be able to respect him if he wasn't. Oh, and smart, like into science so that he'll end up a rich heart surgeon or something."

"You haven't described his looks yet."

I shrugged and made a face. "Fuck, like I care how he looks."

She grinned. "Then I want him to be hot. Preferably blue eyes and maybe even a dimple."

I shook my head, boggled as to why those two things had made the cut and nothing else. Girls were so strange. "Fine," I said. "Whatever."

She snorted out a quick laugh. "You know, we just described a guy who couldn't possibly exist. A sexy, shy, biology-loving athlete. Really, Oren. Never going to happen."

"Well, then I guess we'll just have to grow old together, single and hopeless." Glancing out the passenger side window, I mumbled to myself, "Because I'm certainly never getting laid again."

But my twin heard me, loud and clear. "What do you mean *again*? You haven't—oh my God. Were you at Libby's house when I just called?"

"I was on my way *home* from her house when you called," I corrected.

She gasped. "Holy shit. So you two—" When she glanced at me, her eyebrows crinkled with worry. "Oh, no. Your birthmark freaked her out, didn't it?"

I zipped her a hard stare. "How the hell did you know that?"

She shrugged. "I don't know. I just…guessed. I mean, I've never actually seen a real live penis aside from yours when we were younger, but I've heard girls talk, and none of them mention bright purple spots on the side."

I sank lower in my seat, wanting to just fucking die. "Well, thanks for cluing me in on that…after I'd already fucking humiliated myself for life. She's going to tell *everyone*, you know. She's going to say what a freak I am, and I'm never going to have sex again in my entire—"

"Oh, whatever." Zoey snorted and rolled her eyes at me. "Not every girl out there is as callous as Libby, the slut, Lawson. One day, you're going to meet an amazing girl— that I can actually stomach—and she's going to love everything about you, even your colorful pecker."

I arched an eyebrow. "I was actually hoping I could get as much pussy as possible before *the one* came along and I had to settle down."

Zoey gasped and grabbed a wadded napkin that had been sitting in the center console before she flung it at me. "Don't you dare end up being such a player, Oren Michael Tenning, or I'll—"

"*Watch out,*" I shouted as we entered an intersection. The vehicle to the left wasn't obeying their stop sign.

Zoey slammed on the brake, but it was too late. She screamed my name, and I screamed hers.

I was still shouting her name when I woke, thrashing in my sheets. "Zoey," I choked out, only to jump out of my skin when a pair of hands grabbed my arm.

"Ten. Hey, Ten. Wake up. You're having a nightmare."

I jerked upright and panted, out of breath as my two roommates backed up a step from my mattress, eyeing me as if I was rabid. Sweat rolled down my temples and bare chest.

I gaped up at Ham, remembering every detail of the last conversation I'd had with my twin. The first moment I'd met him, I'd almost shit my pants with disbelief. He'd been the very image of the guy Zoey and I had described. I think my sister would've actually liked him too...if she'd ever gotten the chance to meet him.

The fact that he'd ended up with a woman named Zoey had almost been too eerie to take at first. Blondie was the antithesis of how my sister had been, but still...with the same name and the way she'd hooked up with Hamilton, I hadn't been able to brush off the brotherly feelings I'd grown for her.

"Are you okay?" she asked, climbing onto the bed with worried eyes to sit beside me. "You were yelling my name."

I shuddered. "Was I?"

"It freaked us out." Ham sat on the corner, his expression matching his woman's.

I cleared my throat and glanced away. "Yeah, well... sorry about that."

"You were dreaming about your sister, weren't you?"

With a glare at Ham for even asking that and an internal cringe at myself for once admitting to them that I'd had a sister named Zoey, I then glanced away and gave a nod.

Blondie took my hand. "Do you want me to change my name? I would. For you."

"That's sweet," I said and sent her a small smile as I squeezed her fingers thankfully. Then I pulled her toward me and gave her a hug. "But, no. I'll just keep calling you Blondie."

She nodded. "Okay. I like Blondie. It's way better than Milk Tits."

I pulled out of the hug to scowl at her. "Milk Tits is a kick-ass nickname."

She laughed and shook her head. "No. It's actually really awful." But as soon as her smile started, it settled. "Do you want to talk about it? Your nightmare."

God, no. The last time I'd talked about this shit, I'd ended up with this very nightmare. I was done talking. I shook my head. "No. I'm good. You guys can go back to sleep."

"Are you sure?" Ham asked. "Can we get you some water or anything?"

Damn. These two. Their sweetness was beginning to make my teeth rot. "Mom. Dad." I lifted my hands. "I'm fine. Seriously. I'm sorry for waking you. Now get back to bed."

And finally, they relented. Blondie had to give me another hug and Ham patted my shoulder, but once they were gone, I couldn't get back to sleep. I tossed and turned and before I knew it, I was grabbing my phone off the nightstand and zinging a text off to Caroline.

After writing, *Nobody puts baby in a corner,* I sighed and tossed the phone back onto the counter, only for it to immediately ding with a response. Not expecting her to write back at this time of night, I picked it up, thrilled to see it really was from her.

Why are you sending me a Dirty Dancing *quote at two in the morning?*

I grinned, and immediately, my chest felt looser. I could breathe easier, and the headache that had been forming behind my eyes abated completely. *I've been studying up. I wanted to wow my sexy movie-expert girlfriend with my new knowledge of movie one-liners.*

Well, I'm not wowed. Everyone knows THAT line.

So, I typed, *Frankly, my dear, I don't give a damn.*

To which she typed back, *Clark Gable.* Gone with the Wind. *Send a real challenge already. I'm yawning over here.*

A grin lit my face. *Maybe you're yawning because you're up at two in the goddamn morning. Maybe someone needs to...make you an offer you can't refuse.*

GODFATHER. And you're the one waking me up at two in the goddamn morning. What's up with that?

I was leaving a message for you to read when you woke up. I didn't mean for it to actually wake you, Rosebud.

Well it woke me, Citizen Kane. What're you doing up now, anyway? You didn't work tonight.

I debated over whether I should tell her, but then I shrugged. What the hell? *Bad dream,* I typed.

Two seconds later, my phone rang. I shook my head and answered. "Yes?"

"What were you dreaming about?"

"It was nothing," I started, only for her to talk over me.

"It was about your sister, wasn't it? We had that big heart-to-heart on the roof earlier and it brought up a bunch of memories. Damn it, I should've suspected this might happen."

"A misdiagnosis from Dr. Caroline?" I gasped. "I think I'm going to need a refund from our last session."

There was a pause before she said, "I don't even know what that means. You're not regretting that sex on the theater roof, are you?"

"Fuck, no." I laughed, and damn, it felt good to laugh. I was actually glad my text had woken her. Just hearing her voice was already making me feel better. "I don't know what I meant," I admitted. "It just sounded good."

She snorted. "Is this how your brain works every night at two a.m.? I think you need more sleep, bud."

"Well, maybe I could sleep better if I had a soft, sweet-smelling blonde to cuddle with."

She sighed. "Well, *maybe* if you went to your front door and unlocked it, you'd find one already waiting for you."

I paused and blinked. "Wait? What? You cannot be here, now, outside my apartment."

"Why not?"

"Shit? You're *here*? *Now*?" I threw off my covers and marched through the house to fling open my front door.

A real-live Caroline, her hair full of bedhead and her clothes wrinkled and clearly thrown on in haste, smiled up at me. "Surprise."

"What the hell?" I snagged her around the waist and dragged her inside. "What...please don't tell me you walked here in the dark." And how the hell had she made it here so fast if she had?

"No." She hugged me and kissed my cheek. "I pinched Aspen's keys and left her a note."

I grinned. "Well, you devious little woman, you. Do you know what I do to wily women?"

"You...leave them panting and boneless after a world-class orgasm?" she guessed.

"Why, yes. Yes, ma'am, I do." Picking her up, I carried her back to my room and kicked the door shut behind me.

And the only dream I had the rest of the night was a dream come true.

CHAPTER 20

TEN

THINGS CHANGED after that night. And it wasn't just because I finished college and put on a cap and gown and walked through a stupid line so my parents could take a crapload of pictures of me shaking hands with some important dipshits. I just felt...different.

My applications were sent off, my future was wide open to explore, yet I feared leaving Ellamore more than ever. And it was all because of one sexy, saucy little blonde who'd flipped my world upside down.

It certainly didn't help that she liked to fuck with me at the worst possible times, either, like the sexy little text she sent right before I started a shift on a ladies' night.

Just wanted you to know I'm touching myself right now and imagining it's your tongue instead.

The glasses I was supposed to be stacking behind the bar were instantly forgotten. I whimpered, hard as a rock as I began to type in my response. *You have a dirty mouth, little girl. I know exactly what you need to clean it out with.*

So...69?

I shook my head as desire rippled through me. "Minx," I muttered aloud. I started to type back when a voice from behind me startled the fucking shit out of me.

"Wow, who's texting you that has so much of your attention?"

I spun around to gape at Gam. Then I sniffed. "None of your fucking business." I lowered my face to the text, but now the moment was ruined by big brother.

"Seriously." Gamble made a grab for my phone, but I was quicker, holding it away from him. His gaze shot to mine. "Who're you texting? Why won't you show me?"

"Because it's your sister." I used one of my typical smart-ass answers because, hell, I don't know. That's something I would say, and...shit, I didn't think he'd really believe me.

I typed, *Wear that red thing again. I want to rip it off you...with my teeth this time—* just as the bastard jabbed me in the gut with a fist and yanked the phone from my hand. I doubled over, groaning. When I straightened as much as I could, clutching my belly, I noticed a worried-looking Ham had paused to watch us. His eyes were wide because he knew I hadn't been lying about it being Gamble's sister on the other end of my texts.

Caroline never sexted me from her personal number, though. She still used Midnight Visitor's number. I'm not sure why, but I had to admit it was always hot to see that name pop up. Told me I was about to read something explicit and sexual. At the moment, I was doubly glad she did it, because it had just saved our asses from the wrath of Noel Gamble.

He snickered as he started to read through our private correspondence.

"Pervert," I muttered, grabbing my phone back and glaring at him. "Those weren't meant for your eyes, jackass."

Gam lifted his eyebrows in surprise. "That was your midnight visitor friend."

I rolled my eyes. "Really? I had no idea."

He set his hands on his hips, frowning. "I thought you said you weren't hooking up with her anymore."

"Well, I guess we still text around. Why do you care?"

"I don't. I'm just surprised you're being so secretive about it."

With a full laugh, I shook my head. "I'm not being se-cretive. Since when does not wanting you to ruin my mood by butting into a smoking hot conversation make me secretive?"

"Since you usually shove them in my face to read every fucking line of them. What is up with you, man? You always give details, usually more than I ever want to begin with."

"Well, *maybe* I'm actually beginning to listen to you about keeping my shit to myself. Did you ever think of that? Your little Ten is growing up and learning something called privacy and responsibility and respect, and all that decent shit."

"Yeah, right," he said dryly. "You grew up that much in...how long has it been since you started fucking her? A few weeks ago? A month?"

I bristled. I didn't like how disre-fucking-spectfully he was treating my relationship with Caroline. I knew he wouldn't be saying that shit if he knew *who* he was talking about, but damn...it still made me want to wrap my hands around his neck and just—

"Yo, Gamble," Hart called suddenly from the other end of the bar. I glanced over to see him with his phone in his hand and his palm over the receiver. "Your sister's on the phone for you."

What? Why the hell was Caroline calling him in the middle of sexting with me? And why had I not heard the phone ring? Whatever the reason, Gam moved away to answer her summons, dropping our argument flat.

I blinked at Hart as he shook his head at me when he passed. "You're welcome," he muttered.

"What?" Confused, I turned to follow him.

Hart sighed and glanced over my shoulder to watch Gamble talk on the phone. "You need to be a little cooler around him, man."

I stopped short. "What the fuck does *that* mean?"

"It means you're kind of being an ass. *You're* the one fucking him over right now, sneaking around behind his back. Yet you're acting like it's the other way around."

"Are you kidding me?" I muttered, digging a finger into my own chest. "*He's* the reason Caroline and I have to keep everything hush-hush in the first place. I think I have a pretty damn good reason to be irritated with him. And—wait. What the hell?" I stepped in closer and grabbed his shirt to yank him into the opening of the hallway. "You know," I hissed. "How the fuck do you know?"

The fucker just grinned at me. "Know what?"

I ground my teeth and glanced around to make sure no

one was listening in on us. "Don't fucking play with me, man. How did you find out?"

He shrugged, still looking too pleased with himself. "I figured it out the night you got your first text from...what do you call her again? Your midnight visitor? Caroline asked me to sneak your cell phone back to you after she and Zoey had taken it."

"Zo—*Blondie* was involved in that, too?" Ooh, Blondie and I were going to have some words after this. "Holy shit. So, you knew before *I* even knew?"

"Yeah." Looking proud of himself, Hart chuckled. "I'm pretty clever that way."

"You're pretty dead." I shoved him against the wall and scowled. "Why the fuck didn't you tell me you knew that night?"

Hart merely shrugged, seemingly unconcerned by the fact that I was a split second from maiming him. "I knew you'd figure it out eventually. And Caroline went to a lot of work to fool you. I didn't want to ruin all her plans."

He was Team Caroline. I didn't like that. Just how much did he adore her? Frowning, I scowled as I stepped back to give him room. Starting up a tune to whistle, he winked and slid past me, exiting the hall and reentering the bar.

I followed him slowly, warily. Him knowing too much was not cool. Nothing—absolutely nothing—was keeping him from telling Noel everything, right this second.

"So, Ten..." Asher grinned at me as he swung a chair off a table. His smile was too conniving.

I narrowed my eyes. "What?"

"How about you and I make a little wager tonight?"

Forgetting the glasses I'd been stacking, I moved to the table next to the one he was working on and took another chair off it to swing it around and sit it upright on the floor. "What kind of wager?"

"Let's see which one of us can get the most phone numbers from women?"

I paused and glanced at him. The twinkle in his eyes as he folded his arms over his chest and rested back against the table told me he knew he had me boxed into a corner.

Behind us, Gamble hooted. "Now that's a competition I'd like to see."

Shit. I glanced back at Gamble and mentally bitch slapped the piss out of Hart. What the hell was he getting me into? I couldn't turn him down now, not with Gamble listening in; he'd know something was up if I rejected a challenge like this.

"Me too," Hart said. His grin spread a little too wide and a little too knowingly. "Unless you have a reason why you'd have to say...no."

My mouth fell open. What a prick. He must really like Caroline, enough to fuck with me tonight in some evil plot to get her away from me.

I nodded and mumbled, "Whatever," because I couldn't say no in front of Gam and no way in hell was I voicing the word *yes* aloud.

But the first second I had after we opened the doors and Gamble was busy at the bar, I shoved the prick from behind. "Go up to the bar where Gam can hear you and call this fucking bet off."

"What?" He looked startled. "Why would I do that?"

Because I'd kill him if he didn't. I lifted my hands and sent him an incredulous glare. "Why do you think? I can't fucking hit on other women. I'm with someone, numb nuts."

"Then *you* call it off."

"I *can't*. Gamble will realize something fishy is going on, like I'm sleeping with his sister behind his back."

"Well, you are, so—"

"Fuck you." I shoved him in the chest. "We're going to tell him. Someday. But first, I want to show him I can grow up and take care of her before I drop the big bomb. Maybe that way, he won't kill me quite so fast when he finds out. Except playing a dumbass game to accumulate phone numbers won't show him any such shit."

"Then call it off, man. Show him you're growing up."

I growled. "Like he'll believe that. Everyone knows I couldn't grow up that fast. It has to be a slow progressive change to maturity."

"Oh God." Hart rolled his eyes. "You're giving me a headache."

I shoved him again. "Just call off the fucking bet."

Except he didn't. And so...the night started with his stupid bet itching at my conscience.

"Any numbers yet?" Gam asked a half hour into our shift as I approached the bar with a list of drinks to fetch for customers.

I lifted my face to where he was watching me from behind the counter. "Huh?"

He rolled his eyes and snapped his fingers in front of my face. "Chicks. Numbers. The bet. Any of that ring a bell?"

"Oh, right. Yeah, no. No numbers yet."

"Really? You must be off your game tonight. Hart already has three."

"Does he?" I glanced around to a table where Hart was grinning down at the table of girls. The fucker. I narrowed my eyes at him before turning back to Gam. "Must be the musician thing?"

"Hmm." Gamble eyed me censoriously, as if he knew better. Then he folded his arms over his chest. "I was sure you'd get something from the table you just served."

If I'd actually been playing in Hart's damn game, yeah, I probably would have.

I glanced back at them. "They all had boyfriends," I said.

"And how the hell could you tell that?" Gamble asked. "You barely talked to them long enough to take their drink orders much less gain relationship statuses."

I set my empty serving tray on top of the bar—a little too hard—and sent Gam a glare. "Why the fuck is this bet so damn important to you? Jesus, it's like you're trying to relive your bachelor years through me now, or something."

"*Excuse me*?" Gam wrenched back at my outburst, and I realized I'd gone too far. Shit. "Christ, man. I don't know what's got your pussy so dry and irritable lately, but there is definitely something up with you. Now... *what* is going on?"

I leaned in to rest my elbows on the bar and then I buried my face into my hands. I just about told him everything, then. I don't know why; I hadn't discussed it with Caroline, but I was seriously fucking tired of keeping it from him.

"Or is it because of her?" Gamble's question made me lift my face. I glanced over my shoulder to see Caroline passing clearance through the doorman.

My face drained of color.

Shit, shit, shit. What was she doing here? What if she learned about the bet? What if she thought I was cool with it and had willingly volunteered to participate? What if—

"Jesus, you really do have it bad for Hamilton's woman, don't you?" Gamble murmured.

"What?" I glanced at him, confused, until he pointed

Caroline's way again. That's when I noticed Blondie was with her. The fucker really thought I'd been staring at her instead of his sister.

I groaned. This was not working. I opened my mouth to call off the bet with Hart and tell Gamble in no uncertain terms that I was *not* carrying around a flame for Hamilton's woman when Hart cursed from behind me. Then he spoke up louder, saying, "Hey, Ten. I'm closing the bet, now. I got four numbers. Can you beat that?"

I glanced at him, scowling. "You're stopping it *now*?"

When he nodded, I rolled my eyes. "You all piss me the fuck off. You know that?"

Fed up with the both of them, I whirled away from the bar and marched off. I wanted to go to Caroline, but I couldn't. Which only infuriated me more. When she caught my eye, I kept walking, feeling shitty about having to blow her off.

I'd just taken an order from another table when Hart caught my arm. "Man, I didn't know Caroline was going to show up tonight. I'd never do anything to hurt her."

"Fuck off." I shrugged him away and marched back to the bar to put in my orders. I made sure to stop at Lowe's end instead of Gamble's, though. As he fixed me up with a full tray to deliver to my customers, I glanced around the place. I spotted Blondie where she'd waylaid Ham and was greeting him with a hug and kiss. But Caroline was no longer with her. So I kept scanning. Where the hell had she gone?

When I finally spotted her, she'd already found me. She strolled through the crowd of people and tables as she headed in my direction, and dear God...I had no idea she owned a skirt that short, or top that tight and low-cut. My insides heated. I wanted everyone else in the place to just disappear so I could lay her out on top of the bar and feast upon her.

But Gamble called out her name and crooked his finger beckoning her to him. She turned away from me, and something inside me growled with displeasure.

I watched her skip to her brother at the other end of the bar. He crossed his arms over his chest as he spoke to her, probably giving her some kind of lecture. In return, she set her hands on her hips and said something back, something smart-mouthed and defensive would be my guess. But instead of growing pissed, Gamble merely chuckled and then reached for her to pull her half across the bar so he could hug her, which made her skirt ride higher up the back of her thighs to damn near show the entire club what color of panties she was wearing. As she smiled and hugged him back, I glanced away.

It was times like this that made it so much harder to do the shit I was doing behind his back. If only his sister had been anyone but Caroline, I was sure I never would've had a problem keeping my hands off her. But she was just so...*her*.

"Here you go." Lowe set the last of my drink requests on my tray and I picked it up, sending one last longing glance Caroline's way. She was looking my way again, sadly, as if she was beginning to realize I wasn't going to approach her. Not here.

I turned away, more miserable than ever.

When I returned to the bar, she was no longer there. I had to scan quickly before I caught sight of her near a table full of men and women, where some ugly motherfucker was looking a little too interested in her tits as he smiled and laughed at whatever she was saying.

I cracked my knuckles, wanting to slaughter him, whoever he was.

But then Hart approached their table and stole her attention away from the ugly mo-fo. Except that didn't settle my jealousy in the least.

Seriously, the fucker was openly flirting with her, right in front of Gamble. And Gamble—the douche—did nothing, didn't even twitch an eyelash. I couldn't mention Caroline's name around him without him nearly busting my balls and warning me away from her, but Hart could damn near stick his hand up her short little skirt in front of him and he completely ignored it?

It was no fucking fair.

I stewed and ground my teeth as I took another order. I'd just delivered a round of slippery nipples to a group of rowdy drunk chicks—one of whom grabbed my ass when she slid my tip into my back pocket—when I spotted Caroline entering the hall that led back to the offices and bathrooms.

Not about to let this opportunity slip by, I hurried after her.

CHAPTER 21

TEN

THERE WERE ABOUT a dozen people blocking my way, but I dodged around them and caught Caroline's arm right before she could enter the ladies' room.

"Wha...?" She spun around to confront me, her eyes flashing wide when she saw it was me.

Changing directions, I tugged her along until we reached the door to Pick's office. I didn't even bother to turn on a light. As soon as I had her inside and the door shut, I pushed her against it and pinned her there. Then I kissed the piss out of her. Her mouth clung to mine and her fingers clutched my shirt.

We attacked each other until I had to come up for air.

"What the fuck are you doing, coming here, dressed like that?" I thundered and kissed her again, hard, not giving her a chance to answer. While I spiked my tongue into her mouth, my hands roamed her thighs until I had them up her skirt and was palming her ass cheeks through her panties. After I managed to pull my mouth away, I pressed my forehead to hers. "Or did you just want to drive me crazy because you knew I couldn't talk to you, or touch you, or kiss you after those fucking, stirring texts you sent me?"

"You used to talk to me in public before," she argued,

even as she ran her fingers through my hair and cupped my head in her hands. Then she yanked me in for another kiss.

I ground my pelvis into hers and kissed her back, only to come up for air so I could keep arguing. "Yeah. *Before*," I muttered. "When it wasn't fucking impossible to keep my hands off you. I don't know how the hell I'm ever going to survive being in the same room with you and your brother again, not without letting something slip."

Caroline laughed. "You mean something like this." When her hand wandered toward my throbbing erection, I snagged her wrist.

"Oh, no you don't. You don't get to play with the magic stick after the way you just totally flirted with Hart."

"*What*?" Her incredulous exclamation came a second before she shoved me in the chest. "I was not."

"Really? And here, I could've sworn he told you how good you looked tonight, how you put every other woman in the place to shame, and in return, you smiled up at him and batted those goddamn beautiful lashes *his* way."

"Oh. That." She cleared her throat discreetly. "Well, I wouldn't exactly call that flirting. It was more like—"

"Flirting," I deadpanned. "He fucking *flirted* with you. And you flirted back."

"That's just how we talk. It didn't mean anything. I certainly didn't grab *his* ass the way that one girl did to you when she slid your tip into your pocket, now did I?"

I barked out a harsh laugh. "You're comparing? Really? Then you should note I didn't smile and bat my lashes at that chick after she touched me. I looked around for *you,* and I saw you going down the hall, so I followed you, and bam. Here we are. Jesus, but you make me horny when you're jealous."

I kissed her again and she was just as eager to kiss me back. She crawled up me until she'd wound her legs around my waist.

"Damn it. I want to be inside you so bad right now."

"I know." She whimpered and ground her core against my erection. "But I don't want to leave a mess in here. Do you have anything?"

I shuddered. "Yeah, but...shit, baby. I'm working. Your brother's..." Hell, I couldn't even finish listing all the reasons why this was a bad idea. I ripped her panties off and plunged a finger inside her. She immediately lit up, and

I almost went off with her while I was still tucked in my pants.

"Wait, I...fuck." I couldn't see shit in this dark-ass office.

While Caroline was still coming against my fingers, I searched the wall for a light switch. Once I found it, I flicked it on and caught the last of her orgasm as she rested the back of her head against the door and panted. Perspiration misted her brow and upper lip. She was so damn beautiful I once again almost came.

Spotting the couch across the room, I carried her to it and laid her down. Then I dug my hand into my pocket and whipped out my wallet. As I fumbled for a condom I was sure had to be inside, Caroline sat up and unzipped my pants. I groaned as she pulled me free.

She flitted her fingers over my birthmark first, as was her way, smiling softly as she touched it with a gentle kind of reverence. Then she kissed it before she licked me from base to tip and lapped up a drop of pre-cum at the end.

I wondered why this didn't feel strange. I'd spent years freaked out about my spotted dick and had gone to great pains to keep it hidden from everyone. But a month with Caroline and I had no qualms whatsoever about whipping it out in front of her. She actually made me feel more special because of it.

Her mouth covered me completely before her face bobbed forward and she took most of me down her throat.

Goddamn. That felt good.

I grabbed a handful of her hair. When she moaned, I tightened my grip. "Shit. You're really good at that." She sucked a little harder and pulled me deeper into the hot, cavity of her mouth a little deeper. "Damn. How do you make me ready to come so easily?"

Caroline popped her lips free and grinned up at me. I wanted to sob from the loss of her mouth, but yeah...I was a little too dazed by that smile. "Just call me Caroline Gamble, renowned cock whisperer."

I laughed. "You got that right. My cock definitely knows how to obey your every command."

Her amazing smile only grew. "And what would your cock do if I gave this command?" Letting go of my hips, she lay back onto her spine and spread her legs open until her little skirt fell up to her waist to remind me I'd taken off her panties already. When she touched herself, separating her pussy lips to show me how wet she was, I shook so hard I almost couldn't tear open my condom package fast enough.

"Fuck, woman. You're going to kill me."

"And here I was only aiming to please you."

I paused between her legs and glanced up into her eyes. When she smiled again, I felt sucker punched hard in the chest. "You please me," I said, meaning it more than I'd ever meant anything I'd said in my life. "You please me so fucking much."

I grabbed a handful of her hair at the base of her neck and kept her head captive so she was forced to look into my eyes. As her gaze widened with a knowing kind of shock, I pushed inside her. She pulled in a surprised gasp.

I thrust slow and steady, making sure she felt every fucking centimeter of how much she satisfied me.

"No one's ever pleased me the way you please me. Every time with you is better than the last. I can't even...God, Caroline. You own me."

"Oren." She sobbed my name and threw her head back. When her inner muscles began to milk me, I ground my teeth.

"Damn it. Not yet."

"I can't...help it. Can't stop." She tried to restrain her orgasm, but it took her anyway, and I was unable to hold back either. Kissing her hard and running my hands over her face and hair, I emptied myself inside her.

We clung to each other, riding the chaos until the room settled again. Then I panted out a breath and slumped on top of her, burying my face in her neck, right where she smelled the best.

I have no clue how long we stayed like that. I was nearly unconscious and probably growing heavy on her, though, when she nudged my shoulder and giggled under me. "Oren. Baby, don't fall asleep on me."

"Why not?" I slurred, burrowing into her a little more and making her giggle again.

"You're working, remember?"

I lifted my head from her shoulder to look around Pick's office. "Fuck." I'd completely forgotten where we were. And I'd never locked the door, either.

I jumped up off her, giving myself a head rush in my hurry. Then I tossed the condom and tucked myself back into my pants. As I was zipping up, I turned to Caroline in time to watch her fetch her panties off the floor. There was no way she'd be able to slip the shredded cloth back on, and I couldn't help it; I grinned smugly.

She scowled at me and waved them in my face. "Thanks a lot, asshole. You ruined them. What the hell am I supposed to do now?"

I snatched them from her, glad to have the memento, and stuffed them into my pocket. "Looks like someone's going commando for the rest of the night. Just make sure you don't flirt with Hart again while you're not wearing panties, or I'm really going to lose my shit and go all caveman on you. I'll probably toss you over my shoulder and drag you back to my lair, chain you to my bed and spank you daily."

She grinned and cupped my face in her hands. "I love it when you get jealous."

I snorted because I didn't love it at all. I pretty much hated it. Jealousy was only hot when *she* wanted to cut a bitch for touching me, not the other way around. "You don't know how douchebag Hart fucked with me earlier tonight, so I have a good reason to be pissed at him."

Her brow puckered in confusion. "*Asher* fucked with you? How?"

Feeling like a petulant child who was tattling on a bully, I rested my face on her shoulder and slipped my hand around her waist, only to let my palm wander down until I had it under her skirt and smoothing across her bare bottom. "He figured us out when you enlisted him to help break into my phone. So to give me a hard time tonight, he tried to start a contest with me to see who could get the most chicks' phone numbers by the end of the night, knowing I couldn't say no in front of your brother."

When she tensed against me, I caught her elbow to keep her from going anywhere. "Don't worry. I didn't get a single number. I didn't even try. The fucker just pissed me off for making the challenge in the first place."

When I looked up, I saw relief on Caroline's face. Beaming at me, she murmured, "My poor Oren. It's tough being a reformed man-whore, isn't it?"

"Yes." I puckered out my bottom lip to make her laugh.

Actually, the reformed part wasn't so tough at all; it was pretending to my best friend that I still was one that sucked ass.

"So you promise not to flirt with him ever again, right?" I pressed.

"Hmm?" She seemed too distracted with kissing her way across my jaw to answer. I scowled and snapped my fingers in front of her face.

"Focus, Caroline. Hart. The flirting. You're done with that. Right?"

She blinked and looked up at me with raised eyebrows. "Wow. You're *really* jealous of him."

"I'm not jealous," I muttered. But she seemed so happy about the idea that I let out a long, drawn-out sigh. "It's just that you seem so...fucking close to him."

She shrugged. "Well...I am. I guess. I mean, we're friends."

"Friends," I repeated in a dry tone as I lifted my eyebrows to stare right back at her.

The damn woman *laughed* at my irritation. "Well, you're awfully close to Zoey," she reminded me.

"And you know exactly why," I bit out, loathing this conversation the more it played out.

With a nod, she smiled. "I do. You think of her as a sister. Well...the same holds true for me and Asher, I guess."

I couldn't stop a snort of disbelief from blurting out. "You think of him as a *brother*?" When she nodded, I cocked her a look, totally not buying it. "So you don't find him attractive at all."

"Oh God, yes. Asher's freaking gorgeous."

"*Gorgeous*?" I wasn't expecting her to use *quite* that strong of a word. "That pencil-thin stick of a musician?"

Her fingers trailed up my jawline, distracting me. "Mmm. He has a very arresting face."

I lowered my nose and rubbed it along hers. "But you like my face better."

It was a question even though I worded it as a statement. Caroline's grin spread. "What do you think? It was *your* room I snuck into so I could be with you, not his."

Hearing her say that made me feel better. But I caught her hand to keep it from distracting me. "I think I'm fucking confused. He's the one with the gorgeous body, the *arresting* face, the perfect voice and awesome attitude. I'm an asshole. So, why *was* it my room you chose?"

Her hand broke free of my grip to slide into my hair, and the other followed until she'd caged my face in her palms.

"Because you're the one I want."

I loved hearing that. God, how I loved hearing that. But as she leaned up to kiss me, I caught her again, stopping her.

"But why?" She could do so much better than a fucked-up jackwad like me. "Why *me*?"

She paused when she realized I was serious. Her gaze softened and her lips tipped up into the most beautiful smile. "Do you remember the day we met?"

It was seared into my brain forever, so I nodded. "Yeah."

"You went out and bought us all breakfast," she started.

I'd been starving. As soon as I'd gotten off work the night before that, Gamble had gotten his distress call from home. He'd needed to borrow my truck, since he didn't have any wheels at the time. I'd been worried about him, so I'd gone along for the ride. We drove all night to get to her and Colton and Brandt. I'd needed food before I passed out, and no way was I going to eat something from that nasty place, so I'd taken the two young brothers over to a nearby McDonalds and gotten everyone breakfast while Noel had taken care of Caroline, because her abortion had left her so sick.

Caroline drew in a breath. "While the boys and I ate on the couch, you and Noel went outside to talk, but the window was open, so I heard almost everything you said."

I winced, trying to remember that conversation with Gam. "What'd I say?"

She smiled fondly. "Well, first you cracked some kind of joke about karma-sutra, or something like that."

I chuckled softly. "Okay, yeah. I remember something like that."

"And then you started teasing him about how...how hot you thought I was."

Groaning, I tipped my head back and closed my eyes. "Oh, damn. I did, didn't I? Sorry about that."

"No, I liked it. I liked how you could tease him, how you were trying to get him out of his funk after the shock he'd just come home to." Her smile smoothed out into an expression of supreme appreciation. "But then you got serious with him and made him talk out his problems. When he told you he wanted to just bring us all back home with him, you encouraged it. It didn't matter that doing so meant three more people would suddenly be living in the apartment you shared with him and you'd mostly likely have to find somewhere else to live. You didn't even pause to think it through. You just...supported him, and I don't know if he would've gone through with what he did for us if you hadn't been there to tell him he should. I just..." She shook her head, gazing at me as if I was something special. It made my chest feel all tight and strange. "I remember thinking I wished I had a friend like Oren Tenning."

Unease flooded me. Yeah, I was some friend. I lied to Gamble's face every time I saw him these days.

Caroline seemed to think I was honorable, though. She beamed up at me. "Every time you were around after that, the room just got...brighter. You were always this upbeat ray of optimism. Even when you were trying to be polite to me at the beginning, you'd have something funny to say, something a little off color, a little naughty, but always, *always* entertaining. I craved the times you'd come around. I swear, you got me out of my depression more than anyone. Laughter is a lot more healing than you'd think."

A strange memory caught me off guard at her words. Caroline saw the change in my face, and tipped her head to the side. "What?"

I started to wave her off and tell her it was nothing, but then, I don't know...I stopped myself. "You know that game you play as a kid where you make funny faces at someone to see who'll laugh first?"

She grinned. "Yeah. Noel and I used to play it, and then Brandt and I did after he left."

I nodded. "I was just remembering...what you said reminded me for some strange reason..."

"Of what?" she prodded.

I shook my head, but then I went and confessed, "Zoey and I used to do that too, except we used words. You know, whoever said the funniest thing to make the other person laugh first, won."

It seemed to take her a moment to realize which Zoey I was talking about. Then her lips parted and eyes flared. "Let me guess. You won every time."

I gave a quiet laugh. "No, actually she did. My sister was so fucking hilarious. She always knew how to do or say just the right thing to make me smile whenever I was upset. I just...I guess I felt honored to hear I'd done that for you. Like some part of her is still here, living through me."

"Oren?" Caroline murmured softly. She touched my face and I looked at her.

"I gotta get back to work," I said.

She nodded but whispered, "Thank you for telling me that."

I cleared my throat and tipped my face down to hers. "Yeah, well...thanks for telling me why I'm so much better than Hart." When I winked, she groaned and rolled her eyes. I pressed my mouth to hers just as the office door swung open.

We leapt apart, but it was too late. We were already exposed. Expecting to find Gamble hovering in the doorway, I blinked when I saw Pick instead.

"What the fuck are *you* doing here?" I blurted out.

He glanced from me to Caroline and then back to me. "It's *my* office," he finally said, his voice mild, but his eyes narrowing with displeasure.

"But it's midnight," I argued without meaning to. "Shouldn't you be tucked in bed with your little family right now?"

"Hmm." Pick glanced between us again. Caroline grew more uncomfortable, crossing her arms over her chest and kicking at the toe of her pumps. I shifted slightly to block his view of her.

"Yes, I really *should* be in bed, wrapped around my gorgeous woman right now, but some unfinished paperwork I left here was making me toss and turn, so Tink kicked me out and told me not to come back until I'd taken care of it."

"Oh." Well, that explained that. I blew out a breath, glanced at Caroline, and turned back to Pick as I clapped my hands. "I guess we'll get out of your hair and let you get to it, then."

I stepped aside and motioned Caroline toward the door. She lurched into action, only to pause when she reached Pick still standing in the doorway.

He sent her a warm smile and stepped aside. "Caroline. You look lovely this evening."

She bowed her head and mumbled, "Thank you."

Patting her arm as she passed, he said, "Have a good night."

I started to follow her, but my fucking boss stepped into my way, blocking the exit. Then he moved toward me, forcing me to back pedal. Once he was fully in the room, he shut the door behind him and glared into my face.

"Are you out of your fucking mind?" he growled.

I merely stared back, my eyes daring him to do whatever he was going to do: run to Gamble and tell him everything, beat my ass, lecture me, whatever. I was ready.

"You stupid fucker. I knew you wouldn't be able to stay away from her forever, but Jesus, Noel is just down the hall. And this is my office, man. My *office*. You probably did it on the couch too, didn't you? That was Tink's and my special couch. You've ruined our special couch."

"It is pretty damn comfy," I had to admit.

Pick growled and gave me a little shove, offsetting my balance until I stumbled a step back. "Don't piss me off more than I'm already pissed off. I don't appreciate coming in here and finding an employee, getting it on while he's *working* and stabbing one of my very good friends in the back in the process."

I gritted my teeth, because I absolutely refused to apologize for what had just happened, even though I knew I was totally in the wrong. I could never be sorry for any time I had with Caroline.

"Look, if you're going to fire me, just fire me already, all right?"

With a scowl, Pick muttered, "I'm not going to fire you. Jesus, just...don't ever do that in my office again...or anywhere in the club, and especially not while you're on the clock. I can't believe you and Caroline..." Shaking his head, he blew out a breath.

"Are you going to tell Gamble?" I asked.

That question made him laugh. "You think I'm insane? I'm not getting any more involved in this mess than I already am. He's going to find out eventually, and when he does, I'm going to be as far away from the both of you as geographically possible."

"Okay," I said. "Well...thank for not telling him yet." With a grateful nod, I started for the door, but Pick grabbed my shirt, stalling me.

"Just tell me she means something to you."

I shook my head. Pick was ever the lady's protector. I had to like that about the guy. But still, "Jesus, man. No. She's just a worthless lay I plan to completely blow off tomorrow." When he scowled at my sarcastic answer, I shoved at his arm to dislodge his hand from my clothes. "What the hell do you *think*? I'm risking the wrath of Noel Gamble to be with her. She means fucking *everything* to me." When Pick's mouth quirked with appreciation, I sighed. "Now, can I get back to work, *boss*?"

"One more thing," he murmured. "Can you at least wait until after Skylar's birthday party this weekend to tell him?"

I blinked, totally not expecting to hear that request. "Huh?"

"My little girl's first birthday," he reminded me. "Tink and I invited you all to come for a cookout."

"Right," I said. "So what?"

"So I thought one more time seeing the entire gang together before you break us up, and we're forced to pick sides, might be nice. Plus, I don't want you fucking up her birthday with all your drama. Tinker Bell's gone to a lot to plan this."

With a roll of my eyes, I snickered. "Yeah, sure. For Milk Tits, I'll refrain from telling my best friend I'm boinking his sister. Got it."

"Jesus, you are so freaking vulgar. I have no idea what poor Caroline sees in you."

Caroline saw past the vulgar, I wanted to tell him, but I didn't bother, because he was too busy adding, "And stop calling Tink Milk Tits already. Damn."

I left his office, laughing. No way could anyone keep me from calling Eva Mercer Milk Tits, but that had been a nice attempt. I was still in a good mood when I strolled back into the bar and got to work. I spotted Caroline minutes later, closer to Blondie. When she sent me a worried glance, I winked and showed her a thumbs-up, which made her shoulders slump with relief.

We still had time before Gamble found out the truth, and all the shit drama hit the fan.

CHAPTER 22

TEN

I HAD NO IDEA what to buy a one-year-old, but I walked into Pick's backyard that Saturday afternoon with what looked like a puppy's chew toy. Milk Tits had cursed me out a few months earlier when she and Pick had thrown a birthday party for their boy. She'd sent me out to get him something and ordered me not to return until I'd gotten the rug rat a gift. So, this time around, I came prepared.

Milk Tits cheered her appreciation as soon as she saw me carrying the stupid pink gift bag.

"I can't believe it," she gasped, coming to me and thankfully relieving me of my gift. "Ten-Ten *can* be taught manners."

"Yeah, it's a fucking miracle." I scowled at her as I tugged at the collar of my shirt. "Where's the beer?"

Instead of pointing me in the right direction, Milk Tits folded her arms over her chest and arched an eyebrow. "Before you drink anything, you and I are going to have us a little chat."

Shit, that didn't sound good. Pick must've told her about me and Caroline. "I'm guessing you're not going to tell me you want to name your next kid after me."

She snorted. "No. My next kid is already named, but

thanks. What I want to know is what you think went through my head the moment I walked into Pick's office the other day and found a used condom sitting in the top of his trash can."

My eyes flared wide. "Oh, shit. I am so sorry." I totally hadn't even thought of that scenario. But then I frowned. "Wait, you didn't really think he'd cheated on you, did you?" She and Pick were about as attached as Gamble and his woman, Hamilton and Blondie, Lowe and Buttercup. Those couples just didn't cheat.

Milk Tits scowled even harder. "For a half of a split second, there was a moment when I felt a smidgen of unease." She shuddered. "It was the worst half a split second of my life. So, thank you very much, you asshat, for making me experience it." She shoved me in the shoulder and stormed off to talk to Lowe and Buttercup, who were turning burgers on the grill. Hamilton and Blondie were also around, playing with Pick and Eva's two toddlers. And Hart was over by the coolers of beer.

I started his way, needing a drink bad. When he saw me coming, he grinned.

"Hey, Ten. Check this out. I've been practicing."

He flipped an empty alcohol bottle into the air and caught it behind his back. Once he had it in hand, he brought it around to the front and pretended to pour it into an invisible cup. With a grin, he glanced up to gauge my reaction. "Think that'll get me more tips if I do it at work?"

It was actually a kick-ass move. But I scowled as if unimpressed. "You just always gotta work to be better than me, don't you?"

He laughed. "Work at it? Not really. It just comes naturally to be better than you."

"Whatever."

I started to turn away, but he called after me. "Not a fan of *Cocktail*, huh?"

Pausing, I glanced back. "Cock-what?"

"*Cocktail*. The eighties movie. Tom Cruise. Elisabeth Shue."

I shook my head. "Never seen it."

"What about *Coyote Ugly* then?" He proceeded to flip the bottle over his hand and catch it again.

Damn show-off. I shook my head. "*Coyote Ugly*?" I echoed stupidly. "Is that another movie or something?"

Okay, I'd actually watched that one because it had advertised hot chicks, but I wasn't about to let him know that.

Hart sighed and shook his head. "Man, you're hopeless. Ooh, Caroline." Glancing past me, he grinned. "Check it. I taught myself."

I tensed, surprised to learn she'd come up behind me and I hadn't even sensed her. As I turned to glance at her, she watched Hart do both his *Cocktail* and *Coyote Ugly* tricks.

"Oh, cool." Her smile for him made me grind my teeth. "That's from *Cocktail*, isn't it?"

"Yes. *Thank you.*" Hart arched me a look, but I rolled my eyes.

"That's not fair. She's a fucking movie geek with a *filmmaking* major."

Her mouth fell open "Did you just call me a geek?"

I grinned and shifted a little closer to her. "A hot geek."

Her face lit with pleasure before her eyebrows wrinkled. Realizing just how close I'd gotten to her, she gasped and widened her eyes before darting a quick, cautious glance toward Hart. "Oren," she warned under her breath.

"What? He already knows. In fact," I glanced at everyone already at the party, "I'm sure everyone here knows. Pick clued in Milk Tits, who probably told Buttercup, who would've told Lowe. And Zwinn's been in on it from the beginning. I think Gam is literally the only person who doesn't know, and he just called saying he was running late, which means...." I caught her by surprise and grabbed her around the waist. "I can totally do this."

Yanking her toward me, I tucked her spine against my front and buried my face into the side of her throat where I proceeded to nibble on tender flesh. She yelped out her surprise and clutched the arm I had wrapped around her.

"And this." My hand strayed up as if I was going to cup her breasts right through her shirt.

"Oren!" Scandalized but still laughing, she grabbed my wrist, stopping me. "Cut it out." She spun out of my arms to face off with me. "You're playing with fire." Then she went and jabbed her finger into my gut.

I laughed and dodged away when she came at me again. "Woman," I warned. "Don't poke me."

With a playful laugh, she charged. "Don't be such a baby.

I like it when you poke *me*."

As I caught her and imprisoned her arms, I threw my head back and roared with laughter.

Hart covered his face with one hand and groaned. "Jesus. She's got as dirty a mind as you do, Ten."

"I know." Pressing my cheek to hers, I grinned proudly and swayed back and forth with her. "Isn't it great?"

"Yo, Ten," Lowe called from across the yard. "Noel's walking up the front driveway."

I lifted my face and frowned at him. "What? But he just texted, saying he was running late."

"Well, he's on time now, I guess."

I growled out my frustration. "Shit." With a last, quick kiss to Caroline's cheek, I murmured into her ear, "Lick you later, baby."

My arm slid from around her, and I moved away. A little ache spread in my chest as I did, but I made sure to act cool about it. I meandered toward Ham where he and Blondie were playing with the two toddlers.

"How's the babysitting going?" I asked, watching the Gambles from the corner of my eye as they entered the backyard. Gam and his wife carried plates of food toward Pick where he was setting shit set up, and the younger brothers went to Caroline where I'd left her talking to Hart.

I didn't want to resent my oldest friend for showing up sooner than he said he would, but shit, if I wasn't annoyed out of my mind because he'd shown so fucking early. But I'd promised Pick I wouldn't cause any drama at his kid's party, so I stayed away.

"Hey," Ham said, thrusting one of the kids at me. "Hold Skylar for me, will you? I'm going to help Mason set up the horseshoes."

My eyes went wide, but I caught the kid so it wouldn't fall. Holding it at arm's length from me, I called after him. "*Hey*! Hey, what am I supposed to do with this thing?" He just chuckled and kept walking. When I saw Blondie snickering at me, I turned to her, still holding the baby as far away from me as possible.

"Blondie," I hissed. "Stop laughing and just tell me what to do?"

"I don't know. Maybe you should, you know, sit down with her on your lap."

"Her? So this one's the girl?"

"The pink dress didn't clue you in, huh?"

"Shut it," I muttered. I couldn't think straight with the responsibility of a goddamn kid on my hands.

Blondie laughed at my distress. But her too-kind heart had her patting my shoulder soon after. "Just breathe. You'll do fine. And seriously, you should sit. You look like you might pass out otherwise."

I sat as I was instructed and gulped heavily when the chubby-cheeked little thing with dark, wispy curls gazed up at me with the most serious big blue eyes.

"This is the birthday girl," Blondie introduced. "Her name is Skylar."

"Right." I looked up at her for guidance. "So...now what?"

She shook her head. "I don't know. Try talking to her."

I growled out my frustration and glanced across the yard, checking on Caroline to make sure she didn't see me kidding it up and think I wanted one or something now that she knew she couldn't have any. But she was busy talking with Aspen and Hart. I turned back to the kid.

The little thing *was* kind of cute with that ever-serious expression.

"Hey," I said, not sure what the fuck I was supposed to talk about with a one-year-old. "Uh...happy birthday."

Skylar reared her head back at my voice as if surprised that I'd finally decided to talk to her. Then her lips twitched, and she smiled. At me. Something shifted in my chest and fuck, who knew one little baby smile was so damn powerful? I think I fell I love.

"Blondie. Hey, I think she likes me."

"Of course she does." Blondie grinned up at me. "You're a likable guy."

"Yeah." I nodded. "Fuck, yeah, I am. Chicks dig me." This caused another smile to spread across Skylar's face, and yep, I'd probably die for her. She had caught me, hook, line and sinker.

Blondie stayed nearby, holding on to the boy's hands as he toddled across the grass. "Can you do that?" I asked the girl. "Walk like your brother?" They weren't blood related, but they were being raised together, and since they were so close in age, they'd be raised pretty much the same way my sister and I had been. Like twins.

Skylar sent me a secretive smile at my question. I smiled

back. "Yeah, I bet you can do anything he can." My sister had been competitive enough to make sure she always kept up with me, even though I'd been taller, faster, and stronger. She had still kicked my ass in more competitions than I ever wanted to admit.

"Hey, Blondie," I started in again, needing to share this cool-ass moment with someone.

But the very second I turned her way, she decided to gather up the boy and stand. Problem was, she'd been kneeling close enough to me that her pointy bent elbow whacked me right in the eye as we collided into each other.

"Motherfucker," I howled, momentarily seeing stars as my eye exploded with pain.

"Oh my God," she shrieked. "Oh, Ten, I'm so sorry. Are you okay?"

"No." I saw nothing but a blinding white light as the bundle in my hands squirmed and started to cry. "Is she okay?" I asked. "Fuck, I can't see shit. The kid's okay, right?"

"She's fine." Pick's voice came from my left. "I've got her." The screeching baby was tugged from my arms and she instantly calmed down.

No longer needing to worry about the girl, I doubled over and clutched my throbbing eye. "God...damn."

"Ten, are you okay?" Buttercup asked as she touched my arm.

"Never better," I muttered.

She laughed but then quietly said, "Then give a thumbs-up or something, because Caroline looks worried enough to race over here and check on you."

I immediately lifted my arm, my thumb in the air. "I'm good," I called. "It'd been too long since I had a black eye. Thought I'd get caught up again."

Someone started clapping. "Way to go, Zoey. You can now officially join the Gave-Ten-a-Black-Eye club with Quinn, Pick and me."

"Shut up, fucker," I yelled back to Gamble as Buttercup and Blondie grasped my arms and guided me toward the house. "I bet Blondie's bruise will spread a lot bigger and darker than the little dink *you* gave me."

After the girls fashioned a baggie of ice for me, I returned to the party and found myself talking to Pick and Mason because they seemed to be located the farthest away from Caroline. It was as if everyone was trying to keep me away from her. I didn't like that. So I didn't listen to much of anything the bastards said, too busy keeping track of everything she did across the yard.

This was miserable, and it got even worse when Lowe grinned and clasped me on the shoulder as he spoke to Pick. "Just look at that puppy-dog expression on his face while he watches her."

Pick grinned rather smugly. "Ten, man. You've got it bad."

"Shut it," I muttered and just kept staring as I drank my beer.

The rest of the party seemed to drag by. But seriously, one year olds took freaking *forever* to open their damn gifts. They actually wanted to play with their toys as soon as they opened them without the slightest urge to move along and see what else they'd gotten. Seriously, what was up with that?

I was leaning against a fence post, trying to encourage her brother to toddle over there and help her rip apart wrapping paper when from the corner of my eye—where my Caroline radar was blaring strong—she grabbed her stomach and pitched forward, doubling over. My full attention immediately zoomed to her, and I pushed away from the wall. Her gaze met mine, her eyes wide with shock and pain.

"You okay?" I mouthed the question.

She nodded, but she was getting paler, and sweat was slipping down the side of her face. She wasn't fucking okay at all. Suddenly, she dashed to a nearby bush and heaved over it, upchucking all her lunch.

"Shit!" I leapt forward, but Ham grabbed my arm, stopping me.

Glaring up at him, I tried to pull free. "Don't fuck with me, man."

He shifted closer. "Noel's here. He'll take care of her."

My breathing escalated. I wanted to shrug him off and go to Caroline anyway. Pick, and Hart, and Gamble's wife were crowding around her, as were all three of her brothers. What would be wrong if I went over there too? She was *my* woman, damn it.

"This would be the worst time ever to expose your relationship," Ham murmured.

So I paced on the other side of him, feeling like a caged animal, as I watched from too fucking far away, while Caroline continued to empty her stomach.

"What the fuck is wrong with her?" I muttered, starting to panic. She'd been fine only *minutes* ago.

Ham shook his head. "I don't know. I don't think—" He broke off when Buttercup slapped a hand over her mouth and darted inside Pick and Eva's place right before Lowe followed her, cradling his stomach.

"What the hell?" A second later, Brandt started puking on the lawn too.

"Food poisoning?" Blondie guessed just as Gamble's wife lifted her arms and called, "What did everyone eat?"

CHAPTER 23

Ten

I GUESS IT WAS a good thing I didn't like shrimp. It saved me from a severe case of diarrhea and vomiting. But it didn't keep me from worrying my ass off.

After the worst of the food poisoning passed from Caroline and her brother, Gam scooped her into his arms and carried her away. When his wife went to help Brandt stand, Quinn started forward. "Here, I'll help." But I grabbed his arm.

"Stay back, fucker." Shoving past him, I jogged to Brandt and Aspen. "I've got him," I said.

The kid looked drained and limp. I sent him a sorry-I'm-only-doing-this-to-get-close-to-Caroline grimace and picked him up. He groaned once but wrapped an arm around my neck to steady himself. "Thanks," he finally managed to rasp as he leaned heavily against me.

"No problem." I grunted from the strain. He was probably heavier than Caroline, but I didn't care. Doing this was going to get me close to her. When Gam backed out of the backseat of the car where he'd placed her, all my efforts became worth it.

Gamble blinked at me in surprise, but said, "Thanks for getting him," as I helped Brandt into the backseat next to his sister. Once I had him settled, I leaned into him and then right past him, making him protest as I pressed against him maybe a bit too hard. "Hey!"

But I didn't stop until I had my mouth on Caroline's temple. "Get better," I murmured, meeting her blurry-eyed gaze as I pulled away.

She sent me a weak smile, so I backed out of the car and straightened. Gam—who hadn't seen a thing—patted me thankfully on the shoulder, and I waved him and his family off as they left for home.

The party was pretty much over at that point. I drove back to my apartment behind Zoey and Quinn, who also hadn't eaten the shrimp. But I still couldn't settle my nerves. Finally, I left and drove to the spot down the street from Gam's house where I always picked up Caroline for our midnight rendezvous. I sat in my truck, watching his place until it started to get dark. And then I sat a while longer.

Was she still sick? Getting enough fluids? Resting? Damn it, I couldn't take this shit. I needed to see her. It was late enough that some members of the house might be in bed, so I climbed out of my truck and moseyed my way to Gamble's backyard. I paused in front of a window I was pretty sure was her room and began to tap on it. Just a light tap so as not to alert anyone else to my presence, but I didn't let up until a blind lifted and a pale Caroline peered out.

Her eyes widened. I waved, sent her a sheepish grin, and jammed my hands into my pockets as I waited for her to unlock the window and slide it up.

"Oren! What the heck are you doing here?"

"I'm checking on you, what's it look like?"

She shook her head, confused. "Have you heard of a cell phone?"

"Sure. I even have one. But I wanted to *see* you. Think you can get this screen out? I'm coming up."

"*What*?" She glanced behind and came back around with wide eyes. "Are you insane?"

"Yes. Now let me in. Please."

She sighed as if deliberating her choices. But finally, she shook her head and eased the screen away from the window. Once she had it popped free, I started my ascent. It wasn't easy, but I was a determined motherfucker. Some scrapes and bumps and a handful of newly invented curse phrases later, and I was in.

Sighing my relief, I pulled her in for a gentle hug. "How're you feeling?"

"Better," she admitted, resting her head on my shoulder. "My stomach's still not right, but I don't think I'm going to throw up anymore."

"Good." My hand went to her forehead because she felt so warm against me. "You feel hot. Are you running a fever?"

"A small one. But Aspen's already set me up for the night." She motioned toward her nightstand where she had water, aspirin, a thermometer, washcloth, tissues and such. Then she turned back to me. "I can't believe you just crawled into my window to check on me."

"Why wouldn't I? You're sick. I can't exactly make you come to my place to take care of you."

After I took her arm and steered her back to the bed where she'd pushed her covers aside to answer my window call, I helped her back down onto the mattress.

She must've still felt pretty crappy because she let me pamper her without a fight. As soon as her head hit the pillow, she sighed in thanksgiving. Then her lashes fluttered as she studied me. "You don't have to worry about me. I'll be fine."

"Too late. Already worried, already here. You're just going to have to deal with me." I went to work, fitting the window screen back in place and then closing and locking it. Then I kicked off my shoes and pulled my shirt over my head. As I shimmied out of my pants so I was in nothing but boxer shorts, Caroline simply blinked at me.

"If you think I can perform right now, you're sadly delusional."

"Funny," I murmured and lifted up one side of her sheets so I could crawl into the bed behind her and spoon up against her. "Didn't I already tell you I can survive one night without sex?"

Her voice was throaty and tired. "Yeah, but...wouldn't this constitute as a second night?"

"Nope, because you ended up giving it to me that night, too. So I'm claiming this as my one and only abstinent night."

"Thanks," she mumbled, burrowing back against me. "I

appreciate it, because I don't even want to move."

I kissed her shoulder. "Good, because you don't have to. I'm here to take care of you."

When I started to lightly knead her shoulders, she groaned. "Oh God. That feels good. I swear every muscle in my body is sore."

"Poor thing," I cooed and kissed her hair. "I'll massage it all away." And I damn near did too—I kept rubbing long after she'd gone to sleep on me. Then I just buried my nose in her hair and held her.

I fell asleep holding her and was still holding her when tremors began to wrack her body.

"Care?" I murmured, half out of it as I blinked myself awake. "Caroline? Shit, what's wrong?"

"So...cold." Her teeth chattered and shoulders shook.

"Yeah, well you're burning up." I sat up so I could reach across her and snag her pain reliever. "When's the last time you took this?" I calculated the hours after she told me, and it wasn't quite time to give her another dosage, but I said, "Fuck it," and sprinkled two tablets into my palm.

I helped her sit up, and she had to lean against me to swallow and drink some water. When I made her take another gulp of water, she frowned but obeyed. Her cheeks were flushed with fever, and that worried me.

"What can I get you?" I asked as she lay back down and closed her eyes.

"Blankets," she mumbled.

So I scoured her room for every extra blanket and, hell, a couple sweaters I could find. After I piled them on top of her, I burrowed back in with her. It was hot as fuck under the covers and right up against her. But she appreciated my heat, so I held her close and let her take all the warmth I could give her.

After sweating my balls off and listening to her breathing even out, I threw off half the blankets covering me and hung a leg out one side as I gasped for cooler air. Then I set a hand on her back and listened to her breathe, hoping she didn't take a turn for the worse. I fell asleep with one leg hanging off the side of the mattress and one hand on her back.

The next time I woke, I was soaking wet. Caroline's fever must've broken because she was sweating all over me. I sat up and removed most of the covers. Then I found a towel and dabbed her dry as best I could without waking her.

I was just sponging up her damp forehead when I heard something across the room. My gaze shot up to find a frozen, wide-eyed Aspen halted in the open doorway.

"Sorry," she whispered, holding up her hands as if surrendering. "I was just checking in on her and Brandt. How's she doing?"

There was no reason to try to think up any excuses for why I was there. I was already caught, red-fucking-handed. But Gamble's women wasn't screaming her head off, so I kept it casual and just answered her concerned question. "I think her fever just broke. She's sweating like a whore in church."

She smiled and nodded. "Good. That probably means it's out of her system. It looks like you have everything handled, so I'll leave you to it. Good night." She eased out of the room, closing the door behind her.

I sat there a second, waiting for her to wake her husband, so he could storm in and kick my ass, but thirty seconds passed and nothing happen. Then a minute went by.

Gam's wife wasn't going to rat me out.

Relief swamped me, but then so did sadness. Even his own wife knew better than to tell him about us. Everyone must know he would not take the news well.

I sighed and lay back down beside Caroline. I probably should've gone home then, but I was tired as fuck after being up and down so much throughout the night. Another couple hours with her wouldn't kill me. Besides, I didn't want to leave.

More hours passed. A gray dawn filtered into the room as I came to. The feeling of being watched nagged at my conscience, so I opened my eyes and nearly shit my pants to find myself eyeball to eyeball with Colton.

"Motherfucker," I hissed, springing upright. "Shit, don't do that to people. It's creepy as hell."

He merely cocked his head to the side. "What're you doing in Caroline's room?"

"Well, I *was* sleeping," I muttered irritably. "What're *you* doing in here?"

"I had a bad dream. I always sleep with Caroline when I have a bad dream."

"She's sick, man. Can't you pick on someone else, go

creep them out this time, instead of her?"

The stubborn little fucker shook his head. "No. I need Caroline."

I grumbled a few seconds before lifting my side of the sheet and sighing. "Then crawl in over here. Just don't bother her; she needs her rest."

He didn't move when I motioned him over. He shook his head and pointed to a different spot on the mattress. "I want to sleep in the middle."

"Jesus Christ, kid. This isn't a slumber party. You're lucky I'm letting you in at all."

"And you're lucky I'm not telling Noel you're in here right now."

I narrowed my eyes at him in the most intimidating glare I could muster. He narrowed his eyes right back.

I cracked. "Damn it. Get in the middle, you little shit. But crawl in on this side, and don't wake your sister."

Grinning, he skipped around to my side of the bed and kneed me in the gut when he climbed over me to claim his spot.

"Fuck. Watch your pointy knees, will you? Those things are deadly." When he wiggled some more to get comfortable, he accidently jabbed me again, in the spine this time, and forced me further to the edge of the bed until I was half hanging off the damn thing. "You better not be elbowing Caroline over there," I warned after the third time he caught me in the center of the back.

In answer, he rolled in toward his sister and dragged half the blankets with him, leaving me with a tiny square of coverage over my hip.

"Comfortable?" I asked, my voice loaded with sarcasm.

Colton sighed peacefully. "Mmm hmm." I rolled my eyes just as he said, "Ten?"

"What?" I muttered.

"Will you come over later on and play catch with me, because I want to play catch?"

I snorted. "Yeah, I don't think so. You just stole my spot next to Caroline."

"Well...do you want me to tell Noel about you and her?"

What the hell? "Hey. You already blackmailed me to get into this bed and sleep in the middle. You can't ask for more."

"Why not?" the spoiled little brat asked.

Shit, I didn't have an answer for that. "Why you greedy little—"

Colton pulled in a breath as if he was going to shout for Gamble right then. I growled and slapped my hand over his mouth. "Fine. I'll come over later and play ball with you. Whatever."

His grin was instant. "Thank you," he said, all sweet like, as soon as I removed my palm from his mouth.

"Good," Caroline said, her back still to us and her voice filled with sleep. "Now can we all get back to sleep? Please?"

Shit, we'd woken her.

"Caroline," Colton cheered, good-naturedly. "You're awake."

She sounded worn to the bone when she answered. "It was a little hard to sleep through you two bickering."

I reached across Colton, making sure I caught my armpit right in his face, so I could rub her arm. "How're you feeling?"

"Much better, aside from the fact my bed's turned into Grand Central Station. Seriously, how are we all fitting on my full-sized mattress?"

"No idea," I said. "But I'll get out so you can have room. I should probably get going anyway."

As I slipped off the bed, I met the kid's gaze. He smiled up at me so smugly I had to mouth the word, "*Fucker,*" at him, to which he mouthed right back, "*Asswipe.*"

Damn, I was turning him into a potty mouth. That couldn't be good.

After pulling on my clothes, I went around to Caroline's side of the bed and knelt beside her, touching her hair. Her eyes opened slowly.

"I'll call later, okay?"

When she nodded, I touched my mouth to hers gently. "Take it easy today. I'll see you when I check in for blackmailing duty with shit-breath over there."

"I have to work this evening."

I frowned. "Maybe you should take the day off to recuperate. That food poisoning kicked your ass, baby."

Her chapped lips only widened as her smile grew. "Listening to you worry about me is hot."

With a wistful sigh, I stroked her hair some more. "If only I took advantage of sick chicks."

"That bruise around your eye is sexy too."

Leaning in close until my nose touched hers, I grinned. "Then I'll keep it perpetually black and blue, just for you."

"Are you guys going to kiss goodbye already?" Colton complained. "I want to go back to sleep now."

"We already did, punk." I nudged the back of his head. "Now quit being a Peeping Tom and let me say goodbye properly."

He snorted, and Caroline and I grinned at each other. "I don't want to leave," I admitted on a whisper.

"I don't want you to either." She reached out and touched my jaw. But her eyes were growing drowsy.

"Get some sleep," I told her and kissed her hair.

Her eyes were already closed by the time I pulled back. "'Kay," she mumbled.

"Okay," I said right back as I stood. "Love you."

"You too," she slurred.

I stood there a moment, watching her and her brother curled up together and falling fast asleep against one another. I glanced at the window but knew I couldn't leave that way; no one would be able to close it behind me, so I held my breath and tiptoed to the door. I peered into the hall as I cracked it open. It was fairly dark still, so I stepped into the shadows and darted toward the opening that led to the kitchen. I half expected to find Gamble there, sitting at the table and drinking coffee, just waiting for me, but the room was empty. I escaped out the back door, and hiked to my truck.

After I made it home, I crawled into my own bed, but I couldn't sleep. Everything felt wrong without Caroline next to me. I was tossing and turning when a sudden thought struck me. "Holy shit." I bolted upright, my eyes widening.

I'd told her I loved her. It hadn't even occurred to me what I was saying when I said it. It'd just come out as natural as breathing.

I'd never told any female, besides my mother and sister, that I loved her.

I have no idea why I was so panicked by the idea. I'd known it was true for a while, but still, I didn't have to go just blurting that shit out to everyone.

Maybe she hadn't really heard me. She'd been half asleep and had mumbled back her answer as if she was talking to her brother, or something.

Wait, shit. She'd said she loved me back. I wondered if

she'd remember *that*?

God, all this thinking about it was giving me a headache.

I crawled out of bed and ran to the nearest fast food-restaurant. After buying enough to feed me and my roommates, I jogged back to my apartment. Zwinn was surprised by my generosity when they finally woke up, but they ate and hung out with me, distracting me from my swirling thoughts for a good hour. But then they went their own way, and I fidgeted around the house most of the day. I sent off a few more applications and tried to watch some television. Then I received a return call from one of the places I'd applied to electronically. But mostly I just watched the clock.

I spent a while texting my woman and flirting with her. She'd ended up taking my advice and calling in sick to work and she mentioned nothing of the l-word I'd dropped earlier, so I assumed she didn't remember. Needing to see her anyway, I showed up at her place in the early evening just after I knew they'd had their supper.

CHAPTER 24

TEN

GAMBLE'S WOMAN answered the door.

"Ten," she said in surprise. "Uh...Noel's not here this evening. He's working—"

"I know." Rolling my eyes, I muttered, "I'm here for the kid. The littlest one."

Her eyebrows shot up. "Colton?"

"Yep. That one. He wants to play..." I sighed heavily, "*catch.*"

"O...kay." Opening the door, she stepped aside. "Come on in then...I guess. I'll go get him."

I stepped inside and she disappeared from the room to find the kid. Shoving my hands into my pockets, I glanced around the front room as I waited for—

"Took you long enough to get here," a voice hissed. I spun to find Caroline in a baggy T-shirt and sweatpants hobbling toward me. She looked tired and had bags under her eyes, but she was still so beautiful; I can't even describe how it felt knowing she was going to be close enough to touch again.

My fingers actually tingled when they made contact with her cheek. "What're you doing out of bed? How do you feel?"

She leaned against me, and I gave her a warm hug. "My stomach's still giving me twinges, but I feel a million times better than last night. Your black eye looks really dark. Do *you* feel okay?"

I actually had a bit of a headache, but I said, "I'm fine. You'll never guess who called me today?"

She lifted her face. Shadows filled her eyes. "I don't know. An ex-flame?"

"*What*? No." I lowered my voice and leaned in closer. "Lake Tahoe."

Her eyes widened. "Oh, wow. You got an interview with them?"

With a nod, I blew out a breath. "I wanted to tell you in person."

Leaning up, she kissed me on the cheek. "This is so amazing. Congratulations."

I was watching her face closely, so I swear I saw a bit of fear cross her eyes. Or maybe I was just imagining it.

"Are you excited?" she asked.

I snorted. "Scared shitless is more like it." I stepped in closer to her until I could drive myself crazy with her smell. I almost told her I wouldn't go if she didn't want me to, but Colton raced into the room.

"Ten! You really came."

Straightening away from Caroline, I snapped my heels together so I could send the little shit a salute. "Reporting for blackmailing duty as requested, sir."

He giggled and then grabbed my hand to drag me from the living room, away from Caroline. I glanced back at her with a mopey goodbye wave.

She grinned and rolled her eyes, but blew me a kiss.

The football the kid found me was going flat, so we spent a good twenty minutes digging up a hand pump for it and filling it with air again. It was also covered in dust. "Well, shit. I guess you don't toss a ball around much with your big brother, do you?"

Colton ducked his face at the mention of Gam. "He's pretty busy," he mumbled.

"Oh, yeah?" I wasn't buying it. His family meant the world to Gam. I don't care how busy he was, if he knew his kid brother wanted to play catch, he would've played catch with him. "You ever *ask* him to play?"

Colton shook his head, still staring at the ground.

"Well, you should, you know. He taught me how to do this." The kid glanced up in time to watch me spin the tip of the football on the top of my index finger.

His eyes lit up. "Cool."

"I know, right?" I flipped the ball into the air and caught it with one hand behind my back. "Head over there and get ready to catch this." After he followed my instructions, I called, "You want to know how awesome Noel was at football?" I lobbed the ball his way.

He scrambled but was able to catch it against his chest. "How awesome?" he asked as he jetted it back.

I snagged the ball from the air before it slammed into my knee. "He was so awesome that he could launch a football *forty* yards while running away from a horde of linebackers bearing down on him in below zero weather with five seconds left on the clock while we were three points behind, and he'd *still* manage to win us the game."

I continued to wow him with highlights from Gam's college years on the field. He started to get better with his throwing and catching as he listened, and he even asked more questions, growing increasingly curious about this mysterious big brother of his.

Twilight was beginning to fall when someone else joined us, walking around the side of the house into the backyard and lifting a hand to wave hello.

I frowned, wondering who the hell this preppy, conceited-looking dipshit was. "Can we help you?" I asked, instantly suspicious.

When Colton turned and saw him loitering at the edge of the yard, recognition lit the dude's eyes. He stepped toward Colton. "Hey there, little guy. Do you remember me?"

Instead of answering, the kid bolted to me. I caught him by the shoulder and protectively pulled him against my side. Then I set my hand on his head to reassure him. Instantly not liking whoever this douche was upsetting him, I said, "You know he's nine, right? Not two." But seriously, who talked to a nine year old like that, giving him the baby voice and even trying to crouch down to his level? Fucker was fishy if you asked me.

The stranger sent me an irritated glance before asking, "Are you Noel?"

I snorted. "Do I look like a fucking Gamble to you?"

He shrugged. "Like I would know. None of you have the

same dad, do you?"

Yeah, I *really* did not like this nut sack. There was just something about his prissy, arrogant attitude and Abercrombie and Fitch clothes that pissed me off.

That's when the back door swung open and Brandt strolled out. "Hey, I heard you guys were playing..." His voice trailed off when he saw the visitor. "*You*," he snarled as he balled his swinging hand into a fist and stalked forward. "I owe you a black eye for the one you gave me, asswipe."

As he swung, I easily caught his arm. "Whoa, whoa, whoa," I chided mildly. "No one's punching anyone until I know what's going on. Now someone get me up to speed." I snapped my fingers. "And go."

"He's Sander Scotini," Brandt said.

My mouth opened, but no words came out. I turned to stare at the guy who'd messed up Caroline's life. I wanted to laugh. This puny little pipsqueak was Sander Scotini? And then suddenly I wanted to punch him. This puny little pipsqueak was *Sander Scotini*?

"Oh, is he?" I murmured.

When Brandt tried to move toward him again, I blocked him one more time, stepping easily in his path so I could face off with good ol' Sander myself. "Why don't you let me take care of this one?" When I met the fucker's gaze, I smiled widely and gave him a chin bob. "Hey there."

I knew my almost-flirty greeting skeeved him out. He sent me one of those untrusting scowls and edged away.

Good. I liked unsettling him.

"What brings you by, Sander?" I asked, strolling casually his way. "A little far from home, aren't you?"

He sent a nervous glance toward the house, but he must've known he wasn't getting anywhere near it until he went through me. With a sigh, he scratched the back of his neck. "I need to talk to Caroline."

I shook my head and bunched up my mouth as if I had to think about that. Then I said, "No. You really don't."

The idiot puffed up his chest—all twenty centimeters of it—and lifted that prissy combed eyebrow of his. "I came all this way to talk to her, so I'm going to talk to her. I'd like to see you try to stop me."

Oh, game on, bitch. "Gladly."

I grabbed the front of his pink—yes, *pink*—collared,

polyester shirt and flung him around until I'd slammed his back against the side of the house. Then I pinned his windpipe in place with my forearm and lifted my eyebrows in challenge. The gurgling sound that came from his throat as he floundered helplessly was music to my ears. It must've freaked Colton out, though, because he yelped in fear and raced for the back door of the house.

Brandt, on the other hand, bounced on his toes, his eyes lighting with delight before he murmured an awed-sounding, "Cool."

I leaned close to the fucker, who was obviously hard of hearing, so he could catch every word I had to say. "Now, here's what you're really going to do, *Sandy*. You're going to walk out of this yard and crawl back under whichever hole you came from, and you're never going to contact Caroline again. *Capiche*?"

Before he could choke out an answer, the back door came flying open.

Damn.

Eyewitnesses.

"What in the world—" a wide-eyed Caroline started while Aspen filled the doorway behind her.

But I cut her off by growling, "Get back inside," maybe a bit too harshly.

And yep, that was entirely the wrong way to say it. Her eyebrows lifted in outrage. Setting her hands on her hips, she stepped onto the porch. "What did you just say to me?"

"Care—" I started, but the little fucker flapped his arms, catching her attention.

"Caroline...help."

She jerked to a stop and blinked at the guy I was pinning by the throat. "Sander?"

When he opened his mouth, I shoved him roughly back into the wall. "You are not allowed to talk to her. You are not allowed to look at her."

"What the hell is going on?" she demanded.

"Who is this guy?" Sander choked out, trying to motion to me. "Is this your brother?"

"Hey!" I grabbed a fistful of hair and thunked the back of his head against the vinyl siding. "Didn't I just say no talking to her?"

Caroline sighed and folded her arms over her chest. "Oren, seriously. Let him go."

I snorted. "Right. Like that's going to happen."

She lifted her hands as if she thought my rejection of her request was ludicrous. "And why not?"

"Because I really *like* pinning him to this wall right now. Because I still can't get over the fact that this pathetic little fucker's had his ugly shriveled-up little girl dick inside you. In fact, I'm so bothered by it I just want to grab his greasy, gross hair in both hands." To demonstrate, I let go of his throat so I could grab two handfuls of Scotini's hair. "And I just want to kick him...right in the nuts."

Unable to help myself, I jerked my knee up and caught him hard between the legs. Scotini groaned and doubled over.

"*Oren!*" Caroline surged forward, her eyes wide with shock.

"Ooh," Brandt cried out in amazement before he covered his mouth with his hand and started laughing. "Awesome."

I let go of the douche and lifted my hands as I stepped away from him in an attempt to forfeit all culpability over hurting him. He fell over onto his side, holding his crotch.

Caroline stopped beside me and winced down at him. Then she slid an accusing gaze to me. "Did you really have to do that?"

I nodded. "Yeah, I *really* did. I feel better now, too. Thanks for asking." I motioned to Scotini. "You want to take a turn?"

Caroline studied him a moment, looking tempted before she nodded and stepped forward. "Okay."

I grinned, impressed, but Scotini groaned, making her stop and change her mind.

I snorted. "He's kind of fragile, isn't he?"

"He's definitely not football player material," she agreed, glancing sideways at me.

I cocked her a pleased grin. "Oh, so you go for the football player type, do you?"

"Caroline," Scotini gasped from the ground, a plea for help thick in his voice.

I sighed and grabbed his shirt before hauling him to his feet. Then I slid my arms around him and got him in a headlock from behind before turning him to face Caroline. "Okay, baby," I told her. "Have at him."

But instead of coming in for a physical jab, she cringed and took a step back. Then she shifted uncomfortably as her groaning ex tried to slump against me because he was in so much pain. I kneed him in the ass to keep him from touching me too much.

"Sander, what're you doing here?" Caroline finally asked, her voice tired.

"My parents disowned me." He paused to cough and pant through his pain.

"Really?" My woman arched her eyebrow, seemingly not very interested. "I'm so sorry to hear that." I grinned because she didn't sound sorry at all. "But why did you come all this way to tell *me* that?"

"You have...any of that...twenty thousand... left...that they gave you?"

I sputtered. "Wait, did he say twenty...holy shit." I glanced at Caroline. "Did he say twenty *thousand*? As in twenty thousand *dollars*?" When she just sent me a look, I jostled the fucker. "Hey, pretty boy, you want to knock *me* up?"

"What the fuck?" He struggled against me some more, but yeah, his attempts to escape were laughable. "What is this? *Deliverance*?"

With a grin, I murmured into his ear. "I bet you can squeal like a pig."

"Okay, first of all," Caroline broke in when Scotini just whimpered. She pointed at me and cracked a grin. "Wow. You nailed that *Deliverance* line perfectly."

I beamed, preening happily. "Why, thank you."

"And secondly..." Her smile turned into a grimace as she focused on her ex. "Sander, oh my God, did you just pee your pants?"

"What? Shit!" I leapt away from him, immediately letting go of my headlock. When I saw a wet stain spread across the front of his slacks, I shuddered in revulsion. Wiping my hands against my jeans, I felt contaminated. "Aw, sick, man. *Really*?"

Brandt seemed to think it was hilarious, though. As Scotini fell to his knees and returned to cradling his wet, injured junk, the kid pointed and hooted. "Oh my God, that is so freaking funny. I can't believe you racked him, Ten."

"Hey." I pointed at him with a serious glance. "When someone hurts your sister, you hurt him back wherever you think it'll be the most painful."

"Sander, get up," Caroline ordered, sounding very

annoyed. "I can't believe you actually thought I had any of that money left. I mean, *hello*, look around you. Do you think this house was free? Do you think my three brothers are cheap to take care of? It's been a *year*. That money is long gone."

"Not that she would've given any of it to you anyway," I felt the need to add.

"Shit," Sander hissed just as the back door reopened and Noel stepped outside.

I was so happy to see him I damn near giggled.

"Hey, honey!" I called brightly. "You're home early. And here I didn't even get to put a bow on the gift I have for you."

Scotini glanced from Noel to me and then sent Caroline a scandalized glance. "Oh my God. Your brother's *gay*?"

Really? I turned to her too, and with the same tone, I said, "Oh my God. Is he fucking *stupid*?"

She just sighed, looking a little ashamed, as if embarrassed she'd ever had anything to do with such a brainless douche.

"Ten?" Noel strode over, scowling hard. "What the hell are you doing? Aspen called at work, saying you were beating the shit out of some stranger in our backyard. So, I come home to find *this*. Who *is* this guy?"

I couldn't help but smile. "Well, why don't I introduce you, buddy. This here is Sander Scotini."

Noel pulled back in shock and stared at Scotini before a small smile lit his face. "Is he really?"

I nodded. "And Sandy," I said, picking the little shit up off the ground, by his hair. "Meet Caroline's overprotective, homicidal big brother, Noel Gamble."

The back door opened again. "Noel?" Aspen called, looking worried while Noel cracked his knuckles and stepped menacingly toward Scotini. "Is everything okay? Should I call the police?"

"Who's she?" Scotini asked.

"That's my wife," Noel intoned. "Don't fucking look at her." Then he called over his shoulder, "No, baby. We got this."

Scotini glanced at me. "If he's Noel; who're you?"

"I'm Ten."

He blinked, honestly clueless. "Ten what?"

"Ten seconds away from putting your parents out of

their misery for having an idiot for a son. Jesus. Catch up, already."

"Wait, did he piss his pants?" Noel asked, suddenly taking a cautious step back.

I lifted my hands, proud of myself. "Of course he pissed his pants. I'm a badass motherfucker. I got this intimidation shit *down*."

Noel shook his head, seemingly disappointed. "Well, hell. I can't hit him now."

"Can I hit him?" I asked.

"Ooh." Brandt eagerly jumped forward. "I want to hit him, too."

Noel sighed and set his hands on his hips as he gazed at the pathetic-ness that was Sander Scotini. "What the fuck is he even doing here?"

"Mommy and Daddy finally got tired of his shit, I guess, and cut off his play money, so he came crawling to Caroline to beg for some of her hush-hush-go-away payment."

"Oh, hell to the no," Noel murmured. "You are not getting one cent from her, you little fucktard. And if you want to live to see your next breath, you will leave here now and never come back. In fact, if you ever try to contact Caroline again, you're dead. Got it?"

When Scotini didn't respond within two seconds except to glance beseechingly at Caroline, Noel growled. "Damn it, you looked at her. Brandt, go inside and get my gun."

"Shit!" Scotini yelped, holding up his hands and backing away. "Oh, fuck. Don't shoot. I'm sorry. I'm so sorry. I'll go. I'll never come back again. I'll never talk to her again. I swear to God."

"Then *go*," Noel roared.

Scotini turned tail and half sprinted, half hobbled from the yard.

After he was gone, Brandt glanced up at Noel. "I didn't know you had a gun."

Gam shrugged. "I don't."

We all had to chuckle about that. When I couldn't help it any longer, I let my attention slide to Caroline. She seemed to be okay after what had just happened, but I still hated the fact that I couldn't physically go to her.

As if feeling my gaze on her, she blew out a breath and looked up.

"How much of that money do you really have left?" I

asked, needing a reason to talk to her.

Her scheming grin was downright gorgeous. "Oh... about fifteen grand."

My mouth fell open. "Holy shit." Then I smiled and shook my head. "Sweet." I held out my hand for a congratulatory fist bump. I wanted to grab her, yank her close and kiss the fuck out of her when she pressed her knuckles to mine. But yeah...Gamble was right there.

"Why don't you two go inside," he ordered Brandt and Caroline, motioning them toward the door as if he were herding cattle. "I gotta get back to work. I left Quinn at the bar alone."

Caroline sent me one last glance but finally nodded and followed her brother into the house.

I watched her go as a sinking feeling struck that Gamble was going to start talking the moment the door shut, leaving the two of us alone out here. Scared he'd seen something in the way I'd looked at her or could tell how I felt about her from the way I'd treated Scotini, I sucked in a bolstering breath and faced him, ready for a punch in the gut, or face, or—God I hoped not—the junk.

Instead, he stuck out his hand. "Man..." After his own serious sigh, he added, "Thank you."

"Thank you?" I echoed stupidly.

"Yeah. Thanks for being here for my family when I couldn't be. You're a real friend."

I stared at his hand, feeling so shitty and fake I could scarcely draw in a breath. When I didn't shake with him within five seconds, he furrowed his brow. "What?"

I shook my head. "Nothing." After grabbing his hand and pumping, I pulled away. "But I didn't do anything," I finally added.

"Yeah, you did. You kept him from coming into our house. You kept him away from Caroline. You kept him here until I could show up."

With a shrug, I glanced away. Yeah, I'd done all that. But I hadn't done it for him. I hadn't even thought of him.

It struck me like a wrecking ball through the chest that I no longer valued my relationship with him more than I valued my relationship with Caroline. He wasn't more important than she was to me. If I lost my friendship with Gamble after this, I could survive it. If I lost her, it would destroy me.

Him finding out was no longer the biggest thing I was afraid of. So I opened my mouth, on the very brink of saying, *I'm in love with your sister,* when he blew out a breath.

"You know what pissed me off the most about what he did to her?"

I shook my head. "What's that?"

"That he kept her such a fucking secret. Her first boyfriend, and she probably wasn't even allowed to talk to him in public, or fuck, even hold his hand."

My mind flittered to the moment I'd first taken her hand before introducing her to my parents. She'd been so unsettled by it; I knew he had to be right. Guilt crept over me. She still couldn't hold her man's hand in public, could she?

"She's probably never even been on a real date. Done anything the proper way it's supposed to be done."

I closed my eyes. No, I'd never taken her on a date.

Fuck.

Noel clapped me on the shoulder, making me jump out of my fucking skin. My eyes flew open.

"What're you doing here, anyway?" he asked, eyeing me strangely.

"I, uh..." My mind raced. I suddenly couldn't remember why I was here. All I could see was Caroline's face every night that I'd picked her up at the curb a block from her house. She always looked happy to see me, but there *had to be* a part of her that remained disappointed, rejected. Did she think I thought of her as some kind of dirty secret?

"Ten?" Gamble waved his hand in front of my face.

I blinked. "Sorry. I was...I was playing catch with Colton. He wanted me to come over."

"Oh." Gamble's shoulders slumped, then his eyebrows lowered. "I didn't know he was into that. He's never asked *me* to play catch with him before."

"That's because you still scare the shit out of him." I shrugged. "Me, he thinks of as some kind of fun older brother."

"But I *am* his older brother."

With a sigh, I patted his shoulder. "Except you got a shit deal and had to be his parent too. He hasn't had a great history with parents, so...naturally he's going to be wary of you for a while."

When Gam's face filled with pain, I bumped his shoulder again, a little harder this time. "Don't sweat it, man. He's already starting to come around. I was telling him about a few of your amazing football highlights earlier while we were tossing the ball around, and he seemed pretty impressed."

Gam's lips tipped up, and hope entered his gaze. "Really?"

I snorted. "Fuck, who wouldn't be? Just give him a little more time. All right? He'll warm up to you."

He nodded but had to add, "He took to Aspen almost immediately."

"Probably because she's a hell of a lot prettier than you are."

This time, his mouth gave in to a full smile. "True."

With a slug to the shoulder, I waved him away. "Now, get back to work, asshole. Your family is safe and sound inside. You have nothing to worry about." *Except maybe an asshole best friend who's completely defiling your little sister behind your back.*

Fuck, I was worse than Sander Scotini, wasn't I?

With a nod, he murmured, "Thanks, man." Then he turned and trotted off.

I watched him go, feeling like shit all over again. Okay, so I feared losing Caroline more than I feared losing him, but damn...I'd prefer not to lose either of them before this was said and done. Gamble was my best friend. And Caroline was my heart and soul.

But I didn't see how I could keep them both.

CHAPTER 25

Caroline

OREN DIDN'T contact me after Sander's visit. I expected a text, a call, *something* that night.

I'm sure there was plenty he wanted to say, like, "*What the hell did you ever see in that douche?*" Or, "*Please, fuck, tell me I'm better in the sack, or hung lower, than him.*"

Anything! But, nope, he went radio silent.

I wasn't sure what that meant. I wanted to talk to him, was dying to tell him that watching him toy with Sander had been sexy. He'd reminded me of a great lounging lion, or panther, one of those huge jungle cats, the type that didn't just beat the shit out of its prey, but played with it first, picking it apart limb by limb. I have no idea why I thought that was hot, but I did.

So now, I wanted to know if he was so disgusted by my past choice of boyfriends that he was done with me now, or what. Why wasn't he freaking talking to me? To go from multiple texts a day to nothing scared the shit out of me.

When he finally texted me fifteen hours after kicking Sander out of my backyard, I was a little too scared to read his message. What if it said something like, *We need to talk*? I didn't want to have one of those talks. I wasn't done with him yet.

But I pulled on my big-girl panties—or at least my college-girl panties—and cracked open one eye to read it that way. When it said, *Let's go out today,* the other eye popped open.

"Huh?" Instead of texting back, I dialed his number. "What the heck are you talking about?" I demanded as soon as he answered.

"What do you mean, what am I talking about? It wasn't a complex question. Do you want to go out or not?"

"What do you mean by *go out*?"

"Out," he repeated, sounding stumped. "Like...out. Outside. Out in public. Just...out."

"But...what...we can't go *out*."

"Why not?"

"B-because!" I sputtered. "What if someone saw us and told Noel? Heck, what if *Noel* saw us?"

"I swear, *Noel* is the only person left on earth who doesn't know about us by now, and I'm beginning to wonder *why* he doesn't."

My mouth fell open. Had he just said what I thought he'd said? "What're you saying? Do you *want* to tell him?"

"Well, eventually, yeah."

"B-b-but do you want to tell him *now*?"

He sighed before answering. Then he said, "Let's just say I'm ready to tell him whenever you are."

Oh my God. My stomach churned with sudden nerves. I pictured Noel jacking Oren in the face and not stopping until my boyfriend landed in the hospital. Fear clutched my throat, and my palms went from hot sweat to cold panic. "So you're ready to tell him?"

"No," he said steadily. "I'm only ready whenever you are."

I shook my head. "That's not an answer."

"Well, tough shit, because it's the only answer I'm giving you."

"Well, fuck you. I don't like being put into the position where *I'm* the one making this decision."

"Well, I don't like this conversation, period. I didn't call you to fight. I just want to spend the fucking day with you because I didn't get to see you all fucking night. I'm irritable and jealous as hell after meeting that fucktard you used to date, worrying myself crazy that you're second-guessing your relationship with me after seeing him again, and I just want to spend the goddamn day with you. *Okay*?"

He had diarrhea of the mouth or something. The words just started vomiting out of him until he had my head spinning.

I finally lifted my hand and said, "Wait. Why would you even once think I'd second-guess our relationship after seeing *him*?"

"I don't know," he muttered. "He was your first love, or whatever. You chicks get all sentimental and shit when it comes to your first loves, don't you?"

Why, yes. Yes, we did.

"But Sander was *not* my first love. He was just some...stupid boy who smiled at a young, vulnerable, lonely girl starved for a little attention. He was a user and left me used. The only thing I feel for that douche is supreme satisfaction that you kicked him in the junk for me."

"Really?"

I smiled and rolled my eyes. It completely boggled my mind that cocky, confident Oren Tenning was acting so uncertain. But then I remembered this was the first time he'd dared to open himself up to anyone and attempt a relationship since his sister's death, since that one stupid whore who'd first had him had shattered his ego. Thinking of it that way, yeah, it made sense he'd have a few doubts.

"Yes, really," I murmured. "And yes, I'd love to spend the day *out* with you." If Noel discovered us, I guess that was just a chance I was willing to take to show Oren I most definitely wasn't having any second thoughts about him. Because he was my first love.

"Cool," he murmured as if trying to piece together his doubts and return to being confident Oren. "I have just the place to take you. There's this park about an hour from here, near my hometown. It's really nice and should be far enough away that your brother won't learn about it. It's by a river and there's a carnival and little food kiosks, and—"

"You mean Rainly Park?"

"Oh, you've heard of it?" Disappointment filled his voice.

"Yeah, sure. Noel's taken us there a few times for family outings."

"That fucker," he exploded. "I'm the one who took *him* there first. How dare he take you there before I could?"

I grinned. "If it makes you feel better, I bet I'll have a much better time there with you than I ever did with him."

"You're damn right you will."

I laughed and he finally chuckled along with me.

"Pick you up in an hour at our spot?" he asked.

Pleasure bloomed in my chest. "Sounds great. I'll see you then."

"Yes, you will. Lick you later, baby."

HE TOOK ME TO get corn dogs first, because he was starving, and while he snarfed down three to my respectable one (okay, fine, I stole half of his last corn dog), we meandered around the craft booths, watching a few artists freestyle paint before I came across a vintage video stand.

After flipping through a pile of old DVD and VHS cassettes, I found a readapted version of Disney's *Child of Glass* and nearly wet myself. "Oh my God, I've been looking everywhere for this movie."

Checking out the cover, Oren snickered. "Wow. With the glasses that kid is rocking, I can see why it had your panties all wet."

I smacked his arm. "Hush. It's a seventies movie. Everyone had tacky fashion sense back then."

"Yeah, I can tell. Honestly, if I ever wear a shirt like that, please shoot me and put me out of my misery."

"It was the storyline that hooked me, not what they wore."

"What was it about?" Oren took the DVD out of my hand and flipped it over to check out the back.

I frowned. "You know, I can't remember."

"Sounds titillating," he intoned.

I scowled and nudged his arm again, just to make myself feel better. "I was really young the last time I saw it. It was some kind of Saturday afternoon movie special on TV. I only got to see it once, but I remember just adoring it. I loved the name of the ghost. Inez Dumaine." With a sigh, I grinned. "I built this dream in my head that I'd name a little girl Inez Dumaine if I ever had children."

Remembering I never would have children, my smile faded. Oren looked up from reading the back cover, and I could tell from his expression that he knew exactly what I was thinking.

So I cleared my throat and kept talking. "Anyway, I loved her accent too. I loved the way she said the main boy's name who was helping her. And I wanted to watch it again the next day, so Noel took me to our nearby movie rental place to get it, but they didn't have it. We looked everywhere. I finally wrote a letter to Walt Disney and asked if I could buy a copy from them." With a scowl, I added, "That bastard never wrote back."

"I'm going to kick his ass," Oren promised, sounding dead serious.

I cracked up and grasped his arm. "It doesn't matter anymore. We have the movie now."

"Well, let's buy this som'bitch and watch it tonight when we get home."

As he carried it to the vendor to pay for it, reaching into his own pocket for his wallet, I stayed back and stared after him, amazed. Once the transaction was complete, he returned to me with my new movie and a proud grin on his face.

"What if it ends up not working?" I said, suddenly leery as I bit my lip. "Or what if it does work, and it ends up being an awful movie? I was young, it's been years since I've seen it."

He playfully batted my nose with the tip of his finger. "Frankly, my dear, I don't gave a shit how the movie ends up. It's making you smile now, and that's all that matters."

My heart melted, metaphorically wrung itself out into a gooey pile of mush, and just liquefied at his feet. I let out a startled breath. "Damn, Oren. You have no idea how your little unexpected acts of kindness turn me on. I'm so wet right now I could probably sit on your face and come the second your tongue touched me."

He sucked in a groan and grabbed my hand, squeezing almost painfully. "I know just the place."

As he walked so fast that I nearly had to run to keep up with him, I giggled and pressed against his side. "Are we really going to find a place to be together...around here?"

He sent me a hard, serious glance. "Fuck yes. You can't say shit like that to me without paying the consequences, woman. I'm hard as a fucking boulder right now."

We hurried out of the little market of booths and across an open lawn where families were picnicking, where Noel had brought us to picnic in the past. When Oren veered off into an overgrown footpath, I clutched his arm. "Where the hell are you taking me?" A sign up ahead read, *Trail Closed*.

"To a spot I never took Noel, so I'm sure he never took you." He sounded a little smug as he gripped my waist and lifted me over the sign onto the other side and then leaped over it after me. "There's a waterfall at the end of this trail."

"Really? Oh, cool."

"Yeah, it's pretty sweet, but they had to condemn it a couple years back because of severe soil erosion. Every once in a while the banks just...collapse."

My eyes flared wide. "And *that's* where you're taking me to mess around?"

He grinned and flashed me a wink. "Trust me, baby doll, there'll still be plenty of room to do what we have in mind."

I did trust him, and he proved me right. From that day forward, I'd never look at a waterfall the same way again.

CHAPTER 26

Caroline

I SAT ON OREN'S bed with one leg tucked under me and the other swinging off the side as I watched him pull a suit jacket from his closet and then cough as he brushed dust bunnies off the shoulders.

"Maybe you ought to consider getting it dry-cleaned before leaving for your interview," I suggested, trying not to laugh...and failing.

He sent me a dry scowl. "Gee, you think?"

I shook my head, giggles still blurting from my closed lips. "When was the last time you wore that thing?"

He eyed it with distaste. "High school graduation, I think. Wait, no. My grandpa's brother died three years ago. I had to wear it to his funeral."

"And you really think it'll still fit?" I lifted my eyebrows, not buying it.

"Hey, are you calling me fat, woman?" He loomed over me with an indignant scowl that only made me smile.

"Fat? God, no. But I imagine you grew a few new muscles throughout your college career of playing ball. Like this measly little six-pack here."

When I licked my lips and ran my fingers over his abdomen, he moved closer. "Why do I have a feeling this isn't as much about you worrying over the fit of my suit as it is about you just wanting to see me naked?"

"Oh, but I'm very, very worried about the fit of your suit," I murmured, reaching out to unsnap the top button of his jeans and then slowly draw his zipper down. "Watching you strip to try it on is only an added benefit."

He groaned and clutched my hair when I leaned forward to kiss his six-pack through his T-shirt. "Damn, I love your dirty little mouth."

"I bet you'll really love what dirty little thing I want to do with it right now."

"Fuck, yes."

I started to lift his shirt out of my way when Zoey appeared in the open door. "Hey, guys, the pizza's here— *Oh God.*" When she realized what she was walking in on, she yelped and lifted her hand to cover her eyes. "I'm sorry. I'm so sorry. I thought..." She didn't bother to finish the sentiment as she started to back out of the room.

"We'll be out in a minute," Oren told her. "Until then, shut the door for us, will you?"

"Oren!" I gasped as Zoey reached out and blindly fumbled for the doorknob before yanking it closed.

"What?" he asked, turning back to me as he flung his suit jacket aside and crawled onto the bed with me. "When my girl's promising to do dirty things to me with her dirty mouth, pizza can fucking wait."

I BIT INTO MY slice of pepperoni and moaned in delight. "Mmm. This tastes so good."

Oren grinned up at me from the floor, where he was sitting against my leg with one arm draped over my thigh, and quietly murmured, "Even better than spotted pecker?"

I flushed, glancing toward Zwinn to make sure they hadn't heard, but they were off in their own world on the couch. I shoved lightly at his shoulder and scolded, "Don't be uncouth."

"Why?" He leaned down to playfully bite my thigh. "You love it when I'm uncouth."

I flashed him a little growl. "Only when it's just the two of us."

He didn't seem chastised. Hitching his head toward Zwinn, he said, "As if those two even realize we're here right now. They're too busy making babies with their eyes."

"We heard that," Quinn said, scowling our way.

Oren bit into his own pizza. "Good," he muffled out around a mouthful. "Then listen to this, and promise me you'll stay out of your love bubble long enough this weekend to keep Caroline company while I'm gone, will you?"

An ache spread through my chest as he mentioned his trip to Lake Tahoe. The architectural firm had paid for air travel and lodging for him to fly out there and interview for the position. I knew it was the opportunity of a lifetime. Anyone willing to take on an inexperienced kid fresh from college and give him the kind of benefits and pay they were advertising was something no one could turn down.

I was beyond excited for him, and yet I dreaded his trip even more. What if he got the job? What if he moved away and I never saw him again. What if—

"Actually," Zoey said, wincing. "We were kind of thinking of flying out to see my dad this weekend."

I looked up at her, surprised. "You decided to visit him, then?" Damn, I really needed to stay up to date with my best friend. Since I'd started my secret affair with Oren, Zoey's and my friendship had kind of fallen by the wayside.

She nodded and looked up at Quinn. He took her hand. "She wanted to see if she could learn a little bit of her heritage," he explained.

"But what about Caroline?" Oren demanded, scowling. His hand tightened around my leg.

I rolled my eyes. "I'll be fine." We hadn't discussed how much I'd miss him while he was gone, or how nervous I was that he'd actually get the job. But he must've sensed something if he was acting this way.

That made me feel shitty. I didn't want him to worry about me when he was being presented with the freaking opportunity of a lifetime.

"My entire family is here, and I have my job plus next semester to get ready for." Okay, so I wouldn't have to worry about my next semester of college during this one little weekend while he was away, but I was thinking about when he left permanently, after he got the job.

He eyed me for a moment, saying nothing, his gaze full of concern before he turned back to Zwinn and focused on

Zoey. "You said your dad was staying in California this summer, right? How far away from Lake Tahoe is he?"

"You know..." She tipped her face thoughtfully to the side. "I don't think it's actually too far. A couple hours, maybe."

Oren nodded and ran his top teeth across his bottom lip as he always did when he was hatching a crazy plan. "You booked a flight yet?" he asked.

Zoey shook her head and looked up at Quinn. "We just decided this evening to even go."

"You should take Caroline with you," he answered, glancing up me as his eyes lit with mischief. "She's your best friend on earth. You'll need her moral support during this difficult time."

"Oh, but I—"

"And you should book a flight with the same airline I'm using, then see if you can get a room at the same hotel. Then after you see your dad and I have my interview, the four of us can party on the beach before we head back home the next morning."

My mouth fell open. "Oren, don't be insane. I can't come with you on your interview trip."

He looked up at me. "Why not?"

"Because..." I shook my head and laughed. His entire idea was crazy, though it made me giddy to even consider it. "I can't just hop on a plane and spend a few days with you all the way across the country. If I take that kind of money out of my savings for a ticket, Noel will wonder—"

"Then I'll pay for your ticket."

"*Oren.*" I was about to turn him down again when he grasped my hand.

"I want you there with me." The look in his eyes told me he wasn't kidding around. "I *need* you there."

MY STOMACH roiled as I watched Oren stow our carry-on luggage in the cubby above our seats. I couldn't believe we were really doing this. I almost expected Noel to come charging onto the plane any second and pack me away like a misbehaving child.

I was beginning to feel as childish as I knew I was acting

by hiding my relationship from him, but I was just so worried about what would happen after he found out. The two things I knew were that I didn't want to lose Oren, and Noel didn't want us together. And those two truths weren't going to cohabit peacefully once they became aware of each other.

But I pushed my worries aside to snicker at a middle-aged woman who couldn't stop checking out Oren's ass as his shirt rode up while his arms were over his head. I shook my head, not blaming her for her interest at all. Then I began to chew on my fingernails as all my fears resurfaced.

Oren lowered his arms from the luggage bin and turned to me with a grin. "You want the window seat, babe?"

Ogling Lady nudged my hip. "Ooh, you better take it, honey. Ain't too often a man gives up the beloved window seat for his woman."

Oren turned his grin her way. "It's her first time flying," he said. "I thought she should have the full experience."

"Well, aren't you the sweetest thing." I could just see her insides melt as she gazed at him. The idiot had totally unleashed poor Ogling Lady's inner cougar, and she was no doubt picturing him drizzled in her favorite wine so she could just...lick him clean.

He ate it up, too, being extra chivalrous as he gently took my arm to help me get to my seat.

"You better cut it out," I whispered to him as he sat beside me. "You're going to make her ovaries explode."

His lips twisted with sexy amusement. "But, *honey*, I haven't detonated anyone's ovaries all day."

I snorted and shook my head.

In the two seats directly across the aisle from us, Zwinn were also getting situated. Bumping my elbow in Oren's, I murmured, "Never mind. She just noticed how hot Quinn is and forgot all about you."

"*What?*" He zipped his attention to Ogling Lady. When he saw that she was indeed watching Quinn, he scowled but leaned close to me to murmur, "She's probably just wondering why he doesn't look nearly as good as I do."

Throwing my head back, I laughed. And that's when I decided, no more worrying. I was going to have fun and just enjoy the trip.

I watched Oren untangle his lap belt so he could click it into place. A drunken giddiness stole over me. He hadn't been lying when he'd told the woman I'd never been on a plane before. This was indeed my virgin flight. I'd never even been this far from home before. I kind of wanted to bounce in my seat and squeal. What was better, I was doing it with Oren.

He looked good with his hair sweeping across his forehead as he scowled and muttered at his seat belt, finally getting it untangled. His shoulders were so yummy as they shifted and flexed under his crisp gray button-up shirt. I wanted to pop all the buttons and run my hands up his chest, lick my way across his beard stubble and just...bite his throat.

I leaned toward him and whispered into his ear. "Want to join the mile-high club?"

His hands stilled on his seat belt. Then his face came up. "Fuck, yes."

Grinning, I really did bounce in my seat. "So do I!"

He glanced around. Across the aisle, Zwinn had settled in and were holding hands, leaning against each other as they talked quietly amongst themselves. Turning back to me without actually looking me in the eye, Oren started talking quietly. "First we gotta wait until the plane is actually in the air, and then you go first. When I get there, I'll knock twice. Only twice. Got it?"

I nodded and grabbed his hand, squeezing.

He squeezed right back. "This is going to kick ass."

Ten

OKAY, SO MAYBE the mile-high-club thing turned out to be an epic fail. But we can't say we didn't give it our best shot.

Minutes after we were in the air, Caroline stood up, pretended to yawn and stretch, and shimmied past my legs to reach the aisle. There was a moment when her sweet ass was right in my face, and I was tempted to reach up and cup each blessedly taut cheek, but I told myself, *patience*. I'd have them both in my hands very, very soon as I thrust into her a freaking mile off the ground. Or thirty-thousand feet off the ground. What-ever. The point was, we were going to be so fucking naughty, and I couldn't wait.

Clearing my throat, I watched her make her way up to the front, and I had to resituate myself because my boner was digging into my lap belt.

I tapped my fingers against my knee for a good thirty seconds before I couldn't wait any longer. Then freeing my seat belt, I lurched to my feet and accidentally made eye contact with Blondie as she glanced up at me, frowning suspiciously. After a flirty wiggle of my eyebrows, I headed to the restrooms. There were two doors, and both said occupied, so I wrapped twice on the first, only for a very male, very un-Caroline-like voice to bellow, "This's one taken."

So I started to move to the next door, but it slid open before I could tap on it. A snickering Caroline peered out at me. When I started for her, her eyes went big and she shook her head. "Oren, I don't think—*mmph*."

I backed her into the bathroom and then stopped short because there was nowhere left to move her. "Damn, these things are small."

"I know," she hissed. "This is insane. There's no way we can fit—"

I picked her up by the waist and set her on the edge of the sink, which barely gave me enough room to enter the bathroom with her. Then I shut the door and almost couldn't even turn back to face her.

She slapped her hands over her face and began to giggle. "There's no way," she finally said. "There's just...no way. We don't even have enough room to take our clothes off."

"Speak for yourself, woman. All I gotta do is unzip."

"Well, *my* pants are staying on. I can't possibly get them off."

I glanced down at the adorable black skinny pants she was wearing with a pair of boots and a long, swishy top thing. And yeah, there was no way anyone would be flexible enough to remove them in this kind of space.

"Bet I could still make you come through all that cloth," I decided. I set one hand on the wall beside her head and the other high on her thigh. "We can at least fool around, right?"

Her smile told me she liked that idea, so I leaned in to

give her a soft kiss, when someone pounded on the door.

"Sir. Ma'am," some guy called through the thin door. "This is Jon, your flight attendant. Could you please step out of the bathroom?"

"Oh my God," Caroline gasped, looking up at me with wide eyes.

I blinked right back before whispering, "Busted."

Her face flooded with color. "This is so freaking embarrassing."

Taking her hand, I helped her off the sink. "Don't worry. I got this."

She crowded against my back, seeking protection, as I eased open the door and peered out at the scowling dude in the attendant's uniform. "Sir," he said so seriously that Caroline had to muffle a giggle against my vertebrae. "There's a one-person only occupancy limit for each bathroom. You two will have to separate."

"Yeah, sorry about that," I apologized. "She was... feeling sick. I was just checking on her."

Jon narrowed his eyes. "Is that why she can't stop laughing right now?"

"Well, you know." I shrugged and flared out a hand. "Upset stomachs make her...hysterical."

"Oh my God," Caroline groaned in absolute mortification.

"Sir." Jon was not amused by my lie. He folded his arms over his chest and glared up at me. "I wasn't born yesterday. I know exactly what you two were doing. And those kinds of relations are not permitted on this commercial flight."

"So...you're saying we should've gone with Southwest instead?"

He huffed out an aggravated sound. "This is not the least bit amusing."

"Oh, come on, man." I sniffed and lifted my hands. "What're you really going to do? Throw us in *airplane* jail?"

Jon puffed out his puny little *attendant's* chest and gave me *the look*. "Sir, we are still close enough to turn this plane around and return you to O'Hare."

I had a feeling he was bullshitting me. I couldn't see them turning around just for two horny misbehaving kids, but damn he had his poker face down flat. I gulped, sensing he might just be telling the truth. "Well, shit."

"Oh my God, *no*!" Caroline skipped around me and

shook her head rapidly. "No, please, you can't do that to him." She clasped Jon's arm desperately. "He's on his way to an interview. The interview of a *lifetime*. Please." She pressed her hand to her chest and drew in a deep breath. "It was my idea. This was all...my idea, and I'm so, *so* sorry. Just...please don't do this to him. You can take me back to O'Hare instead. Just me. Not him. I'll take all the punishment. He just...he *has* to get to Lake Tahoe."

When tears filled the edges of her eyelashes, I lost it. "Damn, baby, no." I pulled her to me and sent asshole Jon a scowl for making her cry.

His eyes bulged with worry as I stroked Caroline's hair. "Don't cry, princess. If you can't go, then I won't either. This was your first trip across country, your first *plane ride*. I'm not going anywhere without you."

She looked up, and one of her hovering tears slid down her cheek. "But your interview."

"Fuck the interview. My heart wouldn't be in it if you weren't there." I clutched her face and looked deep into her eyes. "You jump, I jump. Right, Rose?"

She really started sobbing then. "Oh my God. We're about to be sent to airplane jail and you're quoting *Titanic*?"

"I'm sorry," I instantly apologized. "God, baby. I'm so sorry. This was my fault. I should've—fuck, I don't know. I only said the movie quote to make you smile."

"It worked," she swore even as more tears flooded her face and the tipping up of her lips looked anything but happy. "It was so beautiful, and I loved it. I just...I didn't mean to get us into trouble. You've been so amazing, and I'm just fucking it all up."

"No...no, you're not in any trouble, ma'am." Jon patted her shoulder hesitatingly, his expression full of worry. "I didn't mean to make you cry. Here." He thrust a wad of tissues at her.

"Oh. Th-thank you." She sniffed and gingerly took a tissue before wiping her face. "So...you're not...you're not going to kick us off the plane?"

"Of course not. I am sorry for scaring you. I just wanted you to be aware of the rules."

She nodded and blew her nose. "It's okay. I'm aware now. We're very aware."

He still watched her warily as if ready to catch her in case she fainted or some shit. "Are you sure? Are you okay now?"

"Yes. Thank you. Thank you so much. If you don't mind, I...I think we'll go take our seats now."

"Sure." He touched her shoulder again and was lucky I didn't snap his hand off for it. "I'm going to make you something warm to drink and bring it out to you, okay?"

"Thank you. That's so kind."

I lifted an eyebrow as I watched their byplay. When Caroline glanced up at me, her cheeks were still wet from crying, but not a single new tear filled her eyes. She took my hand and led us back to our seats. Without saying a word, we clicked on our seat belts and sat there, facing forward.

"You okay?" I finally asked, dipping my face to get a look at hers.

She turned to me, completely casual. "Of course. Why?"

I blinked. And then it hit me. "Why, you sneaky little shit. You just totally played him." And me too, apparently.

Her devious grin slipped across her face. "Well, I had to do *something*. Your petulant smart-ass attitude wasn't getting us anywhere."

My mouth worked a moment before I hissed, "Holy fuck, woman. How the hell can you just turn the tears on like that?"

She lifted her eyebrows. "I have three brothers. Years of practice."

"Oh my God." I threw my head back and laughed. "You are so awesome. I'm not worthy." Shaking my head, I gazed at her in awe. "I am *so* not worthy."

She blushed and smiled but quickly dropped the expression when she glanced over my shoulder. Elbowing me, she whispered, "Quick. He's coming with my drink."

As much as I tried, I could not stop smiling. I dropped my face instead so *Jon* couldn't see my smirk.

"Here you go, ma'am."

"Thank you so much." Caroline reached past me to accept her complimentary drink. "Warm tea. Mmm. It smells delicious."

"And I apologize again," Jon gushed. "I didn't mean to upset you."

"It's fine. Don't worry about it. I've learned my lesson."

I was so close to busting a gut laughing, and Caroline knew it because she suddenly clamped her hand around my thigh and dug her nails into me to keep me quiet. But shit.

We'd been the ones to break the rules, and here Jon was, apologizing to *her* and fucking serving her tea. She was hands down the most entertaining, dynamic, devious, beautiful, amazing woman I'd ever met.

If I wasn't already crazy in love with her, I would've fallen in that very moment.

CHAPTER 27

Caroline

A MAN WITH A sign that read "*Oren Tenning*" waited for us when we stepped off the plane.

Holding my hand, Oren slowed to a stop when he saw the guy. "Hi," he said hesitantly.

The round little fellow looked up at him. "Mr. Tenning?"

After Oren answered, "Uh, yeah...I guess," the man beamed and held out his hand.

"Lance Stanley. I'm with Booker and Finch, and consequently your ride to the hotel."

"You...*are*?" Oren's smile fell as he glanced down at me and then back at Zwinn. "I wasn't...this is...unexpected. I just....I guess I thought I'd find my own way to the hotel."

"Oh no, sir. This is the full-service interview experience. And can I say it is an honor to meet you? Everyone's been raving about your portfolio since your application came in."

"Really?" Oren blinked before he shook his head and cleared his throat. "I mean, thanks. That's...cool."

Mr. Stanley turned to me. "And you must be Mrs. Tenning. I recognize your face from some of the free-drawing samples your husband added to his portfolio."

"You..." Too flabbergasted to get past the *Mrs.* Tenning part, I looked up at Oren for help.

He stepped in, lifting his hand and shaking it. "Oh, no. She's not...I mean...not *yet*. She's..." He glanced at me, his expression desperate. "She's my fiancée."

My eyes widened as I gaped up at him. He squeezed my fingers tighter. "It's okay that I brought her, right? I was going to pay out of pocket for all her—"

"Oh, sure. Sure." Mr. Stanley waved off Oren's concerns. "Of course, she can come along to check out the area, give her nod of approval. Congratulations on your upcoming nuptials, ma'am."

When the small man sent me a smile, I gave a weak smile back. "Um...thank you. It was..." I glanced up at Oren, "quite a surprise."

Mr. Stanley leaned in to wink. "The best proposals usually are." Then he straightened and turned back to Oren. "The baggage claim's this way."

Oren nodded and tugged me along as we followed Mr. Stanley. Then he glanced back with an apologetic wince toward Zwinn for abandoning them. Quinn sent him a thumbs-up, letting us know they'd find their own way to the hotel, no problem.

And thus started our evening of being wined and dined as a nearly married couple by Oren's prospective employer, though we found out over dessert that Mr. Stanley was more of a glorified secretary than an actual executive with the authority to hire Oren. The worst part was that he tried to sell the town to *me*, telling me about all the perks of living around the lake.

Oren played along, telling Mr. Stanley I was a filmmaking major, which had the poor guy's face lighting up. "Well, California is the best place to be for that kind of major. You would be coming to the right area for sure."

"So, all her credits would transfer with no problem if she came out here next semester?" Oren asked, actually looking interested in the answer.

I sent him a strange glance, which he completely ignored.

"I'm sure they would."

By the time Mr. Stanley dropped us off at the hotel for the evening, my nerves were plumb shot. I silently followed Oren up to our room after we checked in, and I didn't say a thing until he'd rolled all our suitcases into our suite and shut the door. Then I just stood there and stared at him as he dropped the luggage on the bed and immediately went to the window to check out our view.

Finally, I cracked. "Would you care to tell me what the hell just happened?"

He glanced back and winced. "You're talking about the fiancée thing, aren't you?"

I whimpered out a sound at the word and nodded my head.

He sighed and came to me. "I don't know. That just...blurted out. I wasn't expecting anyone to actually meet me at the airport, to meet *you*. Telling him you were only my girlfriend sounded kind of irresponsible, as if I'd only brought you with me to party on Lake Tahoe."

"Oh, so...*lying* to him first thing seemed so much more responsible, huh?"

"Fuck, I didn't know what to do. I was kind of worried they wouldn't let you come with me if I didn't make us sound more...permanent. So I improvised. Seriously, you're not *that* pissed, are you?"

Slowly, I shook my head. "No, but...if you end up getting this job because I made you look more like the responsible family man, then you owe me a cut of every paycheck you get."

Grinning, he pressed his forehead to mine. "You got it, babe."

With a sudden laugh over everything we'd gone through today, I grinned up at him. "First, I'm your fake girlfriend to your parents, now your fake fiancée to your prospective boss. I can't wait to play the fake wife next."

Oren took my hand and kissed my knuckles. "And I'm sure you'd make the best damn fake wife there ever was. Now, come here and check out this view."

He led me to a window, and I sucked in a breath as I looked out at the sandy beach lit with tiki torches and the most colorful sunset ever glistening off the slow-rippling water of the lake.

"Wow," I breathed as Oren wrapped his arms around me from behind and rested his chin on my shoulder. "Okay, we can move out here."

Chucking in my ear, he turned his face so he could kiss my cheek. "We could build our fake home right on the beach and live fakely ever after."

My heart thumped hard in my chest as I substituted

different words for all the fakes. But then I just shook my head, reminding myself it was all...fake. If Oren moved here, I would not be coming with him.

OREN CALLED Quinn, who reported that Zoey was queasy after the plane ride; they'd just see us at breakfast. So Oren and I took full advantage of our accommodations. He ordered a bottle of champagne up to our room, and we lounged on the bed, sipping from our bubbly fluted glasses while watching movies until we started kissing and then made love on the king-size hotel bed.

I woke naked and relaxed the next morning sprawled half on top of him. One of his hands rested limply on my ass and the other was tangled in my hair. I woke him by kissing my way down his chest. He groaned, then growled, and then moaned when my lips wrapped around his morning wood.

"Woman," he muttered, sinking his hands into my hair. He let me suck for a few minutes before tugging me off him and hauling me out of bed, only to carry me into the bathroom and take me hard and desperately against the hotel's enormous shower wall.

After he spent himself inside me and I was panting out my release on his shoulder, he kissed my cheek and asked, "Does it ever feel like I'm wearing your pussy out? I mean, shit. What if I start to rub you raw in there from doing you so much?"

When his hand lowered to pet me gently between the legs, I laughed and pressed my forehead to his. "Does it ever feel like my pussy's rubbing your dick raw?"

He grinned. "No."

I shrugged. "Then there's your answer."

With an amused chuckle, he wrapped his arms around me and pressed his cheek against mine. "I love the way you think."

I loved him, period.

AFTER WE DRESSED, we met Zwinn downstairs in the

dining room for a continental breakfast. Zoey looked sheet white as she sat with Quinn at a table, sipping from a cup of what looked like apple juice.

"Holy fuck, you look like shit," Oren blurted.

I bumped his arm and sent him a look.

"What?" he asked as he motioned to her. "She's as pale as a fucking ghost."

I was worried about her too. It'd only been a few months since she'd had a kidney removed when she'd donated it to her wicked half sister. I hoped to God she wasn't having a bad reaction from that.

But she shook her head and offered us a wan smile. "I'm fine. Just...a little nervous. My dad left me a cryptic message last night. Something about Cora."

Oren growled, not liking Zoey's half sister at all. "If that bitch is there, you fucking leave, you hear me?" He glanced at Quinn. "Don't let them suck you guys into any more of her drama."

"Oh, you don't have to warn *me*." Quinn took Zoey's hand supportively. "We're fully prepared to turn right back around and return to the hotel if she shows up."

"Good." Oren nodded and blew out a breath. He glanced at me, and I saw swirling unease in his gaze. When I touched his leg under the table, he quietly took my hand. But the unease didn't abate. It seemed to grow and fester the longer our breakfast lasted.

By the time Zwinn announced they were going to get on the road and head to her father's place, Oren even had sweat beading across his brow. With a nod, he glanced at me. "I guess it's time for me to drag my monkey suit on."

It hit me then. He was nervous about his interview. After I followed him up to his room and he went into the bathroom to change, I flipped through a notebook the hotel had left in the room, boasting of their local entertainment. Then I tossed it on the bed, deciding I'd just sunbathe on the beach with a fruity drink that had an umbrella in it most of the afternoon. God, this was going to be the longest day of my life, hoping he sucked on his interview as much as I hoped he kicked ass, all the while worrying about Zwinn's trip.

I was just reaching for the television's remote control to keep myself occupied when the bathroom door opened, and a freaking stranger stepped out.

Oren had shaved off all his scruff and even smoothed his hair back. His freshly dry-cleaned suit was sharp and made his shoulders appear impossibly wide. My mouth dried as I stared at this devastatingly hunky businessman.

"Oh my God," I said, my mouth falling open. "I want to blow you so hard, right now."

When he smiled that cocky smile I adored the most about him, I slid off the bed and sauntered his way.

"It's the tie, isn't it?" he asked, touching his throat.

"It's everything about you, Oren Tenning." I sank to my knees in front of him and stared at the front of his pants until it started to tent. Then I gazed up into his gleaming eyes. "I have a feeling Mr. Grey will see me now."

When I unzipped him, he drew in a breath and grabbed the doorframe of the bathroom with one hand. "I'm guessing that's a movie quote."

"Mmm. Very good." Pulling him, hot and throbbing into my hands, I licked the pre-cum off the head and then kissed his birthmark before taking him into my mouth.

His dry-cleaned suit was so crisp and clean, I didn't dare do anything that might dirty it. So when he warned me he was about to come, I swallowed until he was done. When I pulled away and looked up at him, he stared at me with a dazed look in his eyes, and he leaned heavily against the doorframe.

"That was...that was...shit, woman. I don't even know how to tell you what you do to me." Reaching down, he pulled me up off my knees and into his arms. "Here I was, flipping the fuck out about this interview, and you just...completely relaxed every jittery nerve in me. Now do you see why I had to bring you?"

Honored he felt that way, I cupped his face in my hands and looked him in the eye before saying simply. "You're welcome."

He laughed softly and closed his eyes before pressing his forehead to mine. "I'm going to miss you today." When he pulled back, his concerned gaze was searching. "You going to be okay around here by yourself?"

I nodded. "Oh yeah. Sure. I plan on getting the suntan of a lifetime."

My DAY OF SUN tanning on the beach worked out better than I thought it would. I'd turned a golden brown by midday, so I walked to a nearby cabana, ordered myself some lunch, turned down a drink from a guy watching me at the bar, and then went to my room and fell asleep to a movie I found on TV. And I didn't worry about Oren once.

Okay, fine. I worried the entire fricking day away, but everything else I did was true.

The ringing of my cell phone woke me late in the afternoon from my nap.

"We're back," Quinn announced in my ear. "Ten's phone went straight to voice mail so I figure he's still at his interview. Do you want to hang out in our room until he's back?"

I glanced around the lonely suite. "Yes, thank you."

"No problem." He gave me their room number, and I found it a few minutes later on the floor below mine.

Zoey was sitting on the bed, staring at the wall when Quinn opened the door for me. I glanced at her and then back to him as I entered, feeling instantly uneasy. "How did...how did everything go?"

Quinn gave an uneasy shrug. Zoey looked up at me, but the shock in her eyes made it seem as if she didn't really see me. "Oh. Um...fine."

I sat next to her and took her hand, glancing at Quinn for an explanation.

He shrugged again. "Her dad offered her a million-dollar trust fund he'd just taken away from Cora, and oh...her sister's in a nut-house...after trying to commit suicide."

I looked between the two of them before squawking, "*What*?"

Zoey waved a hand toward her boyfriend. "What he said."

Quinn sighed and collapsed onto the bed on the other side of Zoey, lying on his back with his feet on the floor. He looked as shell-shocked as Zoey did. "I guess Mr. Wilder decided to really crack down on Cora and try to get her to behave. He ended up taking away her entire trust fund, and...she didn't like that. So she went a little..." He sent a worried glance to Zoey.

"Crazy," Zoey said for him as she turned to me. "She

went freaking insane, like tried to kill herself, slit her wrists, took a bunch of pills. She just...she's a mess. And now she's at a rehabilitation center, under observation. Oh, but not only do I have that to feel guilty about, but then our father goes and tells me he's giving all the money he took away from her to me."

"Wait. What do *you* have to feel guilty about?" I asked.

"Her dad took her away from Ellamore because of me. I uprooted her entire life. I stole her boyfriend. I—"

"You did *not* steal me," Quinn growled, sitting up to take Zoey's face into his hands and making her look him in the eye. "We fell in love."

But Zoey's bottom lip trembled. "None of this would've happened if I hadn't come to Ellamore."

"Yeah, and she'd probably be dead right now," I broke in, making both halves of Zwinn turn their attention to me. "You gave her a kidney, Zo. After all the shit she put you and Quinn through, you still saved her life. You did nothing wrong. If Cora cracked, it's her own damn fault, and I say she deserves everything she gets."

"Amen," Quinn said quietly as he kissed Zoey's temple.

Zoey leaned into him, set her hand supportively on his thigh, and turned her gaze to me. "I just...I don't really want that money. *Her* money. It feels tainted. I mean, look what it turned *her* into."

I lifted a censorious finger. "First of all, she turned herself into a wicked bitch. Money had nothing to do with the evil in that girl. And secondly..." I shrugged. "You don't have to take any money you don't want to. Don't ever let rich people try to control you with cash. But..."

When her eyes sharpened as if she really wanted to hear my but, I smiled and paused. Then I murmured, "I'm sure you could always find something useful for it. Charities...or maybe a new trust fund for your future children."

She gnawed on her lip thoughtfully. "I guess you're right."

Quinn began to rock her back and forth with his arms tight around her. "I'm with Caroline. You could do whatever you want with it. And you're too good inside to let any kind of money turn you into something you're not. But as long as it never gets back to Cora, I'm happy."

After another moment of thought, Zoey nodded. "You guys are right. Maybe I will take it."

Quinn kissed her hair, and I squeezed her hand. "Damn right, you will."

My cell phone rang, making every muscle in my body tense. "It's Oren," I announced, my stomach leaping with nerves when I saw his name. "Hey. How'd the interview go?"

"God, your voice sounds good," he answered. "But where *are* you? Our room's empty."

"I'm down in Zwinn's room. They just got back, and holy shit. I have a feeling you're going to *love* the news about Cora."

"Oh, yeah? What about her? Please tell me she's in a nut-house."

I laughed, wondering how the hell he'd guessed that. I was filling him in about how she'd cracked when the door to the room came open and he walked in.

"It's about time Whora finally got what she deserved," he announced as he strode to me. Picking me up off the bed, he kissed me hard. He was still wearing that hot suit, so I grabbed his tie and held on to it as his tongue spiked possessively into my mouth.

"Does this mean your interview went well?" I asked when I breathlessly pulled away for air.

He closed his eyes and buried his face in my hair. "Yeah," he said, sounding a little reluctant to admit it. "It went...great, actually."

Pain sliced through me. I knew it was awful of me to have a small part that secretly hoped he had crashed and burned so he couldn't leave me, but I couldn't help it. It was going to hurt like hell when we had to part.

"I'm so happy for you." I kissed his chest, and his lashes flickered open.

His gaze was unreadable for a moment before he glanced around the room and announced, "Let's get drunk."

ZOEY WANTED TO change before heading down to the beach, but Oren was antsy to get his party on, as he called it. I wanted a moment alone with my bestie to see how she was really holding up after her trip today, so as the guys left ahead of us, us girls found some appropriate beachwear to change into.

"So, really?" I asked as Zoey tied a beach wrap into place around her one-piece bathing suit. "How're you doing?"

She sighed. "Really? I have no idea." Then she looked at me and laughed. "I'm kind of relieved and yet feel awful for Cora, and yet I'm glad she got what was coming to her, but then I totally feel guilty for thinking that, and—"

I caught her hand to calm her. Then I smiled. "It's okay. I get it."

She nodded. "I think Quinn's okay too. He looked really surprised when Mr....I mean, my *dad* told us about her, but...I think he's okay."

"I'm sure he's feeling most of the same things you are," I agreed. "I mean, Cora screwed him over almost as much as she screwed you." Then I grinned at her. "But I think it's adorable how worried about each other you two are." With a pat on her arm, I declared, "You're both going to come away from this just fine."

She finally agreed, and I took her hand to lead her from the hotel room. I told her about how hot I thought Oren had looked in his suit as we strolled down the cobble steps toward the opening at the beach, and she rolled her eyes before telling me I was hopeless. Then she pointed. "Oh, there's the guys."

I looked up to find both Quinn and Oren just ahead of us on the path. They'd changed into T-shirts and board shorts and were being waylaid by three women who'd stopped in front of them.

One of them was lowering the top of her bikini and flashing Oren and Quinn her tits. "Are you boys looking for some fun?"

"Whoa." Quinn immediately turned away. His eyes were wide with horrified shock as he faced our way and saw us coming toward them. But Oren didn't bolt in the least.

Of course, I couldn't see his expression from the back, but it was obvious he stared at her exposed chest for more than a few seconds.

Then he finally said, "You know...you shouldn't be so proud of those things, honey."

The woman's mouth dropped open, clearly insulted. "Excuse me?"

Oren snorted. "Too small." He pointed at the woman to the right. "Too fake." He hitched his chin toward the one on the left. Then he pointed at the one still exposing herself in the middle. "And too fucking saggy. I mean, really. If you want to see a set of full perfect, natural breasts, you should see my girlfriend's." He whistled, long and loud. "Now *hers* are grade-A prime tatas."

Quinn chose that moment to clear his throat and elbow Oren in the arm. Oren glanced at him. "What?"

Quinn pointed to us, and Oren swung our way. When his gaze met mine, his grin grew. "There," he called. "Come here, baby."

When I reached him, he grabbed my wrist and swung me around until I was facing the stunned ladies still gaping at him. Swooping his arms around me from behind, he cupped my breasts in both his hands. "Check this shit out." His fingers kneaded me through my clothes. "Now *this* is perfection. Best breasts ever."

While the three ladies gasped in stunned shock before scurrying away, I glanced over my shoulder at him only to wince at the potency of his breath.

"How much have you drunk already?"

His grin was a little glassy. "No idea, but we're going to have fun catching you up with me."

CHAPTER 28

TEN

I SWEAR, AN eighteen-wheeler is what woke me the next morning, as it rammed its headlights straight into my skull and then backed up before slamming into it again.

I groaned and then winced from hearing my own too-loud voice. "Holy...fuck."

It'd been a while since I'd woken up with this kind of hangover. I lay on the sheets a second before I could be sure I was in one piece. Light from the crack in the window curtain continued to irritate my headache, but there was no way I was moving anytime soon to go slide it all the way closed.

"Oh my God," a voice croaked from my left. "Why is there so much sand in the bed?"

I managed to roll my head that way and was eternally relieved to see Caroline beside me because I remembered nothing—not a fucking thing—from the night before, except vague visions of dancing with her on the beach at some party with a bunch of strangers.

"From the amount of sand in my ass crack," I slurred, "I'm going to go out on a limb and say we probably had sex on the beach."

She whimpered and clutched her head before begging,

"Please...make it stop."

I was in no condition to get off the bed, but my woman was miserable, so I rolled until I fell off the side and landed in a heap on the floor. Cursing my sore muscles and pounding head, I grabbed the nightstand and used it to help me crawl to my feet. Naked and tangled in the sheets, Caroline watched me from blurry, bloodshot eyes.

"I got you," I mumbled and scooped her up, more stumbling sideways to the bathroom than walking a straight line.

She slumped her cheek against my shoulder and clung to me in a weak, limp kind of way. Grateful there was a bench to sit on in our shower, I sat her down and started the water, making sure I had the right temperature before turning it on her.

Sighing in gratitude when the spray hit her, she cracked open her eyes and sent me a tired smile, only to frown at my arm. "What...?"

I looked down at whatever had caught her attention, shocked to see a patch of gauze taped to me. When I lifted my hand to the area, a familiar sting told me exactly what had happened.

"Ah...fuck." Fisting my hand and setting it against my pounding head, I cursed a little more before admitting, "I think I got another goddamn drunk tattoo." I sent Caroline a weary cringe. "It never turns out well when I get a drunk tattoo." The last time I'd gotten a football championship tattoo with Gam, we'd lost the game the next day.

I scurried out of the shower and went to the mirror to ease the bandage off my bicep. The word inked into my skin appeared backwards in the reflection, but I could still tell exactly what it said. As my mouth fell open with shock, Caroline called, "What is it?"

I just kept staring, not sure what to say. "Uh...it's, um..."

"You didn't get anything girly, like a heart, or rose, or butterfly, did you?"

"No..." I blinked at the tattoo. "It's...actually a word."

"Well, what does it say?"

"Nothing," I was quick to answer. Too quick.

"Nothing?" she repeated. "As in, it literally says the word nothing? N-O-T-H-I-N-G?"

"Yep. It says nothing."

"Why would you get a tattoo that said nothing?"

"Probably because I was stupid drunk. I don't know. Why do we ever do anything? Why is the world round and rotates in a circle? Why does the sun come up in the morning and the moon out at night?"

"Okay, now you sound weird." Caroline pulled open the shower door and opened her mouth, only to stop cold when I turned to her and she saw my tattoo for herself. Her eyes widened. "That's my name."

"Yeah..." I said slowly. I had her name embedded into my skin...with permanent ink.

I constantly ragged on Pick for tattooing his woman's name onto his skin. I told him it was bad ju-ju. He'd end up losing her somehow—she'd leave, she'd die, she'd get dragged away by flying monkeys—and then he'd just be stuck with a bittersweet reminder of what he no longer had. And yet, here I was, copying the son of a bitch. He'd never let me live this down.

I cracked my eyes open and caught Caroline studying it quietly.

"What?" I asked.

She shook her head before she smiled. "It could be worse. You could've gotten falling-down drunk and slept with some other girl, but instead, you thought of me, and got *my* name branded on you."

I sighed. Yeah, I guess it could've been worse. But I still felt sick with worry, because seriously, it was never good luck when I got a drunk tattoo. Though I was a little thrilled by seeing her name stamped in my skin, and even more thrilled to see how much it pleased her, I also remained as uneasy as hell, because fuck, what if this piece of bad luck ended up making me lose her?

I STILL WASN'T too pleased by the time we finished cleaning up and limped our way down to breakfast. Wearing a dark set of shades and leaning a little against Caroline to keep me upright—while she leaned back for the very same reason—I pointed as soon as I spotted Ham.

"*You*, you motherfucker. What the hell happened last night?" I lifted my hands as I stood over him. He glanced up from his breakfast, and I arched my eyebrows. "You let me get a fucking *tattoo*?"

I knew he had to have been sober the entire night. Not only was he not much of a drinker to begin with, but since his woman couldn't drink a lot after her kidney donation, he'd follow the same path for her.

He just smiled and shook his head. "If you knew everything I kept you from doing last night, you'd realize the tattoo was actually very minor."

"Oh God." I slumped into a chair and cradled my head in my hands. "What else did I do?"

If he told me I tried to pick up some other chick, I'd puke. It wouldn't be so hard—I already felt like I might. When Caroline sat next to me and touched my back, I set my hand on her leg, bracing for the worst.

Hamilton and Blondie glanced at each other before they shook their heads and smiled. "Man, you two definitely know how to have a good time," was all he said.

But I needed a little more information than that. "What?" I demanded. "What did we do that could possibly be worse than a tattoo?"

"Where should we start?" Hamilton chuckled. "First I had to keep you from beating the tar out of some guy who was looking at Caroline. I guess you learned that he'd offered to buy her a drink earlier in the day, and..." He whistled under his breath and shook his head. "After I pulled you away from him, you made a big spectacle of telling everyone we passed that she was *your* woman. I swear, people in Nevada, and Oregon and Arizona heard the announcement that Caroline was with *you*."

"Okay," I said slowly. I could handle telling a bunch of drunk strangers that Caroline was mine. "Is that all?"

"Not even close." Zwinn exchanged another amused glance amongst themselves. "There was a point in there you decided you were going to tell Noel about..." He motioned between Caroline and me. "You know."

I glanced at Caroline. She was wearing sunglasses too, so I couldn't see her eyes, but she did cover her mouth with her hand, obviously horrified.

"Shit." I glanced at Ham. "Please tell me you stopped that?"

He nodded. "Of course. I confiscated both of your phones and kept them for the rest of the night. Here." He motioned to where they currently sat on the table and nudged them our way.

"Whew." I blew out a breath and reached for Caroline's hand. "Well, thank you for stopping that." The worst thing I could've done was tell Gamble over the phone I was with his sister while I was drunk and had her halfway across the country.

Ham nodded. "And that wasn't even the best part."

"Oh God," I moaned. "What else?"

"Well...we came across this wedding party further down the beach. I guess there's one of those twenty-four-hour insta-wedding chapel things nearby. They accept walk-ins and will even marry you right on the beach."

I frowned and scratched my still-aching head. "I thought they only had those things in Las Vegas."

Blondie giggled, so I scowled at her. "What?"

"That's exactly what you said last night," she informed me. "When you were completely wasted."

"And right before you decided you wanted to marry Caroline," Ham added.

Caroline leaned forward. "I'm sorry, *what*?"

"I tried to get *married*?" I repeated, lifting my eyebrows incredulously. "*Last night*?"

Zwinn nodded, and burst out laughing.

"But you stopped us, right?" When they nodded again, both Caroline and I let out similar relieved breaths. "Well, shit. Okay, I can see why you settled for letting me get a tattoo after that."

"Actually." Ham rolled up his own shirtsleeve to reveal the word *Zoey* scrawled on his bicep. "The tattoo was *my* idea. You're the one who copied *me*."

I shook my head. Wow. Apparently, I'd been a busy little boy.

"You designed this for me at the tattoo parlor," Ham went on proudly as he gazed adoringly at his own ink before grinning at Blondie.

"Wait." I waved my hand. "I was blind-ass drunk, and you still let me design a tattoo you're going to have on your skin for the rest of your life? Man, that's whack."

Quinn just shrugged. "It came out good, so I didn't have a problem with it."

I turned to Caroline and shook my head.

After a second of staring back, a slow grin spread across her face. "I think this is the best trip I've ever been on."

Once we returned to Illinois and I had to give Caroline back to her brother, I think I went through a fucking mini-depression or something. I still drove over most every night to pick her up at our spot and got to see her damn near every day, and talked to her constantly via text, but it just wasn't the same.

At Lake Tahoe, I hadn't had to hide her, hadn't needed to sneak. I'd been able to keep her all night long and wake up the next morning beside her. Fuck, according to Ham, I'd been able to claim my feelings for her loud enough in public that people three states away could hear.

But here...fuck, here it was still a secret. And I hated that. Caroline Gamble was not my secret. She was my heart and soul, and I just couldn't do this shit much longer.

I'd been trying to wait until she broached the subject and made it her idea, so she didn't feel anxious or scared when we finally told him, but I just...I couldn't hold out much longer.

Besides, other things were forcing me to make decisions sooner than I expected.

So about a week after Lake Tahoe, I walked her to my room after picking her up at our spot, sat her on the bed facing her, and I said, "There's something I have to tell you."

She blinked and pulled back in surprise. "O....okay," she said slowly. "This sounds serious."

I nodded. There were actually about three serious things we needed to discuss, so I took both her hands and looked into her eyes. But when I opened my mouth, something rattled the wall of the hallway just outside my room.

"What the hell?" Caroline and I exchanged worried glances and simultaneously rushed to the door. "Blondie?" I called.

Ham was gone to work, so it had to be—

"Oh, shit." She lay on the floor, half slumped against the wall and unconscious. Heart lurching in my chest, I leapt at her. "*Blondie!*"

"Oh my God. Zoey?" Caroline was right beside me, falling to her knees with me, as I reached out with shaking hands, afraid of what they might find. When a pulse fluttered against my fingertips as I touched her throat and her breath fell on my arm, I sat back on my haunches with a relieved pant.

"What's wrong with her?" Crouching on Blondie's other side, Caroline gently brushed Blondie's hair out of her face.

"The fuck if I know. I think she just passed out."

"But why? Do you think it's something from her kidney transplant?"

I glanced at her, and we shared similar expressions of worry. "Let's get her to a hospital." I leaned forward to scoop my arms under the limp figure on the floor.

"Call—"

"Already on it." I looked up just as Caroline finished dialing and was pressing her cell phone to her ear.

"God, you're a damn fine woman."

She winked at me but then began to chew on her lip as she waited. "Come on, Quinn. Pick up. Pick up."

"No way is he going to be able to hear his own phone in that place. It's a miracle when we hear the *landline* ring."

"Then I'll call Noel and have him personally drive over and *get* Quinn."

"Good idea." I grunted when I straightened with all of Blondie's dead weight in my arms.

"Damn fine woman, remember," Caroline said, redialing the phone. She hurried ahead of me to open the front door. I thanked her with a quick kiss on the cheek before passing through.

"Noel?" she started, then frowned. "Hello? Noel? *Damn it.*" She shook the phone and scowled at it. "Crappy connection. I wonder where the hell he is."

"Did you tell him you were hanging out with Blondie tonight?"

"Yes. Thank goodness." As I paused to rest a shoulder against the wall and try to redistribute Blondie's weight, Caroline glanced back and stopped. "You okay?"

"Yeah. Just...okay, let's go." I finally had a firmer grip.

Caroline once again surprised me with her forethought when she led us to Blondie's car and unlocked it with a set of keys she'd snagged off the hook by the wall before we'd left the apartment.

Blondie woke up on the ride to the hospital where we had her stretched out in the backseat with her head nestled in Caroline's lap.

"What's going on?" She sounded disoriented and sleepy. "Where are we?"

"You passed out, sweetie." Caroline pressed her hand to Blondie's forehead after she helped her sit up. "We're taking you to get checked out."

"I *did*?" It was Blondie's turn to press her own hand to her forehead. "That's so strange. I've never passed out before in my life. I remember feeling woozy, so I headed to the kitchen to get a drink when the hall just kind of tipped sideways and everything faded to black."

"Do you think it has anything to do with your kidney transplant?"

Blondie stared at Caroline for a moment before slowly shaking her head. "I don't know. I wouldn't think so. After the initial recovery, I haven't had any side effects at all. And honestly, I feel fine now. We don't have to go to the hospital."

"Tough shit," I called back to her. "We're already here. And we're going to find out what the hell just happened to you."

"Ten?" she said, blinking at me behind the wheel of her car as if surprised to see me there. Then she glanced at the empty passenger seat next to me. "You look funny up there all by yourself."

"Yeah, don't mind me, driving my two Miss Daisy's to the store."

Blondie looked over at Caroline, who beamed back. "He really is getting so much better with his movie quoting, isn't he?"

I chuckled and found us a place to park outside the ER. But after I got out and opened the back door for my two ladies, Blondie resisted. "I don't...really. What if we found out something *is* wrong?"

"Then it's better to find out about it now rather than later." Caroline gave her a nudge from behind and when Blondie tumbled toward me, I grasped her hand and helped her the rest of the way from the car.

Her fingers clamped down around mine, and panic lit her face. "I want Quinn."

Caroline's phone appeared in her hand. "Don't worry. I'll get him for you."

"No, wait. You know, this is nothing. I'm sure I'm fine.

Don't call him. I don't want to bother him at work because of some false alarm."

"But what if—" I started, only to shut up when Caroline sent me a warning glare.

Blondie lifted worried eyes to me, so I cleared my throat and nodded. "Okay, we won't bother him. Yet."

So, we sat in the waiting room for damn near an hour and a half with a sighing Blondie continuously telling us this was ridiculous because she felt fine.

I was never so happy to hear someone call her name. "Thank fucking God."

The three of us stood and when they led us back to the room where she sat on a cot, Caroline took one side and grabbed one of Blondie's hands, while I did the same on the other side. I gave her fingers a supportive squeeze as the nurse started to ask her the routine questions and checked her vitals.

As the questions slowly got a little more personal, Blondie's face quickly got a lot redder.

"How have your menstrual cycles been?"

And fuck. This time, I turned beet red with her. I coughed into my hand and caught Caroline snickering at me. I scowled at her while Blondie lowered her face and admitted, "They've been pretty light the past few months. I mean, a lot lighter than usual. I...I'm not even sure I had one last month."

The nurse nodded as if she suspected as much. "Is it possible you're pregnant?"

All three of our jaws dropped pretty much simultaneously. Finally, Blondie shook her head. "No...I...I'm taking birth control. That's not possible."

The look the nurse sent her told us it was entirely possible. "Have you been sick lately? Vomited any?"

"No," Blondie started, only to pause. "I mean, way back in March I guess I did. I had a stomach bug, but it only lasted a day."

"It only takes one missed pill to get pregnant, and if you vomited a pill..." She shrugged, telling us that was that.

"And you got nauseous on the way to Lake Tahoe," Caroline chimed in, implying the beginning of morning sickness.

Blondie glanced at Caroline and then me, her expression beyond panicked.

I lifted my hands. "Well, let's find out if she's pregnant."

The nurse pulled up a plastic cup and instructed Blondie to go pee in it. While she was gone, Caroline came to me. I pulled her into a tight hug, kissing her hair. "Well, at least it might not be something life threatening," I said, relieved out of my mind.

But when Caroline looked up, her gaze was still concerned. "Are you sure? I mean, is it okay for her to get pregnant this soon after her operation?"

"Oh, shit." I closed my eyes and gritted my teeth. "I forgot about that. I don't know."

Blondie returned then, so we shut up about our concerns and flanked her once more.

Moments later, her doctor entered, smiling. "Congratulations," he said, lifting his smile to encompass both me and Blondie. "You two are having a baby."

Blondie squeaked out her shock. Caroline sprang toward the door that led to the hall, already tugging her phone from her pocket. "I'm getting Quinn," she called as she fled the room.

And I looked at Blondie before turning back to the doctor. "Well, damn, that's impressive, since I've never had sex with her."

"I...I'm sorry." The doctor flushed and stuttered a moment before asking, "So, you two aren't...?"

Both Blondie and I shook our heads. Then I looked at her. "She's...my sister," I finally said and gave a warm squeeze to her hand.

"Oh! Well..." The doctor's smile eased. He consulted his chart. "It looks like—"

"Wait." Blondie lifted her hand, stopping him mid-word. "I...I...no. I can't get pregnant right now. I donated a kidney five months ago, and they said...they said I needed to wait at least three to six months before I could get pregnant."

The doctor winced. "Yeah...that definitely makes a difference." He checked the chart. "And you said your periods have been light recently, plus you missed a pill in March, so you could be as far as two months along. Add that to the fact that you've been taking birth control the entire duration, and that puts you in a definite risk category."

"Oh God." Blondie covered her mouth with both hands. She looked so scared that I wrapped an arm around her shoulders. She leaned against me, clutching my arm. "So what...what're we supposed to do then?"

"Well..." The doctor blew out a breath before glancing over a rack full of pamphlets hanging from the wall. Then he pulled one free. "If you're asking about termination, there's some information about that here, places to call for locations and...and...ma'am?"

Blondie recoiled from the pamphlet he was trying to give her and burst into tears. "Are you saying...oh God...I have to get an...an abortion?"

"What? *No.*" The doctor shook his head. "Of course, no one would force you. It's just...you might possibly have a very dangerous pregnancy, and I thought you were asking...I assumed you wanted...honestly, I was just trying to give you all the information there is so you're fully aware of your options."

I lifted my hand to shut him up. Then I gently reached out and pushed the pamphlet out of Blondie's eyesight. "Clearly, that it not an option she's willing to pursue." I even said in a calm, rational voice.

But the idiot just lifted the pamphlet again and thrust it back at her. "But—"

"Are you deaf, asshole?" I roared. "Get that fucking thing out of her face. *She's not killing her baby.*"

As soon as the shout cleared my lungs, Caroline appeared in the doorway. My eyes met hers and I knew, I just knew...I'd fucked up. Big time.

A moment later, her pale face was gone again, completely disappearing from the doorway as she fled.

CHAPTER 29

Ten

My hands wouldn't stop trembling as I led Blondie back into our apartment. She'd stopped crying, but she was still shaken to the core. Caroline must've gotten hold of someone who'd driven to the club and alerted Quinn to trouble, because he'd called my cell phone as I was taking his woman home from the hospital...without Caroline.

I told him to meet us here so Blondie could explain everything, and then I hung up on him because I just couldn't talk.

Blondie had been understanding. She'd looked up at me as soon as Caroline had darted out of the hospital room, and she'd said, "You should go after her."

I'd merely tightened my arm around her shoulders. "You really want me to leave you here alone right now... like *this*?"

With a shudder, she glanced at the doctor and then whispered, "No," from blanched lips.

"Then I'll find Caroline later," I told her.

But shit, it was later, and I was antsy as hell. I couldn't shake the memory of the devastated look on her face when I'd yelled that shit about baby killing.

I was such a fucking idiot.

"I...I'm going to go to my room," Blondie told me, her voice small and scared.

I nodded, but at the last second, I grabbed her and gave her one final hug, planting a kiss on the top of her head. "It's going to be okay, kiddo. I know how determined Hamilton can get. And he's not going to let anything happen to you or your baby, all right?"

She looked up at me from green, tearstained eyes. "Neither am I," she promised. "But thank you. Thank you for the reassurance, and thank you for staying with me."

I smiled and let her go. Seconds after she disappeared into her room, the door flew open and a breathless Ham exploded into the apartment.

"Where's Zoey? What happened? Is she okay?"

"She's in your room. She'll tell you everything. I gotta go."

"Wait." He caught my arm as I reached for the door. "Where're *you* going?"

"I have to find Caroline." I started to pass him, only to pause and bump a fist lightly against his shoulder. "And by the way, congratulations."

He shook his head, utterly confused. "Huh?"

I grinned at him as I let myself out of the apartment, but as soon as I shut the door, the worry set right back in. Fucking hell, how was I ever going to get Caroline to forgive me? I'd seen the desolation on her face; I'd hurt her badly.

I made it to the Gamble house in five minutes, when it probably should've taken ten. I didn't bother to knock but ran around to the back and eased open the rear door. When I slipped into the kitchen, I was immediately accosted.

"You big...*jerk*." Colton scowled up at me a split second before winding back his arm and punching me right in the nuts.

I sucked in a breath as the pain exploded through my nads, making my stomach roil and try to upchuck its contents all over the floor. I went down, my knees buckling, as I choked out a short whimper.

"What the hell did you do to Caroline?" Brandt demanded as he pulled back his own arm. When he jacked me in the eye, I barely even felt it; my junk was still hogging all the pain.

"What the hell?" I gasped, sitting on the floor and resting my back against their kitchen counter while I cradled both my aching eye and swollen nuts.

"You said if anyone ever upset Caroline, we should hurt him back where it hurts him the most."

"Well, congratulations." I still wanted to cry from the agony, but I managed to keep the tears in. "You succeeded. *Shit*...because that really fucking hurt."

Colton finally approached me, looking worried. "Are you okay?"

"No," I growled. "I came here to make sure Caroline was doing fine, and you little fuckers beat the shit out of me. How do you *think* I am?"

Now Brandt began to look uneasy too. "You mean *you're* not the one who made her cry?"

No way could I own up to that, so I said, "Just help me sneak back to her room so I can make this all better again."

The two brothers glanced at each other before they turned back to me. Then they held out their hands simultaneously, palms up.

"What?" I said before it struck me. "Oh, you've got to be fucking kidding me. You don't really expect me to *pay* you after you kicked me in the nuts and gave me another fucking black eye, do you?"

"Yes," they said together.

Muttering, I hiked up my hip, wincing when it caused me to jostle the family jewels. "This is fucking highway robbery is what this is. I'm a wounded man, and you're *still* blackmailing me. Where's the humanity?" I pulled out two bills. "I only have twenty bucks."

"That'll do." Each boy took a ten-dollar bill and smiled smugly at me. As they started out of the kitchen, I hissed. "Hey! Are you going to help me sneak past your brother or not?"

"Oh, Noel's not home," Brandt called back to me. "He and Aspen ran to the grocery store."

"Motherfucker," I muttered, slapping my foot against the floor, because damn, those two definitely knew how to damage a guy and then kick him while he was down.

With another curse, I grabbed the counter to pull myself up. I couldn't believe I'd just gotten played by those two little punks. They kind of made me proud...in the most irritating way possible.

As soon as I gained my footing, I gasped for breath because more blood rushed to my balls with a tender urgency. "Holy shit." I breathed through my teeth to help abate the throbbing, but every step through the house—with me mostly clinging to the walls—was a torturous son of a bitch.

I didn't knock when I reached Caroline's room. I just grabbed the handle and turned, stumbling inside.

Caroline had slunk deep into the corner of the wall on her bed with her knees up to her chest and her arms wrapped around her legs. Tears poured down her cheeks. Both her eyes and nose were red, telling me she'd been going at it for a while.

She gasped when she looked up and saw me. "Wha... how did you get in here?"

"Through the door." Forgetting my own injuries, I went to her, climbing onto her bed.

I was such an ass. Here was my strong, feisty, scheming little spitfire, and I'd broken her. Why the fuck had I reacted so adamantly at the doctor's office when I'd *known* she was in the building, when I *knew* this was the topic she was most sensitive about?

"Damn it." I crawled to her, growling when she shied away from me. "Damn it," I said again, fisting my hands and setting them against my mouth. My heart broke. It just...completely fucking shattered. "Baby, don't," I begged. "Please." On my knees in front of her, I reached for her hair but was suddenly afraid to touch her. I didn't want to do anything to hurt her any more than I already had. "I'm sorry. I'm so damn sorry."

She sniffed and lifted her face. "What're you...what're *you* sorry about? You...you didn't do anything—"

"But I said—"

She shook her head vigorously, shutting me up. "You didn't say anything I haven't told myself a million times. I killed my baby. I—"

"Don't. Shh." I caught her face and finally hauled her into my arms. When she went to me willingly and clung hard, I gulped in relief, so damn glad she wasn't mad at me.

"I would be a mother right now. I'd have a baby, and—"

"And you'd be a total MILF." Okay, so I went for a joke to ease her pain. I thought it might actually work. It'd worked for her before.

But she started sobbing again. "*Oren.*" Burying her face in her hands, she let her inner pain loose. "This isn't funny."

I crumbled. "I know. I'm sorry. I'm so sorry. Shit, see—" I grasped her arms and pressed my forehead to hers. "We all do and say things we regret. For me, it's a lot of things. But big or small, you gotta figure out a way to forgive yourself and move on from that shit. Since we can't go back and change it, we gotta just learn from it. And whether you regret this or not—"

"I do."

I nodded. "Okay. Then you have to...I don't know, fuck. But I can't handle watching you fall apart like this. I mean, look at you. This is not you. You don't cry like this, you don't cower into corners. It totally fucked you up. And I just...I wish I could take it all from you, that I could...fuck! I don't know."

Blue eyes still glittering with tears, she gazed up at me and managed a tremulous smile. "Do you want to know what went through my mind when I saw you yell at that doctor?"

I winced. "That I was a stupid motherfucker?"

She shook her head. "No. I thought...where was this amazing man when I needed him to do that for *me*? Where was he when I was scared and alone, quivering in front of Sander's intimidatingly powerful parents, or when I walked into that clinic feeling sick to my stomach with unease. Why did he have to show up in my momma's trailer the very next morning? Why couldn't he have arrived in my life just one day sooner?"

Devastation swamped me. My throat felt dry, but when I tried to clear it, I had to blink repeatedly to keep my eyes from growing wet. "I wish I could've been there, too," I said in a rusty voice. "I would've taken one look at your face and known that wasn't what you really wanted to do. I would've told all those assholes pressuring you into it to go fuck themselves."

Caroline took my hand and then rested her cheek on my shoulder. "I know you would have. But what bothered me the most was listening to you do that for Zoey and thinking, why hadn't I just done that for myself? Why didn't I stand up to everyone and say no?"

"Because you were scared, and intimidated, and alone, just like you said," I reminded her. I started to rock her back and forth, relieved when she settled deeper into me, relaxing against my chest. "Plus you were young, vulnerable, destitute, and heartbroken from the prick who'd just left you. You didn't feel as if you had a lot of other options left."

She sniffed but didn't answer, just listened to me as I stroked her hair. With a kiss to her forehead, I said, "When I saw you in that doorway of the doctor's office, looking at me the way you did, I thought that was it. You were done with me because I...because of what I said. But I swear to God, I wasn't even thinking about what happened to you when I blurted it out. I just...Blondie was getting upset, and she clearly didn't want—"

"I know," Caroline said simply. She set her hand on my arm, comforting me, and I shuddered with relief. "I knew it the second I heard it. I just...I needed..."

"To get away?" I guessed. "To go to your place?"

She glanced around her bedroom and gave a small smile. "Yeah. I guess I did."

I drew in a breath, relieved her tears had stopped. Her face was still red and splotchy and eyes totally bloodshot, but she no longer looked like she was on the precipice of a total breakdown. Cuddling deeper into her, I rested my cheek against hers and asked, "How can I help you through this? What can I do to ease your pain, because I swear to God, I'll do anything."

Absolutely anything.

She set her hand on my heart and looked up at me, her eyes filled with so much emotion, I swear, some of it overflowed, spilling into me. "Just love me," she whispered.

"I do," I promised. Pressing my forehead to hers, I shifted her around until I had her lying on her back diagonally across her bed. "I love you so damn much it scares the fuck out of me." Hovering above her, I set my lips against hers and gave her a kiss that would've sent a weaker person into a diabetic coma; it was that damn sweet.

But then our mouths opened and our tongues brushed softly. I groaned and buried my fingers in her hair as I settled my weight down on top of hers.

"I had no idea it could be like this," she whispered, only breaking her mouth away from mine long enough to look at me with a measure of awe. "I had no idea I could share so much with one person and feel so...full. Like, I don't know...without you in my life, I'm not sure I'd know how to be me anymore. You've become a part of who I am."

I smiled, understanding her completely. "Yeah, well, you make me want to grow up and straighten my shit out so I can take care of you and be a man good enough to deserve you."

"I'm the one who doesn't deserve you," she countered.

I rubbed my nose against hers and smiled. "Do too."

She grinned back. "Have we gotten serious and emotional enough for one conversation? Because I'm really wet right now and—"

"I'm on it," I told her as I slid my hands down to her body and right inside the back of her jeans until I was cupping two cheek-fulls of ass, one in each hand.

Grinding my hips between her legs so she could feel how hard I was, I groaned when she wound her thighs around me and tugged me even closer to her pussy.

"Damn, I could never get enough of you. Not in a thousand years."

I ripped at her shirt, kissing her and panting when she turned just as savage, tearing a bit in the neckline of my T-shirt when she yanked it over my head.

"I want to look into your eyes and face you while you take me," she commanded.

I had no issue with that, so I nodded and kicked off my jeans as she rushed to remove hers. She took me into her hand, making me shudder with desire as I watched her slim little fingers wrap around my cock. When I pulsed into her palm, she drew in a breath and looked up at me.

"I want to feel this inside me...right now."

Without breaking eye contact, I laid her back onto the bed and came over her. Then I thrust hard.

She arched her neck and started to cry out, but I slapped my hand over her mouth. Her eyes widened and then darted around her room before she seemed to realize where she was. Then she ripped my fingers from her face, whispering, "Oh my God, Oren. We're in my bedroom."

I just grinned and impaled her again. "No shit, Sherlock."

She gnashed her teeth and panted, beginning to lose herself to the pleasure. "But...what if...did you even lock the door?"

"Can't remember," I admitted. I'd been preoccupied with other issues. My balls twinged when my nut sack tightened around them, but even the dulled pain of getting racked recently didn't stop me. I was too preoccupied with matters that were way more important.

Caroline grasped my arms, her nails digging into my flesh. "But what if—" Her eyes flared wide. "Oh my God. I think I hear Noel's voice in the kitchen."

I just shook my head and continued to pump in and out of her. "I don't care. I have to pleasure my woman." Then I leaned down to whisper into her ear. "And show her how much I love her."

She sucked in a breath and clutched my face. "I love you too. So much. So...oooohhh...oh God...much."

I kissed her to smother her moans of pleasure. Her pussy contracted around my cock, and that was it. I couldn't hold back any longer. We came together, clutching each other tight as our orgasm rolled through us.

Once I was spent, I collapsed onto the bed, face-first beside her. "Damn, but we're fucking awesome at that."

She giggled and reached out to play with my hair that had gotten damp. "Yeah, we are, aren't we?"

I shifted to my side so I could smile into her beautiful blue eyes. "Have I thanked you lately for sneaking into my room that first night and totally tricking me?"

She shrugged. "Your gratitude's kind of a given."

Chuckling softly, I ran my index finger lightly over the top swell of her perfect breast. "How the hell did you talk Kelly into switching places with you, anyway?"

Her cheeks instantly turned bright red. "Uh, yeah... about that."

"Oh, Jesus." I groaned, already knowing I wasn't going to like her answer. "What did you do?"

"I...might've...insinuated you had...an...STD, maybe."

I closed my eyes, flopped onto my back and couldn't help it. I laughed. "Seriously? Fuck. Thanks a lot. No wonder why I haven't had many women hitting on me at work lately."

Caroline sat up and bit her lip. "Are you mad?"

With another laugh, I shrugged and rolled toward her. "Not since it ended up in my favor, no. But remind me to never piss you off."

"Never piss me off, Oren," she said with a straight face before breaking into a grin.

I opened my mouth to call her a smart-ass when someone knocked on her door. "Care?" Gam's voice reverberated through the wood, which about made me shit myself. "It's time for supper. You ready to eat?"

Both our eyes widened before we scrambled off the bed together and grappled for clothes that were scattered all over the room.

"Uh...I'll be right out," she called, her voice too panicked for my taste. "I just need to...change first."

"Shit, shit, shit," I hissed under my breath as I went commando and jammed my legs into my jeans.

"Okay," Gam answered her. "We'll give you five minutes."

I was dressed in about twenty seconds while Caroline was cursing her twisted bra. I reached out to help, and she threw her hands up in defeat as I straightened it around her breasts and then slid the straps neatly into place.

"I'll go out the window," I said. "Don't forget to lock it after me."

She nodded as she watched me slide up the glass and take off the screen.

"You sure you got this?" I asked.

With a roll of her eyes, she took the screen from me. "I've done it before, remember?"

I nodded. "Right. Thanks. Lick you later, baby."

Her face lit with adoration. "Okay."

We kissed, hard and fast. When I pulled away, I added, "Love you," to which she sent me the perfect smile.

"I love you too. *Oh!* Wait."

I paused and glanced toward her bedroom door. "What?"

"What did you want to tell me earlier? At your place...right before Zoey passed out. Oh, crap! Zoey. Is she okay?"

I nodded, starting to worry that her bedroom door wasn't locked at all. "Yeah, she's doing good. A little freaked out, but she had Ham with her, and..." Shit, I couldn't tell her what I'd been planning on telling her earlier. Not here, like this. Mentioning the call I'd gotten from Lake Tahoe and the thing I'd found in my luggage after returning from there would freak her out.

Unsettling her was the last thing I wanted to do right now, so I went for the third thing I'd been planning to discuss with her. "I'm going to ask your brother if I can date you."

CHAPTER 30

TEN

I KNEW I SHOULD'VE gone home to check on Blondie and Ham, but I still wanted to be around Caroline, plus now seemed like as good a time as any to talk to Noel and ask for his permission to take his sister on a real, live date. So instead of hunting my truck down, I snuck around from the side of the house to the front. After hopping onto the porch, I drew in a deep breath and knocked on the door.

Gam's woman answered less than a minute later. She blinked as if confused when she saw me.

I smiled as charmingly as I could. "Can Noel come out and play?"

"Uh..." She shook her head. "Yes, sure. He's here. Come on in. What's going on? You look..." She glanced at my rumpled, half-torn clothes. "Out of sorts."

Shit, I probably should've groomed a bit before knocking. Caroline had been a little wild this evening.

Oh, well. Too late for that.

I shrugged ruefully. "It's been one of those nights."

"Ten?" Gam's curious voice came from behind his wife.

I peered around her to grin at him. "Hey, man. Ham and Blondie needed the place to themselves for a while, so I'm temporarily homeless. You take in strays here, right?" I stepped inside around his wife and sucked in a big breath, lifting my nose to the ceiling. "Damn, whatever that is cooking, it smells great. I'd love to stay for dinner, thanks."

Gamble leaned a shoulder against the framed opening of the living room and lifted a non-impressed eyebrow as he crossed his arms over his chest. But his wife laughed at my antics.

"It's nothing fancy," she said. "Just tacos. And you're welcome to stay, Ten. No problem."

Ignoring her husband, I flashed her another bright smile. "Why, thank you, Mrs. Gamble. I'll set the table."

My offer made her face brighten, but she waved out a hand. "You don't have to do that, but thank you. And you can just call me Aspen, you know."

As I followed her into the kitchen, I shuddered. "Yeah, sorry. I don't typically call women by their first name. It's some kind of strange tick I can't control." I sent her a helpless shrug.

"Really?" She sent me a knowing little smile. "I've never heard you call *Caroline* anything but Caroline."

"Hmm," I murmured as I opened a cabinet door and pulled down a pile of plates. "If you want, I can come up with a nickname for you."

Eyes flaring wide with horror, she shook her head. "No! Oh, no. I mean, really. No. If it's anything like the one you gave Eva, I'd just as soon pass."

"Hey, I will have you know Milk Tits loves her nickname."

Aspen blurted out a laugh. "Yeah. I'm sure."

"Wait. I have one." I paused with a plate in hand to study her for a moment and draw out the suspense. Then I pointed and said, "Shakespeare."

She instantly gasped. "Oh my God, I love it!' A split second later, she seemed to realize she was acting too girly, so she blushed and covered her mouth. "I mean, thank you. I'll take that one."

With a wink, I went back to setting out the plates. "You got it."

"Noel, Ten just gave me the nickname Shakespeare. Don't you love it?"

I glanced around to find him leaning against the kitchen entrance now, his eyes narrowed as he watched me pull glasses from his cupboard.

"Since when did you two become such good friends?" he asked.

I opened my mouth to tell him that was none of his damn business but Shakespeare said, "Since I helped him with his resume a few weeks ago."

I pressed both hands to my heart and grinned as annoyingly as I could. "We bonded. It was beautiful."

Gamble contorted his face into an expression of supreme confusion. Then he glanced at his wife. "He didn't hit on you, did he?"

She sighed and rolled her eyes. "Noel. Really?"

"Yeah, Noel," I echoed. "*Really?* I was a perfectly respectable gentleman." Then I winked at Shakespeare. "After we put our clothes back on."

Gam's face turned dark red. "You motherfucker!"

"Oh my God, *Noel!*" Shakespeare grabbed his arm and started laughing. "He was joking. It was a joke." She sent me a wide-eyed, cut-it-out look. "I don't think he thought that was so funny, *Ten.*"

I shrugged and snagged a chip from a bowl on the table. "Well, it sure amused the hell out of me, which is all that counts. Some people," I arched my eyebrows at Gam, "just take things way too fucking seriously."

"Where is everyone?" Aspen asked, desperate to change the conversation. "Colton! Brandt! Caroline! Supper."

Colton came torpedoing into the room first with Brandt right on his heels. They both skidded to a stop when they saw me. Their eyes went wide as if they were sure I was going to call them out for what they'd done earlier.

But I simply sent them a big grin. "Hey, guys. Long time, no see."

Brandt cleared his throat, ducked his face and hurried to a chair. Colton followed with similar meekness. I waited until they were both seated before I took the chair between them and slid down. They grew even more restless, and I almost busted a gut laughing. But damn, I loved fucking with them.

As I was settling in, a breathless Caroline swept into the room, only to jerk to a halt when she met my gaze.

She wouldn't stop gawking, so I sent her a cringe and pointed to myself. "I'm sorry, did I steal your chair?"

"What?" She blinked and glanced around at the places. "No," she started, only to shake her head. "Well, actually yes, but you're fine. It's fine." She sent her older brother a puzzled glance. "Uh...I guess we're having a *guest* for supper."

"He invited himself," Gam intoned dryly.

Caroline shook herself again and finally took the last free chair available.

And so began our supper together as one big, happy family.

I was halfway through my second taco when Gamble frowned suspiciously at me and leaned across the table, squinting. I shrank away from him, hoping I wasn't sporting a hickey or anything.

"Do you have a new black eye?" he finally asked.

I totally wasn't expecting that question, so I said, "What?"

Brandt started choking on a tortilla chip. While I patted him on the back, Gamble turned his attention to his middle brother. "You okay?"

Brandt couldn't look him in the eye while he nodded. "Mmm hmm. Fine. Great. Wonderful. Splendorific."

Gamble glanced at his wife. "Why's he acting so weird?"

While Shakespeare shrugged, honestly clueless, Caroline answered, "Probably because he's a dork."

I laughed. "I'll second that."

Caroline glanced at me, her eyes sparkling with mischief. "All in favor?"

She and I both raised our hands. When no one else seemed to catch on that we were voting on Brandt's dork-hood, I grabbed Colton's arm and lifted it for him.

"Three against two," I said. "It's official. Brandt's a dork."

While Brandt cried, "Hey, that's not fair," Caroline and I grinned across the table at each other...until her smile fell. "Oh my God, you really do have a new bruise. Right around your left eye. The one Zoey gave you was around your right."

"See, I thought so." Gamble pointed victoriously. Then he snickered. "Who'd you piss off this time?"

Brandt's head snapped up, his eyes huge. He must've thought I was going to rat him out. But I just shrugged. "It's hard to tell. I've gotten so many lately, it's impossible to keep track without, like, a spreadsheet or something. Honestly, I think they're starting to spawn and have babies together." Colton giggled at that. So I kept going, pointing at my throbbing eye. "I swear this one's the great-grandkid of the one you gave me last year, Gam."

But Gam wasn't amused. Narrowing his eyes, the bastard scowled at me. "Why are you avoiding the question?"

I scratched my jaw and shrugged with clueless abandon. "What question? You didn't ask a question."

"*Who* gave you the black eye?" he asked slowly.

Just as slowly, I answered, "I'm not telling. It's fucking embarrassing, man. Felt like I got slapped by a little girl."

An incredulous sound gurgled from Brandt's throat as he whipped around to frown his offence at me.

"Did Hamilton hit you again?" Gam asked with a sigh. "You hit on Zoey, didn't you? That's why you had to come over here tonight?"

I slapped a hand to my forehead and groaned. "Oh my fucking God. You are so clueless. *Really?*"

"What?" Gam demanded, clearly perturbed.

Shakespeare stood up suddenly, saying, "You know, Colton. I think it's time for your bath."

I wanted to point at her and tell her hubby, *See, even she gets what's going on here,* but I glanced at the kid. "Dude, you still take *baths?*"

He blinked up at me. "Yeah. Why?"

"*Why?* Because showers are so awesome. They're like a million little wet fingers massaging your entire body."

"Wow." Gam snorted out a laugh as he sent me a strange look. "Look who sounds all poetic tonight."

I shrugged and hooked my thumb toward his wife. "It's because of Shakespeare. Some of her literature shit is rubbing off on me."

She tittered and grinned at Caroline. "I so love that nickname."

Gam just sighed. When the phone rang, he pushed to his feet and left the kitchen to answer it. Aspen followed Colton from the room to help him get ready for bed, while Caroline hauled off and smacked Brandt in the arm. "Oh my God, did you *hit* Oren? In the *eye?*"

"What?" he hissed, ducking away from her. "You were crying. I thought he'd made you cry."

"He did *not* make me cry."

"Yeah, I figured that out already," Brandt mumbled. "I'm *sorry.*"

Caroline smacked him again, but I lifted my hand. "Hey, hey, hey. Children, behave." I lifted my gaze to Caroline. "If it makes you feel any better, the younger one hurt me more when he jacked me in the junk."

"He...Colton *racked* you?"

When I nodded, she smiled softly. "Aww, that's so sweet that he was looking out for me."

"What do you think *I* was doing?" Brandt demanded, lifting his hands incredulously.

Caroline scowled and slapped him again. "I guess next time you should know to go for the nuts, too."

"Whoa, hey." I laughed uneasily. "Maybe you all should just leave this area of my anatomy alone completely." I made a sweeping motion over my lap. "It's off limits."

Batting her eyelashes at me, Caroline asked, "Does that include me too?"

I was about to tell her she was the only person allowed in that zone when a scream echoed through the house. I flew out of my seat, prepared to see someone else passed out in the hallway. But when I plowed out of the kitchen, with Brandt and Caroline piling after me, I skidded to a shocked halt when I saw Shakespeare laughing and crying and hugging Gam.

"What the hell?"

"I got the job!" she screamed and let go of her husband to launch herself at me. When she hugged me hard, I stumbled back a step before catching her and hugging her back.

"Well, congratulations, Shakespeare." I patted her back as I untangled myself and passed her to Brandt. "I knew you'd get it, though. You're a kick-ass teacher."

Tears glittered in her eyes as she smiled up at me and hugged the teen. "Really. You think so?"

"Hell, yes. I hate English, and I was actually acing your class before you had to leave." I sent Gam a telling look for fucking up my grade. I'd ended the semester with a freaking B because of the boring-ass replacement they'd sent in for her.

He just scowled back, so I rolled my eyes and then smiled softly as I watched Shakespeare and Caroline hug and dance around. After the women let go of each other, she went back to embracing her husband. When they kissed, Caroline paused beside me.

"This probably isn't the best time to have that talk with him, is it?" I said from the side of my mouth.

She sighed sadly and shook her head. "No. Probably not."

My shoulders slumped. Fuck. I was going to have to wait even longer for my Caroline.

CHAPTER 31

TEN

GETTING CALLED INTO work on karaoke night sucked ass. But Lowe decided he had better things to do than bartend, so Pick asked me to fill in for him.

I'd been planning on spending most of the evening in bed with my woman. Ever since Lake Tahoe, I just couldn't get enough of her. Each stolen moment felt as if our time together was just getting shorter and shorter. I couldn't wait to pin her brother down and have that talk already.

As luck would have it, I had to work with him on karaoke night. I was watching him from the other end of the bar, debating how to broach the subject when Hart sidled up next to me and slugged me companionably on the back.

"So, how's Tenoline these days?" He arched a curious brow my way. "Or do you guys go by Caroten? I wasn't sure exactly how you were shipping it."

I snorted and rolled my eyes. "It's Oreline, mother-fucker. And we're awesome. Why do you ask?" I scowled at him. "You wanting to make a go for my woman?"

He laughed and shook his hands. "No. *No, no, no.* I mean, if I really wanted her, I would've taken her already."

"Oh, you wish, douchebag. You wouldn't have stood a chance."

"I don't know," he murmured thoughtfully. "Caroline and I have always..."

I narrowed my eyes as his voice faded. Jealousy slithered through me, and I just wanted to knock his head against the nearest wall, but a new song started on the Karaoke. I groaned because I was getting burned out by Meghan Trainor's "All About that Bass." But then one of the two girls on stage began to sing and even I had to lift my eyebrows, impressed. It wasn't often that someone who actually had musical talent sang on our karaoke machine.

I turned back to Hart. "Damn, she's not..." But my words faded, because he wasn't listening to me. The guy had that look in his eye. The same look Gamble got when he talked about his wife, or Ham got when Blondie walked into a room. The same look I knew I probably had when Caroline was around.

I glanced back and forth between Hart and the dark-headed girl on stage who had captured his attention, as she wowed the crowd with her husky vocals. The redhead with her finally leaned in and sang along with the chorus, but she was nowhere near as good as her friend. The ladies did a little dance together, wiggling their asses out at the crowd, and I glanced at Hart for his reaction only to break out grinning when his eyes flared and he grabbed the bar for support. A thin trail of sweat slid down his temple.

"Hey, bud. You okay?" I had to ask, unable to stop my smart-ass grin. But seriously, I loved this. He'd gotten such a big, annoying kick out of my obsession for Caroline. It was fucking awesome to see the tables turned and watch him squirm in the presence of some chick.

Hart blew out a breath before giving me his attention. His eyes were glazed with shock. "I think..." He paused to lick his lips and transfer his gaze back to the stage where the two girls were finishing up the song. "I think I just met the girl I'm going to marry. Right there." He pointed toward the stage. "That one. Yeah, she's going to have my babies."

I snorted at his overdramatic proclamation and had to tease. "Who? The redhead?" I actually knew that one's name. We'd made out a few times back in the dark ages.

But Hart scowled before I could add that part. "No. The tall, beautiful Latina." He sent me an incredulous glance. "I mean, did you *not* just hear her voice? Or see that perfect ass?"

I started to snicker, but the hugging girls on stage let go of each other just as some guy approached them. Hart's dream girl leapt off the stage at him, and he caught her around the waist before lowering her enough that she could lean her face in and kiss him. With tongue. Lots of tongue. When they didn't come up for air within thirty seconds, I had to check Hart's reaction.

I nudged my elbow at him. "I think that dude might have a problem with all your marrying and baby-making plans with her."

Horror lit Hart's face as his mouth dropped open and his eyes bulged. Then he glanced at me, absolutely crushed. "That was *not* supposed to happen."

I threw back my head and laughed. I couldn't help myself. It was about damn time some chick caused him a little misery.

"Shut it." He punched his fist into my shoulder, but that only made me laugh louder.

"Oh, damn." I had to hold my belly because I was laughing so hard it hurt. "Shit, man. You should've seen the look on your face when she kissed some other guy."

"Whatever." He turned his back to the stage so he was facing the back of the bar. "I can't believe she's already taken. She has on an Incubus shirt and everything. Seriously, how many women out there are fans of Incubus?"

"I don't know." I scrunched up my face, thinking about it before guessing, "Thousands?"

"Fuck you, man. This wouldn't be so funny if it was happening to you."

"Oh, I do believe it did happen to me, and you were the first fucker in line to haggle me about it, too. So...humph. Payback's a bitch, honey."

"What's a bitch?" Gamble asked, joining our conversation.

"*Nothing*." Moody as all get-out, Asher picked up a tray of dirty glasses and marched out from behind the bar to carry them to the kitchen for cleaning.

Gam arched his eyebrows and glanced at me. I nodded my head toward the stage. "He grew a boner for the dark-headed chick who sang the last song. Felt rejected when she stuck her tongue down some other guy's throat afterward."

"Ah." Gamble nodded and then snorted out an amused laugh. "It figures he'd go for another singer. She did sound good, though."

I shrugged, even though I agreed. When I saw the redhead who'd been on stage with her approaching the bar, I moved in to take her order. Right before I called a greeting, I racked my brain for her name. It'd been something close to Cody, or Jude, or...*Jodi*! That was it.

"Hey, Jodi." Resting my elbows on the counter separating us, I nodded my head in greeting and flashed her a smile.

She glowered back. "Ten."

We hadn't ended so well. Aside from a little oral pleasure, we'd never gone the whole way, and it wasn't because neither of us was willing. She'd turned a little testy about doing anything in the dark, so I'd dropped her flat. And she'd been hateful to me ever since.

"Good job up there." I tipped my chin toward the stage where someone was now slaughtering a Tim McGraw song. "Who was your friend singing with you?"

She sniffed and tipped her chin. "None of your damn business. Are you going to serve me, or not?"

A couple months ago, I would've twisted that question around into something dirty and spit back an answer that really would've pissed her off. Tonight, I was a good boy and nodded my head obligingly. "Sure. What'll you have?"

Jodi gave me her order for three drinks, which told me she was probably buying for her friend too, *and* her friend's man. I set the glasses on the bar in front of her and said, "This round's on the house."

"Good." She sent me another bitter sneer and picked up one glass to down half the contents. "It's the least I deserve for the way you treated me."

"Hey." I scowled right back. "I wasn't that shitty to you."

"And yet I went away, feeling like a complete idiot." When hurt streaked across her face, I shifted, suddenly uncomfortable.

I'd been too freaked out to let anyone see my birthmark all these years, and I'd probably left dozens of women feeling insufficient because of *my* issues. What an awful fucking self-realization.

I opened my mouth to apologize when she kept on, "And after all this time, the first thing you say to me is, 'who's your friend?' Well, fuck you, Ten! Fuck...you. You can't have her."

Her voice had risen in volume. Cringing, I glanced around to see if anyone had heard her, and sure enough, Gamble was glancing our way. When his gaze clashed with mine, he lifted his eyebrows, curious.

Fuck.

I turned back to Jodi, panicked. "Jesus, Jo." I lowered my voice and slid my hand along the counter in her direction. "I'm sorry, okay. I swear to God I never meant to put you through something that's obviously stayed with you this long." She wasn't buying my apology, so I sucked in a breath and went all out. "I was going through some personal issues back then, and I had no business trying to mess around with any girl. It never even occurred to me that hiding something *I* was ashamed of would actually make *you* feel as if you ever did anything wrong. Because you didn't. You were fun as hell to hang out with, and I'm just...I'm sorry."

She stared at me for a moment before slowly nodding. "Okay. When you put it that way, I guess...I guess I can forgive you."

I nodded respectfully. "Thank you. Oh, and for your information, I wasn't asking about your friend for *my* sake. I already have someone. I was asking for...a friend."

"Then...who?" Her gaze wandered around the bar until it landed on Gamble. She leaned in closer, her eyes widening. "Noel Gamble? The big ESU *quarterback* has a thing for *Remy*?"

Remy? So the love of Hart's life was named Remy, huh? That was kind of a cool name for a chick.

I started to tell Jodi no, that I wasn't talking about Gam, but she went on. "Well, sorry, but Remy's not into athletes. She likes musicians...and she already has one. So you just tell Mr. Hotshot Quarterback he's shit out of luck."

"Musicians, huh?" I glanced around for Hart, wishing he could hear the dirt I was gathering on his future bride and mother of his babies. But he still hadn't returned from the back.

"Yep." Jodi looked a little smug as she picked up the three drinks she'd ordered and slid off her barstool. "Her boyfriend's the lead singer of a band."

"Fascinating." I focused my attention across the club until I spotted Remy in her black Incubus tee as she talked to her lead singer boyfriend. My lips quirked. Oh yeah, it would be nothing for Hart to steal her away from that loser if he really wanted her.

As Jodi started away, I was debating whether I should tell him about the intel I'd collected on his dream woman when Gamble moved to my side. "Struck out, huh?"

"What?" I glanced at him, my thoughts still distracted.

He tipped his head toward Jodi.

Realizing he thought I'd been hitting on her, I lifted my hands. "No. I wasn't... No! Been there already, didn't even do that, and have no urge to finish."

Gam snorted. "Yeah, right. Whatever, loser."

He strolled to the other end of the bar to take an order, and I frowned after him. Shit, he really thought I'd been chasing tail tonight. The ass. Gamble was getting on my nerves in more ways than one. Not only was he keeping me from being out and open with Caroline, but he wasn't even noticing how much I'd changed and evolved lately.

The stupid blind fucker.

I almost didn't approach him about Caroline after the bar closed as I'd been planning to do. But then I thought about how much I hated sneaking around. I wanted to be able to kiss her in public, or fuck, even just hold her hand whenever the desire struck. I was damn tired of keeping my distance.

This ended tonight.

"Hey." I caught Gam's arm as we all began to leave after cleaning the place up. "I need to talk to you for a second."

He paused and came back around. "Sure thing. What's up?" I stared at him a moment, not even sure how to say it. His eyes crinkled with concern. "You okay? What's wrong? You look pale."

I shook my head. "Nothing. I just...I want to say..."

Gam lifted his eyebrows. "Yeah?" His mouth fell open. "Shit, you *are* dying, aren't you?"

"No!" I groaned and clasped my hands to my head. "No, no, no. That's not it at all. I just want to ask Caroline out."

I blurted the last line, Band-Aid fast, and wow. Immediately, I felt better. Months of guilt and worry just oozed off my shoulders.

But Gam blinked at me as if I'd spoken a foreign language.

Frowning slightly, I added, "On a date," for clarification, because from the look on his face, I could tell he clearly needed some clarification.

He shook his head, then cracked a grin and pointed at me. "Yeah, right. You're hilarious."

Oh God. Really? "I'm not joking."

His smile died. He shook his head again, suddenly confused. "But...you have a thing for Hamilton's woman."

"No." I shook my head. "I told you—*every fucking time you suggested that*—that I do *not* have a thing for Hamilton's woman. I want...to date...Caroline."

"And I've told you—every fucking time you ever looked at her—no. That's not going to happen."

I stared at him, not sure what to say to that. For some insane reason, I hadn't expected an immediate rejection. I had thought coming to him openly and honestly would shock him into at least considering it. But this...I hadn't planned for this.

Why hadn't I planned for this? He really had told me to stay away from her a million and one times. Why had I thought he'd change his mind if I was suddenly serious?

"Well..." I floundered a moment, with no idea what to say, because I wasn't about to give up. I *couldn't* give up. I wasn't going to stop seeing her, end of story. "I'm sorry, man, but that wasn't a question." Though, okay. Yes, it had been. I'd been asking for his approval *and* his blessing.

Why the fuck hadn't he just given me his goddamn blessing?

"I am *going* to ask her out," I finished, my voice full of conviction.

But my best friend on earth—the fucker—merely said, "No. You're not."

I exploded, throwing my hands into the air. "What the fuck, Gam? You can't just say *no* like that. She's nineteen years old. She can make her own decision."

"So then you're just going to sneak her around behind my back?"

"No." I growled and fisted my hands before pressing them to my temples. "That's why I'm talking to you right now, giving you a heads up and *trying* to do the right goddamn thing."

"The right goddamn thing would be to leave her alone and just stay away."

I worked my teeth over my bottom lip and shook my head because that idea wasn't even an option. "Why do you have such a big fucking problem with me asking her out?"

With a short laugh, Gam pointed at me. "Because I *know* you. And you don't deserve to have anything to do with her."

Okay, that stung. Noel Gamble, the one guy who'd had my back for four years, and even he didn't think I was worthy. Ye-ouch.

"Thanks. Thanks a lot." I took a step back to draw in a breath and recover from the sting.

Obviously assuming our little talk was over, Gamble turned away to leave.

Panicking, because this was my one and only shot to get him to comply to my wishes, I called after him. "Haven't you noticed *any* change in me lately?"

Gam paused and turned back at me. He cocked his head to the side, obviously confused.

I lifted my hands, offended when he didn't answer. "I don't go out fucking partying and drinking every other night, I don't flirt with every piece of ass to cross my path, I don't...*fuck*! I haven't has sex with anyone since..." I racked my brain, wondering who I'd last had before Caroline, when I remembered. "Midnight Visitor."

But that name only made Gam snort and cross his arms over his chest. "Who you still send dirty text messages."

I ground my teeth and started to answer, but he lifted his hand to stop me. "And don't try to pull that abstinent bullshit on me. I've seen you stroll into work a lot lately, wearing your smug, just-had-sex grin. I *know* you're still getting plenty of pussy."

I blinked, stunned. "I don't have a just-had-sex grin."

When I glanced over to find Hart had stuck around to oversee my conversation with Gamble, he shrugged and sent me a sheepish nod. "Yeah, you kind of do."

"Shit." I ran my hand through my hair, feeling my handhold on the moment slip even further.

Gam lifted his brows as if he expected me to give up the fight.

A weary sigh claimed me. I glanced up at the rows of alcohol lining the wall, and then I focused on him again. "As your friend," I said, "I'm giving you a heads-up. I'm *going* to date her."

With that said, I turned away to leave, but my so-called best friend said, "If you even attempt to ask her out, I'm telling her everything."

I snorted out a strange, confused laugh and swung back around. "I don't know what the fuck you're talking about. Everything about *what*?"

"Everything about *you*. About every single woman you ever fucked. Every woman you disrespected, mistreated and then pissed off." His ice blue eyes were hard as he sent me an evil leer. "I mean, you did describe them *all* to me...in detail, didn't you? I think I remember a decent amount of them. Starting with that pissed-off redhead who came up to the bar tonight and cussed you out."

Panic swamped me. I wasn't sure if I was going to upchuck or break down crying. But the thought of Caroline hearing about every sexual escapade I'd ever had sent me into a cold sweat. It would hurt her; it would really fucking hurt her. I couldn't handle her being hurt.

"You're a fucking asshole," I growled.

Gamble spread his arms and gave a hard laugh. "Hey, you're the one threatening to mess with my sister. *You* started this."

I lifted my eyebrows. "Then I guess it's on." I turned away and strode for the exit.

"Hey," he called after me, his voice hard. "Don't take this as some kind of challenge. Caroline is not some prize to be won just to piss me off. You touch her, and I will execute you."

I didn't even entertain him with a response. I just kept storming for the door.

"*Ten!*" he roared. "Are you listening to me, you little fucker? Don't hurt my sister."

I'd cut off my own balls before hurting his sister. But I didn't bother to explain that to him.

I shoved my way out of the empty nightclub, pissed and scared, and just fucking worried out of my mind. Not only had my plan failed *epically* to gently wade him into the idea of me and Caroline together, but now I'd alerted him to my interest. We wouldn't be able to sneak around behind his back the same way anymore. He'd always be watching and probably turn into a suspicious jackass. A strain was going to grow between Caroline and me, and everything we'd worked these last few months to build together was about to be put through the ultimate test.

Wound tight, I climbed into my truck, drove home and

let myself into my quiet, dark apartment. I waited until I was in my room with the door shut before I kicked my dresser drawers and fisted my hands.

"Motherfucking piece of shit bastard asshole."

"What's wrong?"

I gasped and whirled around, not expecting someone to be in my bed. "Jesus Christ!" Pressing my hand to my heart, I gaped at Caroline as she sat up, the sheets sliding down to reveal she was wearing one of my T-shirts. "What the fuck are you doing here?"

"I came over to see Zoey earlier, and just...forgot to go home."

A blinding, uncontrollable love swamped me. Feeling as if the grains of my time with her were slipping away, I hurried to the bed, freshly awed by how beautiful she was to me, inside and out. "And how is Blondie doing?" I asked, crawling onto the mattress with her to lie on top of the covers next to her.

She shrugged and slipped my hair across my forehead with a gentle touch. "She's scared. Both she and Quinn are freaked out. They've gone to three different doctors, and all of them have said she'll probably be put to bed rest at some point in the pregnancy. They're good for now, but I think it's going to be a stressful nine months."

I nodded as I kicked off my shoes. "Yeah. I can only imagine how much this is going to suck ass."

When I arched my face in to kiss her cheek, Caroline pulled back as soon as my lips touched hers. Setting her hand on my jaw, she squinted at me thoughtfully, sympathy filling her gaze. "Tell me what's wrong."

Shaking my head, I gazed into her eyes, scared that soon I wouldn't be able to look into them like this ever again. I'd never be able to stretch out on a bed with her, or pull her hair while I made her come.

"I love you," I said, meaning it more than I'd ever meant it before, feeling it work through every fiber of my being, and realizing this woman was it for me. She was my soul mate.

Her eyes filled with worry. "What's wrong is that you *love me*?" she guessed, probably trying to make me crack a smile, but I nodded seriously.

"Yeah," I said. "I love you, and that's why I felt this irritatingly noble urge to broach the subject of *us* to Noel."

"You..." Her eyes widened. "You told him? About us?"

I shook my head. "No." I knew she didn't want me to do that, so I that's why I hadn't. That was why I'd done what I'd done instead. "But I...might've mentioned that I wanted to ask you out."

She groaned and closed her eyes. "Let me guess. He said no."

I snorted. "And then some."

"Well..." She shrugged. "I guess we tried that way. And while it would've been nice to let him adjust to the idea in slow increments...maybe we should just tell him it's too late."

My gaze sharpened on hers. "You mean, tell him we're already together and have been for months?"

She nodded. "Sure. Why not? It's time, right?"

I groaned and buried my face in my hands. "Yeah, except for the fact that he threatened to reveal my complete past with other women to you if I dared to ask you out. If he learns about *this*, then he'll definitely spill everything."

Worry lit her eyes as she began to gnaw on her lip. "Is it really that bad? Your...you know, your past?"

I shrugged and glanced away. "I don't know," I mumbled. "It's not *good*." Turning back to her, I begged her with my eyes to forgive me. "You already know there have been plenty, and that I wasn't the most considerate, respectful guy, but shit...do you *want* to hear about them all?"

"No." She shook her head immediately. "But...I just..." She blew out a breath. "You know what? Maybe *you* should tell me. Beat Noel to the punch."

I glanced at her as if she was insane. "Are you completely mental, woman? I don't want to confess all that shit to you."

Her eyes swirled with misery. "Better you breaking it to me easily, than Noel trying to blindside me."

With a groan, I buried my face in my hands. "I'm ashamed," I admitted quietly. When I looked up at her, my face felt hot. "What if I disgust you so much you'll never look at me the same again? What if—"

"Oren," she said softly and caught my cheeks in her hands. "I know you better than anyone else on earth. I'm fully aware you're not perfect. Now, please. Just trust me."

I nodded and licked my dry lips. "Okay." Gazing into her

calm, soothing smile, I nodded again. "Okay."

She took my hand and had me crawl under the sheets with her. I was still wearing my bartending gear, but neither of us cared. After I wrapped my arms around her, she nuzzled her face against my shoulder and gave a content sigh.

"So, you know about the first girl," I started. "Libby."

"The night your sister—"

"Right." I was already worried and strained enough as it was; I didn't want to start thinking about Zoey again, too. Shit. "So, yeah. There was also—"

"Tianna," Caroline supplied readily, "who also saw your birthmark."

"Yeah, and then..." Fuck, my mind had gone blank.

"Someone gave you scratch marks on your back last year. Remember? I poured Reese's latte over your head because of it."

I hadn't forgotten *that* part. But I couldn't remember the girl who'd caused all that. After searching my brain a moment, I said, "April. She was an Alpha Delta Pi girl...with Blaze."

"Blaze?" Caroline stiffened against me. "You mean, Blaze from my film class. You slept with *Blaze*?"

God, I did not like this. I did not like this at all. "Mmm hmm," I mumbled and closed my eyes tight.

After a moment, she blew out a breath. "Okay," she finally said. "I hate her fucking guts, but okay. What about...what about Marci Bennett?"

When I groaned aloud, totally giving away my guilt, Caroline jerked away from me and sat up, putting space in the bed between us. "Marci Bennett?" she repeated. "The slut who got Aspen fired from her job, who almost got Noel kicked out of school? *Her*?"

I gave a small nod, and her eyes flared with horror. "Oh my God," she whispered.

I lifted my hands. "Now...I only did that one to get some kind of dirt on her to use as blackmail to keep her quiet."

"And did that work?" Caroline's chest heaved as she began to breathe harder, but she nodded, still keeping herself somewhat calm. Except the more she struggled to stay calm, the shittier I felt.

I nodded. "Yeah. I got some dirt on her. She...posed for me a little...naked. I have the pictures on my phone to use against her if she ever tries to hurt Noel or Aspen."

"You have naked picture of her? On your phone? Right now?"

When I bobbed my head once more, she dove at me and ripped my phone out of my back pocket. "Caroline..." I started, aching deep in my bones.

She came to my passcode screen, then bit her lip, looking momentarily thoughtful. A second later, she clicked a few numbers and got in.

My mouth dropped open. "How the hell did you figure out my passcode?"

She barely paid me any attention as she found my picture app and opened it. "It's Zoey," she said. "Wasn't that hard to figure out."

She started scrolling through all my snapshots, and I panicked, snagging the phone from her hand. "Don't look at them," I said.

Snapping me a hard glare, she set her jaw firmly. "Why not? Is she that much better looking than me?"

"No. Of course not. Jesus, don't do this to yourself, Care. I'll erase them all. Right now. Enough time's passed, I'm sure she's moved on and won't say anything about Gamble."

Caroline stared at me with hurt eyes as I hunted up the photos and deleted every single one of them. "There," I murmured softly, showing her the screen. "They're all gone."

She took it from my hand and began to look through all the pictures. "So, Marci, and Blaze, and Kelly whose place I took, plus at least two of her friends. Who else is there?"

I shook my head. "Maybe we should just stop there. This was a bad idea."

But Caroline seared me with a hard glare. "Just keep talking. Now I *have* to know."

I wiped trembling hands over my face, feeling the shit rise up around me. "Okay," I whispered. "Let's see. There was..." Fuck, I couldn't believe I was going to admit this one. "Cora."

"Zoey's *sister*?" Caroline's eye widened with horror. "Quinn's ex? Oh, Oren. Is that why Quinn gave you a black eye last semester, because you stabbed him in the back with *her*?"

"I didn't cheat," I insisted. Then I ran my hand frantically through my hair. "I mean, not knowingly. I didn't know they were together yet, not until later and then...shit. You know I wouldn't do that to Ham on purpose."

When she just stared at me, pain building behind her eyes, I breathed out an aching breath.

"I did that to Pick too, though, I guess."

"No." Tears filled her eyes as she set her hand over her mouth. "You slept with *Eva*?"

"What? No! God, no!" When I reached for her arm, she recoiled away from me. "His first wife," I said. "The one who overdosed and died. Julian's real mother. She came into the bar one night and I had no idea who she was. But Pick assured me it was okay, he and she never had that kind of relationship."

"But he was still technically married to her?"

I couldn't get my hands to stop shaking or my breathing to settle down. I hated seeing her like this. "Yes," I rasped. "He was still technically married to her...in name only."

She squeezed her eyes closed. "What about the rest of our friends? You've never slept with any of the women in our group, have you? Reese?"

"No," I whispered. "I have never slept with Buttercup or any of our friends."

Caroline sniffed and wiped at her damn cheeks. I went to move toward her, but she held up a hand. "I just...need a second here."

I dropped my hand and blew out a breath, but my ribs felt as if they wanted to cave in on me.

"What's..." She sopped more tears off her cheeks with her fingers. "What's something Noel would think to tell me? Something he'd think is...bad?"

"I don't know." I groaned and scrubbed my face, just wanting this to be over. "Our freshman year, I guess. We'd go to parties, get wasted and bring a girl back to our dorm room."

"*A* girl," Caroline repeated slowly. "A—singular—girl?"

I nodded. "Yeah. Just...some girl, a different one each time."

"And then..." She shook her head, confused. "What?" But a split second later, she caught on. Her eyes flared. "Oh my fucking God. You had threesomes...with my *brother*?"

"No! I mean, not...really. We just...took turns."

"Eww." She gagged and slapped her hand over her mouth. The tears fell harder, and I cursed a little louder.

"Then there was Faith McCrown."

"You know what? No." Caroline lifted her hands in surrender and flew off my bed. "I don't...I don't think I want to hear anymore."

"Caroline." I scrambled after her, but she warded me off.

"No. Please. Don't touch me right now."

"Damn it." I fisted my hands, wanting to hit something or grab on to her and hold on for dear life. "I knew this was a bad idea."

"No, it wasn't. I just...I need some time." She snatched her jeans off the floor and jerked them on under my too-big-for-her T-shirt. "I gotta go."

I watched helplessly as she slammed her feet into her shoes. "You don't have to leave."

She blurted out a miserable laugh and sent me a dark look. "No, I really do." When she stood, I opened my mouth to say...fuck, I had nothing to say to defend myself. I'd been a slutty man-whore, and that's all there was to it.

After pushing her fingers across her damp face one more time, she hugged her arms over her chest and cast me a broken glance. "Bye."

She hurried from the room, and like the complete screw-up idiot I was, I just let her go. Then I slumped onto my bed and whispered, "Bye," as I cradled my head in my hands and tried not to lose my fucking mind.

CHAPTER 32

Ten

Six days passed. I gave Caroline her space...and she fucking took it. She didn't call, she didn't Facebook message, she didn't come over.

I died a little inside every hour she stayed away.

I reached out to her exactly three times. The next morning, I texted, saying, *I'm sorry.*

The day after that, I added, *I love you.*

And on day three, I wrote, *I still trust you.* I trusted her to learn all this shit about me and not break my heart by leaving me. But my fucking trust had been sorely tested, and shredded.

I reminded myself, she just needed time. She'd get over this, and she'd come back to me.

Yeah, I repeated that over and over in my head, not really believing any of it, while I clung to the hope of it anyway.

Caroline fucking hated me now, and she was done with me. My life was fucking over.

She didn't even show up at Forbidden the next Friday to watch Hart's band, and she always came to cheer on Non-Castrato.

After the bar closed, I was putting away the last bottle of

liquor, when I just stopped and stared at it, tempted to drown all my sorrows like a typical brokenhearted douche.

I was still standing there like a complete dumbass, staring at the bottle, when Lowe paused beside me and leaned his forearms on the bar. He watched Hart and his band pack away their equipment before shaking his head. "I swear that one guy in Asher's band, the one with the Mohawk, drops even more f-bombs than you do, Ten."

I snorted, tipping my head to the side as I considered the bottle of tequila from a different angle. "Not even fucking possible," I said before I shrugged and flipped over a shot glass to pour myself a drink. Then I downed the shot with a single swallow.

"I think he's more crude than you are, too."

"Good for him." I poured myself another.

Lowe finally looked at me, frowning. "You doing okay tonight?"

Shot three, down the hatch. "Just fucking dandy. How're you?"

He lifted his eyebrows. "Uh...*Asher*," he called.

Hart looked our way and then jogged over. "What's up?"

Lowe hooked his thumb in my direction. "What is wrong with him?"

Hart studied me for a second, and then returned his attention to Lowe. "Women trouble. What else?" Then he grinned and patted the bar. "Why don't you take care of this one?"

Lowe snorted. "As if I know what to do with a depressed Ten. That's outside my scope of reality."

With a chuckle, Hart seated himself on a stool. I started in on my fifth shot...or was it my sixth? Shit, I'd already lost count how many I'd downed while these two were talking about me right fucking in front of my face.

"So last time I saw you, you were asking Noel if you could date his sister," Hart murmured, thoughtfully.

"I wasn't *asking* for permission," I bit out.

"Whatever." He didn't seem to care. "Noel said no, you argued back, and then he threatened to tell Caroline about all your past...women, if you tried anything with her, so...I'm guessing he told her anyway."

"No." I swallowed more and hissed through my teeth as that one burned on the way down. "*I* told her."

"You did what?" both guys shouted in unison.

"Oh, you stupid idiot." Lowe sat his hand on my shoulder in commiseration. "Please don't tell me you told her about *all* the women you'd ever been with."

"No." I gave a harsh laugh. "She walked out before I could get through the entire list."

Lowe winced. Hart snickered. I shot them both a glare. "It was either *I* tell her or Gamble tell her. I thought it'd be better coming from me."

"How long ago did this happen?" Hart asked.

"Last Saturday," I uttered, feeling the pain of missing every little part of her: her voice, one of her cute little sexy texts, her arms around me, her smile.

"Shit." Lowe shook his head. "Give her at least a week."

I looked up at him. "What happens if she hasn't talked to me within a week?"

He shrugged. "Then give her *two* weeks."

"Then what happens if—"

"Just give her some time, man."

I buried my face in my hands, abso-fucking-lutely miserable. Time was going to tear me apart if I had to spend too much of it away from her. "I'm such an idiot," I ranted. "The last words my sister ever said to me before she died were not to turn into a man-whore, and what's the first thing I did? I turned into a fucking man-whore to fight back the bad memories, and now it's coming back to bite me in the ass." Cupping the sides of my face in my hands, I looked up at Hart and Lowe, who gaped back at me as if I'd grown horns. Somewhere in my head, I realized I'd just spilled a bunch of shit about my sister, but at the moment, I couldn't even care. There was more important shit going on. "What if I lose her?"

Unable to take the weight of this pain, I sank to the floor and rested my elbows on my knees as I concentrated on not falling apart.

"That's it." Hart tugged on my arm, trying to get me to stand. "I'm driving you home."

I shook my head. "No. Can't go home," I mumbled. "My sheets still fucking smell like her." I hadn't been able to sleep at all most of the week because of that. I probably should've washed them, but then they wouldn't smell like her anymore, and that would've broken me even more.

"Then you can crash on my couch. Let's just get you out of here." The next time he tried to pull me up, I let him.

On Saturday, Lowe's advice of waiting a week came. And then it passed. With no word from Caroline.

The next morning, the beginning of day eight, that was it. I knew everything was over. Caroline hated me, and I would never be allowed back into her life again.

Miserable, unshaven, and two days without a shower, I lay slumped on my bed, watching *Child of Glass* on my laptop because she'd left her DVD in my computer.

I hated the stupid movie.

"This has to be the cheesiest fucking thing ever made," I grumbled aloud to myself. "Awful fucking acting, worst fucking music, and not a single fucking curse word in the entire fucking thing."

Yet this was probably the third time I'd watched it today. I couldn't seem to stop watching it.

"*Wait!*" the movie ghost called out. "*Do not go, Alexander. I need your help.*"

I snorted. "And that has to be the fakest fucking ghost ever created."

I turned the volume up to hear the ghost's accent, the one Caroline had loved so much. "It is a damn cute accent though," I had to admit on a grumble.

And just like that, agony rippled through me. My chest felt full and raw as if metal claws had raked across my lungs.

Turning my face to the side, I breathed in the scent that was still barely clinging to my pillow.

God, I missed her.

"Hey, Ten." Quinn knocked on my open doorway and peered in at me with a sympathetic cringe. "Do you want to ride with us to the picnic or drive yourself over?"

I paused the movie and frowned at him. "What picnic?"

"Uh..." Quinn scratched the back of his head before shifting his weight from one foot to the other. "The one at Noel's...to celebrate Aspen getting her new job at the high school."

"Gam's throwing a *party*?" I said slowly. I pushed the laptop off my lap so I could slide off the bed.

"Yeah...didn't you get the text invite?"

I stared at him a moment before shrugging. "It must've gotten lost in the mail. I think I'll drive myself over."

"You mean, he really didn't—" Ham cut himself off before slicing me a worried glance. "Are you sure that's a good idea? If he didn't invite you..."

"What?" I asked. "You don't think I should crash the party? *I* think that's a great idea." I rummaged through a pile of jeans on the floor, picking a few up and sniff testing them before deciding which was the cleanest. "See you guys there, okay? I'm going to shower first."

Stalling, Ham kept watching me. "Hey, just..." He glanced toward the doorway and moved closer to me. Lowering his voice, he said, "Please don't cause a scene or do anything that might upset Zoey. Any emotional distress for her right now—"

I patted his arm. "Don't worry, Dad. I would never do anything to hurt your baby."

Hamilton blew out a breath and nodded, but his eyes were still full of worry. And they should be, because I was *so* in the mood to cause a scene.

HALF AN HOUR later, I strolled into Gam's backyard. Everyone else had already arrived. Most of the woman were gathered around Zwinn and talking baby shit. Blondie cradled her midsection like she did every time I saw her these days, and I noticed Caroline was next to her. Her back was to me as Milk Tits and Buttercup chattered at them, laughing about...fuck, who knew what.

"Ten." Gamble's surprised voice made me glance to my left where he was slowly walking my way.

"Hey." My voice was fairly pleasant for how nastily I glared at him. "Thanks for the invite, asswipe."

I brushed past him and went to his wife, where she was fretting over the food table. "Shakespeare," I greeted with a smile. "Congratulations." I pulled a round block of red wood from my pocket and handed it to her.

"Aww," she said, taking it. "An apple figurine. Thank you, Ten."

"And it doubles as a pencil holder." I pointed out the holes.

She studied it, smiling appreciatively. "That's so sweet. You didn't have to get me anything."

I just shrugged and without my permission, my gaze strayed across the yard.

"Yeah, Ten," Gamble said from behind me. I whirled back to find him slipping an arm over Shakespeare's shoulders. "You didn't have to get her anything, especially if you thought buttering her up would convince her to talk me into doing something I'm not fucking going to do."

I narrowed my eyes. "I told you I wasn't asking for your *permission*."

"And I told you what I'd do if you went anywhere near her."

"Oh...so first I couldn't ask her out, but now I can't even go near her, huh? Pretty soon you're going to kick my ass if I even *think* about her."

"Maybe you shouldn't *think* about her, then," he suggested, grinding his teeth.

"Maybe you should stop being such a dick," I snarled back.

"Or *maybe* we should eat now," Aspen broke in too brightly, wringing her hands as she glanced between us. "Did you hear that, everyone?" She lifted her voice to gain the crowd's attention. "The food's ready, so just... dive in."

Gamble and I shared one last glare before backing away from each other to let his brothers get to the table and start piling their plates.

I wasn't hungry, but I didn't exactly move away from the food line. Caroline was approaching with the women, so I wasn't going anywhere.

I'm not sure where Lowe and Hart came from, but I found them flanking me as they started a conversation with each other about fuck knows what. I didn't listen to a word they said. I didn't look at Caroline directly either. I stared at the ground in front the food table, and settled for focusing on her from the corner of my eye. When she had to walk right past me after filling her plate, she didn't look at me, though. I lifted my eyes in that split second she moved by and she completely fucking ignored me.

I drew in a long breath, but I don't think I got any air. I felt like I inhaled only a lungful of agony.

"Ouch," Hart murmured quietly beside me.

I ignored him and turned to Lowe. "A week?" I said,

lifting my eyebrows.

"Two weeks," he revised, glancing after Caroline and wincing. "Definitely two weeks."

"Fuck." I wasn't going to survive this.

"Oh crap," I heard Caroline's voice. "I forgot my fork."

Darting to the table, I snatched the first plastic fork I saw and extended it her way. She jerked to a surprised halt when she turned and found *me* there.

"Oh!" She sucked in a breath and pulled back.

"Here you go," I offered quietly.

She immediately lowered her gaze. "Thank you." When she went to reach for it, I refused to immediately let it go. Her face veered up, flaring with panic. "Oren. What're you doing?" She tugged the fork free.

As she started to turn away, I asked, "Are you not even going to say hello to me?"

She froze before slowly glancing back. "You can't do this here," she whispered the warning. But I couldn't *not* do it...anywhere. I needed to talk to her; I needed my woman back. I needed to know she was going to forgive me...if not today, then *some*day.

"It's been *eight* days," was all I could think to say. I couldn't help the way my gaze pleaded. I'd get down on my knees and beg if that's what it took.

Understanding filled her expression. "I..." But she didn't say anything else.

I was on the brink of losing my shit. "Does this mean you're done then?" I asked.

She shook her head, confused. "Done?"

I jabbed a finger into my chest. "With *me*?"

"Hey, what're you two talking about over here by yourselves?" Gamble asked as he strolled toward us. His voice sounded casual and curious enough, but I could still detect the censure.

Caroline jumped at his voice and immediately turned his way, but I couldn't take my gaze off her, not until she answered me. Still ignoring Gamble, I hissed, "*Caroline?*"

Nervous and jumpy, her eyes darted my way. "No," she breathed out so quietly, only I could hear. "Of course, I'm not done with you." Then she returned her attention to her brother and flashed him a big smile. "Maybe we're telling secrets about you," she teased.

"Secrets?" he repeated. When his gaze slid my way, I just

stared back, daring him to even start.

The fucker must've accepted my challenge because he wrapped an arm around Caroline's shoulder and smiled. "Oh, I could give you all kinds of secrets...about Ten here."

"Gam," I said under my breath. The warning clear. I wouldn't just stand here and take this shit. Caroline's face had already drained of color and she looked stiff and upset. "Don't."

He shrugged. "Don't what?"

I glanced around at everyone who'd paused what they were doing to watch us, all of them extra alert. "Don't tell her about any of your secrets? Not even about Tianna?" After a low whistle, he spoke directly to Caroline. "I don't know what he did to that poor girl, but I've never seen anyone hate a guy as much as she hates him, and Tianna loves *all* the guys."

"Noel," Aspen called, hurrying our way. "Do you think you could help me carry out more potato chips?"

"In a sec," he answered, not taking his gaze off me. "Oh, and do you remember Faith McCrown? Didn't you pop her cherry our sophomore year?"

With a quick glance at Caroline, I gritted my teeth. She kept her chin high, though, and that made me proud. But still pissed as hell.

Nodding, I sent my good ol' buddy ol' pal a hard smile. "Yeah, you know, I *do* remember her. I remember how *you* took her over after I gushed about how flexible she was."

Gamble's mocking smirk died cold. I cocked my head to the side. "Wasn't she the one who got so hooked on you she became damn near suicidal after you dropped her cold for her best friend? Or was it her archenemy you fucked? I can't recall which."

Beside him, Aspen started to cough, and I glanced at her, suddenly remembering she was right there.

Shit.

Pressing her hand to her chest, she batted her eyelashes like crazy and stepped in reverse away from us.

"Aspen?" Gamble reached for her, but she darted another step away.

"I...I...I'm sorry. I think I have some dust in my..." She coughed again when tears filled her eyes. Whirling away, she murmured, "Excuse me."

As she hurried off, Gamble shot me a murderous glare.

"You fucking prick." And then he hurried after his wife.

I squeezed my eyes shut. "Shit." I'd fucked that up.

When I opened my eyes, an incredulous Caroline was in my face. "Why the hell did you do that to Aspen?"

"I wasn't thinking about her," I admitted. "I didn't mean to hurt *her*. I was just so...pissed at *him*."

"Well, you did hurt her. You hurt her a lot."

"The fucker needed to shut up, so I shut him up. He was hurting *you*, and I couldn't handle that. I didn't think it through; I was too focused on getting him to stop upsetting you to think about anyone else. I'm *sorry*."

"But he didn't know what he was doing to me."

"Then maybe he *should*," I snapped. "No, there's no maybe to it, anymore. He...should...know. It's past fucking time. Everyone else knows. Even my *parents*. He is the only person who doesn't know."

"But—"

I grabbed her shoulders and shook her lightly. "Why don't you want him to know?"

She shoved at my chest and yelled, "Because I'm scared."

I didn't believe her. Still worried she just wanted to drop me after what I'd told her, I shook my head. "He won't take anything out on you. You're his sister. He'll always love you, no matter what. *I'm* the one at risk of losing my best fucking friend. So what're *you* so scared of?"

I just wanted her to admit she was over me if that was the case, but instead she shrieked, "I'm afraid he'll do or say something that'll convince you I'm not worth the effort. *Okay*?" Tears flooded her eyes. "What if he breaks us apart? I'm not ready to lose you."

Pummeled in the chest by her words, I gaped at her. She wanted to stay with me. She wanted...fuck. I inhaled sharply. My anger instantly oozing from me, I stepped close and cupped her face in my hands. "Baby, there's nothing he could say or do to keep me away from you."

"Is that so?" Noel asked from behind us.

CHAPTER 33

TEN

I SPUN AROUND to find Gamble only ten feet away, his face flushed red, lips curled back in a snarl, and his eyes narrowed in hatred.

"You son of a bitch."

He charged, and about twenty things happened at once. Pick, Lowe, and Hart shouted for him to stop as they leapt on him, catching his arms and chest and keep him from getting to me.

I stepped in front of Caroline so she couldn't get between us, and Blondie leapt forward to drag her away. But Ham wasn't having anyone near his woman, so he hovered over the two girls, while Milk Tits and Buttercup tried to usher the babies and two youngest Gambles into the house, except Colton and Brandt refused to go. Aspen darted out the back door and skidded to a halt to cover her mouth with her hands.

"Damn it," Gam roared, managing to glare me down as he struggled against the three men. "Let me go. I just want to kill him."

"You can't kill Ten," Pick explained, sounding strangely levelheaded for a moment like this.

"Yeah, why don't you have him sleep with *your* sister

behind *your* fucking back and say that to me again."

I growled at him. "I'm not just sleeping with her, fuckface. We're actually dating." I glanced toward Caroline, who was covering her mouth with both hands and watching us from worried eyes. "We have been for a couple months."

"Dating? Are you kidding me?" Noel turned his attention to Caroline, too. "How many dates has he taken you on?"

She blinked at him, obviously not understanding. "What?"

He rolled out his hand, encouraging her to talk. "How many times has he taken you out to eat? To the movies? Dancing?"

"That's not fair." I shifted toward him, balling my hands into fists. "We couldn't do any of that shit because of *you*."

"Yeah. Whatever. The truth is you're no better than Sander Scotini."

Oh, that fucker. He just had to go there, didn't he?

Rage flooded my veins. But what hurt more than hearing he thought I belonged anywhere in the same category as that worthless pussy was that I agreed with him. I hadn't been fair to Caroline. I'd hidden our relationship in fear of the consequences, in fear of Noel finding out. I'd been just as big of a pussy.

But I pushed all my blame on Gamble.

"You bastard," I roared right before I charged.

Hamilton wrapped an arm around me from behind and picked me up off my feet, while Hart, Pick and Lowe regathered their efforts to keep Gamble at bay.

Still pissed as hell, I struggled in my roommate's impenetrable hold. "Take that back! I'm nothing like that piece of shit. I actually *love* her. And the only reason I didn't tell you sooner was to protect her, because I knew you'd fucking overreact, and she'd get hurt. I mean, *fuck*! Just look at her."

I didn't know she'd started to sob, but I could feel it in my bones. And yep, when I glanced over and pointed a finger in her direction, the tears were streaming down her face as she clutched Blondie for dear life. It tore a hole through me.

"Damn it," I rasped, my voice breaking. "We're making her cry."

"Noel," she sobbed. "Please." The pain in her eyes killed me. I just wanted to strangle Gamble and make him see reason.

He squeezed his eyes closed as if trying to block out the effect her pleading had on him. Then he gritted his teeth and shook his head.

"It's not his fault," she begged. "I tricked him. I snuck into his room in the dark when he was expecting someone else."

"Oh, fuck...me." A sickened revulsion clouded his face. "You're Midnight Visitor." He turned to me and pointed accusingly at his sister. "*She's* Midnight Visitor?"

"He had no idea it was me," Caroline said.

Gamble snorted. "Oh, I bet he didn't." His gaze narrowed on me as if he knew better.

"He *didn't*," Caroline cried in self-righteous defense.

"Actually," I admitted with a sigh as I glanced guiltily up at the sky. "I did."

"What?" She spun to me, her mouth falling open. "No, you did not."

I looked her straight in the eye. "Yeah...I did."

She blinked. "No...no, you didn't." Except she suddenly didn't look so sure. "But...y-you got mad at me when you finally found out. You were...pissed because I'd tricked you. I forced you to betray your best friend, remember?"

I shrugged. "I still knew. I mean, you called me Oren. You forgot to disguise your voice too many times, and...fuck, you *smelled* like you. I knew it was you. I just...denied it."

Confusion seized her expression. "What do you mean you *denied* it?"

"Easy. I told myself it wasn't you. Knowing it was really you would've made it wrong, and I didn't want it to be wrong, so...I convinced myself it wasn't you."

She shook her head, unable to believe my statement. "How the hell do you do something like that?"

"I don't know, but I can. I did a damn fine job of denying the fact I had a twin sister who died a horrible death four years ago, now didn't I? I'm like the king of denial."

"You had a twin sister?" Gamble's jaw fell open and his eyes grew wide, but I was too busy staring at Caroline to pay him much mind.

She gave another confused shake of the head. "But...if you knew it was me, then why didn't you stop me?"

I laughed softly. "Because it was you."

As her lips parted, realization lit her face,

I was so intent on watching her expression I didn't realize Gamble had broken free of Lowe, Pick and Hart until he shoved me. I went sprawling across the yard until I lost my footing and landed on my ass in the grass.

"You fucking prick!" he roared. "First, you're fucking my sister behind my back, and now you have some *twin* I've never even heard about? It's like I don't even know you. And why the hell are you guys holding me back like you're trying to protect *him*?"

He shook away Pick, Lowe and Hart when they tried to restrain him again.

Pick held up a calming hand. "Noel, man. You just need to calm down."

"Calm down?" His mouth fell open before he looked down at me where I was keeping myself planted on the ground and then back to the men around him. "Holy fuck," he breathed. "You really are protecting him. He betrays *me*, and you take *his* side. Thanks, guys. Thanks for having my back."

"It wasn't about siding with you or him," Hart spoke up. "Caroline wanted him, and he treats her right, so..." When he shrugged, Noel narrowed his eyes.

"You say it like you've known about this for a while." His eyes flashed wide. "Holy shit. You've known about this for a while. How the hell many of you have known about this?" When he glanced around, everyone lowered their gazes. A sound of denial crackled from his throat.

A worried-looking Colton glanced up at Brandt. "Does this mean we have to give back all the money Ten paid us to keep quiet?"

Gamble shook his head and laughed hollowly. "And you even paid off my brothers? Nice, man. Nice. Next you'll be telling me my own *wife* knew."

When Aspen shifted a step back, he zipped his gaze to her. She covered her mouth with her hands, and his eyes flared wide.

"Oh God," he croaked. "*Aspen*?"

"I'm sorry." She shook her head as if to deny it even as she kept apologizing. "I'm so sorry. But Asher's right. He made her happy again. Caroline was so sad when she first came here, and then suddenly, she was happy. Ten...he's good for her."

"Yeah, he just so fucking great. He had to sneak her around like a cheap, dirty slut that she's *not*, but no...he's awesome." He spun away and stalked out of the backyard.

Aspen buried her face in her hands and started to cry. As Brandt and Colton moved to comfort her, Caroline tore herself away from Blondie. She hurled herself at me, and I caught her around the waist, then buried my nose in her hair. "Are you okay?"

"No. Oh God. How could I be okay? He was so mad. Did you see how mad he was?"

"Yeah. I saw."

When tears fell from her eyes and she sniffed, I lost it. Anger infused me.

Why did he have to go and be like that? Didn't he even care I was who Caroline *wanted*? Or try to find out if I was any good for her or how I treated her? I was supposed to be his best fucking friend, and yet he so easily assumed I was another Sander Scotini.

Well, fuck him.

Unable to help myself, I untangled my arms from her. "I'll be right back." After kissing her hair, I raced after Gam.

He was striding down the sidewalk away from his place when I caught sight of him in the front yard.

"Hey!" I yelled.

He slowed and gradually turned around.

"I'm supposed to be your best friend. Why is it so awful to think of me being with her?"

"Because I *know* you! I've known you since the first day I came to this town. And in the four years I've known you, not once have you ever shown a single iota of respect for any woman."

"What the fuck ever. I respect plenty of women. What about your *wife*?"

Noel barked out a harsh laugh. "Oh, yeah, you respected her enough to hop onto a coffee table and ask a crowded room full of her *students* if she liked to dress up in schoolgirl clothes so I could play the professor. That was *so* respectful."

Fuck, maybe Shakespeare had been a bad example. "Man, I was drunk."

"She ended up getting fired from her job, and the coach posted a topless picture of her on the locker room wall."

"Okay, fine." I lifted my hands to shut him up.

Shakespeare was definitely a bad example, no matter how much I'd made up with her.

I changed tactics. "What about Ham's woman then? I let her fucking move in with us."

"Oh, you mean the girl you went on a date with where you got her drunk for her first time until she was flirting with a guy who was already dating someone else and then ended the night by puking up her guts in the club's bathroom. Yeah, great example."

Fuck, I really wasn't going to get anywhere with him, was I? I thought of my sister, and uncertainty filled me. The one girl I'd loved more than anything, and I'd failed her; the worst thing in the world that could possibly happen to her had happened. Who the hell did I think I was to try to be anything to Caroline?

Stomach churning, I took a step away from Gamble. "So what did I do to Caroline, then?"

He shook his head as if he couldn't believe I even had to ask. "The fact that you had to hide what you had with her and didn't even have the balls to let me know about it tells me everything I need to know. She's just not that important to you."

"That's complete bullshit. She—"

"She wouldn't have become your dirty little secret if you'd been *open* about it from the very beginning. That's all she was to *him* too. That first prick who knocked her up. She was just his trailer-park-trash dirty little secret. And you're making her go through that all over again. If she'd meant anything to you, you wouldn't have gone behind my back, you wouldn't have hidden your so-called *feelings*. You would've fought to be with her openly instead of sneaking around like a fucking coward."

"Jesus, man." I shook my head. "If this is the way you've always thought of me, then why were you ever my friend?"

"Because I'm not a *woman*. It never bothered me what you did to complete strangers, but I sure as hell wouldn't want you to become involved with a girl who's important to me."

I shook my head slowly. It was enlightening to learn what some of the closest people in my life really thought of me. And not in a good way. I didn't know what to say to him. Not even one of my stupid, smart-ass comments came to mind. It felt as if he'd just handed me my ass and no matter how I tried to reason it in my brain, I didn't belong with Caroline. I didn't deserve her. I'd never treat her right, and if I really cared about her, I'd stay away.

But the very idea made me want to puke.

Not sure what to even do, I just turned away and walked off in a strange daze.

Caroline

FEAR CROWDED my stomach like a noxious gas, giving me a painful case of indigestion. It was hard to even function I was so scared.

Last week, I'd been hurt. Every time I'd thought about Oren, I'd envisioned him with a new girl in some awful kinky position, and agony had wracked me until I was dizzy with it. So I'd stayed away to protect myself, to heal, and get over my own pity party.

I'd spent a lot of time with Zoey, helping her deal with her pregnancy fears, and I'd begun to calm down. Then I began to miss him. But I also grew uncertain because I wasn't sure how to approach him and apologize for running off and doing exactly what I'd promised him I wouldn't do.

Seeing him in my brother's yard today had been a blessing as much as it had been terrifying. It'd been too long since I'd seen him, talked to him, kissed him. I wanted to run over and tackle him, drag him to my bedroom and have my wicked way with him. But then the nerves had instantly knotted in my stomach because I didn't even know how I was supposed to face him after I'd left him last week. I'd been so ashamed of myself for letting my tender little feelings get the best of me.

Ignoring him had seemed like the only option until he'd forced my hand, until he'd made me look into his eyes and face the truth. He'd missed me too. He'd hurt without me.

From that point on, everything spiraled out of control. I hadn't been able to let him think I didn't care. Noel hadn't been able to stay away, and he'd tried to keep us apart. And Oren hadn't been able to step back and be meek about it; he'd yelled right back at my brother, making everything explode.

When he'd chased after Noel and then didn't return to the backyard when Noel did, I knew they'd had more words.

"Gamble," Pick started, but Noel held up a hand. "Why don't all you backstabbing motherfuckers get out of my yard? The party's over."

"Does he mean us too?" Colton asked Aspen.

"No." Noel pointed to them. "You guys...inside."

Aspen was pale as she ushered Brandt and Colton away. I grabbed my brother's arm. "Noel."

He wouldn't even look at me. He shoved his palm in my face. "I don't want to talk about it."

"Well, too bad." I tightened my grip. "This isn't going to go away just because you want it to."

He glanced at me, his jaw stiff and eyes flashing. "Caroline."

But I didn't heed his warning. "I did this," I said. "I started it. I came on to him multiple times before I had to resort to trickery and sneak into his room."

Wincing, he turned his face away. "I don't want to hear this."

"Tough shit," I growled, giving his arm a yank. "We're talking about it. *I* pursued *him*, and I wasn't going to stop until I wore him down and he eventually gave in, because I *love* him."

"Love?" Noel sneered and shook his head. "You have no idea, little girl. I've seen what you thought love was, and it ain't even close."

Sucking in a pained breath from that jab, I closed my eyes briefly, but then I looked up at him, steeling my resolve. "I know you totally lost faith in me a year ago. I know you thought I became something that couldn't be trusted with my own heart, but believe it or not, I actually *learned* from my experience with Sander. And Oren is *nothing* like him."

Noel snorted and shook his head, not believing me. I yanked on his arm again. "I'm serious," I said. "He may not have taken me on a conventional date, but he was more considerate and attentive than I ever could've imagined a boyfriend could be. I never started a day without some kind of message from him, letting me know he was thinking about me. He took me to Rainly Park and even showed me a hidden waterfall there."

When my brother shot me a startled glance, I nodded. "We did all kinds of things in the apartment with Quinn and Zoey. He even introduced me to his parents."

Noel glanced around the yard, probably to send Quinn a scowl of betrayal, but all our friends had left, respecting his wishes.

"Honestly, the only person we didn't tell was *you*." As Noel fumed, I lifted an eyebrow. "Why do you think that was?"

Shaking my head, I left him in the backyard to stew. Then I hiked to Oren's apartment. But when I didn't find him there, Zoey let me borrow her car to drive to his hometown. I wasn't sure how I knew he'd go to his place, but I just knew.

When I reached it at dusk, he was sitting by himself, his arms wrapped around his knees as he watched the colorful sunset.

He didn't acknowledge me as I sat beside him, so I didn't say anything either.

"Did you listen in on the conversation I had with your brother in the front yard?" he finally asked, turning his face to consult me.

I shook my head. "No. They kept me in the back while you two were supposed to *iron* it out. But you didn't iron it out, did you?"

He laughed softly. "Not even a little."

I reached for his hand. He didn't pull away, so I tightened my grip around his fingers. "What did he say to you, Oren?"

"Oh, you know..." He blew out a breath and returned his attention to the sunset. "He just verbally bitch slapped the shit out of me with a couple of hard-to-accept truths."

"Like what?"

"Like I'm no good for any woman, least of all you. And if I ever cared about you and wanted what was best for you, I'd let you go to find someone else who deserves you a hell of a lot more than I do."

"So then..." I shook my head, not sure what he was trying to say to me. "It's over between us? Because of what he *said*? You're letting me go? Just like that? After you *promised* me nothing he said could break us apart."

"Damn it," he muttered as he spun to me. "Since when do you know me to do what's best for anyone else? I do what makes *me* happy, with no care how it affects those around me. And what I want more than anything is *you*."

"Then why did you just leave me there?" Tears filled my eyes without my consent.

"I didn't—fuck." His expression flashed with worry. He reached for me and tugged me tight into his arms. "I'm sorry, baby. I wasn't thinking. I'd just lost my best friend. I wanted a few minutes to myself. I just...I thought you knew none of this had changed anything we have."

I clutched his shoulder and buried my face in his neck. "Well, I'm sorry, but I don't know anything right now. I don't know up from down, if my brother hates me or forgives me, if you..." My voice choked up, and he pulled me tighter against him before he grasped my chin and made me look up at him.

"Here's one thing you can take to the bank. I love you. And that's not going to change. Ever."

"Say it again," I demanded.

Cupping the back of my head, he urged my face up until his earnest gaze was focused on nothing but mine. "I love you, Caroline. You've had me from the moment your brother carried you out of the bathroom in that run-down old trailer house. And no matter what happens, I'm going to keep on loving you."

Sobs took me over. "I love you, too," I admitted through my tears. "I just can't help it. There were so many reasons to stay away, to hate you, but...it's like you're a part of me or something."

"Yeah," he murmured with a small smile. Then he kissed my eyelids. "I know exactly what you mean. And that's why I really need to show you something."

I sniffed, blinking at his serious tone. "W-what?" This didn't sound good. At all.

"Do you remember Lake Tahoe?" he asked.

I sucked in a breath "You got the job?"

Oh God. He'd gotten the job and was going to leave. Against my will, more tears fell.

He wiped them away and shook his head. "Not that part. Do you remember when we got really drunk on the beach, and how Zwinn told us they had to stop us from going to that walk-in wedding chapel and getting married?"

I wrinkled my nose and frowned. "Yeah?"

"Well...I think we might've snuck back over there

later...after they fell asleep."

I blinked. "What?"

Oren lifted his hip and reached into his back pocket to pull out his wallet and unfold it. With trembling hands, he pulled a sheet of paper free and handed it to me. "I found this in my luggage after we got home."

He handed it to me and watched me from worried eyes as I unfolded it.

I stared at the document for a full minute before pointing at it. "This is a marriage license."

Oren blew out a breath. "I know."

Eyes widening, I stuttered a second before blurting, "This is *our* marriage license. Oh my God. Is this real?"

"Yes. I called around until I got a hold of someone in some courthouse in California. We were legally fucking married that night." He slipped the license from my limp hand and carefully smoothed it open flat.

"Oh my God," I uttered. "We're *married*."

He blew out a cheek full of air. "Yeah. Pretty much."

Panic flooded me. He watched it fill my face. Grasping my shoulder, he silently urged me to look at him, even though I couldn't focus too well.

"We were drunk," he started in a calm voice. "We can annul it, no problem, if that's what you want. This doesn't have to impact you at all."

"If it's what *I* want?" I repeated incredulously, shaking my head. "But what about you? What about what *you* want?"

"I..." His gaze bored into mine. "I'll respect whatever decision you make."

Stunned speechless, I shook my head. "But what if I don't want to annul it? Would you respect *that*?"

A slow grin stole across his face. "Hell, yeah."

My mouth fell open. "Holy shit, you *don't* want to annul it, do you? You...you want to stay married to me."

"Kind of," he answered with a shrug.

"*Kind of*?" I laughed outright. Oh my God. I was married, and it looked as if I might stay that way.

"Kind of...a lot," Oren murmured into my ear, pressing his nose against my cheek.

Even though a giddy warmth stole through me, I shook my head. "But I'm only nineteen. I'm—"

He took both my hands. "We don't have to be

traditional. Fuck, the very word gives me hives. We can take this slow and any way we want to. We can keep on how we are now for a while if that's what you want."

"You mean with me living with Noel and you staying with Zwinn?"

He shrugged. "Sure. Whatever you want. I mean, I'm sure Gamble's had enough of a shock for one day. We can keep this under wraps for a while until we're ready to deal with it."

"What about a ring?" I asked, starting to really get into the idea.

A grin split across his face. "Do you want a ring?"

"Kind of." Then I smiled big. "A lot."

He pulled me into him and kissed my hair. "Then I'll get you the biggest damn ring I can afford."

"Oh my God," I gasped. "We're really married. We're—oh my God, wait. What about Lake Tahoe? Your interview. You—"

"I didn't get the job," he said immediately.

My shoulders fell because I didn't already know this. "You didn't? Why didn't you tell me?"

He glanced away. "You weren't exactly speaking to me at the time, so..."

I took his hand, feeling like an absolute bitch for staying away as long as I had. Sure, it had hurt to learn everything I'd learned, but I'd asked to hear it. I'd...I was just a total bitch. "I'm so sorry."

He shook his head, unable to look me in the eye. "No, it's fine. They, uh, they had someone else in mind, I guess."

"Those fuckers," I muttered, pissed as I was relieved that they hadn't chosen my Oren. "And you said it went so well, too."

"Well, I was still riding a high from that orgasm you'd given me right after I put my suit on, so...yeah. Everything felt pretty damn good that day."

I slugged him in the shoulder. "Jesus, Oren," I started, but my scolding didn't last any longer than that. I hugged him and kissed his cheek. "I'm sorry you didn't get it."

"I'm not." Turning to me, he kissed me full on the mouth and he showed me how sorry he wasn't that he was going to stay around a while longer.

I had to silently admit, I wasn't sorry to see my husband stay, either.

CHAPTER 34

TEN

THE WEEK progressed. I kept seeing Caroline every night I could, except we didn't bother to hide anything. I pulled into her driveway to pick her up now, and we actually went out to see a movie at the theater and then a restaurant the next night.

I didn't see or talk to Gamble, and Caroline barely mentioned him. I asked her every day if everything was okay, but she merely smiled and said, "It's fine. Don't worry. He'll come to his senses and get over it. He always does."

I wasn't so sure, but I let the issue drop.

But I wasn't the only one worried. Pick yanked me into his office the next time I worked.

"You know how much it sucks to be your boss and friend at the same time, right? Am I going to be forced to pick sides between you and Gamble?"

I shook my head. "No, Gamble was right. I shouldn't have kept it from him. He has every right to be pissed at me."

He lifted his eyebrows. "I notice you're saying you shouldn't have *kept it* from him, not that you shouldn't have *touched* his little sister."

"Staying away from her wasn't an option."

Maybe I *shouldn't* have ever touched her but it was too late for that, and I didn't regret a minute of what had happened between us.

"Fuck," Pick muttered, running his hand through his hair in frustration. "So I'm guessing he's still more than pissed at you, and there's going to be a lot of tension when you two work together."

I nodded. "Yeah, pretty much."

"Lovely." He growled out another frustrated breath. "Okay, fine. I'll try to rework schedules to keep that from happening as much as possible. But there will always be Thursday nights."

"I know." I started to shrug it off again when a new thought struck me. "Wait! You're like every woman's personal defender. Why aren't *you* threatening me to stay away from Caroline the same way he his?"

"Because I've noticed how much you've changed lately. You're faithful to her. And she's happier than I've ever seen her before. I think you're both good for each other."

I snorted. "Mind mentioning that to Gamble? He's obviously not spotted any of the shit you have."

Pick smiled and patted my arm. "Just give him time."

God, I hated time. It moved on, though, and Thursday came before I was ready for it. Ladies' Night at the Forbidden Nightclub started, and Gamble worked the bar with Lowe, as he usually did.

For the most part, we avoided each other. I took my orders to Lowe, and it worked out just fine...for a while.

At one point, I saw Gamble talking to some scantily clad chick. He motioned toward me and she looked my way, but I didn't think much of it, not until Gamble told me to go into the back and fetch another crate of Heineken. I still didn't catch on, not until I was in the stockroom, cornered in the last row of shelves next to the wall with my arms lifted to drag down the necessary crate, when a pair of feminine hands wrapped around my waist from behind.

And that's when I finally got it. He'd sent some skank back to set me up in some kind of compromising position.

The Ten of a year ago would've been all over that. Hell, the Ten of three *months* ago might've even fallen prey to her. But the Ten who'd discovered the woman of his dreams had secretly slipped into his room to be with him wanted nothing to do with this cheap imitation.

Jerking away, I threw up my hands, dislodging her hold on me. "What the fuck?!"

Caroline

I SHOULD'VE KNOWN Noel was up to something awful the moment I approached the bar at Forbidden to make sure he and Oren hadn't killed each other yet.

He sent me an evil little smirk.

"Looking for your *boyfriend*? He went back to the stockroom." When he tipped his chin toward the back hall, encouraging me to go, I knew I'd find something I didn't want to, something about Oren that should change my mind about him.

I told myself not to go, but damn it, I had to know.

I heard his voice even as I opened the door to the storage room. "Did you follow me back here? That's messed up. I don't even know you. And don't ever touch me like that again."

"But that bartender up front said you'd been watching me and talking about me all night. He said if I followed you back here, you'd make it worth my while."

"Oh, he did, did he? Well, he was fucking wrong. I have a *girlfriend*, and I've never even seen you before just now. So, sorry to disappoint you, but you need to step off. Right now."

The woman coming on to him reached out to caress his chest. "You absolutely sure about that, honey? I mean we're already back here...all by ourselves. And I don't see your girlfriend anywhere."

"Then maybe you better turn around, bitch, because I'm right behind you. Get your fucking hands off him."

Oren's eyes went wide as he actually slapped the whore's fingers off his chest.

"Caroline!" he gasped desperately, pushing past her to hurry down the row to reach me.

I wasn't mad at him, but I *was* too mad for any kind of snuggling. So I jerked backward and lifted my hands to keep him back.

"Excuse me," I said through gritted teeth, "while I go kill my brother."

"Wait!" he called after me, but I was already on a rampage.

Noel looked so smug and full of himself when he saw my murderous expression as I marched toward the bar. The bastard actually thought I was this upset with *Oren*.

"Get a nice little show?" he asked.

"Yes, I did." I climbed onto a stool so I could reach over the bar. Then I slapped him as hard as I could.

His head jerked back and he immediately lifted his hand to cradle his cheek. Eyes wide with surprise, he yelled, "What the hell?"

I pointed a threatening finger right between his eyes. "Next time you send someone in to seduce my boyfriend away from me, you should probably pick a better slut who actually interests him, because, sorry, he didn't take your bait."

I spun away, only to find Oren hurrying from the hallway toward me, his eyes lit with concern. I grabbed him by the face, yanked him into me and kissed him as hard as I could. He looked dazed when I pulled away. Glancing back at the bar, I called, "And that, you asshole, only made me fall in love with this man even more."

I started away from the bar, but Oren caught my hand and tugged me back around to him. "What're you doing? Where are you going?"

I touched his face, loving the concern in his eyes. "I'm not mad at you."

He shook his head. "But you *are* mad. I don't want you driving while you're upset. You did drive here, didn't you?"

"I borrowed Aspen's car." I doubted Quinn would let Zoey come back to the bar again until the baby was born, so I'd had to sneak Aspen's keys out of the kitchen.

"Don't drive mad." He pressed his forehead to mine. "I have a bad feeling."

"I'll be fine." Leaning up to kiss him lightly on the lips, I smiled, unable to stay as mad as I wanted to. "I promise."

He didn't look too sure about my claim, but he did kiss me back. "Text me when you get home."

"I will. Now get back to work. I'll see you later."

When I tried to pull away, he didn't let me go at first, but then he mouthed, "*I love you*," and finally released my fingers.

For him, I bottled my feelings all the way home, paying closer attention to the road than I normally would, just so I could fulfill my promise. But I let it all back out as soon I as pulled into Aspen's driveway.

My rage still fueled me as I stormed into the back door of my traitorous brother's house. Aspen was at the kitchen table with Colton and Brandt, building something that looked like a mini volcano with red foamy stuff oozing over the sides. The boys were cheering it on, and Aspen looked just as into their experiment as they were until she glanced up and saw my face.

Smile instantly dropping, she popped out of her chair. "Are you okay? What happened? Did you and Ten—"

"Oren and I are fine!" I yelled, glaring at her. "How could anyone think he'd ever do anything to hurt me? He's the most amazing boyfriend I've ever had. Does no one care that he actually makes me *happy*? That for the first time in a year, I look forward to each new day, or that I've been able to forgive myself for the things I've done? He *healed* me. He never *hurt* me."

Storming past her and my shell-shocked-looking younger brothers, I hurried to my room and immediately knelt on the floor to yank my suitcase out from under the bed. Once it was flopped open, I yanked out the top drawer of my dresser. When I turned back to the suitcase with an armful of bras and panties, I found Aspen in the doorway, looking scared.

"I-I..." At a loss for words, she blinked at me and began to wring her hands at her waist. "I'm sorry, Caroline. You just looked so upset. I didn't mean to automatically assume it was Ten's fault." She shifted to the end of my bed and motioned toward my rushed pack-job. "What exactly is going on here?"

I hissed out a breath, forcefully calming myself. Blowing up at my sister-in-law wasn't going to help anything. It wasn't her fault my brother had been a complete asshole tonight.

"I have to leave," I said. "I can't stay here a second longer with your fuckface husband. He just... He..." I shuddered and my bottom lip trembled. I bit it hard before I could burst into tears over the way he'd betrayed me.

"Oh, great," Aspen muttered, running her hand over her forehead. "I was worried he would do something ugly and irrational. He *always* does something ugly and irrational whenever he's scared and upset."

"Scared?" I spat the word out on a laugh. "What does *he* have to be scared about?"

She looked up at me, her eyes swimming with concern. "I think he's scared he might lose both his best friend and his sister over this."

"Yeah, well...he *did* just lose his sister."

Aspen's eyes filled with misery. "I probably don't want to know what he did, do I? Fine. Let me help you pack. Then I'll take you wherever you need to go."

Ten

THE SHIFT ENDED, the club cleared out, and only us guys remained to clean the place up. I tried to hold my tongue for as long as I could, but for me, "long" lasted about ten minutes. Everyone in the joint must've sensed our tension, because there wasn't a lot of talking or bantering as we set to our duties. I was wiping down the stools in front of the bar when Noel began to clean the counter behind it. We were facing each other, the bar between us, and working in the same direction, though we avoided eye contact, when my patience shattered.

Slapping my washrag on the bar top, I looked over at him and burst. "You know, even if your fucking plan had worked tonight, the person who would've gotten hurt the most was your *sister*. Did that even occur to you, you prick bastard? Your only little sister. Oh, but don't worry; if that was your goal, I think it worked anyway. It wasn't me who caused her devastation, though, it was *you*. I cannot even believe you would..." Shaking my head as words failed me because I was vibrating with so much rage, I just wanted to leap over the bar and start pounding on his fucking face.

What he'd done to Caroline had been completely unacceptable.

Too close to the edge to trust myself, I glanced at Lowe,

who'd stopped what he was doing to watch us openly. "I'm taking off."

He nodded and made a dismissive gesture with his hand, excusing me. I swear I saw some pride glittering in his gaze as he sent me the hint of a smile.

Without even looking Gamble's way, I turned and walked out of the club.

When I found my wife curled in my bed, fast asleep with her luggage sitting against the footboard, I wasn't all that surprised.

Smiling softly, I stripped down to my boxers and crawled in with her.

I woke the next morning to the end of my bed dipping down as someone sat next to my feet. In my arms, Caroline stirred and her scent rustled up from her hair, filling my nose until I had wood. My arms were already wrapped around her as we spooned, and her ass was tucked into my lap with her back snuggled to my chest.

As someone who liked my space at night, it blew my mind that I enjoyed sleeping with her so much that I actually wanted her this close to me. But hell, I had no idea having her right there would feel quite this nice. My hips arched forward and I instinctively rubbed my hard cock through my boxer shorts until I found the crease in her ass.

She let out a breathy sigh, and I leaned in to bury my face in the back of her neck, enjoying every single second of this moment...until a throat cleared at the end of my bed.

Jumping out of my skin, I sat up, instantly pulling the blankets up to cover my woman. We were already fully covered to the tops of our chests. But I knew she only had on those cute little boy shorts and a camisole top. I didn't want someone else seeing even her creamy bare shoulders.

When I spotted Noel sitting by my feet, I lurched upright. "Jesus. What the fuck, man?"

His back was to us and his hands were laced loosely in his lap, as if he was ready to just hang out and wait for us to wake up.

"I need to talk to my sister," he said, his voice rough with regret and apology.

I sighed out a groan and flopped my head back onto my pillow. "Right this second?" Turning my head, I saw that it was barely seven in the morning.

Damn, Gamble really had lost his mind.

"You know, it's still really weird to think of you two..." He motioned between us over his shoulder. "But actually seeing it with my own eyes is even stranger. I don't..." He shook his head and looked away again. "I still don't approve of this, and I'm absolutely certain you're going to end up breaking her heart."

I just snorted and shook my head. "Yeah, well...after last night, I stopped giving a fuck what you think about it."

Noel closed his eyes and gritted his teeth. "Last night..." he started, only to turn back and open his lashes to send me a sincere stare. "Last night, I was wrong. I know that."

I wasn't going to forgive him since he couldn't even bother to say *sorry*, though he'd gone as far as to admit he'd fucked up. No one messed with my woman the way he had and reached any kind of forgiveness without a shitload of groveling and apologies...and maybe a million bucks.

But then he said, "I'm sorry, Caroline. And I'm not just saying this because I had the worst fight of my marriage with my wife last night, who was eager to tell me everything I've done wrong lately. I really am ashamed of what I did. It was impulsive and very...Ten-like."

I glanced at her to find her eyes open and filling with tears.

Gam sent her the most pitiful look ever. "I don't want you to move out just because I messed up. That is your home and will remain your home. I never...shit." He glanced down at his hands and sniffed quietly. "I never told you how proud I was of you for how much you did for the boys while I was gone. And I never told you that I didn't blame you once for how bad things got. I don't know if anyone—me included—could've held things together as long as you did. And I never lost any kind of faith in you. You are a strong, courageous young woman who I am proud to have as a sister. I will still love you, no matter what."

Caroline glanced at me, and I sent her a bolstering smile before taking her hand and squeezing.

"And Ten," Gamble went on. Caroline squeezed my fingers next, as if she expected him to give me the same kind of speech. Hell, I think even I expected it.

But what he said was, "You're a backstabbing motherfucker. I'll continue to work with you, because I have to, but other than that, just stay away from me. I don't want to be your friend anymore. I don't want anything to do with you. And I will laugh and celebrate the day she finally decides to dump your worthless ass."

"Noel!" Caroline cried, appalled.

He glanced at her, his eyes hard. "I'm sorry, I know I can't forbid you to see him, but I'm not going to pretend to like this. Are you coming home or not?"

Caroline wrapped her arms around my arm. "I am home," she said simply.

The look Gamble shot me told me this had to be the worst betrayal yet, as if I'd just stolen his sister from him.

Then he nodded once, cleared his throat, and stood up. After he left without another word, I looked at a quiet, pale Caroline. I didn't feel so steady myself. It wasn't every day I lost my friend.

"Are you okay?" I asked her.

She blurted out a short, shaky laugh. "Are you?"

I nodded. "I don't regret a single thing. I have you, and that's more than I deserve. It's everything I want." Taking her fingers, I kissed the knuckles. "Now what do you want to do about the rest of our life?"

CHAPTER 35

TEN

CAROLINE AND I started looking for a new place together. Blondie got a little morning sickness, but she hadn't yet had one scare. I kept telling her all the doctors were just blowing smoke up her ass. She was going to have a perfectly normal pregnancy, but I was glad she and Ham continued to take every precaution, just to be sure.

In other news, I put Caroline on my health insurance—swearing Pick to secrecy so he wouldn't go blabbing about our marriage just yet—and Caroline went to the Social Security and the DMV to legally become a Tenning.

Caroline Tenning.

The day her new driver's license with her new name came in the mail, she was so fucking excited. She jumped me on the couch and fucked me right there. It was a good thing Zwinn was at a doctor's appointment. We were pretty loud...and naked.

I loved living with her, I loved waking up to her each morning, falling asleep next to her every night, and even showering with her on occasion. There were adjustments—her clothes were always strung everywhere, longs strands of blonde hair tried to smother me in my sleep each night, and feminine products littered my dresser top—but we survived them and usually had fun in the process.

I continued to show up at the coffee shop every Saturday morning, but Gamble never did. Caroline learned about my Saturday routine and how I kept waiting for him to forgive me and just...show up one of these days, so she came one morning and sat with me instead.

I would never in a million years admit it to her, but I did miss the stubborn son of a bitch Gamble. He'd helped me get over my sister, he'd been with me when I'd started this phase of my life. Fuck, he'd been the one to dub me Ten. He was responsible for a lot of who I was, and I missed just hanging out with him and flipping shit back and forth.

But I wasn't about to give up anything with Caroline to admit that.

When she got a call from him one Saturday evening, I tried not to act interested, but she turned to me after hanging up with him as if she knew I craved every detail.

"They're all going to Rainly Park tomorrow," she said. "They asked me to come."

She looked sad about that, so I frowned. "Well, that's cool. Why aren't you smiling?"

With a sigh, she patted my arm and turned away. "Because I'm not going."

When she tried to move away, I caught her around the waist and tugged her right back around. "What do you mean you're not going? Go!"

She shook her head. "No. Not unless they invite you too."

I groaned and rolled my eyes. "Baby, you know that's not going to happen. Just go and have fun. You haven't seen those blackmailing little shit brothers of yours in too long. Don't worry about me, just go."

That stubborn Gamble blood of hers wouldn't give in, though. It was going to bug her all weekend, and in turn, it'd bug me, so finally, on Sunday morning, I dragged her out of bed and into the shower, saying, "Let's get ready. We're both going."

She brightened after that, and I knew I'd done something right. But the fucking drama started as soon as we showed up.

Noel scowled at me, then his narrowed eyes moved to where I was holding Caroline's hand as we strolled up the front walk to meet them in front of their house.

"This is a family outing," he said, making it clear I wasn't invited.

"And I'm family," Caroline argued, lifting her chin.

He seared her with a scowl. "I didn't say *you* couldn't come."

She glanced at me, and I knew exactly what she was thinking. She was considering whether or not to drop the "we're married" bomb on him, see if he'd deny I was family then.

I shrugged, letting her decide if she wanted to reveal anything or not.

"What?" Noel demanded, noticing our byplay. "What the fuck was that look about? Oh God. Please don't tell me you're pregnant."

A moment of awkward silence followed his question before I exploded. "What the hell, douche bag? You know she can't get pregnant."

Gam immediately closed his eyes and winced. "Shit. I forgot. Sorry." When he opened his lashes, Caroline took a step away from him.

She gave a small shake of the head. Then she glanced at Aspen and her younger brothers. "You guys have fun. I think I'm going to stay behind this trip."

She turned away from them, and me too, but her asshole big brother rushed after her, catching her arm.

"Caroline." His voice was desperate and regretful. He pulled her back against him so he could squeeze his eyes shut and press his lips to her hair. "I'm an idiot. I'm sorry. I'm so sorry. I've been so concerned with getting you away from him so he can't hurt you, I end up hurting you, myself. I don't know how to do this, how to back off. I'm used to being your big brother—and a surrogate parent—it's second nature for me to want to jump in and pull you away from anything I think is dangerous. It's scary as shit to watch you walk into something I can't protect you from. And I don't know how to...I just keep fucking it up. But what I know for sure is that I can't lose you. You're a part of this family. I don't want you to leave us just because I'm having trouble behaving myself. If..." He sent me a scathing glance. "If you want to bring someone else along with you, fine. But it can't be a real family day without you."

Caroline drew in a deep breath. Then she glanced over at me. "Okay, but Oren's coming, too."

Gam lifted his hands in surrender. "Fine."

"Can I ride with Ten and Caroline?" Brandt asked.

"Ooh, me too. I want to go with them." Colton skipped toward his sister to wrap his arms around her waist.

Gamble shot me a look full of hatred, silently accusing me of stealing his entire family from him. I lifted my eyebrows, daring him to say something. He opened his mouth, but no words came.

Shakespeare hooked her arm through his. "Looks like you and I have an entire ride all to ourselves."

When he glanced at her and she smiled up at him, a warmth entered his gaze. I guess the two of them had made up from the biggest fight of their marriage. That was awesome, because I was forever grateful for that woman's presence in his life. No one calmed his moody temper as much as Shakespeare did.

"I guess it's settled then," I announced, clapping my hands together. "Everyone, load up!"

Caroline

I DEFINITELY RODE in the "fun" truck on the way to Rainly Park. We barely got a mile down the road when Oren smacked me lightly on the side of the arm with the back of his hand.

"Padiddle."

I glanced at him, completely confused. "Huh?"

He briefly glanced back. "What? Didn't you ever play car games when you were little?"

Both Brandt and Colton leaned forward curiously from the backseat as I said, "My family never *went* on long car rides."

Sympathy crossed his features before he shrugged and grasped my hand, lacing our fingers together over the center console. Then he sent me a quick smile. "Well, my sister and I played endless hours of car games when we were growing up."

I turned to the side in my seat to face him. "So, how does padiddle go?"

He shrugged. "It's easy. You see a car with only one headlight and slap someone else in the car while you call out, *padiddle*."

I blinked, waiting for the point of the game. Finally, Colton scratched his head. "And that's it?"

With a chuckle, Oren shrugged again. "I didn't say it was an enlightening, complicated, or educational game. But it's a fun reason to slap your sister without getting into trouble."

"Except it's daytime," I said dryly. "And our chances of finding someone with only one daytime headlight is fairly low."

Oren scratched his scruff a second before saying, "My friend's family used to play the same game, but they would thump the roof of the car whenever they saw a yellow car."

"I like slapping arms better," Brandt said just as Colton suggested, "Let's do red cars."

A second later, three different hands attacked my poor short-sleeve-covered arm.

"Padiddle," they said in unison. "Red car."

"What the fuck!" I lifted my hands in self-defense, shying away from them. "Why did you all go after *me*?"

Oren wiggled his eyebrows. "Weakest link."

"Oh, what the hell ever." Spotting a red truck, I swung out with both hands, catching Oren and Colton. Brandt was saved that time only because he was the farthest away. "Padiddle."

And so the war began.

It had to be the stupidest, silliest game I'd ever played, but I was giggling by the time we reached the park. My brothers were talking a million miles a minute as we alighted from Oren's truck.

Aspen and Noel paused midway between unloading blankets and baskets full of lunch. Noel scowled at us—probably for being so happy—and his glower fixated itself on Oren.

Ignoring my crabby brother, Oren skipped toward Aspen. "Here, Shakespeare. Let me carry that for you." As he swept the laden basket from her arms, Noel's glower only darkened.

After filling his own arms with two sleeping bags, Noel hurried after Oren, dogging his heels. "Hey, asshole. Don't you dare try going through her to get to me."

Oren didn't bother to glance back. "Wouldn't dream of it," he said coolly. Then he stopped abruptly, picking our picnic spot for us as he set the basket down.

Noel huffed but dropped the sleeping bags. He faced off with Oren. "I don't know what you're playing at with this nice-guy act, but it's not fooling me."

Oren gazed at him blankly for a moment. "Hmm," he finally said. "Good to know." Then he dropped to his knees and unrolled each sleeping bag for the entire family to sit.

My overly suspicious brother set his hands on his hips and watched without assisting. I knelt down to silently help him. Meanwhile, Brandt and Colton began to chase each other across the grass, playing their own game of tag-padiddle, with squirrels now. When Aspen came bustling up with one last Tupperware container, Noel was still moodily standing watch while Oren and I finished smoothing out the blankets.

"Hey, thanks guys." Aspen knelt with us and began to unload the basket.

Finally, Noel joined in to help her, but the contention he'd started remained in the air. As desperate and determined as I'd been to get Noel to include Oren in the family, I'd also been completely naïve. They were both miserable. Noel wouldn't talk except to pierce glares Oren's way, and even as respectful as Oren was being back to him, I could tell by his own uncommon quietness and politeness that he wanted to be anywhere else but here.

Forcing them together had been a mistake. What had I been thinking, pushing them at each other in the hopes they'd make up?

Brandt and Colton chattered as we ate, and Aspen joined in. I was too busy casting worried glances between the two ex-best friends.

When Oren met my gaze, his brow knit. He leaned in close. "What's wrong?"

I shook my head. "Nothing." But when I glanced away, he caught my arm and made me lift my face again.

"Hey," he said, his eyes full of sincerity. "I'm fine. All right? There's nothing to worry about, baby. It's all good."

I looked him over. The seriousness on his face as he lifted his brows to assure me he wasn't suffering only made me love him more...and yet it reassured me my worry was completely founded. He was definitely in a bad way.

But then he went and pointed past me, saying, "Shit, look at that."

I glanced over, but couldn't figure out what he was trying to show me. "Wha...?" When I turned back, he had half a deviled egg in his mouth. Knowing he'd eaten his own already, I zipped my gaze to my empty plate and gasped. "Is that *my* egg?"

Still holding the last half of it up to his mouth, he grinned and commenced to chew. "You weren't eating it."

Shock made my mouth fall open. "I was saving it for last. Nothing tastes better than Aspen's deviled eggs."

"Then you should've eaten it first...like I did. I mean, what if something happened before you reached the end of your meal? You could've choked and died on your sandwich? A tornado could've come along and blown it away? Or someone could've...stolen it?" Like he had.

I gritted out, "I want my damn egg."

"Here." He smiled way too congenially and held out the half he hadn't finished yet. "I'll share with you."

I snagged it from his hand and popped the entire thing into my mouth. As I chewed, he grinned. But I jabbed him in the gut. With a groan and then a laugh, he clutched his belly and fell backward onto the blanket we shared with Colton. At the last second, he caught me and dragged me down with him.

"Oren," I yelped. But he already had me neatly stretched out on top of him.

"If you wanted more, honey, all you had to do was say so."

He kissed me, thrusting his tongue immediately. I'd always been drawn in by his mouth, so I kissed him back. I forgot where we were and who else was around until Noel rudely cleared his throat.

"*Excuse me.*"

I jerked away from Oren's mouth and rolled off him to sit up, red-faced and embarrassed. As I discretely ducked my face and wiped my lips, Oren lifted his head to send Noel a frown.

"Why? Did you fart?"

Noel wasn't amused. "Do you really have to kiss her in front of me?"

I held my breath as Oren went still. He stared back at Noel before shrugging and lying back down on the blanket as if to gaze up at the clouds. "Guess not," he answered.

I touched his arm in gratitude, thankful he hadn't engaged my butthead big brother in an argument. In response, he reached out and caught hold of my knee. With his eyes closed, he began to rub my calf, from knee to ankle and back again. That seemed to enrage Noel even more though. His jaw hardened and eyes narrowed as he focused on nothing but the movement of Oren's hand, his hand which wasn't even going above my knee.

Needing a break from the tension, I grabbed Oren's fingers, stopping him. "Let's go to the waterfall."

His lashes flickered open and he immediately sat upright. "Okay." A warmth spread over me, reminding me what we'd done the last time we'd been there. But as we went to stand, Noel straightened in surprise.

"Where do you think you two are going?"

I sent him a scowl. "We're going for a walk."

Noel motioned with his hand. "Colton, why don't you tag along with them?"

I set my fists on my hips. "Really?"

Noel glanced at me innocently. "What?"

"We don't need a damn chaperone to keep us from going off somewhere to get kinky. You do realize I *live* with him now, right? We're already—"

Oren slapped his hand over my mouth. "Come on, kid," he called to Colton. "Want to see a waterfall?"

"Yeah!" Colton jumped up, excited.

"Be careful," Noel cautioned immediately.

Oren sent him a withering glance. "Don't worry, big brother. You'll get both your siblings back, safe and sound."

Leaving, him, and Aspen, and Brandt behind, the three of us strolled up the abandoned trail toward the waterfall. As Colton skipped ahead, I grasped Oren's hand. "I am so sorry."

He glanced over, his eyebrows lifted in surprise. "For what? You didn't do anything wrong."

I sighed and rested my cheek on his shoulder. "I should've known better than to expect you two to just...get along."

Oren swept my hair out of my eyes. "If we're ever going to get along again, we're going to have to suffer through a couple of encounters like these first." Then he kissed my temple. "Might as well get them out of the way now."

I still hated watching them not get along because of me, though. "But—"

"Hey, don't get too close to the edge!" Oren yelled above me.

I turned to find Colton ahead of us. He'd already reached the banks of the waterfall, and just as he glanced back at us, the ground under him gave way.

One second, he was there, grinning and waving, the next he was being sucked down into the earth. It happened so fast I could barely draw in a breath between what my eyes saw and what my brain realized had just happened.

Then I screamed. "*Colton!*" I sprang forward, but Oren was faster.

He reached the edge first and held up a hand, warding me away. "Stay back. This bastard is unsteady as fuck."

I skidded to a halt, not wanting to add any more problems. But feeling helpless, I covered my mouth with both hands as tears filled my eyes. The roar of the waterfall was so loud Oren had to yell when he glanced back at me. "It's okay. He's right here. He didn't fall in. He's caught hold of some old tree root and is hanging on."

"Oh thank God." I pressed my hands to my heart, beyond relieved.

A light mist from the nearby water coated my arms and legs. I shivered and hugged myself, wishing I could do something as Oren inched closer to the edge, trying to keep one foot back on more solid ground.

He got down on his knees and stretched one arm over the side, where I hoped he was reaching for my little brother. The ground about five feet away crumbled and plummeted into the water. I gasped when I saw big clumps tumble downstream only a second later. The way it was battered around like a pinball made me pray even more fervently that Colton didn't soon join it.

"Caroline," Oren called, glancing back at me.

I could tell immediately from his gaze that something was seriously wrong.

"What?" I demanded. "Is he okay?"

Oren nodded, but he still looked...sick? Scared? Resigned? "I need...I need you to be prepared to catch him as soon I pull him up. Okay?"

"Okay." I nodded, not understanding what that meant until Oren moved. With a strained grunt, he gritted his teeth and jerked his arm up. As Colton simultaneously came flying up over the ledge at me, the ground under Oren gave way.

Colton banged into me, the force of his impact propelling me backward and onto my butt. I grabbed hold of him and held on tight, crab crawling backward away from the bank. Colton burrowed into me until we were a safe distance away. That's when I pushed him aside and searched frantically for Oren...to find him nowhere.

"Oh my God. Oh my God. *Go!*" I grabbed Colton, jerked him to his feet, and then shoved him in the direction of our picnic. "Get Noel. Quick. Oren's in trouble."

As soon as he nodded and took off, I bit my knuckles and crept toward the ledge.

"Oren?" I screamed.

He'd known this was going to happen when he'd pulled Colton up. He'd known he'd get sucked down. Fearing I wouldn't find him at all, I sobbed when I saw him, only to realized he'd been left in the same predictament Colton had been in, hanging from a root sticking out the side of the steep embankment with the rushing water of the rocky river a good thirty feet below him.

When he looked up and saw me, his eyes flared with panic. "No. Get back."

But the root he was clinging to couldn't support his weight as well it had been able to hold Colton's. It started to slide down the embankment, and as he scrambled to hold on, I lurched forward on my stomach so most of my body was still on solid ground—and then I grabbed for him.

He fumbled for my hand, but when he finally got a good hold, I wasn't prepared for how heavy he'd be, and I started skidding forward on my belly, dragged closer to the edge. Dirt and grass and rocks gouged into my belly and arms.

"You're sliding," he yelled. "No. Let go!"

But no way in hell was I letting go of him. I kicked off my sandals and dug my bare toes into the earth, digging them in and slowing my forward progress, but Oren was still so heavy and my arms screamed in agony.

In the distance, I heard Noel shouting my name. He was coming, running our way. Help was almost there. "Just a few more..." I couldn't finish the sentence, too strained and out of breath to finish.

Oren gritted his teeth and tried to climb his way up, but

each time his shoes dug into the soil, it crumbled away under him.

His face was red with strain, his eyes crazy with panic. Through clenched teeth, he shouted "You're *not* falling in with me."

I just smiled at him, even though tears of exhaustion and fear filled my eyes. "You jump, I jump, right, Jack?"

Grief filled his face. I thought he was going to cry, but he just shook his head, and an emotion that let me know just how he felt about me filled his face.

"God, I love you," he said. Then he let go of my hand.

CHAPTER 36

Caroline

EVEN THOUGH I didn't fall into the water, my stomach plummeted into my knees, and it felt as if everything in my entire world sank and drowned.

"*No!*" I lunged after Oren, trying to dive into the rushing river with him. But an arm wrapped around my waist and jerked me back to the safe part of the bank. I fought it, struggling to get back to Oren.

I'd seen him hit the white, frothy water and watched it swallow him whole. I didn't get to see him resurface; I had to get back to the edge and see if he was okay, if he'd gotten his head back above water, if he could raise his hand, give me a thumbs-up.

But no, the damn arm around my waist was keeping me from my Oren. So I fought it. Noel's voice called my name into my ear as he fought to keep me from plunging forward, but I kept struggling against him. Finally, I broke free enough to stand and peer back into the water, but Oren still hadn't come up, so I looked farther downstream, and then a little farther down. A scream of denial ripped from my lungs when I spotted him. What looked like a log from its immobility, but was clearly human-shaped swished through the currents, momentarily sucked under and then reappearing at the surface again, right before it slammed into a boulder and then was pulled along until I couldn't see him anymore.

"Oh my God. Oh my God."

My limbs went numb as my head went dizzy. I started to hyperventilate.

I wanted to race after him on my rubbery numb legs, but Noel caught my arm. "We can't reach him from here." He already had his phone pressed to his ear. As he spoke to a 911 operator in a calm, level voice, explaining what had happened, I burrowed into my big brother and hugged him hard. My head swam and my body shook. I couldn't believe this was happening.

He hugged me back and kissed my hair. "It's going to be okay," he murmured into my hair, but the shock told me this could in no way be okay.

Noel continued to console me. I might've checked out for a while. All I knew was that Noel was there, always right there, holding on to me and staying strong. I clung to him, gripping his shirt and desperately needing his clarity, because I had none.

At one point, I remember Aspen, and Brandt, and Colton, so we must've returned to the picnic, or maybe they'd come to the banks of the water. Colton sobbed hysterically all over Aspen, and Brandt looked as if he'd peed his pants. I just wanted to get back to the river and look for Oren. We had to find Oren.

I grew disoriented. Though everyone seemed to rush around me, everything moved way too slow for my taste. I must've tried to return to the waterfall, the last place I'd seen Oren—where he'd looked into my eyes and told me he loved me before letting go of my hand to save me. And I must've tried more than once, because Noel finally grasped my shoulders and gave me a hard shake as he yelled my name into my face.

"We can't go back yet. We need help finding him."

That's when I finally heard the distant wail of sirens. It still took the freaking police, ambulance, and rescue workers way too long to arrive. And then it took an extra inordinate amount of time to organize everyone and set them loose on their tasks.

Noel and I ascended on the first police cruiser that pulled into the park. We confused the hell out of the poor guy, both talking and trying to lead him to the place where Oren had fallen in. Finally, he stopped in his tracks, lifted his hands and said, "Now stop. One at a time. First of all, what's the name of the victim?"

The word *victim* rattled through me. Oren had become a victim. It didn't even seem possible.

"Oren Tenning," Noel answered, a split second before I blurted, "My husband."

Noel glanced at me, but said nothing. The officer got onto his radio and began to relay information as we fed it to him. "Six foot two. White male. Twenty-two years old. He fell in at the waterfall at Rainly. Embankment collapsed. Search and rescue requested immediately."

Hearing it relayed in that calm, monotone voice rattled me more than anything. It made Oren sound like a statistic, like a generic case number in a long list of other "victims" who'd fallen into a rushing river, as if he wasn't going to get any special treatment at all, as if no one cared that my entire world had just turned upside down, and the love of my life was in immediate fatal trouble.

When we reached the spot where I'd last seen him, the cop gazed into the water below with a grimace. "The way this current's moving, he could've already been dragged a mile downstream. Damn." He murmured the last part under his breath, so I don't think we were meant to hear it, but the word echoed through my head.

Damn.

Damn.

Damn.

As if Oren was already a lost cause.

I flipped out all over again, and Noel had to once again pull me to him and deal with my hysteria.

They found Oren half an hour later. He actually hadn't gone too far downstream. Maybe about a hundred yards before he became tangled in a piece of driftwood that had gotten lodged between two boulders, which in essence trapped Oren in one spot and somehow miraculously kept his head above water, while the current beat over the rest of his body.

It took them another forty-five minutes to get someone down to him and call up to us that Oren was still alive but unconscious, and then another hour and a half after that to get him out of the water and onto dry land.

I dashed to him, but about half a dozen uniforms blocked my path and held me back, telling me the paramedics needed to tend to him...and that I wouldn't want to see him like this, anyway.

"Don't want to see him *like what*?" I demanded. Just how bad off was he? Was he really alive? Why wouldn't they even let me see him?

And so...I lost it. Yeah, again.

Noel scooped me up and carried me to Oren's truck, where he drove me to the hospital. We damn near trailed the ambulance there, but I still didn't get a peek at Oren once we made it and he was being wheeled inside. Too many freaking medical personnel crowded around him. That didn't calm my worries at all.

Once we were settled into a waiting room, where I paced and Noel talked quietly on his phone, I had a five-minute lull to panic and worry before a nurse came in with a clipboard and asked me, "Mrs. Tenning?"

That was the first time I'd ever been addressed as such. It made tears sprout in my eyes. "Yes?" I sobbed, wiping at my cheeks with both hands.

She sent me a sympathetic smile and held out the clipboard along with a pen. "Do you think you could fill out this information for your husband?"

"I'll try." I took the forms with shaking hands and sank into the nearest chair. At first, the words blurred in front of me. But after a few deep breaths, I forced my brain to calm. Name, address, and birthday were easy to fill out without any hiccups. By the time Noel sat beside me to either help out or just continue being the supportive big brother, I was digging out my wallet to fetch my new insurance card, under my husband's name, and see if I could find anything with his social security number on it.

Noel caught sight of my new driver's license and gasped before he jerked it close for a detailed inspection. "Holy shit. This...You're... I thought you were just..." He shook his head and gaped at me. "You weren't lying just to get close to him, were you? This is..." He jabbed his finger at my license. "This is really real?"

I had no patience or stomach for a lecture from my brother, so I grabbed my license back and jammed it into my wallet. Then I gave the short bark of an answer. "Yeah, it's real."

He continued to stare at me with wide eyes as I carefully entered Oren's insurance information. When I finished filling out the form to the best of my ability, I drew out a breath and finally turned to Noel. "We got married in Lake Tahoe."

"Lake Tahoe?" His mouth fell open. "He took you to *Lake Tahoe* with him?"

"We didn't want to tell you—no, *I* didn't want to tell you because you seemed to be having a hard enough time dealing with the fact I was even seeing him. The wedding wasn't planned...or even remembered until he found the marriage license in our luggage after we got home."

Noel closed his eyes and groaned. "Oh God. You got drunk and went to one of those insta-wedding chapel things?"

I lifted my chin proudly and narrowed my eyes. "And I don't regret it at all." Standing, I cleared my throat. "Excuse me. I need to return this to the nurse."

When I returned, Noel was resting his elbows on his spread knees and cradling his face in his hands. He watched me from dark, troubled eyes as I sat in a chair across the room but facing him.

He didn't say anything. We stared at each other for about thirty seconds. I'm sure my gaze was as defensive as his was disappointed.

His phone rang; he popped to his feet to answer it.

"Hey, baby. No. No word yet." He walked from the waiting room and into the hall so I couldn't listen in on any more of his conversation. But with him gone, and no reason for me to keep playing the obstinate little sister, my worries returned.

Just how badly had Oren been hurt? Why wasn't anyone telling us what was going on? Was he still alive or not?

Right about the point where the panic mounted and I didn't think I could contain myself a second longer, Noel returned. He sat beside me without a word and wrapped me in his arms. I turned to him and buried my face in his neck to weep.

"I should be pissed at you," I sobbed as I clung to him

harder. "The way you've been treating Oren lately, the asshole thing you did at the bar to trap him, the fact that you stopped going to the coffee shop on Saturday mornings and he still does, *waiting* for you to show. I should hate you right now."

Noel sucked in a breath. "He still goes to the coffee shop?"

I nodded. "Every fucking Saturday."

"Shit." He closed his eyes and shuddered out a breath. "I've been a stupid, stubborn, blind ass. I know that. I knew it while I was doing and saying all the shit I did, but I just couldn't stop myself. He made me so mad. I didn't think he'd ever go behind my back like that. I...it hurt."

"That's no excuse for—"

He lifted his hand and shook his head. "I know. I...damn it, Caroline. I'm sorry. I'm so fucking sorry. I made myself focus on everything bad he'd ever done, and I just let it fester."

"I love him," I said simply. "And he loves me. He's good to me, too. No one's ever been as good to me as he is."

Noel kissed my forehead. "I see that...now." Now that it could be too late, he didn't add, but seemed to relay with his tortured gaze.

Closing my eyes, I turned my head to the side. "You haven't said anything about our marriage." I don't know why I pushed that subject. Maybe because it kept me focused on something besides my fear.

Noel blew out a long breath. "That's because I don't know *what* to say. You're just so young, but...I'm not scared. Not for you. Because I...honestly, there's no one else I would trust with you more than him. I lost sight of why he was my friend for a while. But he is, and there's a damn good reason for it. He's *always* had my back, and now I know he has yours, which is so much more precious to me than him having mine." Taking my hands, he looked deep into my eyes, begging. "Do you think you can ever forgive me?"

I gave him a watery smile. "I think I have to, because I really need my big brother right now."

"You have me," he promised. When he hugged me again, I held him tight, grateful for him for about the millionth time in the past couple hours. I probably should've tried to hold on to my anger longer, but I just couldn't, because I really did need my big brother.

At some point, I must've exhausted myself because Noel nudged me awake.

I looked up to find Oren's parents in the waiting room, looking a little lost as they glanced around as if looking for help. When I pulled out of Noel's arms and sat up, Brenda finally focused on me.

"Caroline." She gasped and hurried forward. "You look awful. What happened? Were you with him?"

"Yes. I..." When I stood, she grasped my wrists and spread my arms to see me better. I glanced down, and it was the first time I got a real look at myself. My shirt was grass-stained with flecks of blood soaking through from where I'd scraped my stomach along the ground. And now that I was seeing that, I realized my abdomen and elbows were sore. Then there were my palms, my palms that hadn't been able to keep hold of Oren and stop him from falling. They were scratched and coated with dried mud.

Tears filled my eyes. "I'm sorry. I'm so sorry," I sobbed.

Brenda cooed out a sound of understanding and enfolded me into a huge, comforting hug. I told her everything, about the picnic, and that we took my little brother to the waterfall to show it to him, how Colton fell in, and then how Oren saved both our lives. When I got to the part where Oren told me he loved me right before he let go of my hand to keep me from falling in with him, Noel cursed fluently and buried his face in one hand.

Oren's parents glanced at him. "I don't believe we've met yet," Phil finally said.

Noel looked up, and then straightened. He blew out a breath before holding out his hand. "Sorry, sir. I'm Noel Gamble. I'm the one who called you."

I blinked, startled. I hadn't even thought to contact anyone, let alone Oren's parents. Grateful that my big brother had had the forethought to get a hold of them, I found a smile for him somewhere in my grief, thankful he was here with me, to help me through this.

Oren's parents seemed startled by the introduction. "Noel Gamble?" Brenda repeated. "The Noel Gamble who lived with our son for nearly three years and we never *met*?"

Phil shrugged. "We saw him play ball when we went to Oren's games."

"But we still never—"

"He's my brother," I spoke up, feeling the need to defend him. "Noel's my big brother."

"Oh." Brenda shook her head as if confused. "Well, that explains how *you* met Oren, then."

She patted my hands in a motherly fashion, and I smiled uneasily. I don't know why I felt so uncomfortable. Brenda's hands trembled as if it was taking everything she had to hold herself together. It seemed like I was deceiving her somehow, maybe because I'd lied to her about Oren seeing a therapist the last time I'd seen her. Or maybe I was so strained because it was all my fault he was here and she forgave me so easily. No wonder Oren had so much trouble being around them after his sister died. He'd felt responsible and they'd pinned no blame on him. It'd probably made him blame himself even more.

"So, have we heard any updates at all?" Phil asked.

I shook my head, and the Tennings seemed to wilt with more worry.

Just then, the nurse who'd had me fill out all Oren's paperwork popped her head into the room. "Mrs. Tenning?"

Brenda looked up. "Yes?"

A moment of awkward confusion crossed the nurse's face before she pointed at me. "I...was actually talking to *this* Mrs. Tenning."

She darted to me, holding out another clipboard. "Sorry. There was one more form I needed you to fill out."

I froze as both of Oren's parents whirled to gape at me. I sank closer to Noel, who wrapped a supportive arm around my shoulders. "O...okay." I reached out and snagged the clipboard from her and sat in the nearest chair where I began to write with a trembling hand.

The Tennings kept staring. Finally, Brenda said, "You're married?"

"I, uh..." I cleared my throat and pressed the pen flat against the clipboard. "Yeah. We...uh, we are. Oren and I are...married."

The strap of Brenda's purse slid off her shoulder and the entire thing plopped to the floor, completely unnoticed by her.

Her eyes narrowed with accusation, right before she repeated, "You're *married*?"

I cringed lower into my seat. "Yes." Noel sat beside me and took my hand. "W-we got married in Lake Tahoe."

"Lake Tahoe?" Brenda looked like she might claw my eyes out, so I pressed harder against my brother.

Phil hissed a curse under his breath and shook his head. "I guess now we know why he turned down *that* job."

"What?" I shook my head. "No. No, he didn't *get* that job. He told me..." My voice trailed off as I realized Oren might've lied to me.

"Oh, he got the job." Brenda scowled hard. "He said there were reasons why he couldn't take it right now. He forgot to mention it was because he was *married*."

"I...I..." I looked up at Noel, confused. "He got the job?"

Sympathy filled his gaze as he squeezed my hand.

"Why didn't he tell me he got the job?"

Noel opened his mouth, but Brenda was the one who answered. "Probably because he didn't want to distress his precious little eighteen-year-old bride into thinking he'd leave her."

The truth pummeled me in the chest. Oren had stayed...for me. I wanted to cry all over again. He hadn't even told me what he'd given up for me.

Instead of defending myself, all I could say was, "I'm nineteen now," in a stupid, hollow voice.

"Eighteen, nineteen. Do I look like I care?" Brenda snarled. "My son is way too young to be getting *married*, and now because of it—because of *you*—he's fighting for his very life as we speak."

I flinched and pressed my hands to my chest as it shuddered. Pain rippled through me. The truth had never hurt so much. "I...I'm sorry," I croaked, unable to look her in the eye.

She didn't forgive me. "He could be safely tucked away in Lake Tahoe right now. But no, he stayed behind for you, and ended up saving you and your family. Now, I may lose my one and only child."

She pressed a hand to her heart and tears spilled down her cheeks. "I've already lost one baby. I can't lose the other. No. I just...I *can't*." Grabbing her husband's arm, she glared at me, her chest heaving. "This is *your* fault. How could you do this to me?"

"Hey," Noel started in my defense, but Phil held up his hand.

"Leave her be. She's distraught." But he seemed to agree with her because as he wrapped his arms around his wife in comfort, he sent me an accusing glare.

I shuddered, tears filling my eyes.

"Come on." Noel took my hand and led me out of the waiting room and into the hall.

We collapsed onto a nearby bench, where he rocked me in his arms while I sobbed.

"She was right. It's my fault. If I hadn't suggested we go to that stupid waterfall. If I'd kept a better eye on Colton. If I hadn't stopped Oren from going to Lake Tahoe."

"Shh," Noel commanded softly. "This was not your fault. You did nothing wrong."

"I should've held on to his hand longer. I should've—"

"No. Look at me. You did nothing wrong. And if Ten were here right now he'd say the same thing. He made the decision to stay in Ellamore with you. He made the decision to come today. And he made the decision to let go of your hand to save you."

When I sobbed harder, he stroked my hair and kissed my temple.

"And I'm sure he would've done everything the exact same way again if given a second chance. Because he loved you."

It was the way he said *loved* in past tense that broke me.

Dissolving into grief, I wilted against him and wept myself to sleep.

CHAPTER 37

Caroline

WHEN I WOKE, I was lying on something hard, but my legs were slung over the side with my feet on the floor and my cheek was propped against a leg. It didn't feel like Noel's leg.

I sat up, wincing against the pain in my temples. After shoving my hair out of my face, I focused on Asher. Not expecting him at all, I just blinked.

"Hey, there," he murmured, sympathy ruling his green gaze. "How're you feeling?"

I glanced away and around the hospital's waiting room to find everyone else had arrived while I was sleeping. Zoey lay tucked into Quinn's lap fast asleep. Reese and Eva stood from where they'd been sitting with Pick and Mason. When they started toward me, I held up my hands, warding them away. I couldn't handle anyone else consoling me right now. I only wanted Noel.

Or Oren.

But I couldn't have Oren.

Pain slashed through me.

I glanced around again, but Noel wasn't in the room. Neither were Brenda or Phil.

I sniffed and wiped at my dry, crusty face. "Where's

Noel? Have they brought out any news about Oren? How long have I been asleep?"

"Why don't you lie back down?" Asher's voice coaxed as he reached for me, but I recoiled from him.

Oren wouldn't like me touching Asher.

"Where's Noel?" I demanded, feeling a panic attack coming on.

No Oren. No Noel. I couldn't handle this.

Reese clutched her hands to her heart. "He just stepped out to make a phone call home and check in. And no, there's been no news about Ten. We've been here less than an hour. Noel said you'd just fallen asleep when we arrived."

I nodded my thanks, ducked my face and hurried from the room to find my brother.

I heard his voice as I neared an intersection in the hall.

"No, there's no news yet. He must...shit. He must be bad off if they haven't come out to say anything yet. I just called to check in. No, actually, I had to hear your voice. I wish you were here with me."

His own voice was choked and raw, and it stopped me in my tracks. He sounded about as heartbroken as I felt. It bruised my already tender feelings. Here, I'd been worried about nothing and no one but myself, and Noel was on the verge of losing his best friend.

As I clutched my stomach, Noel said, "No, don't come. You said Colton's still upset. He needs you. I'll be okay. Just talking to you helps. Hearing your voice."

After pausing to listen to a question, he sighed wearily. "She's a complete mess. She's hurting and blames herself, and fuck...I don't know what to do for her. What if she ends up a nineteen-year-old *widow* because of this? I just hold her as she cries herself to sleep, and I try not to lose it myself in front of her. But God, Aspen. He was my best friend. What if he dies and the last things I said to him were—"

He hissed out a breath. "I know, but I still feel like shit. I was such a dick. I treated him awful, and he might die from saving both my brother *and* my sister's lives. He truly fucking loved her, and I was too mad and felt too betrayed to even see that. I can't...I just—"

When his voice broke, tears spilled down my cheeks. I hurried around the corner. His red wet eyes widened when they saw me.

"I'm sorry." I rushed to him and hugged him. His arms immediately went around me. "I'm sorry, I was only thinking about me."

He buried his face in my hair. "No. I'm sorry I was so fucking stubborn."

We hugged and cried, and he finally ended his call with his wife. Time passed, I have no idea how much. Seconds, hours, minutes. It all seemed to be sucked into some surreal vacuum where none of this was really happening. It was just a crazy, awful dream, and I was going to wake up any time now. I'd open my eyes and be back in Oren's bed with our legs tangled and his palm cupping my breast. Light would stream in through the windows and he'd crack open his eyes to send me one of his lazy, sexy morning grins.

"Morning," he'd say. *"I guess you decided to stick around another day, huh?"*

But then Noel pulled away from me, wiping his face, and I was still in a hospital, where I hadn't seen Oren in six hours, not since he'd looked up from where he was dangling and told me he loved me before letting go of my hand.

A shudder of horror passed through me, wondering if I'd ever look into those vivacious hazel eyes again.

Noel sent me a tremulous smile that was full of grief. "I totally didn't mean to fall apart on you like that."

I squeezed his arm. "It's okay. Just do me a favor and stop talking about him in the past tense. He's going to be okay. He's going to make it."

Pain passed over Noel's face, but he washed it away with another sad smile and nodded. "You got it."

With that agreement made, we wrapped our arms around each other and started back to the waiting room, where we realized a doctor in surgical scrubs had arrived. Oren's parents had reappeared, too.

"Here she is." Pick motioned to me when I entered the room.

The doctor turned, took me in from head to toe and then nodded before saying, "Mrs. Tenning, I'm Dr. Wolfowitz, the trauma surgeon who worked on your husband. When Oren came in, he was unconscious and in shock. There was significant damage to the left frontal and parietal bone, which probably occurred when he crashed into the log and boulder he was trapped against until they found him. Though that probably saved him from drowning to death, it's also what caused the most damage. There was so much trauma to the head and spinal cord..."

Was? Why did he keep saying *was* like everything was all past tense? Like *Oren* was past tense.

"Other than the brain injury, he has a dislocated shoulder, fractured leg, and significant, permanent scarring to the right side of the face, though we were able to save the damaged eye and ear."

I gulped and pressed my hand over my mouth. Permanent scarring meant nothing to me. No, actually it meant everything. It meant he was still alive. Saving an eye and ear, that meant they'd saved the rest of him too, right? His heart was still beating?

"So he's alive?" I rasped the words, almost afraid to voice them.

The doctor hesitated. I have no idea why he hesitated. If Oren's eye and ear had made it, then the rest of him had to have made it too.

Finally, the doctor gave a small nod. But then he had to go and chase it with, "We had to put him into a medically induced coma to give the brain time to heal."

"Oh my God." Brenda covered her mouth with her hands and turned to Phil, where he immediately gathered her into his arms.

I stared at them a moment as the word *coma* echoed through my ears. But Oren was in a coma. It didn't even seem possible. The most irritatingly, lively, foulmouthed, loving jerk I'd ever met, and they'd shut down his *brain*?

A numb void filled me, as if my own brain decided to take a little break too. I studied everyone else in the waiting room—Oren's parents clutching each other, Zoey sobbing against Quinn's shoulder as he softly rubbed her abdomen and kissed her hair, Reese and Eva holding hands and looking pale while their men flanked them on either sides, Asher with his hands shoved deep in his pockets and his head bowed as he kicked at a piece of his other shoe, and Noel...Noel looking as if he might start bawling all over again—and I just watched them, feeling sad for them, while inside I was just too...too scared to feel anything at all.

But then Noel grabbed me and hauled me into his arms, and that first painful bite of fear sank its teeth into my jugular. I went cold and started to shake.

"You said medically induced," Phil repeated as he

stroked his wife's arm and nodded to the doctor.

When Dr. Wolfowitz confirmed it, Phil asked, "So that means you'll bring him out of it too? How...how long will he be under?"

"It depends. We'll lighten the barbiturates as soon as the swelling begins to recede. If the level of function is good, we'll bring him out completely."

I shook my head, unable to believe most of this. Oren-not-functioning just wasn't something I could configure in my thought process. He was always on the go, never stayed still, never really stopped talking. He always had a comeback for everything, always had some kind of reaction. Picturing him lying still and unconscious—reactionless—in a sterile white hospital bed just didn't fit with the man I'd fallen in love with and married.

But then I didn't have to picture it in my head any longer. Two hours later, I got to see it for myself. Visitors were finally allowed into his intensive care unit, two at a time and only for ten-minute spans once an hour, but none of us waiting to see him cared about a few rules. We were willing to do anything—wait any length—for even the smallest amount of time with Oren.

The nurse looked to me when she came out to allow the first two people in, but I stepped back and motioned toward his parents, letting them go first. I swear, they went over their time allotment, though. Every freaking second felt like a millennium. When they exited, both their faces were wet and they looked ten years older than when they had gone back. Brenda met my gaze briefly, then quickly looked away again.

I turned to Noel for support. He took my hand and gave me a bolstering nod. "Just one more hour."

I nodded back because I couldn't speak. When our time finally came, my fingers squeezed around my brother's arm as fear squeezed around my heart. I hated the sight of blood and gore, and seeing Oren damaged because of what he'd done to save me made it all that much more distressing.

He was in a coma with permanent scarring, a swollen brain, and broken bones because of *me*.

But then there he was, and I forgot about all that. I was finally able to see my precious, precious man. With a gasp, I let go of Noel and raced forward. A cast covered his elevated leg, and they'd put one arm in a sling while half his head was wrapped in bandages. A tube fed into his mouth, giving him oxygen while IVs and heart monitors led various other hoses into him as well. The part of his face we could see was fairly swollen, but I could still tell it was him.

My Oren.

I touched his fingers reverently, careful not to disturb some of the gadgets connected to the back of his hand. Then I crouched beside him so I could speak into his ear.

"Hey there, handsome. I'm sorry it took so long to get to you. I didn't think they'd ever let me back here. I was about to pull one of my acting tricks and have a major diva fit to trick my way to your side, but they finally complied."

I grinned, remembering the scene we'd created on the airplane. But the smile fell when Oren gave no response; his heart monitor just kept beeping out a steady rhythm, and the cuffs around his ankles kept releasing pressure with a puff of air.

"I'm very upset with you, you know." I kept my voice light as I scolded, I even reached out to gently run my nails over his scruff, but I continued to scold. "You weren't supposed to let go of my hand like that. I mean, if you jump, I jump, right, Jack? You were supposed to listen to that part."

But he didn't respond to the *Titanic* quote either. A sob escaped me. Noel's hands wrapped around my shoulders and squeezed supportively.

"I was supposed to go with you, wherever you went. We're a team. You told me once that I had to have a place. Well, I finally figured out where it is. It's with you. Do you really want to leave me alone, without a place? Damn it, you can't abandon me here to live this life by myself. I'm a complete freaking mess without you. I..." My voice broke, and I shook my head. "I love you, Oren. I just...I want you back."

But Oren wasn't here, and I talked to an unresponsive body. I didn't know what else to do though, and I couldn't leave him. So I gobbled up most of our ten minutes with him, just talking, telling him about everyone outside waiting for their turn to see him and how Noel was no longer pissed at him. There was barely a minute left when I finally realized Noel might want to say something, too.

I stepped aside, and he leaned in close to Oren's ear to murmur something short and sweet. Then he cleared his throat and stood, turning to me.

When our gazes met, I knew this was about the worst moment of both our lives.

TWO DAYS PASSED. I didn't leave the hospital once. I just couldn't. Reese and Eva eventually took control of me and cleaned me up. They borrowed some nurse's scrubs from somewhere and changed me into them, cooing over the bruises on my stomach. After that, Reese brushed my hair while Eva cleaned my face and applied a touch of makeup. Zoey sat beside me, holding my hand and being the quiet, supportive best friend. But she looked so pale, the first moment I saw her flinch and set a hand over her baby, I sent her home, commanding Quinn to keep her in bed and take care of her.

She came back the next day though, as did everyone else. Noel and Oren's parents stayed overnight, camping out on uncomfortable waiting room chairs while our friends returned daily. Everyone eventually took a turn visiting Oren, but they all had the same result with him as I did: unresponsive.

When the doctor told us they were going to begin taking him out of the coma, I became a jittery mess. There was a chance Oren's body wasn't ready for that, that he'd die. I hated all the statistics and percentages people gave; I just wanted someone to say, "He's going to be okay," but no one ever did.

"The swelling is down, brain function looks good, and he's breathing independently. He's still unconscious, as we're gradually withdrawing the barbiturates, but if you want to go in and sit with him, Mrs. Tenning, and be there when he wakes, that may be best for him."

I popped to my feet so fast I almost tripped over them. "Yes," I answered too quickly, but I didn't care how eager I looked. Oren was going to wake up soon. I started to follow the doctor, but then paused when I saw Brenda and Phil across the room.

Slowing to a stop, I watched them huddled together before I asked, "Can his parents be there, too?"

The Tennings and I had called a sort of cease-fire. They

no longer glared or slung blame my way, and I avoided all eye contact with them when they were in the same room, but neither of us talked to each other again after the first day, even though they'd been getting to know everyone else in the group.

As Brenda looked up at me now, though, only relief and gratitude lingered in her expression.

The doctor nodded. "In this instance, we'll let it slide and allow the three of you in his room."

So, Oren's parents and I went to his room together. One side of his face was still thickly bandaged, but he looked more like himself with the breathing tube out of his mouth.

We sat with him for a little over an hour, me on one side, Phil and Brenda on the other, before he moved his face on his pillow, turning it away from me. The three of us watching him sprang to our feet. We shared an excited glance before resting our attention back on Oren. A light cough left his lungs, and I swear, it was the most amazing sound in the world. Then he licked his lips and shifted his face again, turning toward me this time.

His eyelashes fluttered.

Holding my breath, I leaned in. "Oren? Can you hear me?"

"Yeah," he mumbled from cracked, rusty lips.

The doctor had warned us about all the types of brain damage Oren could have. He may have speech problems, memory problems, difficulty with motor skills. There were any number of things that could go wrong, but as he opened his lashes and looked up at me from bleary hazel eyes, the only thing I knew was that he was alive and awake, and the world was absolutely perfect.

My Oren was looking at me.

Tears filled my lashes, but I smiled so hard I'm surprised I didn't break my cheeks. "Hey, there. How're you feeling?"

He opened his mouth, tried to talk again, but only a wheeze came out. After trying to wet his lips again, he rasped, "Water."

"Oh." I laughed at my own silliness. Of course he'd be thirsty. They'd had a tube jammed down his throat for days. He probably felt as raw and dry as a seven-year drought.

I spun away to find a cup of water for him, and his mother murmured his name.

"Mom?" His poor voice was so hoarse I winced as I

brought the cup around to him. It must hurt to talk. And yeah, he looked pale and cringed with pain as he held out his hand toward his parents, moving like a slow, sore old man. "Dad."

Brenda and Phil gathered close and took his hand, the three of them clutching fingers while his parents began to cry and laugh.

Oren glanced around the room, looking completely disoriented. "What happened?"

When his gaze landed on me, I held out the cup, bringing the straw to his chapped lips. He drank a few sips and then closed his eyes and sighed in relief.

I set the cup on the side tray. "Do you want me to raise the bed so you can sit up?" They'd stopped elevating his broken leg, so I didn't think there would be any problem with getting him more comfortable if that's what he wanted.

And he did. With a nod, he murmured, "Yes. Thank you."

I pressed the bedside button and watched his face as his torso was lifted. When he opened his eyes and lifted a hand, letting me know he was good, I stopped. He studied me a moment, his gaze moving over my clothes.

I looked down at the scrubs I was still wearing and tried to think up a reason to give him why I wasn't in my own clothes.

"You don't look old enough to be a nurse," he slurred sleepily.

I started to smile, thinking he was teasing me since I'd just given him a drink and adjusted his bed, but then he turned away from me, completely dismissing me, and I realized he really did think I was a nurse.

My gaze zipped to his parents, only to find they were staring right back, alarm in their eyes. Brenda returned her attention to her son. "Oren?" she said fearfully.

"Yeah?" His soft, raspy voice made me shudder. He reached for his mom again. He'd never once tried to reach for me.

He knew who she was. He knew who his father was. He knew who *he* was.

But he didn't know who I was.

Fear, dark and cold, rushed into me. Oren didn't know who I was. How could he not know who *I* was?

"Where's Zoey?" he asked, glancing around the room.

"Oh shit," Phil whispered.

I covered my mouth with both hands and took a step backward. Oren's parents exchanged a horrified glance before they looked across the bed at me, anguish flooding off both of them. I shook my head, trying to deny it, but one of the worst things possible had happened. He'd lost his recent memory, at least four years of it...because he still thought his sister was alive.

Catching all the distress in the room, Oren said, "What's wrong? Is she okay? What happened? Why am I here? Where's my sister?"

Brenda whimpered and laid her hands on him in reassurance, but he must've sensed her pain.

"Mom?" His voice trembled with fear.

His parents looked to me again, and Oren turned my way, his gaze accusing, as if I was interfering in a private moment that a stranger should not interrupt.

"I, uh..." My voice trembled as I lifted my hands and backed another step away. "I'll let you have your family time."

His parents nodded their thanks, and Oren turned back to them, already forgetting me.

Tears streamed down my cheeks. My legs felt like noodles and in no way able to support me, but I kept walking, letting myself out of his room and quietly shutting the door behind me.

I was halfway down the hall when I heard him scream, "Noooo...*Zoey*."

It was a miracle his vocal chords could be that loud after how hoarse he'd been. But the pain behind his screams let me know he'd found a way to use them regardless.

Noel, and Quinn, and Zoey, and just...everyone flew out of the waiting room just as my legs gave out and I started to collapse.

My brother dove at me, barely catching me. "Caroline? What the hell? Are you okay?"

Another cry from Oren's room had him lifting his face and glancing that way. "What happened?"

I grabbed hold of his shirt as our friends gathered around, looking panicked and worried. Tears streamed down my face and clogged my throat. I couldn't talk.

"He doesn't..." A sob seized me, and I squeezed my eyes closed.

"Caroline?" Worry filled Noel's voice as he stroked my face.

"His memory," I got out. "Lost years. Still thought his sister was alive." I met the eyes of every person gathered around me. "He doesn't remember any of us."

Days of exhaustion, fear, worry, heartbreak, and guilt took over then. I passed out cold, everything going dark and blessedly numb.

CHAPTER 38

Caroline

I WOKE IN A hospital bed. At first, I had no idea what was going on or why I was there. When I remembered Oren, and his coma, and him waking up with only half of his memory, I gasped and sat upright. Then I whimpered and cradled my head because it throbbed like hell.

Noel, who'd fallen asleep in a chair next to my bed, jolted awake. "Hey. *Easy*," he murmured, reaching out to comfort me. "It's okay."

"Wha...?" I slowly lowered my arms and looked down at myself. I was still in the scrubs I'd been wearing for days, but my hands were now bandaged. "What happened? How long was I out?"

Breathing out a long sigh as if he were worn to the bone, Noel sent me a tired smile. He hadn't shaved in days, and his eyes were lined with weariness. But he slid up to the side of my bed to sit by me and comfort me as if nothing whatsoever was afflicting him.

"You passed out after—"

I waved him quiet, wincing when I thought about the horror that had lit through me when I realized Oren had no idea who I was, and the pain that came when I heard him scream for his dead sister.

"Yeah, I remember that part."

Noel nodded and gulped. "The staff brought you in here and looked you over. You're suffering from some severe exhaustion and dehydration, kiddo." He took my wrists and looked down at my bandages. "Why didn't you tell me you'd gotten hurt that day, too? Your scratches could've gotten infected."

I shrugged and glanced away. "I don't know. I didn't really notice, I guess." Or care.

He blew out a breath. "We've both been so worried about him, we haven't been taking care of ourselves. Tonight, we're going home and we're sleeping in real beds and letting Aspen fill us with a warm, home-cooked meal. No arguments."

"But Oren—"

"Still doesn't remember either of us." I choked out a sound of denial, and Noel's face flooded with grief. "We're not doing him any good by staying here and making ourselves sick, Caroline. The doctors said he could get his full memory back in a matter of minutes, hours, days, or—"

"Never," I said, the word echoing through my head.

I'd seen the movie *The Vow* with Channing Tatum and Rachel McAdams. It'd been based on a real, live couple, and she'd *never* gotten her memory back.

What if Oren never remembered me? What if he was lost to me forever?

Fear clogged my throat. Knowing him this last year and developing a relationship with him had defined me in ways I'd stay for the rest of my life. To think all that could be completely erased from him devastated me.

I told myself I should be happy he was alive, relieved he'd made it out of the coma. But the selfish, needy part of me just wanted him to look at me and *remember us*.

"Caroline." Noel's voice was calming as he wrapped an arm around my shoulder. "It's going to be okay."

I nodded, but my eyes still went damp. I wiped at them, tired of crying, tired of hurting. I just wanted Oren. I wanted to burrow into his arms and forget any of this had ever happened.

"How's he doing?" I asked.

"Better," a voice answered from the opened doorway. Brenda hesitated when she met my gaze, but then she stepped into the room with Phil at her heels. "His speech is clear and unhindered. His fine motor skills were slow at the beginning, but they're developing by the hour."

"And his memory?" I asked, glancing away because I still didn't know where I stood with her. It was strange to see her looking at me with such compassion.

Brenda sat on the bed next to Noel. "He's still missing about five years. He thinks he's a senior in high school, and he hasn't recovered anything more since awakening."

I nodded. "That's..." I cleared my throat. "Well, at least he still has the first..." But I just couldn't voice my gratefulness.

His mother took my hands, smiling softly as if she understood my dilemma and forgave me for my sorrow. "I wanted to thank you," she said. "Thank you for not telling him who you were. He was already disoriented and scared. Learning about Zoey devastated him enough. I think hearing he was married and—"

"I know." I nodded and pulled my hands away from her to curl them to my chest. "I would never do anything to hurt him more."

Brenda seemed a little sad that I'd pulled away, but she nodded. "I know that. You love him very much, and I..." She cleared her throat and glanced down. "I'd like to apologize for the things I said to you. I was...I was hysterical and scared. And I needed to lash out and blame someone, but you weren't—"

Since I still felt responsible, I couldn't listen to her pardon me. I lifted my hand and rushed out, "It's okay. I understand."

Her fingers bit around mine sternly. "No. I don't think you fully understand. This was not your fault, Caroline. It was an accident. You didn't cause it, and you tried everything within your power to help him. You were *not* to blame."

My nose burned as I tried not to cry, but it didn't work. Hot, heavy tears filled my eyes. "But if only I'd—"

"No. No more ifs, child. Oren's been suffering for years with all the what-ifs he has when he thinks about Zoey. Don't put yourself through that, too. Just focus on the fact that he was a hero and saved both you and your brother. Okay?"

I couldn't help it, I began to sob. Squeezing my eyes closed, I bowed my head and confessed, "I just want him to remember me."

"Oh, sweetie." Brenda tugged me away from my brother and pulled me into a warm, motherly embrace. "He will. Have faith. Oren always comes out okay. He's our little survivor. He'll get his memories back, and he'll love you again. Don't you worry."

But I did, and I sobbed all my worries out on my mother-in-law's shirt. She just held me, and forgave me, and after a while, the tears finally dried.

NOEL MADE GOOD on his threat. No matter how much I balked, he drove me home that night. I hadn't seen Oren since the moment he'd woken from his coma and hadn't recognized me. Everyone thought it best if he wasn't approached by too many people he'd see as strangers just yet, not until he adjusted to the fact that he'd lost his sister and was no longer seventeen years old.

It hurt to stay away from him. A part of me wanted to sneak into his room and just have him look at me. He'd remember. He had to remember me. *Us*. To me, it was the only thing worth remembering. But I didn't want to confuse him and hurt him more than he already was.

My room at Noel and Aspen's house was no longer mine. Brandt had moved in and none of my things were there. That was okay. My home was with Oren, in his bed. I was tempted to go back to his apartment and sleep in our room, alone. But I knew I'd never sleep and missing him would kill me, so I let Brandt be a gentleman and bunk with Colton for the night while I took over his new room.

But I still couldn't sleep, and when Colton snuck in to cuddle with me in the middle of the night, I was glad for the company, even if the bitter sweetness of it made me cry some more.

OREN APPARENTLY grew restless and frustrated with not being able to remember five years of his life. The next day when Noel and I arrived back at the hospital, his parents seemed frazzled from having to "deal" with him.

Brenda swept her hair out of her face and blew out a breath. "He wants answers, and we don't know what to tell him without shocking him too much."

"We told him he's had concerned friends here, worried about him, and he wants to meet you. All of you."

Noel and I shared a glance. Excitement glittered in his eyes, and I knew my own stomach fluttered with anticipation. I couldn't wait to get back into his room. Nodding together, we turned back to Oren's parents.

"Of course," Noel answered immediately. "I'll get the gang gathered, no problem."

Within a couple hours, we had everyone back at the hospital. "Okay, so..." Noel rubbed his hands together as he took control of the group. "I think we've agreed that it's too soon to tell him he's married unless he remembers, but, uh...everything else is fair game. If he asks about something, we can tell him whatever he wants to know."

Though only Pick, and possibly Eva had known Oren and I were married before the accident, they all knew now.

"Sounds good." Pick placed his hand on the small of Eva's back. "Let's go see our boy."

En masse, we started for his room. I wondered fleetingly if so many strangers at once would overwhelm him, but I also knew everyone would take it easy on him. When we reached the door where Phil was standing to welcome us inside, I stalled and latched on to Noel's arm.

He glanced at me and walked me a few steps away before murmuring, "What's wrong?"

Worry filtered through me. "What if I can't do this? What if I can't keep it together and I just...I start crying again? I don't want to upset him or—"

"Caroline." Noel smiled and kissed my forehead. "If you want to see your husband, then come on. I know you. Once we get in that room, you'll do whatever you have to do to keep it together."

His not-so-pep talk made my lips quiver with a half smile. But then I straightened my spine and nodded. Though my nerves were wrenched with worry, I clutched his hand as he led me into the room behind everyone else.

Oren was awake and sitting up in bed. Half his face was still bandaged, but he looked so much better, alert and conscious with color in his face.

His gaze darted warily over everyone as we filed into his room. "Whoa," he finally murmured, as if overcome. "There's a lot of you."

At his side, his mother took his hand. "These are your closest friends," she said. "They've been here every day, worried about you."

Once again, Oren looked sick with dread. He didn't recognize any of us. But he swept out a hand with a big, encompassing wave and gave a shaky, "Hey."

None of us answered. I think we were in shock that he was treating us like complete strangers.

"We'll let you talk to your friends, then." Brenda sent him a bolstering smile as she stood. "If you need anything, we'll be right outside."

He gave a jerky, nervous nod and followed her from the room with his gaze as if he didn't want her to leave him alone in here with us. Then he blew out a breath and glanced at us again.

"Okay, this is strange," Pick spoke up. "Ten's usually the one to crack a dirty joke whenever we need some comic relief."

While everyone else let out a quiet laugh, Oren shook his head, confused. "Who's Ten?"

Silence answered him, which only made him shift on his bed, looking even more uncomfortable. Finally, my brother said, "You are, buddy. That's what we call you?"

I hovered against Noel's side, clinging to his arm because I so badly wanted to go to Oren and just hug him and soothe his unease. He looked so alone in that bed. Alone and lost.

"You *do*?" Oren murmured, sounding confused. He shook his head. "Why do you...oh. Because of the Tenning part. Got it." Glancing around at us again, and not even pausing at me—which stung every time his gaze flittered over me—he added, "Am I not still friends with any of my high school classmates?"

"I've never met any of them," Noel answered. "And I've probably known you the longest out of everyone here. You and I met freshman year of college. We were dormitory roommates for a semester. Then we got an apartment together until about a year ago."

Oren nodded. "So none of you ever knew Zoey either, then?"

The name caused us to freeze. By now, everyone knew who his sister was and that she'd died, but since we had a Zoey in our group as well, it was strange to hear him say the name.

Noel finally shook his head. "Uh, no. No, sorry, we never got to meet your sister."

"Oh." Deflated by that, Oren glanced down at his hands.

"So…" Noel went on, determined to clear the uncomfortable tension from the air. "You've probably known Hamilton here the second longest, for about two years when he joined the football team with us."

"Football?" Oren glanced up, surprised. "I played football? In college?" He shook his head. "I…I wasn't planning on going out for ball in college."

Noel grinned. "No, but I talked you into it. We kicked ass together, too. Won the national championships this year. You were the best wide receiver on the team."

"Really?" An awed surprise flooded Oren's voice as his lips curved into a smile. "That's pretty cool."

"Yeah," Noel murmured. "And after I got married, you moved in with Hamilton here and his girlfriend—"

"Blondie," Zoey blurted before Noel could say her name. "You call me Blondie." Tears glistened in her eyes as she smiled. "And you like to coax me into cooking you a meal or doing your laundry as often as possible."

I wanted to cry all over again because Zoey and Oren had been so close. It had to hurt her, too, to know he'd forgotten the sibling-like tie they'd formed.

"O…kay," he said slowly, glancing suspiciously between Quinn and Zoey. "So, I live with *both* of you? Strange."

Guilt crept into Zwinn's expression as they glanced my way. But it was best not to mention I now lived with them, too.

Noel stroked my arm to soothe me; his Spidey sense must've kicked in, knowing my tear ducts were aching to start opening the floodgates.

"And Pick is probably the next you met. He works at— actually, he now owns—the bar where we all work."

Oren glanced away from Pick to frown at Noel. "Bar? I work in a *bar*?"

"The Forbidden Nightclub," Pick answered. "All of us guys here are bartenders there."

Oren squinted. "A bar?" he repeated incredulously and

shook his head. "I'm not even old enough to drink and I—I mean..." Probably remembering he was twenty-two now, instead of seventeen, he pressed a hand to his brow, soaking in the news. "Weird," he murmured.

He glanced at Eva standing with Pick, so Pick wrapped an arm around her waist. "And this is my soon-to-be wife, even though everyone already calls us married already—"

"Goddess," Eva spoke up. "You nicknamed me Goddess."

Thinking he'd remember that he really called her Milk Tits, everyone paused, waiting for him to correct her, but he only nodded. "Okay."

Pain sliced through me. This might be Oren Tenning lying in this bed, but the Ten part of him was completely gone. And it had been the Ten part I'd fallen in love with. My perfect Ten.

I shuddered and squeezed Noel's hand harder. He glanced down at me, his eyes lit with the same worry. His Ten, his best friend, was also gone.

Mason introduced himself next.

"And you call me Buttercup." Reese waved at him with a grin that didn't quite reach her eyes. "We shared an art class last year, and had some good times annoying the hell out of each other."

Oren blinked back a confused frown, probably trying to figure out how annoying each other could be considered good times.

"I've probably known you the shortest amount of time," Asher said. "My first name's Asher, but you usually call me by my last, which is Hart."

It seemed so bizarre that we had to introduce ourselves to him. I wanted to escape this room, I wanted to escape this moment. Oren couldn't forget us. He just couldn't.

"Sounds like I nicknamed a lot of people."

"You definitely do the nickname thing," Quinn said. "My first name's Quinn, but you've always called me Ham. And Noel is usually Gam to you."

Oren nodded and glanced up at me before turning his gaze to Noel. "So, what did I nickname your wife?"

"Oh." Sympathy rushed through Noel's gaze as he glanced at me. "No. This is actually my sister. Caroline." He paused briefly, as if waiting to see if that name meant anything to him, but he didn't even flinch, which totally made *me* flinch inside. "My wife Aspen's at home with my younger brothers. But you call her Shakespeare, because she's an English teacher."

"Oh. Sorry." Oren glanced at me, apologizing for mistaking me as Noel's wife. He started to look away again, but then did a double take. Recognition lit his gaze, and I held my breath, yearning, praying he remembered.

I think everyone else in the room leaned in as well, holding a collective breath as they hoped for the same thing.

He pointed at me. "You were the nurse in here yesterday, weren't you?"

I sucked in a pained breath and pulled back, trying not to lose it. Noel squeezed my elbow hard, so I blinked rapidly and nodded. "Y-yes. That was me."

He looked between me and Noel before murmuring, "Oh. Okay, then."

I wasn't going to make it. I needed to curl into a ball and weep somewhere. Soon. I caught Zoey's eyes and her face dissolved into misery. She had to bury her face in Quinn's shoulder to hide her tears.

I lifted my chin to hold strong, but I don't know how I made it.

That was a breaking point for everyone, it seemed.

"We should probably let you rest," Asher murmured, looking as sad as I'd ever seen him.

"Okay." Oren, on the other hand, appeared relieved to see us go.

Noel tugged me against him hard, knowing how close to the edge I was. We all glanced toward the door, but then Eva muttered, "Damn it. I know you don't remember me, but I'm going to hug you goodbye, anyway."

"Uh..." Oren pulled back, his eyes going wide as she stalked toward him with a determined arch in her eyebrows. Then he said, "Okay."

I watched enviously as Eva wrapped her arms around him and hugged him. He even hugged her back with one arm. Then she stamped a quick kiss to his cheek. I longed so hard to go to him, too, to melt into his arms and just hold the love of my life.

Reese glanced at me, winked, and then darted away from Mason. "Well, I want a hug, too, then."

So, she hugged him, and he let her, giving her another one-armed hug back. When she pulled away, she looked directly at me. "Next?"

Zoey reached out and nudged me forward. I stumbled, but caught my feet and lifted my gaze. Oren watched me, letting me step toward him without protest.

I was going to hug him. Oh God. How was I going to stop after a reasonable amount of time and be expected to let go? How was I going to stop with just one hug?

But I leaned toward him, anyway, scared out of my mind that I wouldn't be able to hold myself together.

My arms went around him and they nearly wept with relief, so happy to be enfolding Oren's familiar mass. He didn't smell like Oren, though; he smelled like sterile hospital antiseptics. It helped to remind me that he was no longer mine, and I began to pull away.

Except Oren turned his face toward me so that my hair dragged across his nose as I moved back. He sucked in a startled breath and looked up at me with wide eyes.

I froze, gaping back. He blinked repeatedly, looking utterly confused.

"What's wrong?" I asked slowly, afraid to believe I'd actually triggered something.

Noel moved in closer. "Did you remember something?"

Hell, I think the entire room moved closer. Suddenly everyone was right there, their eyes bright and eager.

"I..." Oren kept staring at me before he shook his head. "Sorry, I just had this strange feeling. You smelled—I mean—" He shook his hands as if the ideas in his head were preposterous. "Sorry," he finally murmured, looking absolutely embarrassed as his cheeks reddened.

"No, don't be sorry," Eva demanded. "Just tell us what you remembered already."

Oren pulled back, obviously startled by the impatience in her voice. But then his gaze drifted back to me, and my stomach coiled with all kinds of things. Need, hope, anticipation, love.

Squinting as if desperately trying to remember, he said, "Did we...?"

"Did we what?" I urged softly.

Again, he shook his head. But then he blew out an incredulous kind of sniff and asked, "Did we ever climb up the side of a building together and sit on top to look at...*stars*?"

Immediate tears filled my eyes. I covered my mouth

with both hands and muffled out the answer. "Yes. Yes, we did."

But that only seemed to confuse him more. "The old movie theater?"

I bobbed my head up and down.

And he shook his. "But why would I take you there?" A nervous laugh rumbled from his chest. "I only go there to be alone. I have never taken anyone there." His eyes suddenly flickered with realization. He glanced at Noel. "Oh, hell. She's not just your sister, is she?"

Noel grinned proudly. "No. No, she's not."

Oren returned his gaze to me. He stared as if trying to read me from the inside out. My heart ticked away at a crazy speed, so happy he'd remembered sitting on the theater roof with me.

"Amazing," Quinn murmured. "Smell is the sense most closely associated with memory because the olfactory bulb is part of the limbic system, but wow. I've never actually seen it work like this before."

With a sigh, Oren rolled his eyes. "What a fucking biology nerd."

A grin spread across my face. He remembered biology was Quinn's specialty. He remembered...

I reached for his arm, unable to help myself. When his gaze laser-beamed to my hand, I stopped and began to pull away, but he caught my wrist and brought it to his nose.

"But he's right. I *know* that smell." His gaze roved back to my face.

Tears filled my eyes as *Ten* slowly began to return to us.

A knowing glean entered his face. "Come here." He crooked his finger, beckoning me closer.

I leaned down, and he asked, "Do you want to build a snowman?"

I blurted out a happy laugh. He'd quoted a movie for me and done our thing. "*Frozen*," I said, naming the movie.

When his lashes flickered open, a look of awe swept over his face. Then he reached for my hair and gathered a handful to his nose. "Holy shit." His gaze shot to mine. "You like it best when your hair's pulled."

I gasped and tugged away from him in mortification. "*Oren!*"

"Of course," Eva muttered dryly. "His first memory *would* be about sex."

"Shut it, Milk Tits," Oren called, never once taking his eyes off me. "I'm trying to get my goddamn memory back here."

"You remember." Tears swamped my face. "You remember everything."

Oren gently brushed the droplets off my cheeks. "As if I could ever forget you. You're my other half. My wife."

When Reese cooed, "Aww. That's so sweet," from somewhere in the room, Oren scowled. "Now, these other motherfuckers, I'll gladly forget them."

"Hey," Mason's offended voice broke in. "That's not very nice. We hauled our tired asses down here every day this week to not even get to see you most of the time, and *this* is how you repay us?"

Ignoring him, Oren tugged me closer. "God, I love you," he murmured and pressed his forehead to mine, only to mutter, "ouch," and pull away.

"Sorry, sorry." I backed off too, pressing my hand to my mouth because I really was sorry, even though I also wanted to laugh and cry with joy because my Oren was back.

Ten was back.

"Jesus." He winced and prodded his bandage gently. "What the hell happened to me anyway? People are just saying an accident. But they're not saying what kind. The last thing I remember..." He paused and glanced at Noel. "You were pissed as hell at me, but you still let me tag along to your family picnic. And...we played padiddle on the way there with the boys, but...that's it." His eyes flared with horror. "Shit. We weren't in a car accident, were we?" His gaze roved frantically around the room. "Where's Colton and Brandt?"

"They're fine. They're home." Noel set a reassuring hand on Oren's shoulder. "We all made it to Rainly Park safe and sound. We had a picnic, and then you took Colton and Caroline off to show them the waterfall."

Oren nodded, but his brow wrinkled in confusion. "And then...I was bitten by a poisonous snake who..." He lifted his arm and eyed it strangely, "...had some wicked awesome ninja skills that put me in an arm sling and leg cast, and mangled my face?"

"And then the soil around the waterfall eroded," I corrected, "when Colton got too close to the edge."

"Shit. Did he fall in?"

"Almost. He caught hold of an old root protruding from the embankment, and you were able to pull him up to safety. But in the process, *you* fell in."

"But the kid's okay?" Oren asked insistently.

"Just a scratch or two," Noel said. "He was pretty upset after you got hurt—thought it was all his fault—so Aspen and Brandt are home with him right now."

"Poor kid." Ten reached for my hand, and I can't even express how amazing it felt to tangle my fingers with his. When his gaze met mine, he blew out a breath. "So, what about me? Am I going to be okay?" Once again, he touched all the bandages around half his face.

A smiled bloomed across my face. I knew he was going to be just fine. "Aside from the brain damage, you just have a dislocated shoulder, fractured leg, and some bad scratches." I paused, drew in a deep breath. "Oh, and the doctor says there will probably be permanent scarring on your face."

Oren's fingers paused on the bandage. "Permanent?"

I nodded and reached for his hand to pull it away. "I bet scars on you will look sexy."

His gaze filled with torment, and I wanted to tell him he'd always be the most handsome man I'd ever known, but Noel spoke up. "The good news is, after you saved my little brother's life, I'm not pissed at you anymore."

Oren glanced at him. Then he sniffed, "Yeah, as long as I give your sister up, though, right?"

Noel just kind of shrugged. "Meh. After you saved her life too, I figure you're stuck with her now."

"Saved her life too?" Oren said slowly, turning his gaze to me.

I wasn't going to answer him, but Noel had to say, "After you started to fall in, she tried to pull you out."

Oren whirled to me. "Christ, Caroline. You didn't? You could've fallen in, too."

"She almost did," Noel seemed eager to blab. "She was slipping toward the edge, but you let go of her hand so she wouldn't."

"You're fucking right I did." Oren nodded as if there were no other logical step.

I shook my head. "I might've been able to save you, hold on long enough until Noel made it to us."

But he shook his head too. "I don't care. What you did

sounds too risky. Never in a million years would I let anything bad happen to you. For that, I guess I can handle a couple scars. I was too damn handsome anyway."

Though everyone else laughed, I stared at him, amazed over how lucky I was to be the woman he loved. I knew I didn't deserve it, but I was going to cherish it with everything I had.

Noel grasped his shoulder. "Hey," he murmured.

When Oren looked up at him, my brother gulped loudly. After swallowing away his pride, he said, "I'm sorry."

My husband frowned and shook his head slightly. "For what?"

"Being a fucking ass these past few weeks."

Oren shrugged. "You're always an ass. So, what's new?"

Noel let out a strangled laugh that sounded as if it might turn into a sob. Then he rasped. "You know what the hell I'm talking about."

But Oren shook his head. "No. I really don't. You thought Caroline was in danger, so you did everything within your power to protect her. I'm not going to forgive that shit. I'm glad you did it. I would've been pissed if you hadn't done anything."

With a shake of his head, Noel refuted him. "You're glad I did all that shit against you?" He didn't sound as if he believed it.

But Oren reached out slowly and grasped my brother's arm. "I'm glad you did it against whoever you thought was a threat to her. But I'm also glad you finally fucking realized I'm not a threat."

"Yeah." Noel wiped his face as if to make sure it was still dry. "Me too." Then he drew in a deep breath. "So...coffee? The next Saturday morning after you get out of this place? I might actually buy this time."

Oren smiled at him before turning his gaze my way. "You got it, bud." Then he snapped his fingers as he kept his gaze on me. "Hart," he called. "Isn't it tradition for you to start singing some bullshit song for us right about now?"

"Really?" Asher's voice was dry. "You're going to make me do that *again*?"

Oren merely kept grinning at me. "Fuck, yeah. I'm the one lying in the damn hospital bed. What I say goes."

"Fine. But you owe me for this." And so Asher began to sing. I laughed as the lyrics to "Sweet Caroline" filled the air.

But Oren didn't laugh. He just gazed at me, his eyes bright with love and awe as he silently mouthed the words to the song. When Eva, Reese, and Pick joined in at the chorus, Oren tugged me closer.

"I love you," he murmured. "Thank you for being here when I woke up and bringing me back to myself."

"I love you, too," I murmured back. "Thank you for coming back."

"For you? Always."

EPIL♥GUE

TEN

FIVE YEARS LATER

IN COLLEGE, drinking games had rocked because they usually meant I could get some drunk chick to do me. Tonight, I wanted to roll my eyes and groan. Oh, wait. I *had* just rolled my eyes and groaned. But fuck, I was an old married fart now. Okay, maybe not old, but definitely aged to perfection. Still, I didn't need alcohol to get laid tonight.

All the couples sitting on the floor in a circle around a hotel ottoman were just as old and married as I was, too. So why were we bothering? There would be no random hooking up after this or me waking up in some strange place with vital pieces of clothing missing.

We'd all just wander back to our respective rooms and curl into bed with our significant others, then wake up before the ass-crack of dawn to catch early flights back home. So why were we playing a stupid fucking drinking game?

"Oh, damn," I grumbled, clutching my side. "I think I just popped my hip out of place from sitting on this fucking floor."

Gam kicked me, in the very hip that I was cradling. The fucker. "Stop being a baby. You sound like an eighty year old instead of twenty-seven."

"Feeling closer to eighty," I complained, glaring at him as I rubbed the spot he'd kicked. "Asswipe."

Next to him, his wife slapped a hand over her mouth and started giggling. The game had her completely lit. I still didn't want to play, but okay, it *was* funny as hell to see Shakespeare drunk. It was her first weekend away from their new kid, and you could tell. The poor woman seemed starved for a little bit of adult freedom.

"Let me hold that for you, babe." Gamble reached for her bottle of chick liquor, but she held it out away from him and leaned the rest of her body his way as she puckered her mouth for a kiss.

"I'd rather you hold *me* instead."

"Ack! God." Wincing, I lifted my hand to shield my eyes from the lip-lock that followed. "Really? You're going to make me watch your porn after I'm already being forced to suffer through this stupid-ass game where Shakespeare's cheating by sneaking drinks between each turn and these two can't even participate?"

I hooked my thumb toward Milk Tits and Buttercup, who were both big and swollen with pregnancy, and therefore banned from drinking any spirits.

Buttercup rolled her eyes as she took a sip from her sparkling grape juice—another cheat, sneaking drinks. "Getting drunk isn't the point."

Frowning, I lifted an eyebrow. "Then what's the god-damn point of a *drinking* game?"

"Reconnecting," Milk Tits answered. "It's been forever since we've all been together. We're just trying to have a little fun, Ten. Gah. Don't be such a fun hater."

I sighed. Stupid games were not my idea of reconnecting or having fun. I thought we'd done a damn fine job of catching up at dinner before the concert, and I'm sure all the guys would've backed me on that...if they'd been willing to go against their wives' opinions.

Whipped pussies.

Appreciating Caroline to hell and back for never making me feel as if I couldn't voice my own fucking outlook, I slung my arm over her knee and stroked the length of her soft calf. She sat on the chair next to me, and I was already leaning against her leg for support.

When her fingers burrowed into my hair in response, I

almost purred contentedly. God, I loved this woman. I would honestly do anything for her, even leave our perfect nest in Lake Tahoe—where I'd eventually gotten another opportunity to apply for that job and accepted it this time, and Caroline had transferred colleges to graduate with a filmmaking degree—to travel all the way back to Chicago and watch Asher Hart and his band Non-Castrato in their first big performance at the Metro.

Okay, so maybe I was proud of the guy, too, and I'd also wanted to watch his concert, which *fine*, had been pretty kick-ass, and the backstage passes he'd sent us had been even sweeter—but I never would've admitted all that aloud. Instead, I had to piss and moan about it because that's just the way I rolled.

But getting together with the rest of the crew in Pick and Milk Tits's hotel room afterward to play "reconnecting" drinking games really did suck ass.

"Ooh, it's my turn." Buttercup was a little too giddy as she snatched a folded sheet of paper from the pile in the center of our circle and opened it. After clearing her throat, she read the message aloud. "I think this game fucking sucks." Tipping her face to the side, she sent me a dry look. "*Ten*."

"Wow," I said, unimpressed, "You figured out that one was mine." Setting my hand over my heart, I fluttered my lashes her way. "You know me so well."

She sniffed. "No, unlike *some* people here, I actually have a good memory. You said that very phrase aloud not thirty seconds ago."

"Oh, you're going to go with the memory bash, huh? That's low, Mrs. Lowe. Just low."

Every once in a while, I still had blanks in my memory. I remembered absolutely nothing from the picnic on the day of my accident, and sometimes Caroline had to remind me of things we'd done when we were dating, but I never forgot how much she meant to me, which was all that mattered. "Next time, just go after my fucked-up face, why don't you?"

Actually, everyone had gotten so used to my scars they usually didn't even see them.

"But they're kind of cute." Buttercup reached out to trace the deepest one down my jawline. "So that would defeat the purpose of trying to make fun of you."

"This one's my favorite." Caroline touched the one that

bisected the corner of my left eyebrow. I grinned up at her.

"I kind of like the swirly one on his chin." Blondie grinned over at me as she wrapped her arm around Ham's bicep and rested her cheek on his shoulder.

When I winked at her, Gamble groaned. "What the hell? The asshole gets mutilated, and chicks *still* dig him?"

"Hey, I'm just a loveable guy." Resting my cheek on Caroline's thigh, I grinned up at her, and she grinned back, letting me know she agreed.

"Yeah, a loveable guy who hasn't stopped bitching and complaining since he entered my room," Pick muttered. He flicked a finger to the pile of paper pieces on the floor. "And whose turn it happens to be."

I groaned. "You all are *really* going to make me keep playing, aren't you?"

"Just pick a damn piece of paper already," Lowe growled.

With a scowl his way, I pulled away from the warmth and comfort of my woman to lean forward and snag a scrap.

Grumbling under my breath, I undid every annoying fold and then widened my eyes before focusing on the words. "I'm pregnant and don't know how to tell my husband," I read aloud, before immediately guessing, "Milk Tits."

Milk Tits frowned at me as she set her hand on her huge belly. "Um...I think it's safe to say Pick *knows* by this point."

"Fine." I rolled my eyes, took a drink, because that meant I'd lost my turn. But then I still had to guess until I got the right answer. "Buttercup, then."

She snorted and rubbed her belly as well. "If you don't think I let Mason know every chance I get that I'm five months pregnant with his *twins*, then you're insane."

"And she really does let me know...every chance she gets," Mason added. When his wife shot him a dark look, he quickly added, "And I love it every time she does." Then he broke off a piece of the chocolate bar he was holding and hand-fed her the chunk. She immediately sighed and closed her eyes, appeased.

Damn, Lowe was good. I'd have to remember that trick for when Caroline—shit. She couldn't get pregnant. I'd been a douche and forgetting that a lot lately. I blamed Gamble completely. Ever since he'd knocked up Shakespeare, I'd been...antsy.

Speaking of Shakespeare, I shot her a curious glance after I took my second slug of beer.

She immediately shook her finger at me. "Don't you even look my way, buddy. I just finished breastfeeding Beau. I am *so* not ready for a second one yet."

So, I transferred my glance across the room to the couch where Parker's wife cradled a sleeping infant in her arms and Parker cradled her in *his* arms. Freaking newlyweds. As the newest couple to our group, they fit in fine, but ever since they'd become parents, they liked to tuck themselves off to the side in their little family bubble. I had to admit, it was kind of cute to watch them together. If Caroline and I had a kid—shit. I had to stop thinking about us and kids.

"I'm not either," Parker's woman, who I'd dubbed Three, spoke up. "So, yeah, stop looking at me like that."

"Damn." I took two more drinks, and everyone in the room swerved their attention to Blondie.

Even Ham blinked at her with a shocked awe. "Zoey?" he asked quietly.

But she shook her head and waved his hands. "Oh, no. No, sorry, it's not me. I think J.B. and Luke are it for us."

She'd had enough trouble getting J.B. here. He'd ended up being born more premature than Milk Tit's first kid had been. When Luke had come along two years later, Hamilton had been a freaking emotional mess, worried about her the entire nine months. But she hadn't even had morning sickness with *him*. Incredibly, both her boys were healthy and hearty now, currently being watched by college-boy Brandt, who was also stuck back at home babysitting Gamble's little boy with Colton—who, Jesus, was now in high school.

"Well, fuck," I muttered after another sip. "I don't know." There were no more ladies left in the room to guess from. "Hart's woman, then."

"How could Remy toss in a turn if she and Asher aren't even here yet?" Pick asked.

Hart had called about half an hour ago, saying he and his wife were on their way, but they still hadn't showed up yet.

I shrugged. "Fuck if I know. There's no other woman to choose from, unless one of you guys *miraculously* got yourselves knocked up."

When silence answered me, I paused from taking a

drink and scowled at them. "What?"

Buttercup jabbed her finger in the direction of the woman I was leaning against. "There's still one woman you haven't guessed yet."

My arm tightened reflexively around Caroline's leg, wanting to protect her. "Don't be cruel." I narrowed my eyes at Buttercup for even suggesting the idea. "Caroline can't..."

But her leg tensed under my touch, and I looked up at her, concerned. When I met her blue eyes, they looked bright and anxious. Her lips tightened into a nervous smile as if she wasn't sure whether to apologize or congratulate me.

"Oh my God," Buttercup ranted. "I cannot believe you, Ten. We came up with this stupid-ass drinking game as a cutesy way to tell you you're going to be a daddy, and you *still* don't get it, even though Caroline is the very last woman in the room to guess. *Gah!*" She looked up at Lowe as if she might start crying, or commit murder. I wasn't sure which. "Sometimes he just...irritates the hell out of me."

"I know, baby. I know." Lowe fed her another piece of chocolate and kissed her cheek. "He irritates the hell out of me, too."

I gawked at them for another moment while my dazed brain tried to catch up. Then I whirled back to Caroline.

My shock pitched into the bottom of my stomach as my jaw dropped open. "Holy shit. *You're* pregnant?"

She slowly bobbed her head up and down as her cheeks flooded with color.

I shook my head, unable to believe it, afraid to even attempt to believe it. "But the doctor said—"

"He said it was unlikely, *highly* unlikely," she was quick to interrupt, "not that it was completely impossible."

I let out a hard breath. It'd been years since we'd bothered to use any kind of contraceptive. I'd just assumed babies were impossible. Finding out I was wrong made my ears ring and my vision blur.

But Caroline was pregnant. My wife and the love of my life was going to have *my* baby.

"Holy fuck." My hands went to my hair to clutch my swimming head.

"Wow, Ten," Pick murmured, sounding impressed. "You must have some kind of super sperm to overcome odds like that."

"You're damn right I do," I said, still dazed.

A hard hand clasped my shoulder. "Hey," Gamble said seriously. "You okay, bud?"

I looked up at him and blinked him into focus. "Yeah. Why?"

His blue eyes crinkled with worry. "You look like you're trying to check out on us. You ready to be a dad, or what?"

Dad.

Dear God, just thinking of that word being applied to me made me break out in a cold sweat. Fuck no, I wasn't ready to be a dad. I wanted to be a good dad, like my own dad was, but how could I possibly do that when I had no clue what being a dad truly entailed? I wanted my kid to have everything amazing. The best life ever.

But then I realized it would; it'd have Caroline as a mother.

With a snort, I rolled my eyes at Gam. "You ready to be an *uncle*?" I challenged right back.

Genuine pleasure gleamed in his face as he smiled. "Oh, I am *so* ready to be your kid's uncle. I'm going to spoil your kid more than you spoil my Beau."

"Bring it," I said, ready to take him on, confident I could out-spoil his kid, no problem.

"Hey, Ten," Blondie murmured softly, jerking my attention away from Gam. When she caught my eye, she zipped her gaze to Caroline.

I looked up at my wife and straightened, instantly alarmed. Instead of full of energy and eagerness as she'd been moments ago, her face had drained of all color.

"Baby, what's wrong?" I tugged her out of her chair and down into my lap, where I pressed my hand to her abdomen.

She covered the back of my palm with cold fingers and looked up into my eyes, worry and fear creasing her face. "*Are* you okay with becoming a dad?"

"Are you kidding me?" I blurted out a surprised laugh and pressed my forehead to hers. "I'm...I'm so far and gone past okay, I'm fucking trembling with it." I cupped her face in my hands. "We're going to have a baby, Caroline. A little piece of you, a little piece of me. I can't...I can't even process this it's so fucking awesome. We're finally getting our Inez Dumaine."

Immediate tears filled her eyes. "Oh my God. You

remember."

"Of course I remember. Why would I forget the name you want to give our daughter?"

"I love you," she sobbed. "I love you so much, Oren Tenning, it almost scares me."

"Not nearly as much as I love you," I shot back.

As my pregnant wife cried and kissed me, I turned a little drippy myself. But shit, this had to be one of the happiest moments of my life, in the arms of the woman I loved, surrounded by my best friends on earth, and hearing I was going to be a father. Who the hell wouldn't drop a tear? I certainly couldn't refrain.

And if any of you fuckers reading this even think about spreading around the fact that I bawled like a pussy when I found out I was going to be a dad, I'll kick all your asses. This is my goddamn happily ever after; I'll cry if I want to.

THE END

NEXT

worthless

KNOX'S STORY

BEFORE, NO ONE THOUGHT HE WAS GOOD
ENOUGH FOR HER; NOW, HE DOESN'T EITHER.

Wait... *Knox*? Who's Knox?
He's a new guy.
Asher isn't quite ready for his turn yet,
so get ready for Knox Parker next!

THANKS TO:

Thank you to my beta/early readers: Shi Ann Crumpacker, Alaina Martinie, Lindsay Brooks, Ada Frost, Ana Kristina Rabacca, Patty Brehm, Chelcie Holguin, Elisa Castro, Jodi Maliszewski, Mary Rose Bermundo, Jawairya, Amanda at Beta Reading Bookshelf, Jennifer at Three Chicks and Book, Laurie at Just One More Page, and Michelle and Pepper at AllRomance Book Reviews.

Thank you to my editor Stephanie Parent, and proofreader Shelley at 2 Book Lovers Reviews!

More thanks to all the supportive people who visit my social media sites and read my stories, keeping me in business. And a huge apology to Soha Khalil for my awful spelling in my last acknowledgement list!

Thanks to my huge family, thanks to Kurt and Lydia for providing me with my own happily ever after, and then finally thank you to God.

I know I don't deserve so much help and support from you guys, so I cherish and appreciate it, recognizing it for the amazing gift it is. Thank you.

ABOUT L. K.

Linda grew up on a dairy farm in the Midwest as the youngest of eight children. Now she lives in Kansas with her husband, daughter, and their nine cuckoo clocks. Her life's been blessed with lots of people to learn from and love. Writing's always been a major part of her world, and she's so happy to finally share some of her stories with other romance lovers. Please visit her at her website:

www.LindaKage.com

ALSO BY L.K.

The Stillburrow Crush
The Trouble with Tomboys
Hot Commodity
Delinquent Daddy
A Man for Mia
The Right to Remain Mine
The Best Mistake
The Color of Grace
A Fallow Heart
Addicted to Ansley
How to Resist Prince
Charming
Kiss it Better

Granton University Series
Fighting Fate
Loving Lies

Forbidden Men Series
Price of a Kiss
To Professor, with Love
Be My Hero
With Every Heartbeat
A Perfect Ten